Praise for
Demon's Grip

'A most exemplary work, a real joy to read. The colour, depth and vitality of both the writing and the narrative is stunningly good: the exploration of motives, outlooks and hopes of the characters quite intoxicating. It ranks as a true work of literary accomplishment.' Clive S Johnson, Awesome Indies reviewer.

'Newland's spectacular descriptions bring her characters' thoughts out into their physical world once again. Demon's Grip is yet another action-packed part of a series full of imagination and fantastic adventure.' Kate Policani Reviews.

'Demon's Grip is more than a standard YA fantasy story; the characters' internalisations and dialogue, and the progression of the plot itself, lead the reader to be more contemplative, even meditative, about the emotional issues involved. Overall, a nicely-paced novel, well-written, with memorable characters and the chance, perhaps, to reflect more deeply on life while enjoying the story.' Kevin Berry, author/editor.

'Just how original Newland's fantastical vision is becomes far clearer in this latest book. As Ariel and Nick's relationship matures so does its complexity. As well as dealing with the turmoil of love, they have to continue to learn how to turn their ordinary selves into superheroes and saviours of mankind. It seems that only they can save us all from the suffocating evil of the black serpentine.' Richard Bunning Reviews

Also by Tahlia Newland

Lethal Inheritance
Stalking Shadows
Eternal Destiny
You Can't Shatter Me
A Matter of Perception

Demon's Grip

Tahlia Newland

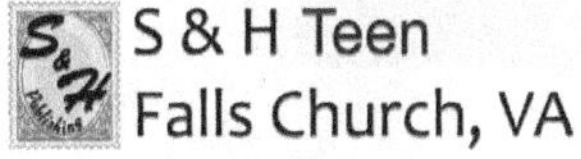

S & H Teen
Falls Church, VA

S & H Teen
Falls Church, VA

ISBN: 978-0-9873231-4-9

Cover design by Velvet Wings Design

For Krisi.
May you be happy and well.

Contents

The Hidden Realm of Diamond Peak

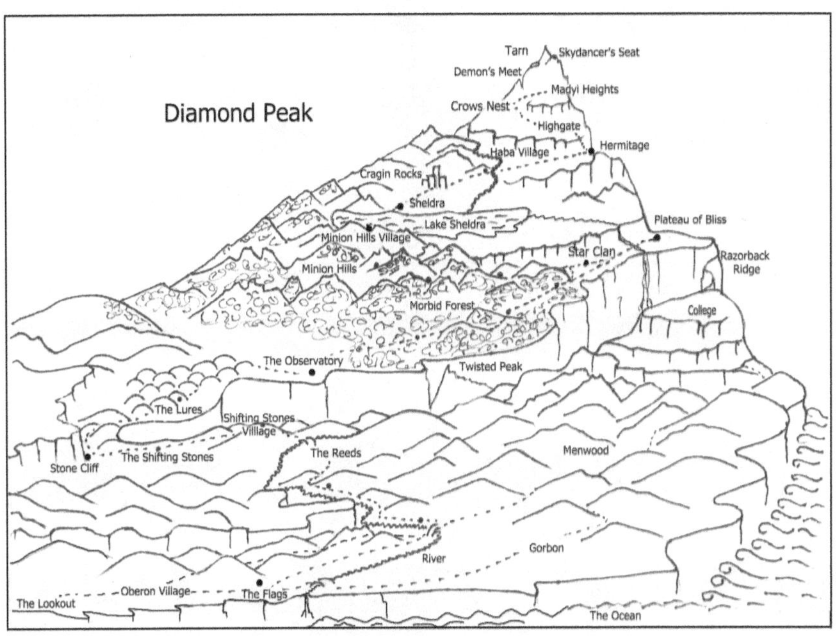

Middle Mountain

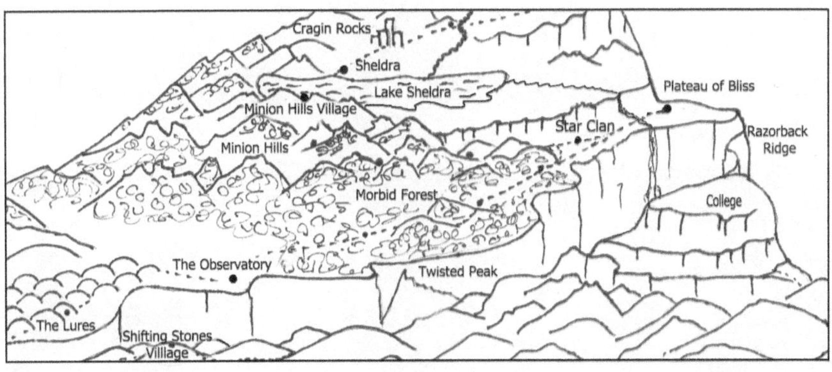

1

Minion Hills

Walnut sat on his feet behind the lattice on the roof deck and cradled Miramar's head in his lap. Her long grey hair, loosened from its bun, lay soft against his hands. His head bowed over the still form of his dead lover, and a single tear dropped from the corner of his eye into the centre of her forehead.

A volley of wand fire crackled like lightning between the houses. It zapped across the rooftops, splitting roof tiles and thumping into the magicians' magic shields like hot punches. Miramar's fine young sons, Blade and Falcon, ducked their heads over the balustrade to return the fire of the rogue magicians who had infiltrated the neighbouring house and killed Miramar.

Never again would she gaze upon him in this life. The energy drained from his limbs and his heart wept for the loss of a remarkable woman. Walnut barely registered the wooden decking he sat on. Though only two metres wide, it flanked all four sides of the turret room on the top of Miramar's house. A shaft of sunlight broke through the early morning mist. It glanced off the big windows behind him, reflected onto Walnut and Miramar where they hid behind the deck's balustrade and bathed them in a pool of golden light.

A fresh wave of wand-fire sounded from the street below.

'Our clansmen have arrived,' Blade said from where he crouched beside Walnut. His olive skin, though light for a Magan, seemed darker in the shadow of the lattice and, once again, Walnut noted the boy's delicate features, a legacy from his non-Magan Grandmother. 'We'll get them now,' he continued, all strength and fire, but Walnut felt his bleeding heart as his own. At fifteen, he was still just a boy.

Let me take it all, and that of Falcon too, so they need not suffer. But even as he thought it, he knew the boys would still have to feel their grief. There was no way around it.

The attack had come before anyone had a chance to erect a magic shield, and as Miramar's life force had drained away, the hands of fate had seized Walnut's heart and ripped it open. He'd known it was too late even before he saw the hole burned through her white blouse into her chest and the glazed, lifeless look of her eyes. He had touched his fingertips to her eyelids and slid them shut.

Nick and his healing power had arrived too late.

Footsteps thundered up the stairs, and men from other Warrior Clans flooded onto the deck and added their fire to the cacophony.

Don't let this begin a war. He didn't think the words, nor did he hear them. It was the wordless whisper of Miramar's Radiance that nudged him into action.

Walnut kissed her forehead, then eased her head off his lap and laid it gently on the wooden floor. He took a deep breath, uttered six syllables, and spread the energy it called forth into a magic shield a good metre from his body. May the Noble Ones throughout all space and time strengthen this magic, he thought, then chanted the incantation to call forth their combined Radiant Power. Strength returned to his limbs, healed his aching heart and filled every cell with light born of vigour. He suspected that he glowed as he rose effortlessly to his feet. Men shouted from both sides, but Walnut's voice rang above them all.

'Stop!'

Those on the roof-deck obeyed the command, but sporadic fire still blasted from the house across the way. A crackle of white fire glanced off Walnut's shield and the Warrior Clan Magans around him ducked behind the lattice-work.

'Cowards,' one of their enemies shouted.

Walnut, however, stood firm. He whipped his sceptre and bell from the pouches on his belt, chanted the incantation for immobilisation, rang his bell and pointed his sceptre at the man responsible for firing on him. Power, greater than any he had wielded before, ripped through Walnut and out of his sceptre. The man froze, arm raised ready for another blast. Walnut smiled; the Noble Ones had heeded his call.

One after another, Walnut froze the Mage Clansmen in the neighbouring house. Many disappeared from the windows when they realised what their fate would be if they remained. The firing soon stopped, and when all was still, Falcon called for the Warrior Clan Magans to take the building. The power, its task completed, drained from Walnut's body and he slid to the floor beside his beloved. Only the ache of loss remained. Footsteps retreated down the stairs, but Blade and Falcon did not follow their kin. They knelt beside the old man, their soft white shirts in stark contrast to their dark leather jerkins.

The three remained silent, heads bowed over the corpse in grief. Falcon, Miramar's eldest son—a young man now sporting a good thick beard—ran his fingers through his black hair and cursed his mother's murderer. His strong features twisted with grief and anger, so unlike his usually calm expression. His leather jacket and matching black trousers rustled against the wooden lattice, their colour harder than Blade's brown ones, like the differences in the brothers' personalities. But Walnut loved them both as if they were his own.

Blade, the younger son, brown-haired and beardless, breathed deeply and drew Falcon into its rhythm. They breathed together, and the anger faded, but, as was its way, the grief remained to sadden their days until they had paid its due.

'I will take her downstairs,' Falcon said when he had calmed. He lifted her carefully and led the way through the turret room and down the stairs. Walnut and Blade followed behind and stood silently while Falcon laid his mother on the couch. 'I feel we ought not to wait before taking her to the square,' he said when he'd laid her to rest. 'The village should know immediately what this feud has cost us.'

Walnut nodded.

'I'll get a stretcher,' Blade said and rushed away.

The boy's distress was palpable and Falcon's no less, his was merely hidden better. Walnut neither hid his pain nor dwelt on it. He simply let it wash over him like the waves in the ocean. Its roar would calm eventually. In the meantime, it flavoured the moment with the deep sadness born of love.

The Chief of Miramar's clan, Lord Terrigal, arrived with four of his clansmen soon after Falcon had laid his mother's body onto the stretcher Blade had prepared. Like Miramar's two boys, the bearded Magan men wore high black boots, swords at their sides and wands tucked into their belts. The chief, Miramar's brother, wore a long maroon jacket with the crest of the Terrigals embossed on the leather over his heart, and the men's jerkins bore the same colour and mark, though smaller to designate their lesser rank. Around their shoulders hung the maroon velvet cloak of their clan.

'We go now,' Walnut told him. He kicked off his sheepskin house boots, dragged his sturdy walking boots over his woollen socks and donned a thick coat, brown to match his trousers. The speckled maroon scarf that Miramar had knitted for him after the boys' father died sat comfortingly around his neck. He gestured to the door.

'I cannot speak.' Grief choked Lord Terrigal's voice.

'There is nothing to say,' Walnut replied and, indeed, they said nothing as Falcon took the stretcher handles at his mother's head and Blade took those at her feet. They set shields to ward against magic and headed to the door. Once outside, Walnut positioned himself on one side of the stretcher and Lord Terrigal took the other. The clansmen drew their wands and placed themselves one in front, one behind and one on each side of the procession. In this way, they carried Miramar through the cobbled streets to the town square.

Though no wand did fire on them, the presence of Lord Terrigal's guard allowed Miramar's sons to grieve in peace without concern for the possibility of attack. Silent tears ran down Blade's smooth face and Walnut thought how it would please Miramar to see that her gentle son was strong enough not to fear showing his grief.

Lord Terrigal began the haunting Magan song of passing, and all in the procession joined in. Blade's tears stopped and his voice grew stronger with each note. Like the others, Walnut looked straight ahead, but he felt people watching them from the windows they passed, heard doors quietly open and close, and voices add to the song as people joined the procession. Falcon's powerful baritone held them all in its embrace, the timbre of his voice expressing what he never would with words. Although he had lived only ten years more than his brother, Falcon seemed older, the result of having the role of head male in their household thrust on him before he had even grown a beard. His shoulders had grown broad to carry the load and he had made his mother proud. Walnut wiped away a tear.

The terracotta tiles on the pavilion in the centre of the town square glowed bright orange in the morning sun, their reflection deepening the bronze of the town bell tucked in its turret on top. The white-washed stone pillars stood out from the mundane grey of the granite walls on the surrounding shops, like Miramar had against the conflict that caused her death.

The song ended as Miramar's sons laid the stretcher on the funeral dais in the pavilion. Walnut, feeling suddenly old, grasped the bell handle in both hands and pulled, once, twice, three times. The clear chimes brought a smile to the faces of the three beneath the bell. They knew how much Miramar loved the sound of the bell when it rang each hour. She would rejoice in the sound, even though this time, it tolled for her.

Walnut, Lord Terrigal and Miramar's sons stood, one in each direction, with heads bowed over the body while the four guards stood outside the pavilion. When the ringing faded into silence, Falcon pulled the bell rope three more times, and when that ringing had ceased, Blade took his turn. Lord Terrigal rang the bell a final time. Called by the bell, people poured into the square from all directions and drew near to see who lay on the dais. Walnut's gaze remained on Miramar's face, tranquil even in death, but the people's dismay, shock and grief carried to him on their whispers.

While the bell rang, black clouds gathered and scurried over the sun, casting the square into gloom. When the last note had faded into silence, Walnut turned and raised his hand. The crowd stilled.

'In honour of Miramar of the Terrigal clan, I call upon all clan chiefs and all their men and women who have care for her to come on the third morning when her pyre will be set alight.' The old guide's voice rang easily across the square.

'What happened?' someone called out.

'An accident,' Walnut replied.

'Wand fire is no accident,' another cried out. 'Someone is behind this tragedy.'

'Indeed they were, but the fire was not meant for Miramar. She died saving another.'

The crowd fell quiet again, and many nodded, as if thinking it a fitting end for a woman who constantly thought of others before herself. Some faces grew red with anger, but thunder drowned any call for revenge. It boomed over the square and unleashed a torrent of rain. The square emptied as people ran for cover, but many stepped under the protection of the pavilion and sat on the benches around its edges to grieve with Miramar's family as rain washed the cobblestones clean.

Walnut turned back to Miramar and began the chant for setting the light. Undiminished by the power of the thunder, his voice, instead, rode on its peals and drew all who heard it into its embrace. Once again, the pure tones of Falcon's voice rang clearly above the others. Despite the pouring rain, many Warriors gathered and added their voices to the chant. Some even stood in the pouring rain as a tribute to the woman so many loved.

A brilliant white light appeared above the pavilion and grew with the chant. It swelled with power, then burst asunder and unleashed a waterfall of liquid light. It poured through the pavilion roof as if the covering didn't exist and washed through Miramar's body and those of the mourners. While the nectar cleansed Miramar of the stains of her life, grief and anger poured like melted tar from the mourners' bodies and dissolved into the stones beneath them.

Gradually, Miramar's corporeal body grew transparent, and her Light Body, all five colours clear and strong, shone through from within. The rain eased as the nectar ceased dripping. The light descended through the pavilion roof and rested at the apex above the body. Miramar's Light Body separated from her physical body, floated upwards into the light and dissolved in it. The light dissolved from the outside in until only a luminescent pin prick remained. In a flash, it too vaporised.

The chanting ceased. Only a corpse remained.

After the prescribed twenty-one minutes of silent mourning, Lord Terrigal sent a man to make the funeral arrangements. Many of the mourners drifted away only to return with flowers—which they set around the pavilion—and food for whoever sat with the corpse until the pyre was complete.

'Who will stay first?' Lord Terrigal asked.

Walnut glanced at the two boys and knew their minds. 'We will all stay.'

The lord nodded. 'I will arrange three bedrolls.'

Falcon sat stalwart on the bench at his mother's head. Blade slumped against the dais with his head in his hands, and Walnut turned to the north and prayed that Nick and Ariel had made it safely across the snake-infested lake.

2

Sheldra

Ariel stood with Nick on the bank on the northern side of Lake Sheldra. Behind them, green grass spread down to the glistening lake, and in front of them lay woodland with the towers of the University of Sheldra peeking over the crowns of the trees.

Sunlight broke through the clouds and sprinkled Nick's rich brown hair with golden highlights. The mist they'd travelled through on the lake and their recent battle with the Amic demons had left it even more tousled than usual. He still wore the black shirt and jeans he'd worn through Magan territory and, as always these days, his sword hung at his side.

Beside them stood Yule, the bright-eyed, sweet-faced scholar with the shaved head, and at her heels stood the baby wombat that had followed her when she came to meet them at the edge of the lake.

'You'll never guess what Maya found when she was in the old part of the library searching for the map,' she said, wrapping her loose maroon coat around her.

'What?' Nick's deep brown eyes twinkled over a charming smile.

'Old Magan scripts! Maya was right,' Yule gushed, 'they did have some knowledge written down. There's one particular

9

gem I can't wait to translate. The bits I dipped into are fascinating, but it's tricky. I need your help.'

Ariel left them to their conversation and squatted in front of the wombat. 'Hi, Spud,' she whispered, patting his head. He bunted his solid little nose against her hand. She grinned. 'It's good to see you.'

Twitchet, the ginger cat who had accompanied them on their boat ride across the lake, peeked around Nick's legs and narrowed his eyes. 'Arrange a bowl of cream for me at lunch,' he declared, then skirted warily around the wombat and raced into the trees.

'Sure thing, tiger,' Nick said, glancing down. 'What *are* you doing down there?' he asked Ariel.

'It's Spud,' she replied, tucking her long auburn hair behind her ear as she looked up. 'He's out of his pouch.'

'You know this wombat?'

'Sure,' Ariel stood. 'He lived at my house before … you know, before they kidnapped Mum. She was rearing him, and I couldn't leave him behind all alone, so Maya took him. She said she'd find him a good home.' Her eyes met Nick's and she felt his pleasure, echoed by hers, at how easy things were between them. She hadn't felt the more shocking aspects of their energetic connection since she'd incited his jealousy on the Plateau of Bliss.

'He came from you?' Yule exclaimed. 'That's wonderful.'

'How do you like raising a wombat?' Ariel asked, wiping her hands on her jeans. *Like the night feeds and the smell of a pouch needing changing.*

'He can be pretty demanding,' Yule replied, 'but I fell in love with him as soon as I saw him, and Maya is really too old to be up feeding a baby at night. He thinks I'm his mother now and follows me everywhere.'

'As they do.' Ariel lifted her pack with one hand, and with the other tried to pull her old leather coat—borrowed from

Blade—down at the back. Nick stepped behind her and lifted the pack, freeing both her hands.

'Ew!' Yule exclaimed, staring at the blood on Nick's shirt. 'What happened?'

'Just a scratch from an Amic,' Nick replied. 'A bunch of them attacked as soon as we got to shore.'

Ariel turned back to the scene of the battle and scanned the lake; no sign of Kestril's boat. The gruff, green-eyed Magan had disappeared into the low mist that hung above the snake-infested water. She saw no sign of the giant water serpents that, had it not been for him, would most certainly have been their doom.

'So close to Sheldra. Oh dear,' Yule said. 'Things *are* getting all topsy-turvy.'

'Ariel took out their boss though,' Nick said.

'That is good news. Well done, Ariel.'

Ariel nodded but didn't turn. On the other side of the lake, the forested slopes of Minion Hills rose above the grey vapour, dark and foreboding. Memories of their tense journey through the Back Ways and fleeing the Mage Clan Magans during their attack on Miramar's house chilled her to the bone.

'But there's bad news too,' Nick said. 'Miramar is dead.'

Ariel only vaguely registered Yule's shock and Nick's explanation of the battle where Miramar had thrown herself in front of Ariel to save her from a blast of Magan wand-fire. Walnut's lover was dead because of her. The old guide would insist that it wasn't her fault, but it was *her* head that the demons offered a reward for. Ariel had no idea why.

'Is that why Walnut isn't with you?' Yule asked.

Nick nodded. 'Last seen, he, Blade and Falcon were in the thick of a battle.'

Yule squinted across the water. 'How did you get across the lake?'

'Let's just say we had magical assistance,' Nick replied.

Her eyebrows rose. 'A Magan? Who?'

'Can't say, classified info.'

'We should go,' Ariel said. A Magan from a Mage Clan would never help a Warrior, but Kestril had, many times. His identity must remain secret.

Yule nodded and let the matter drop. They followed her along a path that led into the woodland, but just inside the trees, she stopped. Spud bumped into her, then stood unmoving with his nose against Yule's calves. He didn't seem to mind her coat flapping around his head. Ariel and Nick chuckled.

'He does that,' Yule explained fondly as she bent down and scratched the wombat behind the ear. 'When he first started following me around, people kept tripping over him, and he's as solid as rock. The medics had all these bruised ankles to treat, but people stay away from me now.'

Ariel smiled. She liked this tiny scholar already.

The young woman's face grew somber. 'If it's classified, then it's a Mage Clan Magan. Should I be hopeful?'

Nick shook his head. 'Before? Maybe. But now ...'

'Miramar's death could set off a war,' Yule finished for him.

He nodded and Yule walked on.

They followed her along a well-trodden path through an open woodland of slender trees. Unlike the dark, wild forests across the lake, light penetrated the small-leafed canopy, and the hand of human care showed in pruned shrubs. Before long, the path emerged from the woodland, and two stories of Gothic architecture hewn from granite and smoothed into regular blocks stood before them.

Ariel smiled. Narrow arched windows, some with stained glass, reminded her of the palace on the Plateau, but this was less ancient and more solid, a place to honour learning not power. Two towers, complete with battlements, rose on each side of the wide, arched entrance. Ariel stared at them in awe until they passed beneath the arch and into the University grounds. Inside the compound, the wide gravel path, flanked by colourful perennial gardens, cut through the centre of a well-trimmed lawn that filled the U-shape between the entrance building and its two wings.

Ariel smiled, a sense of relief eased through her, as if the two arms of this building held her in an embrace. Here she could recuperate and train before continuing her quest to free her mother from Rasama, head of the Rasa demons. Sheldra was supposed to be a safe place, but they'd said that about Miramar's house too and look what happened there.

Ariel had killed Amic—and Bitah before him—but Emot, the next of the Master Demon's bodyguards, would be hunting her now. The Rasas usually waited until a traveller moved on from Sheldra before attacking, but nothing had been usual with Ariel's journey. Emot, or one of his emanations at least, could be on her at any moment, and she hadn't even begun to learn how to avoid an Emot trap. She wasn't here for a holiday.

'I'll go and arrange the practices for Miramar,' Yule said softly. 'You get Ariel settled; she can use the room next to yours.'

Nick nodded and the little scholar strode ahead.

'You have a room here?' Ariel asked as they followed at a more leisurely pace.

'Sure,' Nick replied, 'this is where I live when I'm not on the road.'

'I never thought of you living anywhere.'

Nick chuckled. 'Everyone lives somewhere.'

Even if it was a cardboard box under a freeway? She didn't bother to ask. They probably didn't have homeless people in the Hidden Realm.

They left the granite tower building behind and walked between plain, two-storied sandstone buildings with rectangular windows—no arches or Gothic details to distract the scholars from their studies.

'Dormitories,' Nick explained. 'Most of the single scholars live on this side of the Great Hall. The shops, workshops and services are on the other side, and the teachers and their assistants have various kinds of living arrangements in between. Married couples usually live off site.'

The darker stonework around the doors and windows did little to soften the austere facade of the dormitories. The only ornamentation came from artfully curved hinges on the oiled wooden shutters and door, but since nothing else drew the eye, you couldn't miss the beauty of their design. The very buildings in the place seemed to suggest the clarity of focus required to excel here.

The travellers continued along the road, through well-tended gardens and past several more buildings in the same style. Roads branched off each side of the main street and curved around some distant central point in a perfectly symmetrical layout. Nothing had been left to chance in this ordered environment.

'Where are the classrooms?' Ariel asked.

'On the eastern side of the Great Hall,' Nick replied, pointing to the large building at the end of the road. 'I'll show you later.'

Ariel nodded and gazed at the emerald grass, trimmed shrubs and flowerbeds. "It's so neat, and beautifully laid out, almost mathematical.'

Nick led Ariel to a building that looked similar to the dormitories except that, outside each upstairs room, narrow double doors opened onto balconies with curved wrought iron railings. 'Offices and accommodation for the guides and their assistants,' he explained and ushered her into a spacious entrance hall with a polished wood floor and unadorned white walls. They turned right and walked down a wide corridor past dark doors set on either side. Light shone onto the floor from a glass door at the end, cutting a dazzling path through the gloom.

Nick stopped three doors from the end, opened a door and gestured for Ariel to enter. 'My office,' he said.

She stepped into a large office, complete with laptops, printers and upholstered chairs. 'Pretty impressive for a world without electricity,' she said, looking around.

'Solar power,' he said, easing his pack off his shoulders onto the top of a bunch of filing cabinets. She wriggled out of her pack, lowered it carefully to the floor and stared at the mess of papers on the desk on the left of the large window. 'I share it with Yule,' he explained. Apparently the tidy one on the other side belonged to Nick.

'What's through there?' Ariel asked, pointing to a door in the right hand wall.

'Kitchen, dining, living room; have a look if you like.'

Ariel peeked through the doorway into the next room. A surprisingly modern kitchen with a sophisticated grey and white colour-scheme filled the corner between her and a door into the corridor. A bowl of fruit made it feel lived in, but whoever used it kept the bench and dark wooden floor spotless. Ariel's mum would love that.

A blue sofa, two chairs and a coffee table set on a cream carpet made a cosy sitting area around an old-fashioned fireplace on the opposite side of the room, and an elegant oval dining table filled the space to her left. The muted greens and browns in the wallpaper and light from the cream-draped French doors on the left gave the room the feeling of a relaxed picnic in a forest— one with a very convenient pantry.

'Is it okay if we see whether Tynan's here before going upstairs?' Nick asked from behind her.

'Sure.' Before she turned back into the office, Ariel glimpsed a courtyard and what looked like a wombat pen on the other side of the glass doors.

'Don't worry about the packs. We can pick them up on our way back,' he said.

Ariel followed him across the room. 'How often does Tynan come here?'

'He usually teaches two or three days a week.'

'The art of sword fighting, I guess.'

'And chemistry, physics, and applied electricity and technology. He set up the mountain's electrical installation team.'

'All solar?'

'And water, little hydro-electrical generators.'

'Water wheels?'

'Basically.'

'Does anyone else I know teach here?'

'Maya. She's lived here since she arrived.'

'Arrived from where?'

'No one knows, or at least they're not telling. You know Walnut; he has a wonderful way of avoiding answering anything he doesn't want you to know. I figure she comes from somewhere Off-World.'

'Off-World, as in another planet?'

He shook his head. 'More like another realm.'

Ariel's eyes widened. 'Another realm?'

'Yeah. Most people doubt there is such a thing, but there's mention of them in some of the ancient texts. Those who might know more don't talk about them.'

'Why not?'

'People get sidetracked; like with magic. It's better to leave it until you've defeated Rasama.'

Ariel smiled. 'So after he's dead, I can take a holiday in another realm.'

Nick cocked his head. 'Maybe.'

'If there is such a thing,' she added.

He smiled and opened the door into the corridor, stepping back to allow Ariel to go first. Nick's manners, rare in her off-mountain world, had seemed old-fashioned when she first arrived here; now she found them charming. He led her

down the corridor and stopped at the last door on the right. Its
brass name-plate said T Swiggins.

3

Tynan

'Swiggins! Tynan's last name is Swiggins?' Ariel exclaimed, staring at the name on the door.

'Yeah,' Nick replied. 'So?'

Ariel giggled. 'That's awesome.'

'What is?'

'Tea Swiggins. Get it? Tea; as in swigging tea. He drinks a lot of tea; it's perfect.'

'It's not that funny,' he said, but his lips curled slightly and his eyes crinkled at the edges.

'Sure it is. It's hysterical.'

Nick shook his head and knocked on Tynan's office door.

Ariel regained her composure by staring out the glass door at the end of the corridor. The sun shone fully now, turning the terracotta paving deep orange.

'Come in,' Tynan called.

Nick opened the door and gestured Ariel inside. Tynan, her sword master from the Observatory, sat at a desk behind a huge stack of papers. His bright blue eyes peered at them over his spectacles and his face lit up with joy. His beard was freshly trimmed and his fair hair neatly tied back with a blue leather thong that matched the colour of his trousers—a nice contrast to his loose white shirt. Ariel smiled fondly at the elegant, long-limbed Warrior.

He stood and walked around the desk towards them, arms open in greeting. 'Ariel, Nick, how wonderful that you're arrived safely. Where's Walnut?'

The smiles disappeared from Ariel and Nick's faces. Tynan glanced from one to the other, then at the bloodstain on Nick's shirt. His expression grew grave. 'What has happened?' When neither of them replied, he indicated a grey leather sofa beneath the window. 'It looks like we had better sit down.'

'It's not Walnut,' Nick assured him.

'Thank goodness for that. And I'm hoping that all is well beneath that stain.'

'I'm fine.'

'Good, I will order some tea.' He opened an internal door on the right hand wall and poked his head through while Nick took a seat on the grey leather lounge. Ariel slid in beside him.

'What's in there?' she whispered.

'His assistant's office,' Nick replied.

'Liam, could you bring morning tea for three, please?' Tynan asked.

'Yes, sir,' a boy's voice replied.

Tynan turned back, sat on a matching chair facing them and pushed a wisp of long grey hair behind his ear. His brow furrowed. 'Now then, what's this all about?'

'Miramar is dead,' Nick said. 'Murdered.'

Tynan gasped and searched their faces, as if hoping to find he'd misheard. 'That is terrible news,' he whispered.

Ariel nodded, her heart as downcast as Tynan's expression.

'How could anyone have done such a thing?'

'It was an accident,' Ariel replied.

Nick snorted. 'They attacked us!'

'Start from the beginning,' Tynan said.

Nick sighed and in muted tones told the story of their journey through Minion Hills. Part way through, Liam, a slender teenager in the loose maroon coat and shaved head of a scholar, brought tea and biscuits laid out on fine china plates. Tynan introduced the boy. They exchanged the usual pleasantries and waited until Liam had left before Nick continued. When he'd finished the story, Tynan sighed heavily, and they sat in silence for several minutes. Although Ariel hadn't eaten since early that morning, the memory of Miramar's last minutes severely curtailed her appetite. She only sipped her tea and nibbled unenthusiastically on a biscuit.

'Don't say anything of this until Walnut is here,' Tynan said finally. 'I don't think it would be good to have a lot of scholars arriving in Minion Hills right now. Like many here who knew and loved her, I would like to go to her cremation, but the situation there is too volatile. It is better left as a Magan mourning for now. We can have a memorial service for her later.'

'Yule already knows,' Nick said. 'She's gone to arrange the practices.'

Tynan nodded, then reached for the pen and notebook that sat on the coffee table, scrawled a note and called Liam. 'Give this to Yule. She'll be with the practitioners.'

The boy nodded and left through the door into the corridor. Tynan lay back on his chair and closed his eyes. Ariel and Nick waited in silence until he opened his eyes a few moments later. 'Now then, where were we?'

'A timetable for Ariel's studies, perhaps?' Nick said.

Miramar is dead, but life must go on, Ariel thought.

'It's on your desk,' Tynan replied. 'I wasn't sure if I would be here when you arrived.'

Nick stood. 'I'll get it. You stay here, Ariel, and tell Tynan the good news.'

'Good news?' Tynan perked up immediately. 'Excellent. I am all ears.'

Ariel smiled at Tynan's boyish enthusiasm, and as Nick left the room she continued their story from the time the boat left the wharf at Minion Hills to their arrival at Sheldra.

'May I see it?' he asked after she told him how the giant water serpent had given her a locket.

She lifted the chain over her head and handed it to him.

'It looks like silenite,' he said, 'though I don't understand why you call it a locket since I see no evidence that it opens.'

'So call it a pendant.'

Tynan narrowed his eyes and peered at her over his spectacles. 'When you consider the nature of its discovery and that silenite does not exist naturally anywhere on this planet, it is likely to have some magical properties. Nevertheless, until it reveals itself, it is just a rather dull lump of silenite on a chain.'

At least it's a smooth lump, Ariel thought as she slipped the necklace back on.

At the news of her defeat of Amic, Tynan clapped his hands. 'Ah, another one down,' he beamed. 'Well done, well done. Only three left to go.'

Ariel wished he hadn't mentioned that, but Nick saved her from thinking about the future by returning with a timetable of classes for the crash course Tynan had planned to begin on her arrival. He sat beside her again and spread the piece of paper out between them.

'You have Wrathful Power Application, with me,' Tynan said. 'It includes advanced demon-fighting techniques and shield creation; The Nature of Reality with Walnut; Demonology with Layla; Response Ability with Maya; and a single class each on Diamond Peak History and Terrain. At the end of each day, you will have a tutorial with Nick.'

She glanced at Nick but he was studying her timetable. 'What's Response Ability?' she asked, looking back at Tynan.

'Developing your ability to use the Radiance in response to whatever arises,' Tynan replied.

'It's like what we used in the forest with the spirits,' Nick added. 'Instead of using swords, we used the power of the Light because it was more effective in that situation.'

Ariel nodded, then chuckled. 'You know, I thought I'd left school behind when I came onto the mountain. I hope I don't have to sit exams.'

'There are no exams on crash courses,' Nick replied. 'The indication of whether you pass or fail is whether or not you defeat the demons.'

'Right. If you fail, you die, or become a demon's slave. Mmm, I think I'd prefer exams actually.'

Tynan nodded. 'Everything you need will be provided by your teachers, but don't write notes during the talks.'

'Why not?'

'Because when you face a demon, you won't have time to read them even if they do happen to be in your pocket. You have to listen and remember what you hear, so it's there in your mind when you need it.'

That made sense.

'Now if you don't mind,' he continued, 'I have papers to mark, and you two look like you're in need of a shower and a good rest.' Tynan stood and Ariel and Nick followed. 'Shall we meet for dinner at the usual time?'

'Sure. See you later,' Nick said and they left Tynan to his work.

Ariel's limbs suddenly felt heavy, dragged down by a tiredness she hadn't noticed before. Perhaps it was the food settling in her stomach, or perhaps, more likely, the trauma of the morning weighing on her soul.

They walked along the corridor in silence until Nick opened the door into his office. The modern office equipment didn't fit with the ancient buildings and rustic lifestyle of the Hidden Realm, or even with the old wooden desks they sat on. 'What do you do, exactly?' she asked.

'Translate from the ancient language into modern and vice versa.'

'What sort of things?'

'Texts and talks. It's so the Magans, the Haba and others who speak the ancient tongue can have a copy of the teachings in their own language, and so that those who speak only English can read the ancient texts written by the Pathmaker and other early travellers. For years, no one had the skill or the time to translate them, so they just got left in the bowels of the library.'

'Wow.' It sounded important. 'Who are the Haba?'

'A race of Warriors who protect the path on the Upper Reaches.'

Ariel nodded. She hadn't expected Sheldra to be such a large, busy place, and on top of the terrible morning, it was all becoming just a little overwhelming. 'I don't know about you, but I could really do with the shower and rest Tynan suggested.'

'Sure, follow me.'

They picked up their packs, slipped them on and left the office, closing the door behind them. Nick led Ariel back to the entrance way and up the unadorned stairs opposite the main door. Once upstairs, they turned right and followed the corridor past several doors before Nick stopped outside one with his name on it. 'This is mine. The next one's yours.'

'So this is where you live when you're not on the road with Walnut?'

'Mostly; want to see?'

'Sure.'

'Isn't it sweet that they put us together,' he said with a cheeky grin as he opened his door and gestured her in. 'Just a wall between us.'

Ariel ignored him, her attention taken by the room. Like the rest of the building, it had white painted walls and a polished wooden floor, but unlike the dormitory buildings, a French style double door opened onto a small balcony. It reminded Ariel of her balcony at Tynan's house, but the comparison ended there. Unlike the old-fashioned décor at the Observatory, this room had simple modern furnishings and an airy, spacious feel. A pale wooden chest of drawers, a wardrobe and a bookshelf overflowing with books sat against the walls. A double bed with a black and white cover and a white leather sofa took up the rest of the room. The room wasn't at all what Ariel expected, but then she didn't know what she had expected. She hadn't even thought about Nick living anywhere.

'The sofa was a present from my mother,' he explained as he dumped his pack on the floor.

Ariel's smaller room had the same white walls, but less furniture, just a single metal bed frame and a dark wood dressing table, wardrobe and bedside table. Not a home, just a room. She plonked her pack on the floor with a sigh. 'It'll be good not to have to carry that for a few days!'

'I reckon,' Nick agreed. 'Shall we meet in my office in about an hour?'

Ariel nodded. She hoped the shower would wash more than just the grime away.

***

Just over an hour later, refreshed from a shower and a nap, Ariel made her way downstairs. The door to Nick's office was slightly ajar, so she pushed it cautiously and peeked inside. Nick sat on the edge of his desk, frowning at a sheath of paper. He looked up and smiled.

'I wasn't sure if I was supposed to knock,' she said.

'You're not a student yet.'

Ariel wasn't quite sure what he meant by that, but the thought of him as her teacher in this formal setting made him suddenly seem terribly remote.

24

He laid the papers in a neat pile on his desk. 'Are you ready for the tour?'

Ariel nodded.

Once outside, he pointed down the road to the impressive building at the end. 'The Great Hall awaits your perusal, ma'am.'

They walked side by side towards the ornate three storied building, a stark contrast to the plain dormitories. Here, the richness was clearly considered the focus, not a distraction. A glass dome rose in the centre of the top floor, and a wide veranda, supported by elegant columns, wrapped around the ground floor on all sides. The gardens, lawns and pathways around the building continued the curves of the street layout, and lines of different plants radiated outward in a display of mathematical and aesthetic perfection. Ariel imagined that, if seen from above, the great Hall would be the centre of a mandala made of streets and buildings.

'Where is everyone?' she asked, noting that the spacious gardens and walkways were deserted.

'In class.'

Ariel stopped at the edge of the veranda, awed by the life-sized bronze statues of Warriors with wide eyes and drawn swords that flanked either side of the main entrance's double doors. A richly carved and painted image of Diamond Peak decorated the doors. Though stylised, it managed to convey the majesty and mystery of the realm, as if the essence of it dwelt within the paint—perhaps it did. Colourful swirls and spirals covered the columns, and runes drew Ariel's gaze to the sandstone architraves. Nick gave the great doors a gentle push and they opened smoothly. Ariel's jaw dropped.

Twitchet took that moment to walk between Ariel and Nick. 'Fish!' he declared, staring up at her.

'Why are you here?' she asked, wondering if the cat's manners would deteriorate again now that Walnut wasn't with them.

'Just doing the rounds.' He sounded blasé, but his shining eyes betrayed his enthusiasm for the spectacle of the Great Hall.

Nick squatted down and stroked the little cat. 'You like this place, don't you?'

'I spent a lot of time here once,' he replied.

'When?' Ariel asked.

'Another life,' Twitchet muttered and walked into the hall.

Nick and Ariel exchanged a glance. 'After you,' he said.

Ariel stepped across the threshold into the hushed interior. Golden light poured through the glass dome, three stories up, and illuminated a huge gilded statue that took her breath away. The seated figure rose almost as high as the glass ceiling and stared down with an all-knowing, all-feeling gaze that vanquished her thoughts in an instant. An aisle between chairs set in rows beckoned her towards the base of the statue, but she stayed rooted to the spot and continued gazing around. Smaller golden statues sat on either side of the big one, and a wide balcony flanked the hall on three sides. Stillness and serenity pervaded the atmosphere.

'I love people's first impression,' Nick said, looking at Ariel with a grin.

'Is that the Pathmaker?' she asked in a whisper, her eyes fixed on the peaceful face of the golden statue.

'Yep. Without that guy, none of this would have happened.'

'It's unreal.' She walked quietly down the aisle between rows of chairs.

The great statue exuded a tangible feeling of peace, so overpowering that Ariel's unease simply melted away beneath the Pathmaker's compassionate, majestic gaze. They stopped halfway down the aisle and stood without moving. Just looking at the statue opened her heart and set her mind soaring. Its presence moved her to her core.

Ariel pointed to the two smaller statues sitting cross-legged at the base of the Pathmaker. 'Who are they?' she asked in barely more than a whisper.

'Great guides from the past,' Nick replied, 'the one on the left is Aya and the one on the right is Larl.'

Ariel wondered at their other-worldly beauty. 'Did they really look like that?'

'I doubt it. They're images of their Radiant Bodies, not their corporeal ones. See how the Pathmaker has a sword. It's the sword of wisdom. Aya has the seven eyes that see and care for everyone, and Larl has the flames of power. Those are the three qualities we need to defeat Rasama.'

Ariel sighed. 'Daunting, isn't it?'

Nick's hand reached out and gently clasped hers, sending a tender energy flowing between them. He smiled at her, his eyes twinkling warmly in the soft light in the Hall. 'Are you ready for lunch?'

She nodded and turned from the statues with a sigh. Lunch she could handle. King of the demons? Not so much. At least not now.

No sooner had they stepped out of the hall than the sound of a huge gong rang out. Shuffling papers, earnest voices murmuring and soft feet pattering on wooden floors broke the silence. Doors opened and people spilled into the courtyards and onto the paths around the classrooms. Scholars and students of all ages, gender, shapes, sizes and races swarmed around them. The scholars had shaved heads and most wore long maroon coats, or jackets with hoods and the words, 'Sheldra University' written on the back in gold lettering.

Nick led her to the dining hall next to the building where they had their rooms. The room, ten times the size of Tynan's office, had a servery at the far end and a kitchen beyond. Heavy-looking wooden chairs sat around large tables, and bench seats lined the walls, all solid and sensible like the rest of the university. People in the queue stepped aside and dipped their heads, letting Nick and Ariel go before them.

'Why are they doing that?' she whispered.

'I'm a tutor,' he replied.

'And I'm new? Is that why they're staring?'

'Something like that,' he replied evasively.

Ariel frowned. Why did she feel that these people expected something of her? What wasn't he telling her?

The smell of food knocked the questions aside and they helped themselves to fresh bread, stew, steamed vegetables and fresh fruit, then sat side by side in the corner, as far as possible from the cluster of people at the servery.

'What do you think of the food?' Nick asked after several mouthfuls.

'Okay,' Ariel replied with a shrug.

Nick snorted. 'You're just being polite.'

'Okay, so it could be better, but it's an institution, what can you expect?'

'I have an alternative,' he whispered conspiratorially.

'What?'

'Remember the kitchen next to my office. We can stock it this afternoon, then we can eat good food in private. I always cook for Tynan and Walnut when they're here, but Yule usually comes here, she feels she should do what everyone else does.'

The idea heartened Ariel. She didn't like being watched, especially not when she ate.

Twitchet suddenly appeared and jumped onto the table. 'What about me?'

'Write a shopping list,' Nick replied.

'Easy, fish, fish, fish and cream. My needs are simple.'

'Get off the table,' Ariel said.

'My paws are clean,' he protested.

'Maybe, but you're causing a minor stir.' Nick tilted his head to the rest of the room. People were staring again.

'Fine. Does your room have a cat door?'

'No, but I can arrange a doorbell at paw height.'

4

Orientation

After lunch, Nick showed Ariel the classrooms housed in plain sandstone buildings, like the dormitories, except with larger windows. Dark wooden desks with matching chairs set in neat rows filled rooms roughly twice the size of Nick's office. Ariel walked into an empty room and surveyed the walls: not a mark on them, and no rubbish on the floors either—unlike her off-mountain school. No whiteboard in sight either, only a huge blackboard and chalk dust.

'You're downright spoilt, you know,' Nick said, leading her out again. 'You have all the best teachers.'

'And the best tutor?' she asked with a grin.

He grimaced. 'No, you got a bum one there.'

'Perhaps Walnut thought I might like to see you once each day.' Ariel only half joked; her schedule had no room for Nick.

He walked back to the entrance way. 'We will have dinner together.'

'Yeah, but just dinner.' She couldn't keep a hint of disappointment from her voice.

He grinned. 'You're not going to miss me, are you?'

'Of course not!'

He chuckled. 'The library's next.'

After showing Ariel the library, the observatory, the art rooms and the training rooms, Nick took her to the grocery store. They loaded their purchases into day packs then wandered back to the kitchen/living room next to his office and stashed the goods in cupboards or the gas-powered refrigerator. As soon as they'd finished, Nick walked into his office without a word. Ariel stood at the doorway looking in and feeling forgotten.

Yule stood staring out the window, Spud like a guard dog at her heels. She turned when Nick entered. 'The practices for Miramar have begun.'

'Not in the main hall, I hope.'

'No, I got Tynan's message. It's upstairs, just the practitioners.' The usually smiling scholar looked sad and drained. Nick wrapped her into a brotherly embrace. At least, Ariel hoped it was brotherly. Not that it was any business of hers, of course.

'Let's have a look at that manuscript,' he said when he released her.

A smile lit up her face. 'Way to go, partner!' She jumped over Spud, strode to the messier of the two desks and picked up an ancient, hand-bound book.

Ariel suddenly felt obsolete.

'Can we get that out of here first?' Nick asked, pointing to Spud.

'I'll take him,' Ariel said quickly. 'We can have some quality time together.'

'Thanks.'

'He has an enclosure in the courtyard,' Yule explained.

Ariel scooped the wombat up and took him outside via the French doors in the living area. Head-height sandstone walls made a courtyard the same width as the living area and twice as long. Ariel deposited the now wriggling wombat into the wire-fenced area at the far end, and he ran into the wombat-sized concrete drainpipe in the corner. Someone had covered the gap at the end of the pipe with dirt and covered the entrance with a heavy cloth. Ariel smiled. Her mum would approve of the quarters.

It looked as if Spud's home had been erected over the only patch of garden in the area. Sandstone paved the rest of the courtyard and made bench seats around a table in the middle. Various herbs grew in terracotta pots, and a couple of small shrubs sat on either side of a rustic gate in the centre of the wall. The hinges squeaked when Ariel opened it. She glanced around, but no one came to tell her not to, so she peered outside onto a road with a matching building on the other side. A grass strip, unmarked by footsteps, separated the courtyard from the road. Apparently, Nick and Yule had no reason to use this entrance, but Yule would have to once Spud grew a bit more.

She closed the gate and wondered what to do next. Nick had apparently forgotten about her, so she went to her room to sort out her washing and give in to the tiredness that had settled on her soul.

***

That evening, Ariel helped Nick cook dinner, and they ate a friendly meal with Tynan and Yule. Just as they were finishing, a messenger came from the portal with a note from Walnut.

'He says that all is well,' Tynan relayed as he read, 'and he'll be here after Miramar's cremation early in the morning of the fourth day. He wants to know if you are safe.'

The messenger handed Tynan a note pad and pen. The sword master scrawled his reply and handed it back to the messenger who would take it through the portal to Walnut in Minion Hills. The atmosphere became subdued in the wake of the message, and after a moment of silence, Nick and Tynan stood quietly and began clearing the table.

'Nick's such a gem, isn't he?' Yule said quietly, leaning across the table towards Ariel. 'We all love him here, and he's the best tutor.' She grinned and sat back in silence as Nick returned to the table to wipe it down.

Ariel nodded and smiled. It felt strange to see this other side of Nick, someone with a job and a place to live, someone who obviously had a lot of knowledge and skill and a great deal of respect from his colleagues. She couldn't help looking at him with new eyes. Did she know him at all?

As soon as the dishes were finished, Tynan and Yule excused themselves and left the room. Ariel yawned and Nick gave her an affectionate smile.

'Time for bed?' he asked softly.

'Yeah, but you don't have to come.'

'Yes, I do. Someone should always be with you.'

'So you think Emot might appear before I'm ready?'

'I think he'll strike as soon as he's probed your mind for some ammunition.'

'He does that?'

'His emanations do. They sneak around here, staying out of sight generally, but here nevertheless. I'd like to get rid of them before they have a chance to get inside your head. It takes a bit of preparation before you can face Emot safely.'

'So I hear.' She yawned again.

'Come on.' He led the way upstairs, opened the door to her room, flicked on a light switch and looked inside. 'All clear.'

'I've got electricity,' Ariel said in surprise. 'That's good.'

'Yeah, there's a system for this whole building. It used to be much smaller and just do our office, but Tynan extended it a couple of months ago.'

'So, things are changing on the mountain.'

'Things are always changing. That's why everything is possible.' He grinned mischievously. 'Anyway, sleep well; I'll see you in the morning.' He stepped forward and embraced her as naturally as if they were brother and sister. 'Non-predatory?' he asked.

'Quite acceptable,' she replied, bathing in the warm glow that embraced them both.

'I'll be next door,' he said as they parted, 'so just shout if you need me, and make sure you do a good shield. There are no building shields here; the place is just too big.'

Ariel sighed as she closed her bedroom door. Her quest lay heavily on her shoulders, weighed down by tiredness and a forboding sense of abandonment. In an effort to stay positive, she told herself that she would study diligently so that her victory over Emot would be assured. She would kill him as soon as her course was over so they could set off to the Hermitage at the end of the week. There she would upgrade her skills to Cogin level and take out the last bodyguard. She could do this. Her studies here would ensure it.

By the time she realised the naivety of her assumption that conscientious study was all that was required, it would be too late.

5

Dennis

After breakfast the next morning, a freckle-faced man with ginger hair, dressed in black jeans and T-shirt, met Ariel and Nick outside their building. Shorter and more solidly built than Nick, but of similar age, he shook Ariel's hand firmly when Nick introduced him as Dennis.

'I've been engaged to accompany you throughout the day,' he said in a deep voice.

'Personal insurance,' Nick added with a wry grin. 'Dennis has defeated Emot, so he'll lop the head off any emanation that tries to sneak up on you.'

Dennis nodded and folded his arms over his muscled chest, like a bouncer at a nightclub.

'He's another off-mountain person,' Nick continued. 'So you have that in common, and he's the main reason electricity is coming to the mountain, but I'll let him tell you about that.'

The gong rang across the campus, calling Ariel to her first class.

'See you later,' Nick said and disappeared back into their home building without a backwards glance.

Ariel took a deep breath and headed off to class with Dennis beside her. At least the sun shone today. 'What's your role in getting electricity here?' she asked.

'I'm an electrician. I told Tynan the possibilities. He got inspired and I helped him.'

Ariel waited for more but, apparently, Dennis was a man of few words.

They walked past several teenagers watering the flower gardens. They wore scholars' coats and had shaved heads, and Ariel couldn't tell if they were male or female. 'Why do some shave their heads and others don't?' she asked Dennis.

'Some, like me, would rather embrace a woman than celibacy,' he said impassively.

Ariel blushed. 'Oh. So the shaved heads mean you're celibate.'

'That's right.'

'Are they like that for life?'

'Not necessarily. A lot of people take a vow of celibacy just while they're studying here and give it up when they leave. Others do it for the first degree and drop it after that, like Nick.'

'Nick was celibate!'

'Yeah. I hear that when his hair started to grow, the girls went crazy.'

Ariel nodded, that wouldn't be hard to imagine. 'But why be celibate?'

'Sex can be a big distraction from your studies, and I reckon a lot of them think they can beat Emot more easily if they remove that whole thing from their life.' He shrugged. 'I don't know, maybe it's true, maybe it's not. Anyway, here we are.'

Ariel nodded. At least she didn't have that distraction. She'd worked hard to avoid it though; perhaps too hard.

They entered the classroom to find several people already there, a couple of robust, dignified-looking Magans and various people in ordinary mountain-style clothing who could have come from any of the mountain villages.

All eyes turned to Ariel and heads dipped in greeting. Ariel gave a nervous smile and dipped her head in return. She had that horrible feeling that they expected something from her, something she wouldn't be able to give.

A tall, striking Magan woman walked gracefully towards them. She flicked her black hair over her shoulder as she drew close, exposing the Menhir clan emblem embroidered on the shoulder of her deep purple waistcoat.

'Hello,' she said with perfect diction. 'My name is Kelee, and I expect you are Ariel for whom we have all been waiting.'

'Yes,' Ariel replied. 'I hope you haven't been waiting long.'

'Not at all, you are within two days of your expected arrival, but that is not my interest at this moment.' She paused for a moment and looked pointedly at Dennis. He smiled politely and moved out of hearing, but kept a close eye on the exchange. Kelee continued in a whisper. 'Yule gathered the Magans together late yesterday afternoon and told us of Miramar's sad fate. She didn't tell us the details, but she did tell me personally that it was a Menhir clansman and I am keen to know who it was. You were there, I believe, do you know?'

Ariel's eyes moistened. She didn't know what to say, and she didn't want to remember. The experience was still too raw.

'I'm sorry if you don't want to talk about it, but please,' Kelee whispered. 'I am Menhir's daughter, my clan's deeds reflect strongly on me. I must know.'

'You're Kestril's sister,' Ariel whispered, staring into the woman's startling green eyes. Of course, she saw it now, the same chiseled features softened into a womanly beauty, the same stately bearing.

'Do you know my brother?'

'Umm, I've met him, yes,' Ariel replied, hoping she hadn't said anything she shouldn't have.

'It wasn't him, was it?' Kelee asked urgently.

'No, no of course not.' How much did Kelee know about her brother's allegiances?

'Then who?'

'I didn't see, but Nick said it was Beak.'

'Beak,' Kelee exclaimed. 'That black hearted villain, the worst of the Menhirs. Oh, I am stained by kinship. How can I hold my head high amongst these good people when they find out?'

'They needn't know,' Ariel replied. 'I'll not tell anyone.'

'You would do that for me?'

'And for your family.' She couldn't mention Kestril by name.

The door opened, and Ariel's eyes widened when she saw who had entered.

'The Haba,' Kelee whispered, seeing Ariel's surprise.

Five statuesque, brown-skinned people wearing black leather trousers, fitted T-shirts with swirling designs on the front, and wide, well-stocked weapon belts looked around the room with glistening black eyes. Tattoos curved across high cheek bones and bare arms. Silver studs decorated their earlobes, and chains adorned with charms hung around their necks.

Long black hair, softer features and no facial tattoos marked two of them as women but, though finer, their bodies looked as powerful as the men's. Their noble bearing made a dramatic entrance, and their presence dominated the room. They murmured to each other in the ancient language and sat down.

Kelee nodded to Ariel then joined the other Magans. Ariel watched her walk away with a mixture of awe at her regal demeanor and delight at her clothes. She wore a pale blue Magan-style loose-sleeved shirt and a deep blue velvet waistcoat over narrow-legged heavy cotton trousers. A wide, black leather belt covered with various sized pockets sat around her hips. Ariel was just wondering where she could buy such a belt when Layla entered.

Ariel hadn't seen the pixie-like older woman since the battle at the Observatory, and her bright green hair looked even spikier than she remembered. As usual, Layla wore a green tunic, and this one had an intricate embroidered pattern in more shades of green than Ariel knew existed. Layla scanned the class with shrewd eyes, her copious bracelets and necklaces rattling with every movement. Ariel caught her eye and smiled.

Layla nodded in acknowledgement, then introduced the course by speaking about the Rasa clans and their food preferences. 'The Bitah clan craves hatred and anger; the Amics feed primarily on arrogance; Emots lust after grasping and craving, and Cogins prefer jealousy. We fight them all the same way, but each clan has its own methods of trapping you, and if you can't avoid their traps, you can't kill them, so we'll be working on identifying the ways in which they trap you.'

She repeated her words in the old language for the sake of the Haba and Magans.

'Now we will break into small groups,' she continued. 'Those concentrating on Bitah will go to study room one, those focusing on Amic, room two, and those dealing with Emot will stay here. Groups one and two, your tutors will be waiting for you.'

Most of the students got up and left, leaving Ariel with all the Habas, two Magans—a youngish man and an older woman— a fair haired girl from Observatory, and a man from Terralgo—a village to the west of Observatory. During the introductions, Ariel discovered that the Habas had already defeated Emot but wanted to do the course as part of their training to be teachers for their clan.

The rest of the students in Ariel's group had returned to their homes after a failed attempt at defeating Emot. Now they were considering another push up the mountain and wanted a refresher course. They all spoke some English, but the Haba's vocabulary was limited, so Layla often had to translate.

'Emot is a wily and relentless opponent,' Layla began, 'and particularly good at slipping away and returning when you least expect it. As you know, some of the things that arise in your mind are easier to catch and let go of than others. So we will be looking at the sort of things he is likely to hit you with personally.'

'What's the difference between wanting something and craving it?' the blond girl, whose name was Marcia asked.

'Wanting is based on a simple appreciation for the object,' Layla replied. 'You won't fall apart if you don't get it and you can be happy without it. Craving, however, is based on a sense of lack in yourself and on fear that you won't get what you want.

'Wanting becomes craving when instead of simply feeling your desires as they are in the present and letting them pass in their own natural way, you chase after them, stir them up and lose yourself in an imagined future. That is where Emot will catch you, and his barbs are designed to turn your simple desires into desperate cravings.'

Marcia nodded, and Ariel shivered at the thought of the kind of desperation Layla must be referring to. She wouldn't want to be caught in this demon's grip.

'Task one,' Layla continued, 'is to make a list of the things you desire the most and make sure you include all the senses, taste, feelings, sounds and so on.' She handed out notebooks and pencils.

Ariel noticed that Dennis had recorded the talk on a small battery-powered tape recorder.

'What's that for?' she whispered.

'The tapes go to scholars whose job it is to type it all up, then the translators do a full translation in the old language. Then the documents are sent off to the students so they can study the material again. It's only done for the main teachers,' Dennis replied quietly.

Ariel nodded. The university was a well-organised place.

'Are you doing your work, Ariel?' Layla asked abruptly.

Ariel flinched. 'Um, yes.'

Layla pulled a face that said, *you can't fool me.* 'You in particular do not have time to waste,' she said curtly.

Ariel grimaced and put her attention on her task. The first thing that came to mind was her mother. More than anything Ariel wanted to free Nadima from the demons. She only had to think of it and a burning desire for her mother's release rose up in her. No doubt Emot would play with that and try to turn it into craving.

Second on her list was killing Rasama which would free her mother and get rid of the Serpentine infestation in the whole human race. After that, she listed all sorts of things from the Magan skirt belt to Pavlova, the soft-centred, cream-covered meringue cake she loved.

'Now list the things you don't want in your life, or that you don't like,' Layla instructed.

The students wrote again.

Ariel's list went from demons, bullies and murderers to manipulation of people by the media, followed by an assortment of random things ending with the smell of rotten potatoes and Rasas.

'Why do we need to concern ourselves with things like chocolate?' Marcia, asked. 'Surely it's too small a thing for Emot to bother with.'

'Ah,' Layla replied, 'this is a common mistake that people make, but I have seen Warriors resist craving their strongest desires, then fall prey to craving for a simple thing like chocolate. Many are caught on food because Emot can make you feel hungry and tantalise you with the smell or a tiny taste of good things, just enough so that you crave more. It can happen quickly and before you know it, it's Emot feeding on you, not you feeding on chocolate.'

'Do you really taste it or just think you do?' Ariel asked.

'There will not be any chocolate in your mouth, just as your lover will not be truly there if Emot lures you with that, but it will seem to you that it is there, for you will taste it and feel it and see it more strongly than with Bitah and Amic.

'Now, before lunch tomorrow, we will work with food, so you are not allowed to have anything to eat beforehand.'

'That's cruel,' Ariel protested.

'Do you think Emot is not cruel?' Layla retorted.

Heat flushed Ariel's face.

'If we are to prepare you well,' Layla continued, 'we must make it as real as possible.'

When the gong rang to signal the end of class, the students filed out of the room with their notebooks. 'It sounds a bit masochistic, don't you think?' Ariel whispered to Dennis.

He looked at her without the faintest trace of amusement. 'No, this isn't about enjoying pain; it's about not freaking out when you get it.'

Ariel only just managed to stop herself from rolling her eyes. Dennis didn't look like he was going to be much fun.

An old fat scholar called Henry McKay took the next class on the history of the mountain guides. Dennis told her very seriously that Mr McKay ate too many steamed buns, and when Ariel pointed out that the History teacher looked like one too, he didn't even crack a smile. This time, Ariel did indulge in an eye roll.

Despite Mr. McKay's droning voice and bland delivery, Ariel managed to stay awake as he laid out the names of a long line of the distinguished guides that lived before Maya, Layla and Walnut. Each one had brought at least one other Warrior to the top of the mountain before their death, so that there was another master guide to continue the lineage of knowledge and experience that enabled travellers to conquer both the mountain and Rasama.

When McKay began following the ownership of the Blade of Aarod down to the present day, Ariel perked up immediately. This was her lineage, a line passed down from parent to child ever since the first Aarod—the first Warrior to reach the summit and defeat Rasama after the Pathmaker laid out the path.

'This is the only lineage that comes through a bloodline,' McKay explained, 'and each wearer of the blade has become a guide in their own right. The last one to wield this blade was also called Aarod. He was already an established and respected guide and Walnut's finest trainee, and he would have become a great guide had he not been killed in an unfortunate accident on the Far Upper Reaches.'

Ariel stared at the teacher, her skin prickling. She hadn't known her father was a guide, or that he'd died on the Far Upper Reaches, only that it had happened somewhere on the mountain. Only those who had defeated Cogin and were ready for their final battle got that far.

'Many, including myself, thought that was the end of the line of Aarod. There was some whisper of a child but no one saw her on the mountain until recently. Apparently, she had been hidden off-mountain until old enough to battle Rasas.'

Ariel studied her notebook, letting her hair fall over her face, hiding what felt like a dreadfully red face, and praying he wasn't going to say anything more. But the man realised her worst fears.

'The mark of this family is their copper coloured hair and you may have noticed that we have the last of the line in the room with us today.'

Chairs scraped, clothing rustled and Ariel felt the eyes of the class on her. She bit her lip and didn't look up.

'I'm sorry, Miss Ariel, I don't want to embarrass you, but on behalf of everyone I would like to say welcome and tell you how glad we are that Aarod, who I was very fond of, has a living heir and that the Blade of Aarod is once again strapped to the side of someone qualified to use it.'

Ariel nodded but kept her head down.

'Can we see it?' someone asked—a teenage boy by the sound of his voice.

'Now, now, my boy,' McKay admonished him. 'The blade of Aarod is not a museum exhibit.'

Ariel gulped and wished he would get back to the rest of the subject, but apparently, the topic of the heir to the blade of Aarod was to be the end of his lecture.

'We all wish you luck, Miss Ariel, and pray that the lineage will continue.'

'Thank you,' Ariel whispered.

The class erupted into applause and Ariel, completely mortified, closed her eyes. Luckily, the gong rang before anyone could say anything else. She rushed from the classroom with Dennis hot on her heels.

'Are you all right?' he asked when he caught up with her outside.

'Let's just say it's lucky there isn't a demon that's fond of the flavour of embarrassment,' Ariel replied.

Dennis nodded thoughtfully, and Ariel turned her head so he couldn't see her grimace at his appalling lack of humour.

'There's no need to be embarrassed,' he said. 'Mr. McKay speaks for all of us.'

She turned back and looked him in the eyes. 'You don't think that might put the teeniest bit of pressure on me?'

'Maybe,' Dennis shrugged, 'but no one doubts an heir to the blade of Aarod. I'm sure you're quite capable of carrying on the line.'

'Oh yeah, sure,' Ariel retorted. 'Not only am I expected to defeat Rasama but I'm supposed to be breeding stock too. You seem to forget that I could have an accident too, or maybe I don't want to have kids. Perhaps you shouldn't get your hopes up or you might be disappointed.'

Dennis frowned, and Ariel shook her head in frustration and strode off. She checked behind her for Gimps, but apparently her annoyance had been too brief for one of the little demons to appear. Now that McKay had publicly named her as heir to the Blade of Aarod, and now that she knew what that meant, she could hardly be seen with a Gimp trailing behind her. *I'll have to hide in the bathroom next time Dennis annoys me,* she thought with a sigh. If Nick was there, she could have said it aloud and they would've had a laugh.

6

Classes

When Ariel arrived at the training room for her next class, Tynan gave her a wide welcoming smile. She returned the gesture, knowing she could trust him not to embarrass her in front of everyone.

He began by asking them to draw their weapons, but when Ariel drew her dagger and whispered the incantation to transform it into a sword, she heard a low whistle from behind. She swung around. A teenage boy stood staring at her sword with wide eyes. Unfortunately, alerted by his whistle, everyone else stared too. She shot a desperate look at Tynan.

'You boy. What's your name?' Tynan asked in a commanding tone.

'Jamie, sir.'

'Out here then. Let's test your skill.'

The boy gulped but walked to the front of the class as requested. Tynan engaged him in a low-key sword fight during which he pointed out the boy's weaknesses and blunders.

'That is where your focus should lie,' Tynan said emphatically, 'on improving your skills, not on the fancy hardware that someone else may carry. What anyone else does, or is, or wears, is not your business. Is that understood?'

The boy nodded and returned to his spot behind Ariel. No one dared comment for the remainder of the class, leaving Ariel to enjoy the physical exercise—something she especially welcomed after a morning of sitting down. As well as instructing them on sword fighting and projecting power through their blades, Tynan revised how to make curse shields and told them that over the next few days they would also practice strengthening their protective spheres and magic shields.

At the end of Tynan's class, Dennis accompanied Ariel to the cafeteria for lunch. She tried to strike up a conversation with her companion, but he answered in single words, and his complete lack of humour made her long for Nick to come and brighten up her lunch hour. Even the food tasted bland without Nick around to shoot jibes at it.

She told herself that had she been with anyone just slightly more interesting than Dennis, she wouldn't have missed Nick quite so much. As it was, she couldn't help noting that he'd been by her side almost continually since he'd joined her and Walnut four days into her journey. At some point in their travels, she had come to take his presence for granted.

After lunch, she and Dennis arrived with the other students at the classroom designated for Walnut's class on the nature of reality. Of course, Walnut wasn't there, but they all assumed that they would have a substitute teacher. Jamie, the teenage boy who had taken a fancy to her dagger, had just declared that, since no one had turned up, they must have a free period, when Yule walked in with Spud trotting at her heels.

'Sorry to keep you waiting,' she said with her usual smile. 'Your teacher for this class has not yet arrived, so you are to go to the library and withdraw a book called *Stages in Understanding the Nature of Reality*. Until The Precious Guide arrives, you will read this during these periods. Thank you.' She left the room without another word. Ariel didn't even get a chance to say hello to Spud.

Nick had shown her the outside of the Great Library, but they hadn't gone inside, so when Ariel stepped into the cool interior, the smell of leather and paper, the sound of silence and the sight of shelves overflowing with books in a seemingly endless room hit her senses in one breathtaking moment. She smiled with delight.

Plain wooden stairs stood to the left of the entrance, one set going to the basement—the old part of the library—and the other to the first floor. Dark wooden shelves ran between pillars, painted white like the walls, and librarians wearing the University colours of maroon and gold sat at huge desks, one near the door and several more in offices visible through glass windows in an internal partition.

'Follow me,' Dennis whispered.

Ariel followed him down the central aisle, wincing when her sneakers squeaked a little on the wooden floor, but no one paid her any attention. Rows of shelves ran off at right angles on either side, all neatly labeled with names and numbers. Occasionally, the space between rows was double its usual size and pleasingly arranged with leather lounges and desks and chairs.

Dennis found the book she needed and sat nearby when Ariel curled up on one of the couches to read the unfamiliar subject matter. Never before had she read a book that made her question her ability to understand, and she found herself spending a lot of time staring at the table in front of her, trying to decide if it was still a table if it didn't have any legs.

When the gong sounded next, Ariel checked out the book and headed towards the Great Hall for Maya's class. Her companion seemed more relaxed after their time in the library, so she tried once more to strike up a conversation. 'How did you come to be on the mountain?'

'I found *The Mountain Path* in a bookshop and read it. Then I phoned the number in the back of the book and got onto a man called Bob Tingle.'

Ariel waited for Dennis to continue, but he didn't. 'What did Bob do?' she prompted.

'Taught me the basics, and when I said I felt ready to climb the mountain, he told me to pack and meet him at the lookout. We trained there for a while, then he led me up a track, and at the top, there was the Hidden Realm. It'd never been there before, but it was there then.'

'It's a bit of a shock, isn't it?'

'Not really. I was well prepared.'

I wasn't, Ariel thought, but she didn't mention it. 'How did you feel when you saw the Serpentine and the Radiance for the first time?'

'I haven't seen it.'

'But you saw the mountain.'

'I don't think I would've if Bob hadn't taken me,' he replied thoughtfully. 'But I don't need to see the Serpentine to know it's there. I can feel it rise in me, and in others. I can see how it clouds the eyes of people when they're doing wrong, how it shuts them off from others and turns them cold. And I can see the Radiance in the love in people's eyes, in their joy and concern for everyone, and I can feel it in my heart when it's open.'

'That's beautiful,' Ariel said.

Dennis shrugged. 'It's just how things are.'

Ariel smiled. Dennis might be boring, but he had seen something with his ordinary sight that she hadn't noticed until she found her Second Sight.

Maya was already there when Ariel walked into the Great Hall for Response Ability, and the ancient, white-haired woman walked towards her in a swirl of pale floral skirts. A soft white shawl lay over her shoulders and instead of her usual demon-kicking boots, she wore a simple pair of white shoes. Maya embraced Ariel warmly, and Ariel fought back an inexplicable urge to burst into tears. She had no idea why Maya had that effect on her.

'It is good to see you again,' Maya said. 'Tynan told Layla and myself about your journey, and I must say that much of it is quite fascinating.' She looked pointedly at the locket hanging at Ariel's neck.

Ariel smiled. 'Meeting a Gana is for sure the most fascinating thing that's ever happened to me, but terrifying is probably a better word for it.'

Maya's eyes twinkled. 'We shall talk more about it some other time.' She turned her attention to the other students who were filing in. 'Please sit in front of the statue of Aya.'

Ariel sat in silence and let the tranquil atmosphere of the great hall permeate her while she waited for the rest of the students to join them. She stared at the exquisitely-crafted, gilded image of Aya, the woman who, for Warriors, represented love and compassion. The statue sat cross-legged on a huge flower, had wide awake eyes—but with a reassuring softness—and the innocent beauty of a sixteen-year-old. An extra eye sat vertically in the centre of her forehead, and more eyes marked the soles of her feet and the palms of her hands.

One hand held a flower at her heart, the other rested on her knee. She wore a crown of flowers over long hair painted black and bronzed fabric wreathed her hips. Although only a statue, the figure had such a powerful presence that it almost felt alive.

The last of the class joined them and Maya began. 'Response Ability is your ability to respond with empathy in all situations and is one of the qualities of the Radiance along with openness and clarity. It is also the seed of love and compassion and a powerful weapon against the Serpentine and its demons.'

'I didn't need love and compassion to kill Bitah,' Jamie said.

'It was there,' Maya replied, 'you just weren't aware of it. Since love destroys anger and hatred, how could it possibly be absent from the Radiant Power that you used to defeat Bitah, the master of hatred?'

Jamie shrugged.

Maya continued. 'There are two ways we can develop this response ability. One is to always act with a kind heart. The other way is to enter deeply into the Radiance, for in that mind state, we are naturally empathetically responsive to all situations, and love and compassion flow without obstruction.'

'Which is the best way, Miss?' asked one of the blonde girls.

'Both,' Maya replied. 'One works from the outside in and the other from the inside out. Each time you act with kindness, it poisons your Serpentine a little. This makes it easier to tune into your Radiance and the more you can do that, the more you will act with kindness. So each helps the other.'

Ariel frowned. She'd been so busy just getting through Minion Hills and killing demons that she'd practically forgotten about the parasite that made them, and yet it infected her, same as everyone. She thought the incantation for accessing the Radiance and looked through the Ordinary Layer of reality to the Radiant Layer beneath. With this Second Sight, Ariel could see the Radiance shining from everyone in an explosion of rainbows. She also saw the black greasy Serpentine that wrapped around it, hiding most of the Radiant Light. The sight disgusted her. Ariel sighed and returned to her ordinary perception.

The class chanted Aya's incantation, their voices filling the Great Hall. The syllables thrummed through Ariel's body and chased her thoughts away, leaving her mind soaring, as if in a vast cloudless sky.

In the endless blue of this mental landscape, called by the chant, Aya appeared, ethereal like a rainbow. Silk swathed her milk white limbs and brilliant white light poured from the centre of her chest into Ariel. It melted a hole in Ariel's Serpentine, freeing her Radiance and filling her with a fierce kind of joy and a powerful love that she longed to share with the whole world.

The class sat in that state until the gong sounded, then with Dennis trailing behind like a faithful puppy, Ariel set off for her tutorial with Nick.

✻✻✻

'Come in,' Nick called in reply to her knock on his office door. Ariel opened the door and stepped inside, followed by Dennis.

The office looked as it did the day before, except that a laptop sat open on Nick's desk, its screen glowing, and a couple of large books and several papers scrawled with Nick's fine handwriting spread across the rest of the desk.

Nick swivelled his office chair towards them and stood to take the tape recorder from Dennis.

'Thanks, Dennis. I hope you enjoyed your day.'

'I did,' he replied. 'It's great to have such excellent teachers and a distinguished classmate.'

Ariel would have hit him if he hadn't been so dead serious about it. She grimaced instead.

'Come back in half an hour,' Nick said. 'Yule will have finished walking Spud by then and she'll insist I get back to work.'

Dennis nodded and left the room, shutting the door behind him.

Nick burst out laughing.

'What?' Ariel asked.

'You should have seen your face; *such a distinguished classmate*.'

She tried to punch him on the arm but he skipped out of the way.

'It must have been terrible for you,' he teased, 'the famous holder of the Blade of Aarod!'

'Stop it! Honestly, Nick, everyone's so serious.'

'You need a cup of tea.' He chuckled and walked through the adjoining door into the kitchen.

Ariel followed him and sank onto the couch. 'I mean, what I'm learning is important and everything, but it's so intense without someone to lighten it up.'

'Why don't you lighten it up for everyone else?'

'I think Dennis might actually growl at me and everyone else would probably call for psychiatric assistance, scared that the line of Aarod might be tainted with humour.'

Nick chuckled again. 'They're too late, it already is tainted. Badly infected with laughter-producing humour. I'm afraid there's no hope.' The kettle boiled. Nick poured the water into a tea pot, and set it and two cups on the coffee table, then sat beside her.

'Any cookies?' she asked.

He moved a jumper off the table, revealing the jar of large cookies hidden beneath it. 'Not home made. Sorry.'

'They look pretty good.'

'They're okay, but not as good as the ones I make.'

Ariel grinned. 'You sure like your food, don't you?'

'Yeah, and Emot got me on it too.'

'He did? How?'

'Chocolate.'

'You're kidding,' Ariel exclaimed through a mouthful of what she figured was some kind of shortbread.

'I'm surprised Layla didn't tell you. It must have been one of the stupidest failures ever.' He poured them both tea and pushed a cup in front of Ariel, then took a cookie and lay back on the couch, stretching his long legs beneath the coffee table.

'How did he catch you?'

'He threw all sorts of traps at me, but I avoided the big ones without too much trouble because they're so obvious. I don't think he'd done his homework though because the porno films were pretty awful, an insult to my tastes. Then he tried to make me think that I had a chance of being Prime Minister. Can you believe that?'

'I gather that's not on your list of major desires then?' Ariel took a sip of tea and picked up another cookie.

'Not even on it.'

'I think you'd make a great PM.'

'I'd rather be a doctor.'

'Did he tempt you with that one?'

'Yeah, but I was prepared for it. I thought afterwards that maybe he wanted to give me a false sense of security because I remember thinking that the battle was easy, and next thing I knew, he was having lunch on me and I was desperate for another taste of the most amazing chocolate I'd ever tasted. I've never tasted anything like it since either.'

'How'd you get out of it?'

'Walnut blasted him into non-existence.'

'What was it like?'

'What?'

'Feeding Emot?'

'Why are you asking that? You fed Bitah. You know what it's like.'

'I heard it's different with Emot.'

'Hey, don't get into that little lure.'

'What lure?'

'Emot's feeding can feel, well, good. No, not good, pleasurable I guess. People can become addicted.'

'Oh.'

'But forget that for now; tell me about your day.'

'McKay exposed me as the heir to the Blade of Aarod.' She said the last six words with a scathing tone.

'Poor Ariel. McKay knows a lot, but he doesn't do the subject justice. Some of the stories of these guides' journeys are amazing. I'll loan you a book.'

'And when am I supposed to have time to read anything other than what I have to read for Walnut's class?'

'It's a pity Tynan hasn't perfected his time-stretcher yet.'

'His what?'

'Time-stretcher. Didn't he tell you he was working on it?'

'No. Really?'

Nick chuckled.

Ariel grimaced as the realisation hit her. 'See, I'm already spending too much time with Dennis.'

Nick's eyes twinkled. 'I chose him 'specially. I didn't want any competition.'

'I should hit you.'

'Please do.'

'Masochist!'

He smiled her favourite smile, his eyes crinkling upwards at the corners. 'You read in the evenings and lunch breaks, of course. Before breakfast too and probably at two am in the morning. I could read aloud to you then if your eyelids are too heavy. I'd be quite happy to come into your room and help you with your studies.'

She chucked a cushion at him with feigned ferocity and her heart lifted in response to his light-heartedness. She really had missed his company.

'I thought what I studied at home was hard enough,' she complained, 'but there I could forget it all as soon as I had regurgitated it for exams, but this ... remembering this stuff is a matter of life or death.'

'What's important is that you experience it,' Nick said, 'work with it, apply it to yourself and really feel it in your heart, then it's well programmed in and it's there when you need it.'

He gazed into her eyes and, for a moment, Ariel experienced Nick's understanding and glimpsed the world from a deeper perspective. She felt no intention behind the exchange; it simply flowed on the energy that always connected them—always tender these days. Did that mean he had his feral energy under control, that he was safe for her, that she could risk . . .? Ariel squashed the memory of his kisses. She didn't want to go down that road.

'Is there anything in particular you want to discuss about your classes?' he asked.

'No, I'm okay with it all, unless you can tell me when a table isn't a table.'

'When it's a table,' he replied straight-faced.

Ariel narrowed her eyes at him then realised that the twinkle in his eyes wasn't because he was joking. 'You're not kidding are you?'

'No, but don't believe me. I could be wrong. You're supposed to keep looking for the answer yourself.'

The outer door to the office opened and Yule called out. 'Back to work, partner.'

Partner? Only a few days ago, Nick had called Ariel his partner.

Nick glanced at his watch and pushed himself off the couch. 'Tute's over. See you here at six.' He opened the door into the corridor. Dennis stood outside.

Ariel blinked. That was it? 'Oh. Okay. See you later.' Suddenly, she felt terribly insignificant. Here, he was a tutor and she merely a student.

✳✳✳

Ariel and Nick made dinner together, joking about the lack of dried peas and a wood fire. Yule and Tynan joined them and they kept the conversation light and far away from demons, Serpentine and the nature of reality. After eating, Tynan fell asleep on the couch and Yule went back to the office.

'I have to get back to work,' Nick said, not looking remotely bothered about it.

'Haven't you heard of the forty hour week?' Ariel asked.

'Here you do the work when it needs to be done. Sorry.'

'It's okay. I've had a lovely dinner. I felt almost normal there for a moment.'

'Good. I'll see you in the morning.' He smiled, then stepped into his office.

Ariel clenched her teeth. Did he have to close the door quite so firmly? Did he think she'd disturb his precious work? She grabbed the book on the nature of reality, slumped deeper into the chair and tried to pretend that the prospect of an evening without him wasn't as bleak as it felt.

7

Assassin

The next day passed much like the one before, except that the heavy rain returned, dulling the light and turning everything grey. Ariel missed Nick at breakfast. According to Tynan, he and Yule had found a particularly wonderful part in the old text and had gone to the library arguing over the whereabouts of a supporting text.

'Nick's very focused when he's enthusiastic about something,' Tynan explained.

'I've noticed,' Ariel mumbled, feeling as if she'd been passed over for an old piece of paper. Even Tynan was too busy reading to pay her any attention, and since Layla had forbidden breakfast in preparation for her class, Ariel didn't even have food to keep her company. An empty saucer sat on the floor in the kitchen, but she saw no sign of Twitchet. She did find Spud in an enclosure in the garden, but wombats were poor conversationalists.

When Dennis came to collect her from Tynan, she felt like a piece of baggage changing hands and wondered if the children of divorced parents felt like that when passed from the care of one to the other. As they walked through throngs of students and scholars to the Great Hall for Maya's class, Ariel realised that, despite the people surrounding her, the ache in her chest was loneliness and she yearned to be back on the road with Walnut and Nick, even if it did mean facing another Major Rasa.

Maya's second class was similar to the previous one, except that she used photographs of people in terrible situations to arouse the student's compassion and set the responsive quality of the Radiance flowing. Ariel looked at the suffering faces of people who were starving, the agonised expressions of prisoners under torture and the screaming mouths and terrified eyes of people injured in a bomb blast. Any of them could have been her. She could have been born in their situation. They could have been her brothers and sisters, her mother or father.

She imagined she was the woman sobbing over the battered body of her dead husband, and immersed herself in her suffering until the pain felt real. The spot in the centre of her chest softened, and the white light of compassion flowed, deadly poison to Serpentine and Rasas. This powerful magic she sent to all people who suffered, all who were dissatisfied and all who were trapped by the Serpentine infestation. She sent it to everyone everywhere, and when her light came upon the darkness of the Serpentine, it poisoned it with the light of love.

By the time Layla's class arrived, Ariel was starving. Her partner, a Haba girl, gave her a taste of an extraordinarily delicious cream tart from the village bakery, and then refused to give her more, while Ariel watched what arose in her mind.

'First Emot will make you feel dissatisfied because you don't have something you want,' Layla told them. 'Then he will dangle what you want before you to arouse your craving, or he will tempt you with a little taste of something you want, then take it away from you until you begin to crave it.'

Copious amounts of laughter peppered the class, and at the end they ate everything. After food, Layla moved onto the next pleasure on her list.

'Most of you will probably have something on your list that is physical desire,' she said. 'And if you don't have it now, you will one day.'

Ariel looked at her list. *Nothing about that there. I don't have a boyfriend, that's why.* An image of Nick swam into her mind. She rolled her eyes at her wayward psyche and reminded herself that she didn't want him that way.

Layla looked at Ariel's list and frowned. 'Mm,' she said. 'I think we will leave this one for later in the course. We'll look at success for the rest of today.'

✳✳✳

The weather plummeted as the day progressed, the sun chased away by clouds. The grey weighed on Ariel's heart and she gave up trying to talk to Dennis. They ate lunch in silence, which didn't seem to bother him at all. He had the ability to just sit and watch the world go by, but Ariel yearned for something to brighten the day. Nick's face kept popping, like a ray of sunshine, into her mind.

The physicality of Tynan's class helped a lot and she found the Geography lesson helpful, but the highlight of her day—the tutorial with Nick—couldn't come fast enough. They had to dash through pouring rain to get to the library for the last period, and Ariel spent it reading another book on the nature of reality, while Dennis just sat and watched everyone else like a hawk. This time she found herself staring into space as she tried to pinpoint a moment where she was actually solid, a time when there wasn't something in her that was in the process of changing. She failed miserably.

When she finally arrived in Nick's office for her tutorial, he and Yule were bent over his desk, frowning intently at an ancient looking piece of paper.

60

'You're wrong,' Yule said. 'Look here. If they've used it that way there, then surely it's the same here.'

'Not necessarily,' Nick replied. Ariel cleared her throat. He looked up and blinked. 'Oh, you're here.'

'Would you rather I wasn't?'

'No, of course not. I've arranged for Tynan to take your tutorial. I hope you don't mind.'

Ariel shrugged. 'No, that's cool,' she lied.

'We've found a bit about other realms.'

'Other realms?' Ariel perked up at that.

'I knew you'd be interested,' Nick smiled. 'It's difficult to work out though, because there are words there I've never come across before.'

'He's having to wrack his brains on this one,' Yule said with a grin.

'I suggest we talk to one of the Haba.'

'Let's hope one of them is familiar with this kind of thing.'

'If not, you'll just have to take a visit to Habaville.'

Yule chuckled. Nick grinned and Ariel felt completely left out. She'd completely missed whatever they'd found funny.

Tynan poked his head around the door. 'Ah, there you are, Ariel.' He stepped inside. 'Are they boring you with the intricacies of ancient grammar?'

She shook her head. They'd have to actually talk to her to do that.

Tynan turned to Nick. 'Have you worked out who wrote it yet?'

'Yule thinks it's the Pathmaker himself, but I'm not sure. She thinks it says Pathmaker, father of wisdom, but I think it might say, Wisdom, son of the Pathmaker. The word used is Aarod, it means wisdom, so it could be Aarod the first, Ariel's ancestor.'

Tynan nodded thoughtfully. 'Either way, it's a good find, yes?'

'Sure is, but we'll need a Haba elder to verify who's right.'

'Go on then,' Ariel said. 'Get on with it.'

Nick smiled, but something in his eyes told her he questioned how genuine her enthusiasm was. So he should, she thought, as she left the room with Tynan.

✱✱✱

Sometimes, Yule was simply too intense, Nick thought. He had to take a break. 'I won't be long,' he called and escaped the office before she could protest. He turned down the corridor and headed towards the entrance, planning a walk around the building, but the air seemed to thicken around him, slowing him down. In a flash of insight, he recognised the growing feeling of incapacitation from the battle at The Observatory. Magic!

Nick drew on his Radiance and created a halo of Power to protect him from the magic that threatened to freeze him to the spot, but the will of a powerful magician fought against him and he struggled to hold his concentration. His limbs grew heavy, his body sluggish—the magician was trying to squash him like a bug—but he delved deep into the reservoir of Power at the core of his being and blasted it outward.

The magic released his body, but Nick sensed its master in the entranceway, brewing another spell. He drew his sword, sidled along the corridor wall and leapt around the corner. A startled, black-clad Magan in a purple cape—one of Kestril's clan—drew his sword and stepped back, his eyes on the tip of Nick's blade pointed at his throat.

Behind the olive-skinned Magan, on the other side of the open double doors, rain fell in silver sheets. Even in the dim light, Nick recognised the black-bearded man. 'Druid,' he said calmly, raising his voice over the sound of the rain. 'Your magic has

62

failed, so tell me who sent you, or this sword will prise the words from your throat.'

Druid's eyes narrowed and his arm muscles tensed ready to strike. 'How do you know my name?'

'I'll tell you that if you tell me who gives you your orders,' Nick replied.

'You know whose side I'm on.'

'But you don't see Rasama directly. He'd eat you up and spit out your bones. Lord Menhir is it?'

'No,' Druid spat, his face distorted with growing rage.

'Kestril then?'

'Him? Pah! Menhir's precious son who whispers soppy words in his ear? Never.'

'Then who? Tell me, or perhaps you'd rather be a corpse.' Nick pressed the tip of his sword into the Magan's throat.

Druid stepped back. 'You wouldn't kill me.'

Nick stepped forward. 'Are you willing to test that hypothesis?'

Druid stood his ground. 'Warriors don't kill men.'

'That's a dangerous assumption.'

'I'll risk it.' The Magan darted away from Nick's blade and struck out with his own.

Nick took a step back, surprised at the ferocity of the Magan's onslaught, but he parried his every blow and stood his ground. They battled solidly, swords flashing in the grey light that spilled into the entrance hall.

'Emot is it? Nearby, is he?' Nick sprang forward, beat down Druid's guard and aimed a blow at his neck.

The Magan blocked the blow, parried another attack and thrust forward only to be parried in turn. 'He's never far away,' Druid gloated as he thrust again. Sweat dripped from his brow.

Once again, Nick's quick reflexes blocked Druid's attack. 'What does he offer you, Druid? Riches? A bounty for Ariel?'

Druid snorted. 'Kill you and I take her for myself.' His top lip curled in a suggestive smirk.

Disgust, fury and a powerful urge to protect Ariel fuelled Nick's determination and he unleashed his full power, forcing Druid backward. 'Whatever it is, he won't pay up. He never does. He'll keep you hoping, always wanting. That's what he feeds on. You're a fool if you think you'll ever get anything he promises you.'

'Enough words,' Druid growled. He stood his ground, maintaining his guard but unable to take the upper hand.

Nick feinted then cut towards Druid's chest. The Magan parried a little too late and the tip of Nick's blade scratched his side.

'Surrender or die,' Nick said as his sword arced towards his opponent again.

'And end up in a cell! I'd rather be dead,' Druid hissed. He blocked Nick's sword with a clang, then feinted and followed with a vicious chest cut.

Nick slammed the Magan's sword out of the way. 'You're already a slave; a Rasa's slave.'

Druid merely hissed in reply. Their swords bound and disengaged, thrust and parried. Druid slowed, struggling under the weight of Nick's superior swordsmanship. Eventually, Nick broke the panting Magan's defence with a well-timed thrust. He stopped with his sword held steady an inch from Druid's throat. 'Drop it or die.'

'Better I die!' Druid took advantage of Nick's pause, mustered his failing strength and knocked the Warrior's sword away.

Nick sprang back. Maybe he shouldn't have given Druid a choice. The Magan probably thought Nick didn't have the will to kill him. A bad assumption for Nick, for Druid was a skilful opponent. A positive outcome was not assured.

'Gutless wonder!' Druid sneered. His fight had a desperate quality now and Nick's second sight revealed a heavy infestation of Serpentine inside him. Grown to overflowing by the Magan's hatred, black slime dripped from the Magan's brow, and the beginnings of a Rasa demon grew from his back. It arose, snarling and spitting, devouring what remained of Druid.

In many ways the Magan was already dead, a puppet of the Serpentine. Fully fledged and unleashed, it used the human to do what it could not do alone—kill Nick. But Nick was a Warrior and he gave the power of his Radiance full rein. He didn't want to kill Druid, but the Magan had chosen his own fate. With the unconfined power of the Radiance racing through it, the Warrior thrust his sword into the Serpentine puppet's heart.

Druid dropped to the floor with a thud, his sword clattering on the hard stone. 'As you wished,' Nick whispered. 'And I pray it's quick.' The Magan's eyes glazed over.

Nick pulled his sword free and softly chanted an incantation. A white star appeared above the dead man and liquid light poured over him like silver rain. Serpentine oozed from the pores of his skin, his nose and mouth, dripped onto the floor and disappeared. The rain of light ceased and an ephemeral body of tiny particles of multicoloured light rose from Druid's body. It floated upwards and merged with the star, which dissolved into a pin prick of light and vanished into empty space.

Ariel and Tynan's voices floated along the corridor towards him. They rounded the corner into the entrance hall and stopped, eyes wide. Ariel's jaw dropped.

'An assassin?' Tynan asked, staring at the body.

Nick nodded. 'Druid. He chose death.' He took a cloth from his pocket, cleaned his sword then sheathed it and dropped the cloth on the Magan's body.

'You knew him?' Tynan asked.

'He was one of the Magans that attacked us on the way to Minion Hills,' Ariel replied.

Tynan nodded and crouched by the body. Blood already stained the dark polished wood. 'You've called the light already?'

'Yes.'

Tynan nodded his approval. 'May his next life be more conducive to conquering the mountain.' He closed Druid's eyes and stood.

'He's Emot's man,' Nick told them. 'Nearby I'd say.'

'Mmm.' Tynan frowned.

'What are we going to do with him?' Nick asked.

'Stay here. I'll send Liam to the hospital to get a stretcher, and I'll find something to cover him with, then we'll find Kelee and ask her what she wants done with him. He is her clan, and she is the chief's daughter.'

The Menhir's chief's daughter, Kestril's sister, is here? Interesting, Nick thought.

Tynan strode back along the corridor towards his office, leaving Ariel staring at Nick. He turned to meet her gaze.

'What?' The energy flowed calm and clear between them.

'You're so … unshakably calm,' she said.

'Should I not be?'

She smiled. 'Now you sound like a knight from an old movie.'

He shrugged.

'Really. I can feel your compassion for this man, even though he tried to kill you, and the strength of it is . . .' She searched for the right word. 'Magnetising.'

Nick raised an eyebrow. Did that mean she found him attractive? No, he couldn't think about that now. He turned his gaze to the corpse. 'I would rather not have had to kill him.'

'I know.'

Liam ran down the hall. 'I'm on my way,' he said as he sped past them and out the door.

Nick watched him go, then turned to Ariel. 'Do you know where Dennis went?'

'No idea.'

'Mm, you'd better stay with me until Tynan has sorted all this out.'

Ariel sighed. 'I've never wanted muscles like a man before, but right now, I do. If Druid had attacked me, I'd be the corpse on the floor.'

'I won't let that happen,' Nick said.

'You can't be with me the whole time.'

'I can have someone with you though.'

Ariel just shook her head and stared morbidly at the corpse until Tynan returned a moment later with a sheet. He laid the white fabric over the body, making sure that it covered every part. 'Ariel can remain with me for the rest of the day,' he said.

'Thanks,' Nick replied. 'Yule's on a roll. She won't let me stop.' He caught Ariel's grimace before she turned away. Had he said something wrong? He had no time to think about it because a Magan woman walked in. Nick noted the regal bearing and features similar to Kestril's. Liam followed her in and stood against the wall, his face pale and drawn.

'Kelee is it?' Nick asked.

'Yes; and you are?'

Nick smiled; her response was so like her brother's the first time they'd met at the Observatory.

'He's Nick, Walnut's apprentice and my … friend,' Ariel said.

He raised an eyebrow at her hesitation.

'What? I could have said bodyguard, except that it's really Dennis at the moment.'

And yet the vibes Nick got from her hinted at a readiness to be something more than just a friend. He couldn't help a smile creeping across his face.

'Liam told me what happened,' Kelee said. 'Do you know who it is?'

'Druid,' Nick replied.

Kelee sighed, her eyes on the sheet covering the corpse. 'He would never surrender.'

Nick nodded. 'He made it quite clear.'

Kelee bent down, lifted the sheet, looked impassively at the body, then covered it up again.

'I'm sorry, Kelee,' Nick said. 'Did you know him well?'

'No, he was a friend of my cousin, Beak, and I avoided them both. They were cruel men and with the worst motivations. Why would he attack you?'

'Nick has been travelling with Ariel,' Tynan explained. 'Next to Walnut, he is her primary protector.'

'Then Ariel would have been his next target. He would be wanting the reward.'

'And you don't?' The words slipped out before he could check them.

Kelee's eyes narrowed, and she fixed them on Nick. 'Such bounty is only of interest to those with a black heart.'

'Without a doubt,' Tynan agreed.

Nick felt suitably chastised, but his first instinct was never to trust a Magan, even if they wore the guise of a Warrior.

Kelee sighed. 'Can we keep this from the others, please? I am ashamed to be of the same clan.'

'No one need know,' Tynan replied quietly. 'No one has seen the corpse, apart from us, and we and the healers will not speak of it.'

Two healers came through the entranceway carrying a stretcher. The foursome stepped aside and watched silently as the stretcher-bearers moved Druid's body onto the stretcher. The rain stopped, but the fading daylight kept the entrance hall dim. The day would soon be evening, and Nick had work to do.

'Say nothing about this and keep the body out of sight,' Tynan said. The healers nodded. 'Go quickly before the gong calls the scholars from their classes.'

The healers nodded again and carried their burden from the building. A pool of blood remained on the flagstone floor.

'Liam,' Tynan said.

'I'm on it, Sir,' the boy replied and darted down the corridor.

'Do you want him sent home for cremation?' Tynan asked Kelee.

She frowned before speaking. 'Father does not know that I am here, so I cannot send a message, but even if I could, I would not say anything until we know what is happening there now. Father was reticent to move against the Precious Guide, but he was also keen to get the reward for Ariel. For all I know, he may have sent him.'

'I asked Druid who gave him his orders,' Nick said, 'and he denied that it was either your father or your brother.'

'I am pleased to hear that,' she replied with just a hint of a smile of relief.

'Does your brother know you are here?' Ariel asked.

'No,' she replied. 'I do not know my brother well. I don't think anyone does. He spent many years away from home when I was young. He does my father's bidding but … I don't know … Miramar arranged for me to come here. I am only here because of her.' A tear formed in the corner of her eye, but she quickly wiped it away. No one said anything. They all shared Kelee's sadness.

Liam arrived with a bucket of soapy water and a mop and set about cleaning the floor.

'How about a cup of tea?' Tynan asked. 'I could certainly do with one.'

'No, thank you, Tynan,' Kelee replied. 'In accordance with our customs, I will have to sit with Druid, for a couple of hours at least. He has no one else here and he is of my clan.' Her mouth twisted with distaste.

'I can sit with him for half an hour,' Nick offered.

'You!' Kelee exclaimed. 'But he tried to kill you.'

'Yes, but I killed him,' Nick replied.

'Don't you hate him?'

'No. He was badly infected with Serpentine, but his Radiance still shone beneath it. That is the Druid I will honour with my presence.'

Kelee looked at him in amazement. 'This is what it means to be a Warrior,' she said, 'this way of thinking that is so strange to a Menhir. Yet, if I could be like you, I would make Miramar proud and atone for our clan's evil.'

'Follow the training, Kelee,' Ariel said, 'and you'll be like Nick.'

Nick suppressed a smile. Were Ariel's eyes shinning with pride? For him?

'And don't think that you are alone amongst the Menhirs,' she continued. 'Remember that there are good people everywhere.'

Kelee smiled. 'Thank you.'

Nick presumed Ariel referred to Kelee's brother, but he'd yet to be convinced of Kestril's goodness.

8

Message

Ariel couldn't believe how keen she was to see Nick at dinner time. She told herself that she just needed his humour, but when he didn't even look at her when she and Tynan entered the office, then suggested that they eat at the cafeteria without him, the degree of her disappointment suggested that her feelings were more serious than that. Damn. She didn't want to miss him.

'Yule and I'll grab a sandwich later,' he said. 'Just let me know when you plan to go to your room.'

Ariel wondered why he would care, then hated herself for thinking like that.

Several hours later, Tynan walked her back to Nick's office. 'I feel like a baby,' she complained.

Tynan yawned. 'We're just making sure you're safe.'

'I know, but I'm going to do more weights tomorrow and extra sword practice.'

'Excellent.' He opened the door. The office was empty, but voices came from the dining room. They walked through the connecting door and found Yule and Nick side by side on the couch, debating the meaning of a sentence.

'Bedtime,' Tynan said.

'Nooo,' Yule protested.

'Even you have to sleep sometime,' Nick said.

The petite scholar sighed. 'I guess. Can we start early?'

'Sure, what else have I got to do?'

Was he serious?

Ariel was tempted to say that she was quite capable of walking herself to her room, but kept her mouth closed. Tynan said goodnight and left. Nick extricated himself from the couch with a yawn, and after they exchanged bedtime pleasantries with Yule, he escorted Ariel upstairs.

'I'm going to sleep in your room from now on,' he said when they reached her door.

'What?' She searched his face. His expression showed no humour. *He ignores me all day, then wants to sleep with me?*

'Sleep. I said sleep. Okay. In your room, not your bed. Just like round the campfire, only there are walls.'

She checked his energy. He radiated honesty. 'Oh. Right.' A stupid mixture of disappointment and relief sent her heart into turmoil.

'After what happened this afternoon, we can't risk leaving you unprotected, and I am the appointed bodyguard for the night shift.' He opened her door and stepped back to let her inside. She didn't move. 'You wouldn't want someone you didn't know in here, would you?'

'No, but I don't want to be guarding my body from you either.'

He chuckled. 'Then don't.'

She rolled her eyes and shook her head. 'See. You don't give up.'

'The walls are stone, Ariel, too thick for me to hear if anything gets into your room at night and there are no locks on the door.'

A quick glance at the door told her he was right. A nervous flutter danced through her gut.

'I'll be in a protective dome,' she countered weakly.

'That's not enough; domes can be broken with the right magic.'

'You're making me paranoid.'

'Better than dead.'

Ariel swallowed hard, her throat suddenly dry. 'Fine, whatever.'

'I'll get organised.' He headed down the corridor.

Ariel stepped into her room, let out an enormous sigh and sank onto the bed, her legs suddenly like jelly beneath her. Despite her nervousness, the idea of Nick being in her room overnight suddenly seemed very comforting. I could do a lot worse, she thought dryly.

Nick brought in a screen and set it up to provide a private area for changing, then he dragged his mattress in and placed it on the floor between Ariel and the door. After they'd both used the bathroom and changed ready for bed, they made a dome large enough to cover them both.

'Goodnight,' she said, sitting on the bed.

'Wait a minute.' He sat beside her.

She narrowed her eyes at him.

He raised an eyebrow. 'Just a goodnight cuddle.'

She shrugged and he put his arm around her, drawing her close. His proximity sent shivers of excitement through her.

'You know how I feel about you,' he whispered. 'I wish you'd own up to your own feelings.'

'I know what I feel, and I don't need a distraction,' she countered firmly.

He chuckled. 'The resistance is the distraction, not me.' He ran his fingers slowly up her arm, leaving a trail of bliss. 'You might be able to hide it from yourself, but you can't hide it from me. I know what you're feeling right now.'

'You do not,' she countered. Her lips pursed but she didn't pull away. Why didn't she pull away?

'Yes, I do,' he whispered into her neck, blowing sweet breath across her skin, skimming it with his lips, barely touching, teasing.

She stood abruptly. 'You're taking advantage of me.' And she loved every bit of it.

He sighed. 'I just want to kiss you. That's all. I promise.'

Even without the silken tones of his voice and the love spreading from every fibre of his being, the sight of his eyes alone was almost enough to undo her. But she ignored it all and paced the edge of the sphere pouting in agitation. Nick waited patiently, silent. She felt his mind, calm and clear, and his heart reaching out to her, willing her to surrender so she could be done with the pain of denial.

He had a point.

She sat beside him again, letting the strange mixture of irritation, excitement, willingness and fear flow unhindered for him to read. For a moment, he didn't move, then he turned slowly, his eyes searching hers. She glanced away, heart fluttering, stomach churning.

She felt as if she were on the edge of a cliff, on the verge of jumping over. A thick mattress waited at the bottom and a comforting pair of warm arms, but could she trust that the mattress was thick enough, that it wouldn't shift away and that the arms would hold her without demanding more than she wanted to give? She wouldn't be able to jump back up again. And he had ignored her all day!

He stroked her neck, trailed a finger over her lips, then took her chin and turned her to face him. She yearned for what was to come and feared losing herself in it, but she couldn't resist anymore.

He kissed her. Softly at first, gently, searching, questioning. Her lips responded, as if of their own accord, and she kissed him back. As she had feared, the intensity of their connection overwhelmed her, as if all the feelings she'd held back until now suddenly flooded through every cell. She didn't want him to stop, but he did.

'Goodnight.' He stood and walked calmly to his bed, leaving her stunned and confused, blinking at his retreating form. She bet he was grinning.

'You're teasing me,' she accused.

'Only because you're teasing me.'

'I am not!'

'Think about it, Ariel … Now, goodnight and sleep well.'

With a groan, she threw herself on the bed. *Not fair!*

Nick's breathing quickly slowed and deepened, but Ariel didn't succumb to slumber so easily. His last words played on her mind and she found herself reviewing her interactions with him after the debacle at the Plateau. She'd reminded him many times that she wanted to be no more than friends. She'd made that quite clear. So how was she teasing him, or was his accusation just an empty, petulant retort to hers? All the times he'd caressed her, the times he'd held her, and the times he'd kissed her paraded through her mind. She'd always pulled away, hadn't she? When had she teased him?

The realisation was almost painful as it laid bare the extent of her personal subterfuge. Who was she trying to kid? No wonder he never believed her. Every time before she'd pulled away, she'd enjoyed it as much as he had. She'd lingered to taste the pleasure of his presence, his touch, his arms around her, his lips against hers. She tried to tell herself that it was because if she didn't withdraw gently, they'd both get a painful backlash. They'd discovered back in the Morbid Forest that when she suddenly created an emotional barrier between them, his energy bounced off it and whacked him like a punch. It gave her a nasty shock too. But she never truly believed that excuse for a moment.

Nick was right. He already was a distraction. It was too late; perhaps it had been too late since the first time they felt that strongly evocative connection between them. Ariel sighed and tried to sleep.

***

The next morning, Ariel awoke groggy from broken sleep, feeling as if she'd tossed and turned all night. Something unresolved still lurked inside, waiting to ambush her. Nick. She rolled over to face him, but his mattress was empty. The disappointment she felt annoyed her, so did her desire to remember the feeling of his fingertips on her face and his passionate lips on hers.

When Nick came in fully dressed, she was sitting on the bed dreamily running her fingers over her lips. She dropped her hand, hoping he didn't see her blush. 'I thought you were supposed to stay with me,' she accused.

'Good morning to you too.' He turned a cheeky grin on her. 'And I don't think I need to take you to the bathroom with me, do you?'

She rolled her eyes and poked out her tongue.

The clouds lifted that day, giving glimpses of blue sky and periods of sunlight, and the day quickly grew hot. Nick found Ariel in the cafeteria at lunchtime and suggested that she join him for a swim in the lake.

'What, with the snakes?' she asked, horrified.

'Yeah,' he replied. 'The little ones don't bite and they feel sort of nice slipping and sliding all over you.'

'Ew! No, thank you. I'll watch you have a snake bath though.' She wasn't about to let him get away when she'd yearned for his company all morning.

Nick chuckled. 'I was kidding. There's a netted area. It's snake-free. I promise.'

Ariel rolled her eyes at him and shook her head as if he was a hopeless case, but she appreciated the laugh. Dennis declined to join them, saying he would meet them at Ariel's next class.

By the time Nick and Ariel arrived at the pool—created by a net strung across the mouth of a bay—others from the University seeking its cool waters packed the beach. They found a spot near the rocks on the far side, and Ariel lay face down on her towel, not trusting herself to watch as Nick stripped off his shirt and raced into the water. She had to stay focused.

'Hey, Ariel,' he called a short time later, walking up the bank towards her, 'come in, the water's great.'

'It's a lake on a mountain,' she replied, sitting up as he came near. 'It has got to be cold.'

'The Ganas warm it up. They're warm-blooded,' he replied, looking dead serious.

Ariel stared. Not only did she have absolutely no idea if he was joking or not, but he stood bare-chested in front of her, dripping water on her, smiling his most alluring smile. Her heart fluttered like some stupid, helpless bird. Damn it. Nick was right. She did want him. Her body had betrayed her. 'Request permission to clobber you if you're joking.'

'Permission given, Milady,' he replied with a mock bow and a grin.

Ariel leapt up and raced into the water, plunging straight in. She didn't want to dally on the edge, better to get in quick, get the shock over with. But Nick was right, the water wasn't cold. It wasn't warm either, but it was pleasant enough. She loved swimming without the limitations imposed by a small pool and, after practicing every stroke she knew, she stopped to rest on the rocks that marked the side of the pool where the net began. She lay with her chest on the edge, legs floating out behind her, and stared across the lake. Nick sat on a submerged rock beside her, looking north towards the peak.

'The clouds are off the mountain,' he said.

She swung around, pulled her legs in and drifted onto a rock. 'We've come a long way since the Observatory.'

'Yeah.' He smiled and turned to look at her. 'A long way.'

She felt his gaze caressing her and closed her eyes. Yes, she had better add that thing to her list.

'I have to get back,' he said suddenly. 'Yule has arranged for one of the Haba to meet us.'

***

Once again Ariel's class on the nature of reality consisted of reading the book and reflecting on the topic. Ariel decided that she wasn't her body but that she lived in it. The trouble with that idea, however, was that she couldn't find out exactly where she lived. She was sure she was in her brain but where exactly? Scientists had found places responsible for memory, feelings, and various other things, but as far as she knew, no one had found where central control was. If the scientists couldn't find it, it was no wonder she couldn't.

She looked for her mind, but what colour was it, what shape, what size? If she didn't know any of that, then how would she know it if she found it? Those and other questions posed by the book seemed unanswerable, and she found herself staring into nothing, unable to think anymore. When she recovered and returned to the text, she was amazed to read that not finding her mind was, in fact, finding it after all.

Ariel smiled. Just because she couldn't find it didn't mean that it wasn't there. The crazy contemplation had brought her to a lovely, open, peaceful state, the very essence of her mind. She may not be able to find it with her thoughts, but she most certainly experienced it, and it was not nothing, for something so heart-warming that it could only be love filled it to overflowing

As usual, the sword training class with Tynan was the class Ariel enjoyed most and when Nick turned up, it became even better.

'I needed a break,' he whispered as he joined her, 'and something physical.'

She nodded, knowing exactly what he meant. Ariel threw herself into the training as if she could clear away the fire in her veins by pushing her body to the limit. It probably would have worked if the cause of the blaze hadn't been beside her. As it was, his fierce physicality overshadowed every other perception she had. In some ways, it was as if they were the only people in the room. Ariel floated in his aura.

In Demonology class, Ariel added one word to her list of pleasures. Beside the words, physical desire, she wrote – Nick. There, she'd admitted it.

'Ah,' the impish teacher said with a grin. 'Today we will look at one of the strongest of physical pleasures and one that Emot is extremely skilled at using to lure you into craving.'

Ariel grimaced. She wasn't looking forward to this.

***

Ariel took a deep breath before knocking on Nick's office door for their tutorial. Here was her opportunity to practice what she had worked on with Layla, only this wouldn't be something she had imagined. This was the real thing—her and Nick together, alone. At least her studies on the Nature of Reality had confused her enough that she had a question for him.

'Does any of this exist?' Ariel gestured to the room around them.

'Of course it does. It all functions just as it appears. Causes create results, there is this and that, you and me, good and bad, love and hate, but none of it exists the way we think it does. Everything is always changing; things depend on everything else for their existence and they can be broken down into smaller pieces of time or matter, but we don't see them that way.'

Ariel stared at the wall behind him. It was really just a bunch of atoms.

'This table appears solid to us,' Nick continued, gesturing at the coffee table. 'But science tells us that 99.9% of it is open space. That space isn't empty though, it's full of energy, forces and endless dimensions.'

'It's a lot to get your head around.'

'Yeah, but even if we can't understand the nature of reality, we can experience it, which is how it relates to demon slaying.'

'Huh?'

'When we see our thoughts and emotions as something solid and lasting, we easily get caught up in them, and even the demons themselves, though they seem solid, are just energy. The thing is, we can see all that for ourselves when we're tuned into the essential layer of reality. '

'Which is where mind training comes in,' Ariel said, pleased that she finally seemed to be understanding how it all fitted together.

'Yep. And I realised that there's a way to get there that we don't practice in mind training.'

Ariel raised her eyebrows.

His gaze fixed on her. 'Remember what Walnut told us to do?' She shook her head. 'Drop the barriers and completely surrender to each other. Try it.'

She gulped. Refuse, or accept the challenge? Could she do it without getting her hormones in a knot? Who was she trying to kid? Her hormones were already in a knot. She returned Nick's gaze, dropped her guard and plummeted into his being, as he did into hers. Their minds merged, expanded and became crystal clear. Goosebumps rose on the back of Ariel's neck. Her mind went on forever, her heart overflowed and the edges of reality softened. Several moments passed, then slowly, at the same time, they dropped their gaze.

'That was good,' Nick said.

Ariel nodded but kept her gaze on the floor.

'Still trying to pretend there isn't some kind of deep connection between us?'

She shook her head.

'Good. That's progress.' She heard the smile in his voice. 'I'll make some tea.' He went into the kitchen, leaving Ariel floating in a kind of limbo. Things had changed and she wasn't sure where to go from here.

'Why doesn't Maya have dinner with us?' she asked when Nick returned with a tray with a pot of tea and biscuits on it.

'I have asked her but she said she prefers to eat in her apartment. I think she has a special diet and she spends all her spare time in the library looking for maps of the tunnels.'

'Yeah, well, that's important. What about Layla?'

'She goes home every afternoon.'

'Where to?'

'Somewhere on the Upper Reaches. She has pets to attend to.'

'What sort of pets?'

'I don't know. Have a biscuit.'

'You're a real afternoon tea person, aren't you?' she said after finishing a mouthful of biscuit.

'I caught it from Tynan,' Nick replied with a grin.

Yule poked her head around the door.

'Nick, a messenger came up from Shifting Stones and said that your group there was ready to go on and that they wanted you to take them up to the Observatory. Evidently, they're ready to go. Shall I send a message to say you're coming?'

Nick's face fell. 'No.' Then quickly he added, 'Not yet. I need to consider timing.'

'Okay,' Yule replied and disappeared back into the office.

Ariel turned to Nick, 'Does that mean you'll be leaving us?'

'I'll try to get out of it,' he said, but he didn't look hopeful. 'I'll discuss it with Walnut as soon as he gets here.'

✱✱✱

The door to Nick's living room opened. Tynan had arrived for dinner. The lanky sword-master strode in and deposited a parcel wrapped in bakery paper on the bench. 'For you, Nick.'

Nick ripped open the paper and took a long sniff of what looked like a chocolate mousse pie. A blissful look spread over his face. 'That looks suspiciously close to what Emot got me with.'

'I expect there's a demon's recipe behind this one,' Tynan said. 'It's called a chocolate love tart and it is the most delectable thing I have ever tasted.'

'A love tart!' Nick chuckled.

'It's very rich,' Tynan continued, 'but we don't have to have a lot of it.'

'Oh, I like my love rich,' Nick said, studiously avoiding looking at Ariel, 'and I do like a lot of it.'

'It's chocolate,' Ariel pointed out.

'I know. Why? Did I say something else?' he asked, feigning innocence.

Tynan chuckled. 'You said, love, instead of chocolate.'

'Same thing,' Nick said with a cheeky grin. 'Sweet and rich, melts in your mouth, warms your heart, brightens up a dull day.'

'Will you punch him or shall I?' Ariel asked.

Tynan just kept chuckling, bubbling away like a kettle on the boil.

'What's the problem? It's true,' Nick protested. Ariel pulled a face at him. 'Anyway, thanks, Tynan.'

82

Ariel found a suitable-looking plate in one of the cupboards over the bench, and Nick slid the cake onto it as reverently as if it were a precious jewel. After that, they turned their attention to serving the meal, and soon sat around the dark wood table on the sturdy, comfortably-padded chairs.

'How is this translation coming along?' Tynan asked after they'd eaten their frittata in silence for a while.

'The Haba elder we spoke to reckoned that Aarod the First is the author,' Nick replied, 'and after long discussions with him, we decided that the best translation indicated that Ariel's esteemed ancestor was writing about how to transfer to other realms.'

Tynan leaned forward eagerly, his eyes widening. Ariel stared at Nick in wonder.

'Come on, boy, tell us,' Tynan said.

'Look at you two, you're like bees around a freshly opened honey pot,' Nick mocked.

'Nick,' Ariel complained. 'Seriously, we want to know.'

'I know you do,' he replied. 'And I also know that anyone who wants to defeat Emot has to learn to let go of their cravings.' His eyes twinkled over a roguish grin.

Ariel grimaced. 'Fine, don't tell me then.' She placed her chin in her hands and stared at him innocently.

'You'd better tell me though,' Tynan said, resting his hands on the table, twiddling his thumbs and trying to look fierce.

Nick chuckled. 'Apparently in order to travel between realms you have to be able to dissipate and you can only dissipate after you have defeated Rasama.'

'Maya can dissipate,' Ariel interjected. 'I saw her.'

'Then she could have come from Off-World,' Tynan concluded.

'According to this text, it's quite possible,' Nick continued. 'It seems that both the Pathmaker and Aarod the First were able to do that and did in fact make a couple of journeys. This text could also change the way we understand the Pathmaker's death.'

'How?' Ariel asked.

'I haven't done a detailed translation yet, but he seems to be saying that the Pathmaker didn't die, instead he left this world for another realm and didn't return.'

'That's extremely interesting,' Tynan said. 'Having Maya ferreting around in the old part of the library has been exceptionally useful. She also found a reference to the possibility of destroying the Serpentine for all time.'

'That's great,' Nick said. 'What did it say?'

'Not much, I'm afraid, just that the author considered that if there was sufficient Radiant Power focused in the right way then it was possible.'

'Oh,' Ariel said, 'that's not much help, is it?'

'Well, it confirms that at least one other person thinks it is possible,' Tynan replied. 'It also indicates that he thought the amount of power and the way it is focused is a key factor, which is the same as my own theory.'

Ariel smiled, glad Tynan was working on it. It didn't seem fair that even if she did manage to kill Rasama, another Master Demon would grow as soon as someone fed their Serpentine root to excess. To get rid of the demons forever, the shock waves of Rasama's death had to destroy the root of the Serpentine in everyone, not just in the victor.

At bed time, Ariel and Nick set up a protective dome around their room and, after a shower and changing into her pajamas, Ariel slipped into bed and waited for Nick to finish his shower. Now that she had admitted her feelings for him, her heart pounded in anticipation of a bedtime kiss, but it didn't come. He simply walked into the room and stretched out on his mattress on the floor.

Disappointment replaced expectation. Was he distracted by his stupid old book, or was he just not interested in her tonight, or had he felt the change in her and realised that he'd already captured her heart, so he didn't have to try to seduce her anymore? Ariel didn't know what to think, so she didn't bother thinking anything; instead she applied Layla's training and simply felt what she felt. Her disappointment faded in the light of acceptance.

'Ariel?' he whispered suddenly, 'are you still awake?'

'Yes.' She heard him get up and come towards her.

'I forgot to say goodnight. ' He bent over and kissed her gently—and platonically—on her forehead. 'Goodnight.'

'Goodnight.' Had he waited until she'd stopped wanting his attention? For a moment, part of Ariel wanted to run far away from this man who felt too much of what she felt, who read her too well; but she stayed frozen in her bed, listening to him breathing, incapable of taking herself away.

9

In Miramar's Honour

Walnut, Falcon and Blade had camped beneath the Pavilion in Minion Hills' town square for three days, their needs provided for by Miramar's clan. Lord Terrigal and others had joined them from time to time, and when not sitting in silent contemplation on the fragility of life, they had spoken of the times they'd shared with Miramar. Occasionally, Walnut had sung her favourite songs, the clarity and vibrancy of his voice portraying a moving mixture of sadness at her loss and joy at the beauty of her life. Falcon sometimes sang or told Miramar's favourite Magan stories, the strength of his voice showing his pride in his ancient culture, and Blade sat with shining eyes, watching his older brother with something akin to hero worship. Falcon often gave his brother a hug, exactly, it seemed to Walnut, when the boy needed it most. Like many Magan men, Falcon had more sensitivity than he was inclined to show.

Under the direction of their chief, women from Miramar's clan had come and bound the body with cotton and herbs, and men had bought special hot burning wood for the pyre. Miramar's sons had joined in the building while Walnut had chanted the appropriate incantations to ensure a swift fire. No shops had opened in the town square. If any had business to attend to, they had undertaken it elsewhere, or delayed it while the watchers stood vigil over Miramar's body. The sky had remained clouded, as if it too grieved, and occasionally rain had fallen like tears. Each evening, the threesome had set a protective dome around the pavilion and kept the chill away with copious blankets and warm soup.

On the third morning, the sun rose above the clean cobblestones in a sky clear of clouds and breathed new life into the square. Buds in the window boxes blossomed into flowers glowing with colour, their sweetness scenting the breeze, and even the granite walls of the surrounding buildings seemed more vibrant.

The completed pyre—a wooden platform on top of well stacked firewood and a red cloth canopy above—sat in the open space behind the pavilion where Central Park adjoined the town square. People of the Terrigal clan gathered and watched in silence as Falcon and Blade lifted the flower-bedecked stretcher bearing their mother's corpse and laid it on top of the wooden platform.

The other clans—marked by the colour of their velvet cloaks—streamed into the town square behind their chiefs. The Warrior Clans, guards and ordinary people alike, arrived first— the Conjurs, the Julars, the Swifts, and the Fardells—followed by the larger of the unallied clans—the Carvells and the Eaglans. Finally, the Mage Clans marched in with grim faces. Lord Menhir came first with his son, Kestril, in his rightful place at his side.

The bearded men wore their usual jerkins over full white shirts and narrow trousers tucked into high boots. The middle-aged women wore wide-brimmed straw hats, shawls and calf-length embroidered skirts, and the younger ones favoured dress more akin to the men, but with wide pocket-belts instead of jerkins. Like the men, their swords and wands hung at their hips. All wore velvet capes in their clan colours.

Walnut caught Kestril's eye with a silent question. *Are the other Mage Clans coming?* The affirmative answer came with the sound of many footsteps, and a few minutes later, Lord Donarth led his people into the square, followed by Lord Torens and his kin, and last of all the Doharvens. Although many of them had travelled far, they left their horses in the grazing paddocks near the gates of the town and came respectfully on foot.

The Warrior Clans stood on the right hand side of the square facing the town hall where Walnut sat waiting, and the Mage Clans filled the left side. Between them, like the rift between the clans, lay the pavilion and Miramar's pyre. Walnut rejoiced that her memory could draw the clans together in this way, for at no time since the death of the last King had all the clans gathered in the same place. The only ones not present were those who lived far away in the back blocks of Minion Hills—the Rorocks and other small unaligned clans.

When the crowd grew still, Lord Terrigal's men brought Beak, Miramar's murderer, out of the shadows and into the square before the assembled clans. Chains shackled his hands and feet, but his face portrayed no emotion.

Walnut rose and stepped forward into the sun at the top of the town hall steps. 'Chiefs of the clans,' he said in a voice that, filled with the deep strength of his being, carried easily across the throng, 'by putting aside your differences and coming together to pay your respects to Miramar, you have proven that Magan dignity is as alive today as it ever was.' At these words, the chiefs straightened their spines and drew back their shoulders. 'I thank you, for myself and on behalf of Miramar and all the Magan people for your presence here today.' Behind him, the ancient granite of the town hall, its carved columns a monument to nobler times, gave extra gravity to his words.

'This woman,' Walnut continued, indicating the pyre, 'mother to Blade and Falcon, wisdom holder and honoured elder, was a friend and healer to all, truly a queen amongst our beloved women, yet here she lies, her death another cruel result of this split in the Magan clans.

'Beak of the Menhirs stands here as the perpetrator of this crime, but why would he do such a terrible thing, when he too has seen Miramar's kindness? His intention was not to kill Miramar, she died protecting someone else, but why did he raise his wand against someone in her company?

'Unfortunately, it was not for some noble reason, but for the lure of riches. Rasama, King of the Demons, posted a huge reward for the death or capture of Ariel, daughter of Aarod, and some, like Beak, thought this a good enough reason to kill her. But they were seduced by demon lies. I ask you, clan chiefs and good people of Minion Hills, do you truly think the Rasas would pay up if you kill or capture Ariel and hand her over? Even if they did, where would they get the money unless they had stolen it from you first?'

Walnut scanned the faces in the crowd. Many nodded their heads or murmured their agreement. Others set expressions of nonchalance, though their feet shifted uneasily. 'Now look at the result of playing the Rasas games,' Walnut continued. 'We have lost a precious gem, one of the true treasures of Minion Hills and one that was for all clans. Miramar thought that Ariel's life was so valuable that she willingly traded her own for it. Why? The answer is the same as to the question of why does Rasama want her dead. It is because she has the ability to defeat him, and you know, every one of you, what freedom we will all gain when the King of the Demons is dead.

'The Rasas are our enemies, we are not enemies of one another, and when we put our energy into fighting Magan against Magan, we let the true enemy prosper. Miramar knew that the Serpentine and the demons are the real enemy, and she fought against them in everything she did. Her every action diminished the Serpentine; her every care poisoned it; her every intention rendered it impotent and her understanding undermined its existence. She fought the Serpentine with a courage and fortitude that is an example to every Magan, regardless of clan. I seek to honour her life by forging a new era for the Magan clans, a new alliance based on Miramar's example, Magans united against the demons.'

Smiles broke out on the faces of many from both Warrior and Mage Clans, but others frowned and turned to their neighbours in discussion. A murmur of unrest grew amongst the Mage Clan Magans. Walnut raised his hand, signaling for quiet, but the talk continued. Voices rose as some Magans' unease turned to outrage.

The brown-cloaked chief of the Doharvens raised his hand and the Mage Clans fell silent. 'This is just another excuse to try to break up the Mage Clan alliance,' he shouted with disgust. 'We have heard the old guide's tired words before and I will have none of it, not even in honour of Miramar.'

'Nor I,' Lord Donarth added in a booming voice. 'Miramar was a good friend to us—it is true—but she knew nothing of politics and I would not follow her example there. I would honour her in other ways but not through such a drastic move.'

All eyes turned to Walnut, curious to hear his response. 'The aim of Miramar's life was to bring peace and freedom from the demons to the Magan people. What could please her more and bring greater honour to her name than to forge an alliance for peace, and against the demons?'

No one replied. Everyone who knew her knew it was something she wanted with all her heart.

'An alliance for peace would mean she did not die in vain,' Walnut continued. 'It is the only thing that would give any meaning to this terrible loss and,' he turned to Beak, 'would even redeem its perpetrator to some extent.' The young man stared back at the old guide. His face gave nothing away, but his thoughts broadcast clearly to Walnut. Part of him wanted such redemption, for Miramar had once saved his mother from death.

Many in the crowd murmured their approval, and a tentative hope rose in Walnut's heart when he saw that some of it came from people of the Mage Clans. Miramar's fearless love had broken down boundaries forged in the iron of politics; boundaries Walnut had tried and failed to break with reason and logic.

Lord Menhir, an imposing figure in his royal-purple cloak, raised his hand, silencing the crowd. His voice rang with authority. 'Unfortunately, it was one of my clan who did this terrible act, and since it leaves a stain on all Menhirs, as chief, I must claim some responsibility for reparation. Whatever the Precious Guide and Miramar's sons decide as fitting punishment for Beak, we will carry it out.'

Walnut nodded. 'Thank you, Lord Menhir. Falcon, Blade and I have discussed this matter.' He turned to Falcon, and the young man joined Walnut on the steps of the town hall.

'It is our opinion that Miramar would not want a brutal punishment for her killer,' he said, 'but, rather, that he redeems himself by continuing her work. We request that Beak join the building crew on the new wing of the hospital and work without pay until it is complete.'

Beak's jaw dropped and he stared at Falcon with a mixture of disbelief and relief. It would not have been unexpected for the aggrieved family to ask for his death, which would have been carried out swiftly by knife to the throat. Lord Menhir's eyes widened, a slight smile crept into Kestril's countenance and whispering broke out amongst the crowd.

'Quiet!' Lord Menhir's voice boomed across the square. 'Miramar was an unfailing and constant source of healing and comfort for our people, not least of all myself at the time of my queen's death. I scoffed at many of her radical ideas as unpractical, but this decision, I know, is what she would have taken for herself had she been able to tell us. Therefore, I accept the punishment as wise and true, and the Menhirs will administer it.'

Lord Terrigal made the formal reply. 'I accept this as payment of the debt your clan owes mine for this tragedy.' The two lords bowed to each other, and Walnut continued.

'Now, I ask you, Lords, you who care for your clan, where is the benefit for your people in the present way, when so many of you are engaged in almost constant warfare, in petty squabbles over money and lands? Some of your grandfathers lost sight of your ancestors' aims and chose to fore-go the path up the mountain and pursue magic and riches instead, but you do not have to choose the same today. Consider the nobility of your ancestors who honoured true courage, the courage to face demons for freedom.

'Look at Miramar and ask yourself: which courage is greater and more worthy of a lifetime's commitment, hers for peace and freedom from the Serpentine, or yours for riches which brings warfare and enslavement to the demons? Ask yourself, Great Lords, which is better for your people? I call on you to embrace a new order, a new alliance of all Magan clans in the name of peace, and in memory of Miramar, the beloved.'

The old guide paused to allow the lords to discuss the proposition with their heirs and advisors. Kestril spoke earnestly with his father, no doubt urging him on. The other Mage Clan chiefs merely frowned and shook their heads.

Menhir held his hand up for silence and spoke when the crowd had quieted. 'I am moved by the pointlessness of this death, by the memory of this woman who is beloved by all clans, by the wars my people have suffered in recent times and by the proliferation of demons in the midst of our village. I am willing to reconsider my alliance.'

Cries of horror, surprise and joy erupted from the crowd. Kestril caught Walnut's eye and smiled. The old guide's heart soared and he mentally communicated his gratitude and respect to his ally. Kestril suffered mistrust on both sides for his role as double agent, and regularly struggled to find solutions that didn't fail either his father or the Warriors.

Walnut bowed to Menhir, then turned to the other Mage Clan Magan chiefs and raised his hand for silence. The discussions stopped and all eyes turned to Walnut again. 'Who else of the Mage Clans stand with Lord Menhir?' he asked. None of the Mage Clan Chiefs spoke and several heads shook, so Walnut continued. 'I have petitioned for many years for an end to the division between the clans, and waited for the Chiefs to come to this wisdom of their own free will, but I have waited too long for your free decision, and now my queen Miramar is dead. Therefore, if you do not agree to this new order in her memory, I will bind you.'

Lord Torens, bristling with rage, drew his wand, followed by his men and those of the Donarths and Doharvens. 'How dare you threaten us?' he growled.

Walnut's hands blurred as they flew to the pouches on his belt and whipped out his bell and scepter. With a flick of his wrist, the bell chimed, and with the help of an incantation, his scepter froze them all. They stood like statues, rage etched upon their faces. 'It is not a threat,' Walnut said. 'It is an assurance, so that no clan need feel in fear of those who do not agree. After peace is established, I will review the binding and release those who agree to peace of their own free will, but those who remain stubborn in the old ways will be bound again.'

'That is fair,' Lord Eaglan, chief of one of the smaller Warrior Clans said.

The sound of horses' hooves galloping towards the square halted further discussion. Heads turned to the street leading from the town's main gate, and the crowd parted as a group of twelve Magans wearing the colours of the Rorock clan rode into the square on foaming horses. Adrianne, daughter of Lord Rorock, rode at their head, leading two horses with bodies strapped across the saddles. The majority of the group halted at the edge of the crowd, but Adrianne plus the horses bearing the bodies and two other riders rode directly to the steps of the town hall. With a gesture, she bade her men untie the bodies.

'Bring them here,' Walnut said, and the men carried the bodies onto the top steps and laid them beside Walnut where all could see that Chief Rorock and one of his kinsmen had died from a Rasa slash.

Wanting to see their reaction to Adrianne's tale, Walnut unfroze the Torens, Donarths and Doharvens. They glared at him, but said nothing, for the moment more interested in the events unfolding before them than in arguing with Walnut.

10

Adrianne of the Rorocks

Adrianne stood beside Walnut on the top step of the town hall and raised her hand for quiet. Eager to hear the tale, the crowd stilled, their eyes on the strong-limbed girl. 'A crowd of silver-eyed Rasas attacked us on the way here,' she cried, brushing a strand of long black hair from her face, 'and though my father fought bravely, the Rasa that attacked him was Bitah himself. He grew huge in size and strength and defeated my father. Hence, I am now chief of the Rorocks.'

'How did you escape alive?' someone in the crowd called.

'I beheaded his killer a moment after my father fell,' she replied and many voices murmured their approval. 'But not before this loyal man died and several others were wounded. They need healers.' Several Warrior Clan healers made their way towards the wounded horsemen. Adrianne looked up at the funeral pyre and continued her speech. 'Let all hear my first words as clan chief.' Even the children stayed still and watched with wide eyes, for Adrianne had a commanding presence. 'The Rorocks are no longer allied to the Mage Clans,' she said. 'We stand alone, and we stand for peace.'

Again, the crowd murmured, some in concern, others in delight at Adrianne's courageous declaration. Walnut's face broke into a smile and the hope in his heart strengthened. The old order was shifting. 'You do not stand alone,' he said. 'The Warrior Clans stand with you, and I think also the Menhirs.'

Adrianne glanced to where Kestril stood with his father. He nodded slightly. Walnut wondered if perhaps he had Kestril to thank for this unexpected ally. 'Then they have seen wisdom also,' she said. 'But some are suspicious, so let me explain why I have taken this step.' The crowd stilled once more. A baby cried and was shushed by its mother.

'Look what this commitment to riches and boldness in taking it has cost us—the death of Miramar. What clan has she not befriended? Who has she not helped or healed? She came to us when no other would, when many were dying from the war with our neighbours and we were still under attack. She risked her life to heal our injured, then she risked her life again crossing the lines to do the same for our enemy. Some thought this wrong, but such boldness, such courage, cannot be denied. She embodied the Magan quality we all admire, that of standing firm for what you believe. As you all know, it was not riches she desired but peace, and she brought peace wherever she went. And so does our precious guide here, yet I hear that some also attacked him. We are lucky, Magans, that we did not lose two of great wisdom in this foolishness.'

'We have given up peace to fight over riches,' she continued, 'and I say it is a poor trade and that any chief who honours it does not look after his people well.'

Shouts of disagreement broke out amongst those in the Mage Clan Alliance. Walnut raised his hand for silence, but the grumbles only fell away when Lord Doharven shouted for quiet. Though he obviously disliked her words, Walnut sensed a healthy dose of respect for Adrianne in his glare.

'For some time I have watched the plight of my people as we fostered warfare in the name of riches,' she continued. 'Rewards came, for sure, but mostly only for a few families, and the cost was great for all. Many had loved ones die or be injured, but worse I think was the infiltration of the Rasas.'

Many people on both sides of the square nodded or murmured their agreement.

'They wander amongst our people and feed easily and grow stronger and bolder while those who feed them grow weaker. And when they are too weak for fodder, the demons kill them and grow even stronger on their deaths. They are rarely challenged, for too few of our people have the skills to defeat them. Meanwhile, the Serpentine infestation increases, spreading like wildfire and thickening dangerously in many. These people become outlaws, a blight on our society, killing and stealing, raping and slandering their own kin as they wish. Our lives within the walls of our own village become a reflection of the policies of our chief, we live in a state of war with each other, and no one is safe.'

'She speaks the truth,' someone shouted.

'Hear her well,' another called.

Adrianne continued. 'This is what our acquiescence to the demons has cost us, and now they grow so bold that they have even taken my father, the chief of our clan. He tried to bargain with them. He said, 'Let me go and I will bring the girl to you,' but the demons only laughed. 'A clan chief is good strong food,' they said, 'preferable to others.' Think on that one, clan chiefs. Even if Rasama kills the daughter of Aarod, the demons will still need to feed, and even before your people are wasted wrecks, they will turn their attention on you, and all the riches in the world will not protect you.

'I challenge you to turn your minds to the welfare of your clan over and above your desire for riches and status. That will be my focus and I pledge my commitment to this by accepting the precious guide's offer. I will train as a Warrior and, like Miramar, I will test my tenacity and courage not against other Magans but against our true enemies, the Rasa.'

The majority of the crowd erupted in applause and Walnut beamed at Adrianne. He could not have said it better himself—and she had the extra power of being one of them. The Mage Clan chiefs' eyes narrowed as they surveyed their people. Many ceased clapping when they saw their Chief's gaze upon them, but the ordinary folk had made it clear that they were sick of war. Menhir, with his son standing proudly at his side, turned to his people and acknowledged their opinion. They cheered even louder.

It seemed that Miramar and Chief Rorock's deaths had not been in vain.

Adrianne raised her hand once more for silence and added. 'We will not attack, but be warned, we will defend.' Then she walked down the steps with a determined stride. The crowd waited for Walnut's response.

'Well spoken, Adrianne,' he said. 'You have shown yourself to be a person of great courage and an excellent Chief for your people. Your father would be proud if he could have heard you today, even if he disagreed with your decision, but I think that in his death he would see the folly of the old ways.

'Now, noble leaders of the Magan clans, it is time to throw out the old order for it no longer serves your best interests. It is time to form a new alliance, an alliance against the Rasa who, as Adrianne saw in her wisdom, are your true enemies. I call on you now to state your allegiance to peace amongst all Magans. If we all commit, then no one need fear a breach, and a new era of freedom and prosperity will come to Minion Hills.'

Lord Menhir raised his hand. 'The Rasa attack on chief Rorock is a warning to us all, and Adrianne's ideas are not new to me, for my son has long whispered in my ear of the benefits of peace amongst Magans. He has held the policy of no attack but strong in defence for many years, and it has not made him weak. On the contrary, he is respected by all and his power is well known. None dare attack him and demons do not feed from him.

In fact, they run from his presence, and he has a calm and peace of mind uncommon amongst my people. The Menhirs commit to the new alliance and seal our commitment with a pledge to send more Menhirs to Sheldra to undertake the Warrior's training.'

Walnut bowed low to the chief of the Menhirs, his eyes glittering with joy, and the Warriors and their supporters gave an enormous cheer. Lord Menhir looked both baffled and radiant as he accepted their praise, but anger and betrayal flashed across the countenance of Lord Doharven and other leaders of the Mage Clans. Walnut raised his hand again, and when the crowd had fallen silent once more, the chiefs of the Warrior Clans, Lord Conjur, Lord Jular, Lord Swift, Lord Terrigal and Lord Fardell committed their allegiance.

Lord Carvell raised his hand. 'Together we can drive out the bandits,' he said. 'I commit.'

'And trade freely in fair competition,' said Lord Eaglan. 'I too commit.'

With the two non-allied clans declared, Walnut turned to the remains of the Mage Alliance. He nodded first at Lord Donarth. 'I will ask my people,' he said.

Walnut inclined his head in respect and the crowd murmured in surprise, for this was a radical move for a Mage Clan Chief.

'What say you, my people?' Lord Donarth asked, turning to the members of his clan. 'Do you want peace amongst Magans and war on the Rasa?'

'Peace,' they shouted, though some said nothing and others hesitated, looking about them before they joined the shout. Lord Donarth nodded, then raised his hand and the crowd fell silent. 'The Donarths commit to the new alliance,' he said.

Once again, a cheer rose from the crowd and Walnut's eyes glistened with tears of joy. Ah, Miramar, he thought with gratitude, even in death you do great work, bringing about what I have been unable to achieve in life. The crowd fell silent of their own accord, and all eyes turned to the Torens clan.

Their Chief spat on the ground. 'We do not surrender to the Warrior Clans,' he hissed. 'Or to the inspired oratory of untried chiefs or the magic tongues of old men. Nor are we swayed by oath breakers. We remain true to our commitment to the Mage Alliance and will fight to protect ourselves and take what is rightfully ours.'

'The Doharvens prosper under the present arrangements,' Lord Doharven declared. 'And we see no reason to change. If you want my subjugation, old man, you will have to bind me against my will, for I do not commit to this new alliance. But be warned, even if you manage to complete such a binding, we have powerful magicians and they will work to break the spell even while held by it. You will never know when it is released and then, I vow you will all feel our revenge.' He waved his hand, dismissing his people, but before they had even turned towards the town gate, Walnut raised his sceptre and froze them and the Torens Clan where they stood.

Like most in that square, Walnut stared at the sight of fifty or so people standing like statues and wondered at his power. He had never been able to do that before and likely would not be able to do so again when whoever had lent their minds to his withdrew. 'To bind such a crowd, I need the minds of all Warriors,' he said, then began the incantation for arousing Radiant Power. The Warriors amongst the crowd added their voice to his, and though Kestril said nothing, Walnut felt the strength of his silent incantation.

When the chant rang strong and even, Walnut gathered the power of their joint focus, rang his bell, traced magical signs in the air with his scepter and chanted words of binding. The complex spell would prevent the bound Magans from attacking other clans. It was a tricky spell to cast at the best of times, and the sheer numbers he bound took every vestige of energy he had, but he stayed on his feet until the binding was complete, then he released the obstinate Magans from their frozen state. 'Now our beloved Miramar's death has not been in vain,' he said.

Some in the square clapped and threw their hats in the air, hope for a better future lighting their faces. The nobles remained seemingly unmoved, but their eyes sparkled and their features softened. Walnut gazed at Lord Doharven. The man nodded begrudgingly and though some of his people left in protest, he and Lord Torens and their retainers remained out of respect for Miramar.

Walnut staggered as the minds of the Noble Ones departed. Suddenly, he felt all of his one-hundred and twenty years. Lord Torens ran up the steps and helped him to a seat, then as head of the clan of the deceased, he spoke the Magan words of final farewell.

Falcon and Blade lit a torch each and set them on the funeral pyre. Flames caught quickly and the crowd watched in silence as the blaze raced up the wood and consumed Miramar's corpse. A rainbow appeared in the clear sky above the town, and the Warriors amongst the crowd smiled at the sign of Miramar's greatness. We will meet again, my love, Walnut thought, as the burning structure crashed to the ground.

When the pyre had burnt to embers, the crowd moved quietly away. Walnut accompanied Blade and Falcon home and said his farewell on the roof deck. The boys watched with drawn faces as he sat cross-legged, rang his bell and shot into the sky.

'I will return,' Walnut called down to them as he turned towards Sheldra. Soon the lake sparkled beneath him and the towers of the university beckoned in the distance. He scanned the water below, searching for any sign of the silver scales of the great water serpents, but no elegant necks arched from the lake, until a trespasser sent ripples across the surface of their domain. A bright blue kingfisher dipped to the surface and dragged a small snake from the water. The bird barely escaped the sleek head that burst from the depths and snapped at its tail feathers, but Walnut flew well above the Gana's reach. The serpent slid back into the water, cocked its head at Walnut and winked one glistening eye before diving beneath the surface once more.

Kestril had done well to get Ariel and Nick across the lake unharmed.

11

Nick Leaves

Yule leaned over a paper on Nick's desk, a frown etched on her forehead, and Nick leafed through a thick dictionary beside her. He felt rather than heard Walnut enter the room and looked up into a weary face.

'Walnut,' he said, standing up. 'Thank goodness you're all right.'

Yule gave the old guide a hug. 'I'll make tea and you can tell us all about it.' She slipped quietly through the door into the kitchen.

'The group at Shifting Stones wants me to take them to Observatory,' Nick said. 'I don't have to do it now though, do I?'

'Hello, Nick, nice to see you again,' Walnut replied, 'and yes, I did manage to bind most of the magicians at Minion Hills, thank you for asking. At least those in the town. There are still plenty of rogues in the hills though.'

'Sorry,' Nick mumbled. How could he have been so oblivious of the old man's suffering?

Walnut dropped his battered straw hat on Nick's desk and sank onto his chair, then he rubbed his hand over his bald head and looked up. Dark hollows underlined his eyes and his shoulders stooped a little. Nick sensed a deep weariness in him, and yet when he spoke it was with the same calm and kindness as always. 'A guide has a responsibility to his group; you accepted that when you agreed to guide them, and if they are to trust you, then you must be trustworthy.'

'But I have to be with you and Ariel when you move on,' Nick protested, 'and it will take at least five days to get that group prepared and up to Observatory. And that's if there are no problems. Can't someone else take them?'

Walnut shook his head. 'I know you'd rather be with Ariel, but we can manage without you, and you can catch us up anywhere between here and Crow's Nest. You have an allegiance to this group, so you must go.'

'Crow's Nest,' Nick whispered. His heart plummeted. Surely, it wouldn't take that long. Crow's Nest, far away on the Upper Reaches, was as far as Nick had ever climbed. He couldn't portal any higher. Once Ariel and Walnut left there, he would have no hope of catching up to them. And he didn't want to miss any part of Ariel's journey. He had promised to remain by her side. 'They could wait for a while. I could ask them. I'm sure they'd understand.'

'No. They're ready now, so you must be also. You're lucky they don't expect to go all the way to Hermitage. Besides,' he added tenderly, 'we all need a rest before attempting the Upper Reaches, and Ariel needs to train and study. I expect we will see you at the Hermitage in five days.'

As far as Nick was concerned, even that was too long, and there was no guarantee that his timing estimates were accurate. It seemed especially doubtful when he thought of the dubious calibre of the group waiting at Shifting Stones: Robyn, John and Sarah, and who knew who else they might have collected. 'What if something goes wrong and I don't get back to you before you have to leave Crow's Nest?'

'You will see to it that nothing does go wrong, and you have plenty of time between now and then. Get your things and be ready to leave this afternoon after my talk. Where's Ariel?'

Nick checked his watch. 'She'll be here soon.'

'Good. I will put my things in my room and meet you back here. I expect you will want to hear what happened after you left.' Walnut didn't wait for a reply. He picked up his hat and left the office just as the gong rang, signalling the end of first class.

Nick stood, listening to the sound of the gong fade into nothing, his mind still, but his heart heavy. He hated the thought of missing any of Ariel's journey, not just because he'd fallen irrevocably in love with her, but also because it was his journey now. However, he consoled himself that, thanks to his recent experiences, he would be a much better guide, and there was something about the opportunity to test himself once more on the Stones that appealed. This time, I will not be caught, he told himself. I'll do it. I'll do it well and I'll leave the Hermitage at Ariel's side.

***

Ariel sat in the Great Hall, staring into the calm gaze of the statue while the scholars and students entered without a word. Apart from the rustling and shuffling as they settled in their chairs, the room remained as silent as it had when she'd first walked in soon after Walnut had finished his story and declared that he intended to give a talk. Yule and Tynan had raced off to get everything organised; Walnut had gone to rest and Nick had suddenly found a million things he had to do, none of which involved her, so here she sat.

Anticipation filled the atmosphere, and gradually the rustlings died away as the crowd became still. They sat like statues carved from flesh and bone. Their eyes, unmoving,

105

focused softly towards the dais under the great statue where a rocking chair sat next to a low table. Nick entered and sat at a small table beneath the statue of Aya. Silence held all in its embrace.

A door opened at the side of the hall and the assembly stood reverently as the Warrior's most precious guide entered, Ariel's beloved Walnut. His nut-brown face beamed pure joy, and loving kindness emanated from every pore of his body. He sat gleefully in the rocking chair and rocked back and forth like an innocent child.

'Where's Ariel?' he asked, peering into the audience. 'Ariel?'

She raised her hand tentatively. 'Here, Walnut,' she said when he didn't seem to see her. Heads turned her way.

'Ah', he smiled and waved at her. 'Do you like my new chair?'

'Yes.' Heat rose to her face. Why did he have to single her out?

Walnut grinned and got off the rocking chair. 'Now that I'm off my rocker, we can begin.' His eyes sparkled and his body rippled with glee. A moment later, he grew serious, walked to the edge of the dais and peered into the faces of the gathering. 'You are too stiff. Get up and do this.' He waved his arms in the air and wriggled his body in a mad dance. Ariel giggled as the audience did their best to copy him.

'Enough. Sit down,' Walnut said after a minute or two.

The assembly sat and resumed their silence, more relaxed now. Walnut sat back in the rocking chair, propped himself upright with a cushion and began. 'Many of you know and love my queen, Miramar of the Terrigal Magans,' he said, 'and you should know now that she died three days past.'

A shocked murmur washed over the assembly. Walnut continued. 'This is a terrible thing, but I do not want to talk about how or why this happened but about who Miramar really was.'

He paused while Nick spoke in the ancient tongue, translating Walnut's words for the Haba and Magans in the audience. Everyone sat in respectful silence as his satin voice, bold yet humble, soft yet clear, travelled effortlessly across the Great Hall.

'Who Miramar was, who Miramar is, is in essence, the same as who you are, so I ask you, good people, who are you? Are you your name, a mere label, a sound? No, of course not.

'Then are you what you do? Your job, your hobbies, your roles? You are a son or a daughter, perhaps a mother or a father or a scholar or a merchant. Do these roles define you? Are they all that you are? No, of course not.'

He paused again so Nick could translate. Ariel watched Nick from her place near the back of the Hall. She noted the kindness and humour etched in his face, the clarity in his eyes, the commitment in his focus on Walnut's words and the care with which he delivered the translation. Even when Walnut continued his talk, Ariel found her eyes drawn to Nick.

'Are you your body?' Walnut continued. 'Or are you in your body, and if so, where? Ah, you say, I am my mind. But what is your mind? Perhaps you think you are your thoughts and emotions, but they are always changing. So where is this one thing, this constant thing you call you? Ah, you say, I am the thinker and the feeler. But where is this thinker? Where is this feeler? Where do these thoughts and emotions come from and where do they go?'

After Nick translated, Walnut sat still for some time, and the atmosphere in the room became highly charged with a profound peace and vibrancy. No sound broke the silence and for many moments, it seemed that no one breathed.

'This is our essential self, my friends,' Walnut continued, 'this endless clear awareness, this all encompassing love. But although some of us can see our true self manifesting as a Radiant Body, it is not some thing. In essence, it is open space, empty of all form, free of all ideas of something and not something. Yet we can know it. With our clear awareness, we can know our own essence.'

Again, Walnut sat without moving, his back upright, his gaze soft, then he lifted his arms and, in a wide arc, gestured to everything. 'All this is the dream of the essence. If we know that we are not the dream, then for us there is no death, because death is part of the dream. It cannot touch our essential self.

'If at the moment of death, we can let go of our dream self and remain aware of our essence, then we are free of the Serpentine forever, for it too is part of the dream. Then we are a Noble One, free to choose our mode of existence.

'When Miramar's body had burned to ashes, there came a rainbow in the sky, a sign that she has become a Noble One.'

He paused.

'Miramar is not dead. Miramar is dead. Both are true and neither.'

In the silence that remained when Nick finished translating, Walnut began rocking, and for some time, the only sound was the rhythmical creaking of the chair. Ariel sensed Miramar's boundless love holding them all, as if she was there with them. Some of the scholars wept, whether in joy for her presence or sadness for her loss, Ariel couldn't tell.

Nick drew himself up and sat erect, his bearing stately, and he scanned the audience slowly. From within the dream, Ariel recognised her dreaming. When his gaze met hers, their minds merged as one, and as the deep bliss of their spiritual union washed over her, Ariel realised that he was no ordinary man, she no ordinary woman and theirs no ordinary relationship. It never would be, or should be.

When the audience filed out of the Great Hall after Walnut had left, Ariel made her way against the tide of moving people towards Nick. He picked up the rocking chair but put it down when she drew near.

'I'm glad you've come,' he said. 'I'm leaving straight away. I wanted to say goodbye.'

So soon? 'How long will you be away?' she asked, hoping he didn't notice the quavering in her voice.

He shook his head. 'I don't know. I'm hoping to meet up with you again before you leave the Hermitage, but if it takes longer, it might not be until Crow's Nest.'

'Crow's Nest?' Ariel's heart sank. That was ages away.

He shrugged. 'I don't want to go, but I have to. I'll catch you up as soon as I can.'

Ariel nodded. His eyes met hers and sent the familiar warmth pulsing through her. She smiled, then wrenched her gaze away, floundering like a fish out of water, seeking words that wouldn't come. She had to tell him something before he left, but the new urgency muddled her brain. She needed time to prepare, but suddenly there was no more time.

Nick stepped off the dais to where she stood in a daze. 'Can I have a goodbye cuddle then?' She nodded, and he embraced her warmly, but she felt stiff, still trying to pluck up the courage to make her confession. Before she knew it, the hug was over. He stepped back and grinned at her. 'Oh come on, that wasn't in the slightest bit predatory.'

'No, it's … it's fine,' she stammered. 'I'm just a bit … I don't know. Walnut's talk got to me, I guess.' That wasn't what she wanted to say at all.

Nick nodded, his soft eyes fixed on her knowingly. 'Yeah, that sort of stuff is supposed to unravel us a bit.'

She looked at him in silence and he returned her gaze with a gentle smile. Why hadn't she said something?

'I'll see you later then,' he said.

She nodded.

He turned, stepped back onto the dais, picked up the chair and left the room without a backwards glance.

'Damn,' Ariel muttered, then turned on her heels and strode out of the Hall.

***

Ariel sat on her bed pulling at the roots of her hair and shaking her head in frustration. Nick's door slammed and footsteps strode past her door and down the corridor. Ariel's heart jumped. There was still time. She raced after him and caught him at the top of the stairs.

'Wait,' she said breathlessly.

He stopped and turned towards her, one eyebrow raised, his beautiful eyes crinkling up at the corners.

'There's something I need to tell you,' she confessed.

His eyes met hers and stripped her naked with one look. 'What is it?'

'It's too late,' she whispered.

He smiled and traced the side of her face with a fingertip. 'What is?' The fingers passed leisurely across her lips.

He knows. He's always known. He was right; I've been stupid.

He waited, eyes twinkling. Words still failed her, and clearly he wasn't going to make it easy for her. She stepped closer, her nose almost touching his cheek. Time froze. His breath warmed her cheek. His energy, soft and powerful, yet undemanding, filled her with pleasure. She brushed her lips against his, but he didn't move. He just waited. She planted a kiss on his lips, soft for only a moment before she filled it with all the passion she'd denied herself for too long.

His hand slid around her waist and pulled her close. His lips met hers with undisguised hunger, the power of his response igniting ever deepening layers of abandon. His intoxicating

110

presence swamped her whole being, and she felt her heart would burst with the joy of it. All she knew was his scent in her nose, his lips firm against hers and her body aching for more. He swung her around and pushed her gently back against the wall. She ran her fingers through his hair and pulled him closer. He pressed his body against hers, and she groaned at the pleasure of it. Gradually, the fiery passion became a slow burn, then a deep glow that etched itself deep in Ariel's being and sealed their bond.

'I love you,' he whispered against her neck. Then he planted his hands on her shoulders and stepped back, appraising her with a satisfied but wistful smile. 'But, unfortunately, I have to go.' He kissed her again, quickly this time. 'I'll be as quick as I can. See you soon.' He turned swiftly and strode down the corridor. A moment later, he was gone, disappeared down the stairs.

✳✳✳

Ariel sat on the thick stone ledge and stared morosely out at the landscape as the grey light faded. The rain had ceased and the clouds lifted, but although from her vantage point on the top floor of the college, Ariel saw right across the lake to Minion Hills, the sight did not cheer her. Silt washed down by the heavy rain clouded the lake, turning it grey. Where was the deep blue lake glittering in the sunshine? Joy had faded from sight; only a sense of dull vacancy remained, as if all the sunshine had seeped from her life.

If Nick was with her now, he'd be warming her with his gaze. His eyes would twinkle and his mouth turn up in that familiar little smile of amusement. Maybe he'd come up behind her and kiss her neck or run his fingers gently through her hair.

Ariel sighed. She'd missed his constant presence since they'd arrived at Sheldra, but she'd always seen him for some time each day. Now she wouldn't even have that. He'd only been gone twelve hours, and already she was as miserable as the cold, wet day. It didn't matter how much she berated herself for her foolishness, her heart still wept over his absence. The wound of abandonment, rudely gouged by her mother's abduction, reopened like a gaping hole.

That evening as Ariel prepared for sleep, Yule's presence in her room in place of Nick painfully confirmed his absence, and her mind, encouraged by tiredness, ranged restlessly over depressing possibilities. What if she were never to see him again? The mere thought of it brought tears to her eyes and the black night that descended on the mountain that night perfectly mirrored her bleak despair. She might never see him or her mother again.

***

Firelight flickered on the granite walls of Nadima and Aarod's bedroom at the Hermitage, but it wasn't the fire that warmed Nadima deep inside. Aarod stroked her shoulder, his deep brown eyes smiling into hers. She glowed under his touch and yearned for him never to leave. His finger came to rest against the base of her neck and she shuddered with pleasure.

But something was wrong. No man had a fingernail that long!

Nadima awoke from her swoon with a start and found herself back in her cell deep underground, her back against the rough walls and the stench of a Rasa demon close at hand. The big Rasa sat on the dirt floor beside her, his talon on her neck, feeding from her dream as she craved the touch of her long dead husband. The thin line of the demon's fiery mouth curled upwards and a thick purring sound came from the back of his throat.

He stroked her neck tenderly, igniting the thing she feared most. Tremors of pleasure shivered through her body, but she caught her growing craving for the pleasure of it and released it, leaving nothing for the demon.

'Why do you still resist craving the touch of my talon?' he crooned. 'Is it not pleasurable for you?' When she didn't reply, he traced the edge of her lips with his talon. 'Our bargain does not allow resistance.' He watched her intently, the fire in his red eyes flickering lazily, bright against his shiny black skin.

'Your kind and mine are mortal enemies, Sai,' she answered, pushing his talon away. 'I feed you when you wish it because we made a bargain, but I cannot provide the flavour of craving that you so desire. You are a demon. I am a Warrior. It is not possible for me to crave your feeding.'

'Yes, it is,' he whispered in a horribly seductive tone as he brushed her hair off her face. She turned her head away, but he stroked her neck and rested his talon once more at its base.

In this cruel climate, his tenderness disarmed her. Desire for a long lost intimacy arose, but she feared where it might lead, and let it fade away.

The demon growled. His eyes flared. 'You are wrong. We are not enemies, Nadima.'

She flinched. His voice was too soft. If Emot Sai wasn't a demon, she might think he cared.

'You are more like a pet to me, and I am a good master. I look after you well, and you are a good pet. You feed me willingly, and soon you will provide the flavour I most desire.'

The horrifying truth of his words disgusted her. Was that what she'd become? A demon's pet! A plaything! Despair washed over her and she immersed herself in it. Better he feed on despair than craving for his talon on her neck. But the despair soon wore itself out. And he desired a different flavour.

The sharp tip of his talon pressed into the flesh beneath Nadima's chin and pierced it slowly, drawing a drop of blood. She gasped, tensing against the pain. She could have transformed her anger into pure Radiant Energy and sent it blazing like fire into his talon, but she had to submit to his demands and let him feed. That was the deal.

'This is all very well,' he said, his tone bitter. 'But if you refuse to provide whatever flavour I wish, you void our bargain.'

'Flavour was not part of the bargain,' she replied through gritted teeth, 'only willingness.'

'It is part of the bargain now.' Her heart contracted at his smooth commanding tone, and his words confirmed her fear. 'I demand the pleasure of your craving for my talon on your neck, and you will supply as I demand or I will pierce the flesh of your little friends and make you watch.'

Nadima shuddered. He had spoken the cruel words softly and without malice, but she knew he'd do it. That was how he'd got her to make the bargain in the first place: dragged her down to the cells where they kept the other prisoners and made them suffer until she'd relented.

Once again, his talon stroked her neck, and this time, she relented, giving herself over to the painful yearning invoked by his feeding. She felt his gaze on her and knew, without looking, that a blissful smile wreathed his face. He lifted his talon and the pleasure stopped. It was frighteningly easy to want more. There was no other pleasure in this dismal place.

'At last,' he sighed. 'At last you crave my touch, sweet flavoured Nadima. Give me this when I desire it and I'll never hurt you again.' He fed until satisfied, then stroked her hair gently before gliding from the cell without a sound.

Nadima dropped her head in her hands and sobbed quietly.

12

Emot Bait

The next day, Ariel's studies continued as before, except that Walnut took her Nature of Reality class. She threw herself into her lessons, listening carefully and asking questions, determined to make the most of her time at the University and keep her mind off the absence of what she had belatedly recognised as the best thing in her life. Nevertheless, although the sun shone brightly on the green lawns and blossoming flowers of the University, the weather in her heart remained cloudy and painted her day with gloom.

When the gong rang for lunch, she walked with Dennis—silently as usual—to the cafeteria for their midday meal. She'd given up trying to liven Dennis up, finding more entertainment in watching the many scholars and other students that flooded the walkways and courtyards. A cluster of students passed them by just outside the dining hall and a girl with blonde curly hair caught her eye.

'Susan!' Ariel called, but instead of stopping, the girl hurried away. Ariel rushed after her. 'Wait. It's me; Ariel.' But the petite student disappeared into the crowd.

'It doesn't look like she knows you,' Dennis said, still at her side.

Ariel frowned. Of course, it couldn't be Susan, the girl she'd befriended at the Plateau of Bliss. How could she possibly have made it to Sheldra? It wasn't possible. 'I guess I made a mistake. It must just be someone who looks like her.'

'It happens,' Dennis said.

***

'Is everything all right, Ariel?' Walnut asked that evening after dinner. They sat in the comfy chairs in Nick and Walnut's living room while Yule pawed over books in the office next door.

She didn't look up from the book she'd been trying to read for the last half hour. 'I'm fine.'

'Even without my insight into your mind,' he said, 'I can read your hunched shoulders, downcast face and the far away look in your eyes.' She glanced up and met his eyes. He cocked his head and looked at her with a gaze that told her she couldn't fool him for a moment.

Ariel sighed. It was impossible to keep anything from Walnut. 'Fine. I'm missing him. I got used to him being around.'

'We can get used to having a bad smell around too, but we don't miss it when it goes,' Walnut chuckled.

Ariel rolled her eyes.

'You're not just missing him; you're pining like a lost puppy for its master.'

'What's wrong with that?'

'Nothing is wrong with it, you are just suffering more than you need to.'

'You sent him away!'

'You think it is my fault that you're unhappy?'

'I wouldn't be unhappy if he was still here.'

He chuckled, much to her annoyance. To Ariel, none of this was remotely amusing. 'The reason you are unhappy,' he said, 'is because you want to keep him with you, but you can't, and

116

instead of accepting that and getting on with your life, you keep reminding yourself that you're missing him. Stop going over and over it in your mind. Feel the desire to have him near, feel it and let it move through you, but don't hold onto it, or stir it up, or you turn it into clinging and that is …'

'Emot food. I know. This is why Twitchet didn't want me and Nick to get together, isn't it?'

Walnut nodded. 'He feared that you might become possessive and clingy. Love kills demons, but possessiveness kills love, and feeds demons.

'I'm not clingy!'

'Good, let us hope it remains that way.'

Ariel frowned. 'Did you send him away to test me?'

He chuckled. 'Very perceptive, my dear, but no; it was merely good timing.'

'Now? When Emot wants to get his hooks into me? I don't think that's good timing!'

'That's exactly why it's good timing. You'll get plenty of practice at keeping craving out of your desires.

'If you continually think about the cause of your feelings, or make stories about them, you make them bigger and more solid in your mind, and that gives them power over you. If you're not careful, you become a slave to your emotions.'

'And a slave to the demons.'

'Or at least good fodder.'

'But shouldn't I be making love stronger?'

'Of course, so long as it is love you are fostering and not an impostor.'

'Like lust?'

Walnut chuckled. 'Physical desire can be a natural expression of genuine love, but if you think of the other more as an object for your own pleasure or adornment than as a person, then it is not love.'

Did she wear Nick like a necklace around her neck? No, she'd never particularly wanted a boyfriend, never felt she needed one and had no one to impress, even if she did want to, which she didn't.

'Genuine love is when you want someone to be happy, not when you only want the beloved to make you happy,' Walnut continued. 'Love destroys Serpentine in yourself and others, so strengthen it, and you weaken the demons. Feel your love and concern for others and expand it to include the whole universe.'

Ariel smiled. She knew that feeling from her best mind training sessions, her heart bursting with joy, streaming out in all directions, lighting up the world.

'Enjoy it, but don't crave it, or you will destroy it,' Walnut continued.

Ariel frowned. 'It's just more fun with him around, that's all.'

'Of course, you enjoy his company and you want him back; that is natural. It is only when you constantly think about what you don't have and fear never getting it that a simple desire can become craving, and craving, though it sometimes feels like pleasure, is inherently painful.'

'Except to Emot and his minions.'

'Indeed. For them it is delicious.'

'I do miss him terribly,' she admitted, 'and it's hard not to think about him all the time.'

'How do you get rid of a shadow that's stalking you?'

'Shine a torch on it.' Like I did in the Morbid Forest.

'Exactly, and in the same way, you turn the light of your awareness on whatever thoughts and emotions arise, and you simply let them pass on through. They're just thoughts, just feelings, that's all. Just don't get involved. Say, *hi, nice to see you again*, and *bye, see you later.*'

Ariel chuckled at Walnut's comical expression as he waved at an invisible passer-by.

'This is an exceptionally good opportunity to practice avoiding Emot's traps.'

'I'd rather he was here,' Ariel mumbled.

'That's easy fixed.'

'It is?' Her eyes lit up.

'Yes, Emot will come if you call.'

'Not him.' She narrowed her eyes. 'Nick.'

Walnut chuckled. 'Think about and appreciate what you do have, not what you don't have. He will return, Ariel, you need not be afraid that he won't. Now go and practice.'

Ariel nodded and left the room feeling somewhat conflicted. She knew how to spit out demon food when it rose in her mind, and she knew that imagining the worst possible future was a sure way to make you miserable. On the other hand, fifteen years ago, her father hadn't returned to her mother, so why on a mountain full of murderous demons should she trust that Nick would return to her?

***

Dennis followed Ariel everywhere. When she wanted to be alone, his presence annoyed her, but he did his job well. He knew how to stay far enough away that she didn't feel too much as if she had a dog, and when she went to her room, he always stayed outside. There she could be alone and indulge in her misery without anyone watching, at least until the night shift when Yule slept in her room.

The first Emot emanation appeared early on the day after Nick's departure. Ariel was too involved in thoughts of Nick to notice the odour, and Dennis had little sensitivity to their smell, so it was almost upon them before they saw it. It glided noiselessly up behind Ariel as they walked to the dining hall for lunch, and only when it laid its claw on her neck did she turn. She shrieked at the slimy black creature with his flowing cloak-

119

like skin and flaming red eyes, and Dennis whipped out his sword and lopped its head off. Ariel breathed a sigh of relief as it vaporised. Nick had picked her bodyguard well.

'I thought Rasas didn't come into the University,' she said, shocked by the demon's sudden appearance.

'They don't usually,' her ginger-haired companion replied, 'but I suspect that any heir to the Blade of Aarod is a particularly tasty snack.'

What he was too polite to say was that Ariel was positively oozing Emot food.

After that, they often saw the red-eyed Rasas sneaking about or waiting in the corridors to ambush her. Many times, the Emots ran off as soon as Dennis or she discovered them, and when they attacked, Dennis dispatched them quickly and easily. Sometimes he just locked gazes with them and they dissolved, other times he took them out with his sword.

'They'll have to try harder if they want to get to you,' he commented after one such incident.

'Why don't you let me take one out?' Ariel asked. 'I need the practice, you know.'

'Sorry,' Dennis replied, 'it's the Precious Guide's orders. He says he'll tell me when you're ready for practice. In the meantime, he doesn't want them getting any intelligence on you.'

Ariel bit her lip, embarrassed that Walnut didn't even think her ready to face an emanation. She wondered how much Dennis knew. His face gave nothing away.

'You're a very good bodyguard, you know,' she told him after one such incident.

'Thanks,' he replied. 'I did a stint as one back home. I'm a professional.'

Ariel did try to focus on what she had rather than what she didn't have, but there was something just too tantalising about thinking about Nick. She often remembered their good times together—a shared joke or bit of banter, a timely cuddle, a friendly joust or a delicious kiss. But stupid things also flitted into her mind, and she caught herself almost believing them.

If he really loved her, he wouldn't have gone, and why couldn't he jump in a portal and come and visit? She imagined him falling in love with someone else while she wasn't with him and found her heart pounding furiously at the thought that he wouldn't want her anymore. She knew it was ridiculous, but still those thoughts came, turning them into stories with no basis in reality. When she realised what she was doing, she felt incredibly stupid. The very thing she'd hoped to avoid had come to pass; her brain was turning to mush over a man! But it was too late now; she couldn't go back to pretending she wasn't interested.

Walnut stopped her in the hallway and looked into her eyes. 'Where do you feel love?' he asked.

Ariel pointed to the centre of her chest. 'Here.'

'So why do you look for it in Nick?'

He walked on then, leaving her rooted to the spot, the yearning completely cut through, replaced by a soaring sense of freedom.

Dennis stood respectfully a couple of metres away looking casually away from her.

'Come on,' she said to him a moment later.

'He's good, isn't he?' Dennis commented as they walked on.

Ariel sighed. And I'm stupid. I mean, honestly. How brainless is that? To feel jealous and betrayed over a story you made up yourself. She was a Warrior. She should know better, but the memory of the comfort of Nick's presence was so strong that sometimes she wanted to follow any thought that involved him.

She imagined what they'd do when he returned, or even after all this was over. Perhaps they'd travel. They could go to movies together, and parties, like normal couples. That would be different. She remembered the nightclub on the Plateau and how she'd loved dancing with him. It would be good to do that again without that sleaze-bag Jason around. She wouldn't go back to the Plateau though; she'd take him home, show him off to Tamara. They could even go running together.

She imagined Nick holding her, saying he loved her, and stealing kisses in unexpected places, like change rooms in shops. Her little stories weren't the same as the real thing, of course, but they dulled some of the pain of his absence. And she figured there was no harm in it so long as she knew what she was doing and let the fantasies play like movies across the screen of her mind, but when she reached out for more, and then more again, and she felt like she could never have enough and that there was an enormous hole inside her that only Nick could fill, then the Emots gathered around and she realised that the unquenchable thirst she felt was craving.

As soon as she recognised it, the craving dissolved, leaving a wonderful sense of peace and freedom, yet still she couldn't resist replaying the fantasies, and she hated herself for it.

Where was the great Warrior she was supposed to be?

Sometimes the reason she threw herself on the bed and screamed into the pillow wasn't her yearning for Nick, but her frustration at her failure to apply what she knew. Why did she choose the murk of black clouds over the brilliant blue sky?

'Habit,' Walnut told her. 'You have to break the habit of thinking you need something more and create a new habit of identifying yourself with your greater self, the one that already holds everything in its embrace.'

'I feel like a yo-yo,' Ariel complained, 'high in the sky during training and hitting the ground in between sessions.'

Walnut nodded kindly. 'It will come,' he reassured her. 'Once you can choose the peace, clarity and love of your Radiance over the lure of the touch of a phantom, you'll be ready to defeat Emot.'

Ariel swallowed nervously. She hadn't told him about the fantasies and she guarded her mind carefully around him.

To minimise the times when her mind was left without something to occupy it, the times when Nick's face swam into her mind, Ariel spent more time in the library. At lunchtime on the second day after Nick's departure, she almost bumped into Kelee as she was about to turn into the entranceway. The Magan woman's face looked tense, as if she was preoccupied with something.

'Hi Kelee,' Ariel said.

'Oh. Hello, Ariel.' Kelee's face brightened, but her eyes flickered from Dennis back to Ariel. Ariel glanced at Dennis and he fell back out of hearing.

'He's good like that,' Ariel whispered. Kelee smiled. 'What are you studying today?' Ariel asked as they passed through the door into the quiet of the library.

'I am helping Maya in the old part. We are searching through ancient language books and papers for a map of the Rasas' tunnels.'

'Excellent.'

'She is very keen to find them,' Kelee whispered. 'I don't know why. Do you?' She stopped and fixed her deep green eyes—so reminiscent of her brother's—on Ariel.

'Yes. One of the Rasas kidnapped my mother. We think she is somewhere in the tunnels.'

'Oh, Ariel, I am so sorry. That is terrible.'

'That's why I'm here. If I kill Rasama, she'll be free. But I might fail, or I might be too late. If we can find a map, we might be able to get her out sooner.'

'Then I will find it,' Kelee said, her eyes glittering with determination. 'If I do this, it will help atone for the misdeeds of Beak and Druid.'

'Maybe I could help too,' Ariel said. 'I can't read the old language but I know what a picture of a map looks like.'

'Yes.' Kelee's eyes lit up with enthusiasm. 'I can give you likely books and you can look through them.'

'Great,' Ariel smiled, 'where do we go?'

Kelee led Ariel and Dennis to the far end of the library where she lit an oil lamp then guided them down a set of narrow stairs into the basement.

Dennis stayed close as they entered the gloom of the old part of the library. The oil lamp cast deep shadows and the musty smell of the ancient books thickened the atmosphere. He glanced warily around as they followed Kelee along the eastern wall past rows of bookshelves set at right angles to the walkway.

'Do you have to do this?' he whispered to Ariel as they walked further from the stairs.

'No,' Ariel replied, 'but I want to.'

'I advise against it.'

'Advice noted,' Ariel replied.

'You shouldn't trust a Menhir,' he whispered.

Ariel ignored him.

Deep in the library, they stopped at a small table with several books and a lamp on it, set up not far from the wall. Dennis scouted around the islands of shelves on both sides then found a stool for himself and settled against the wall.

'You can look through those to start with.' Kelee indicated the pile of books on the table. 'I will get out some more.'

Ariel picked out two of the books and took them to Dennis. 'Make yourself useful; see if there are any maps in these.'

He shook his head. 'How can I do my job with my eyes on a book?'

'Oh. Yeah,' Ariel replied. 'You're a professional, right?'

'Right, and you're down here with a Mage Clan Magan in a place with one exit and hardly any light. You're putting yourself in danger.'

'Kelee is a student here and I've had enough to do with her to know where her allegiances lie.'

'Don't be naïve, Ariel; a Magan's primary allegiance is always to their clan.'

'I'm not so sure of that.'

'Obviously, but I suggest you be cautious or that idea could be the cause of your death.'

Ariel sighed. 'I'll be careful.'

He nodded, and she took the books back to the table where she seated herself on a stool and began shuffling through the pages. Kelee returned with another table, and soon had another pile of books on it. They saw no one apart from two scholars who passed by, going deeper into the library, their faces shrouded in hoods.

'They come everyday at the same time,' Kelee whispered. 'Who knows what they are looking for.'

Ariel shrugged and went back to looking through the books, until she noticed the faint smell of rotten potatoes. She strode over to Dennis. 'Do you smell Rasa?' she whispered.

He sniffed. 'No, but my sense of smell isn't that great.'

'It's faint, but I think it's coming from down there.' She pointed down the aisle the way the scholars had gone.

Dennis jerked his head towards Kelee. 'Who's she defeated?'

Ariel shook her head. 'Probably no one. She's new.'

'Okay, let's check it out.'

After telling Kelee what they were doing, Ariel followed Dennis deeper into the library. The smell deepened as they drew closer to the source, yet no sound indicated anyone's distress. Perhaps the Rasa had snuck up on someone and killed them before they had a chance to scream. The thought sent a shiver down Ariel's spine.

A dim light shone from an aisle near the far wall. Ariel and Dennis crept towards it without a sound. He led her down the aisle next to the light and they peered through the gap above the books into the next aisle. Two scholars in hooded coats stood beside a table with a lamp turned low, their faces in deep shadow. Many celibates wore their hoods inside on cold days to keep their shaved heads warm, but the strand of long blond hair spilling from the hood of one of them indicated at least one of these was unshaven. The girl's head tilted to the side and the other scholar rested a long fingernail on her exposed neck. Not a finger nail. *A talon!* The girl stood as if frozen, and the Rasa purred contentedly. His head turned slightly, enough to see the red fire flickering where a person's eyes would be.

Ariel's eyes widened at the sight. Dennis pointed to himself, then at the demon, then indicated that Ariel should stay where she was. She nodded and peered through the gap in the bookshelf, trying to see who the demon had trapped. Dennis carefully unsheathed his sword, crept to the end of the aisle and up the next one until he stood behind the feeding demon. Then he struck, beheading the oblivious demon with one strike. It fizzled into nothing and the scholar fled, racing past with her hood pulled over her face.

'No thanks from that one,' Dennis commented as he sheathed his sword.

'She was feeding it willingly,' Ariel said through the bookshelf.

'Scholars don't feed demons willingly,' he replied.

'This one was. She didn't put up a fight. Maybe she's not really a scholar.'

'A spy,' Dennis whispered. 'I told you it was dangerous down here.'

'The Rasa wasn't after me; he'd come for his daily feed. I've seen bandits feeding demons as if they were pets, and Kelee said that these two came at the same time everyday.'

'Ew.' Dennis's top lip curled up in disgust. 'I doubt they'll come tomorrow, but I'll arrange someone to check it out.'

As they walked back to where Kelee was working, Dennis said, 'Can we get out of here? This place gives me the creeps.'

'Just a bit longer,' Ariel replied, 'I said I'd help.'

Dennis shook his head in defeat.

13

Information

That evening after dinner, Ariel sat curled up on the sofa in Nick's living room, staring at a book and thinking of Nick. Why, she asked herself, when she knew through experience that everything she needed was already within herself, why did she feel so insecure without Nick's arm around her? He did love her, didn't he? Or was that a fantasy as well?

Walnut sat on the comfy chair across from her filling in a crossword, a faint crease on his brow as he considered his answers. He looked up, saw her watching and smiled. 'No matter how much he puts his arm around you, Ariel, the pain will not go away until you give up wanting the pleasure of it.'

'How can I not want pleasure?' she exclaimed.

'Giving up *wanting* pleasure is not the same as giving up pleasure. Enjoy your pleasure when it is there, but if you crave it when it is absent, it will only bring you pain.'

Ariel shook her head. 'I can let the craving go, but it just keeps coming up, again and again.'

'Then be more active. Be courageous. Use the Warrior's weapon. Look directly at it and shatter it with your awareness.'

Ariel sighed. She knew how to do that. She'd killed Bitah and Amic that way, so why was this so difficult?

'And beware,' he continued gravely, 'the wanting itself can become quite alluring. Craving the craving is Emot's most subtle and dangerous trap.'

'I won't fall into that,' she said quietly, ignoring the little voice whispering at the edge of her consciousness which suggested that perhaps she already had.

'Good. Be diligent, for all our sakes.'

He bid her goodnight then and left. She would have to call Yule from next door when she wanted to go to bed, and she wasn't ready for that, so she sat, alone, yet feeling as if she were two people. One, a Warrior with a powerful weapon that destroyed the enemy the instant she used it; the other, a teenager with all the angst of her first love. Why did she have to be a Warrior? Why couldn't she just be normal and indulge her emotions and make mistakes like everyone else? It hurt to want Nick with her all the time, but the pain had a sweetness to it, and the intensity of it made her feel alive. Even though she knew Walnut was right, something in Ariel rebelled at the old man who insisted she let it go.

Twitchet strolled in, jumped onto the coffee table and stared at her with a feline version of disdain.

Ariel stared right back. 'Don't say it, okay. I really do not need to hear it.'

'Say what?' the cat replied. 'That I told you so? No; I won't say that, but now you can see what I was trying to save you from.'

'Save me from what?' Ariel retorted. 'From loving Nick? No, I'd rather have that and any pain that goes with it than the cold heart you laid on me.'

'So be it,' Twitchet replied. 'What's done is done. But you will have to learn to love him without possessiveness or he'll be what drags you to your death.'

'Thanks, Twitchet,' she replied sarcastically. 'You're so encouraging.'

'Just telling it as it is. You've put yourself in a dangerous position.'

'I get that. Okay?'

'Do you? Really?'

'Get out!' She threw a cushion at him. It missed. He leapt from the coffee table to one of the chairs, then sat still again, looking at her with unblinking eyes.

Yule poked her head through the connecting door to the office. 'Are you all right?' she asked.

Ariel picked Twitchet up by the scruff of the neck, opened the door into the corridor, threw him outside and slammed the door behind him. 'I'm fine,' she declared.

Yule pointed behind Ariel. 'You do have a Gimp, though.'

Ariel turned. A red, spiky-haired Gimp stood on the sofa behind her, eyes bulging, little fists held up ready for a fight. 'Leave me for a minute,' she said. 'I'll be wrestling a Gimp.'

Yule frowned. 'Is that some secret training method?' Warriors didn't wrestle Gimps; they ignored the little demons, vaporised them with a glance or melted them with a friendly smile.

'Um. Yeah.' Ariel's own personal, I'll-indulge-it-if-I-like method.

Yule looked sceptical but she left and closed the door behind her.

The Gimp bared his teeth and hissed. Ariel returned the gesture and added a deep-throated growl. It crouched, ready to spring. Ariel copied it, a faint smile dancing at the corner of her mouth. The Gimp started to fade.

'Don't you dare go away, you nasty, horrible little thing!'

The Gimp re-solidified, stuck out its tongue and leapt at her. She ducked. It hurtled over her head and landed with a thump on the floor behind her. Ariel spun around and threw herself on it, knocking it to the floor. They rolled over and over, each trying to get on top of the other. By the time they hit the sofa with Ariel on top, the Gimp had grown to her shoulders and almost matched her in strength. She sat on top of him, pinning his arms to the floor, glad of the additional muscle tone she'd gained in the gym. He kicked and struggled, but she held him firm and enjoyed the tussle. Her frustration ebbed away in the physicality of the game. When she burst out laughing, the Gimp looked astonished and dissolved beneath her.

'Thanks, little Gimp. I needed that.'

***

Ariel vigilantly kept a clear mind around Walnut and Twitchet. The fact that she could do that helped allay her fears that her fantasies might somehow trap her. She felt a little guilty about her subterfuge but assured herself that there was no harm. The stories were under her control, not the other way around. *I can stop them whenever I want,* she told herself.

Her chance to test her theory came when Dennis escorted her back to Tynan's office on an afternoon that threatened rain. Ariel felt as gloomy as the day and couldn't help thinking how Nick would brighten it up. He would hold her hand—though he never had—and kiss her when she didn't expect it. Her fantasy was not only infinitely preferable to her present reality, but also, so well created that, mentally, it almost became her reality.

The clouds grew darker and the first spots of rain appeared. Dennis hurried Ariel along, but as they turned the corner into a walkway, an Emot suddenly stepped out in front of them. Dennis whipped out his sword, but Ariel felt the cool, alluring touch of another Rasa's talon on her neck.

The shock woke her up. She jerked back, spun around and drew her sword at the same time. With his meal forfeit, the Rasa—an Emot, of course—went for the kill instead. His talon sliced through the air towards her, but Ariel parried the blow.

'He's here,' the demon purred. 'Behind you.'

The Warrior in Ariel took control and shone her awareness onto her desire for Nick's presence. The desire dissolved before it could turn to craving. 'Liar!' She thrust her sword into her opponent's chest, and the demon vaporised just as the head of the other rolled on the ground. 'Yes,' she shouted. 'We can tell Walnut I'm ready for real practice now.'

Dennis merely nodded. Not even a high five. Ariel sighed, but even Dennis's lack of enthusiasm couldn't dampen her sense of confidence. She could keep her fantasies and kill Emot as well.

After that, Dennis let her try to defeat the emanations herself. Sometimes she succeeded and sometimes she didn't. He never waited long though, stepping in well before she was in any real danger. Several times, she shouted at him to back off, then finished off the demon herself. Once, one of the beasts scratched her arm. Dennis, mortified, rushed her to the hospital where a healer fixed her up in a few minutes.

'It's no big deal,' Ariel said. 'I've had a lot worse.' She lifted her T-shirt enough to show him the scar from her tussle with Amic. The blush on Dennis's freckled face kept her giggling for the rest of the day.

✳✳✳

Late in the afternoon on the third day after Nick's departure, Walnut called Maya, Tynan and Ariel into his room across the hallway from Tynan's office. Though similar to the other offices in décor—white walls, polished wood floor and dark wooden furniture—Walnut's room was a bedroom, office and kitchenette in one—Ariel presumed that the internal door led to a bathroom—and looked somewhat bare of personal possessions, as if he rarely lived there.

'It is time to mobilise the Warrior Army, Tynan,' Walnut began once they were all seated on the various chairs set around

132

a small coffee table. 'Our inside sources have informed me that a large number of Rasas and Domos will mass on Craggin plain within the next few days to prevent us from going further up the mountain. I suggest we ride out as soon as possible, at least as far as the rocks. We don't want to risk them taking cover there.'

'Who told you this?' Tynan asked.

'Kestril,' Walnut replied, giving Tynan a challenging look.

'Then it could be a trap,' Tynan pointed out. 'They may be there already waiting to ambush us.'

'But we are prepared,' Walnut replied. 'And please remember that although Kestril is a Magan, his allegiance is most certainly with Ariel.'

'Walnut speaks the truth,' Maya said.

'We don't know that for sure,' Tynan argued. 'He kidnapped you to hand you over to the black magicians.'

'And he freed us. It was a ruse, Tynan,' Walnut reminded him, 'to draw the Mage Clans away from our path, which he did, and at considerable risk to himself, I might add.'

'But someone told the Mage Clans of your whereabouts in Minion Hills.'

'Enough of this, Tynan! Not only has Kestril proved my trust on many occasions but he swore on the body of Ariel's father that he would protect her with his life. He deserves your trust and you need to trust him. But please, do not speak of it; a Magan's oath is a private matter.'

Ariel's heart fluttered and the skin at the back of her neck prickled. 'Was he there when my father died?' she whispered.

'Yes,' Walnut replied.

'Then how? I never heard.' Ariel's words tumbled out in a rush.

'You will have to ask him yourself.'

'All that's for another time.' Maya put her arm around Ariel and gave her a squeeze.

'Did he say anything else?' Tynan asked.

'There will be many Rasas from all clans, as large a force as they can muster. I flew out for a quick look and estimate that there could be as many as five hundred on their way already.'

'Five hundred,' Ariel exclaimed.

'Rasama could have command over every Domos clan on the mountain, and if Amic and Bitah have been able to build their numbers back to full capacity, we could be facing over one thousand demons if we include the Cogin. Kestril isn't sure if they'll be involved or not; his informant thinks they're too arrogant to fight with the lesser Rasa clans, but if commanded by Rasama they will have no choice.'

'Then you are correct; we must ready for battle,' Tynan said. 'Your little company could not pass through such a force alone. No matter how many of the Major Rasas you have defeated, the sheer numbers could kill you, or at least exhaust you sufficiently to render you helpless before Emot when he comes for you,' he turned to Ariel, 'which he undoubtably would.'

'For me?' Ariel asked.

'You're the one with the price on your head, the one he doesn't want anywhere near him.'

'But why?'

'How many Warriors do we have?' Walnut asked before Tynan could reply. Ariel opened her mouth to protest the interruption, but Maya placed a hand on her arm, and somehow Ariel knew that she would find out when Walnut wanted her to know.

'Around six hundred and fifty of varying capacity,' Tynan replied, 'including some who are untested against Rasa Majors, but I can use them against the Domos. There may be one hundred mixed experience Warrior Clan Magans, and the Haba, if they come, could probably bring another one hundred and fifty.'

'Don't forget the Light Brigade,' Maya put in.

'What's that?' Ariel asked.

'My Warrior magicians,' she replied. 'We work with the light instead of the sword. We will be able to weaken the Rasas with the Light of the Radiance. There are about twenty of us.'

'I included you already,' Tynan said.

'Even with the Haba that's only nine hundred,' Ariel said bleakly.

'Yes,' Tynan agreed with a sigh, 'we will certainly be outnumbered if the Cogins come.'

'Or if the Haba don't come,' Ariel said gloomily.

'They will come,' Walnut said. 'I will visit them as soon as we have finished here. I will explain that if they do not come down and fight the demons mid-mountain, there may be no one left to ascend to the Upper Reaches for them to protect up there. Also there is the Star Clan. I may be able to convince them to send some to help.'

'Who?' Tynan asked.

'A hidden clan of non-demonised Domos,' Walnut replied.

Tynan raised his eyebrows. 'I didn't know one existed.'

'We should plan to be without them, however,' Walnut continued before Tynan could ask more. 'It will probably be too much to ask for them to reveal themselves in this way, let alone fight against other Domos.'

'What about Nick?' Ariel asked. 'Will you find him? He'd want to be there.'

'He can't just leave a group of travellers where they are,' Walnut replied. 'We'll leave a message for him at The Observatory.'

'Don't be concerned about numbers,' Tynan reassured them. 'We can be out-numbered and still be the stronger force, because the Rasa clans have one major weakness, if we kill their major, they all die. All we have to do is pick off the majors and, even with Cogin, there are only four of them.'

'They won't show their faces though,' Ariel said, 'just like Bitah at the Observatory.'

'We will have people searching for them off the field,' Tynan replied. 'They won't be far away.'

'It's a race then, isn't it?' she asked. 'A race between getting the Majors before they get the Warriors.'

'Yes,' Tynan replied, 'except for one complication.'

'What?'

'You.'

'Me?'

'If you want to try to defeat Emot here, then we should leave him for you. The question then is, how much time do we give you to kill him? Because our Warriors will have to fight his emanations until you do.'

Ariel sighed.

'Are you ready to try at all?' Tynan asked.

'I might as well. Walnut can get rid of him if the Warriors are struggling.'

'I agree, but our primary goal must be to show the demons that this sort of strategy will not work. We must wipe them all out as quickly as possible, so we will not give you long, Ariel. The other Rasas will also have their targets, and that will complicate matters, but I think we have a fair idea of who they will be and can position them to our advantage.'

'There won't be many Amics anyway,' Ariel said, 'I only killed him a few days ago. He can't have made many emanations since then.'

'Ah yes,' Walnut said. 'That is perhaps the most distressing news.'

Ariel shivered at the grave tone of Walnut's voice.

'It seems that when Ariel defeated Amic,' he continued, 'one of the Amic emanations didn't dissolve because he was feeding off a prisoner at the time. He became the new Amic, and because food was readily available in the cells, within twenty-four hours he became strong enough to create more emanations.'

The group absorbed the disturbing news in silence, but it struck Ariel like a blow to the head; all a Rasa major had to do to facilitate almost instant regrowth was to leave one emanation with a human they had imprisoned or enslaved.

'This makes freeing the prisoners much more urgent,' Maya said. 'We cannot leave the Rasas with a stable full of fodder for the purpose of regeneration.'

Ariel flinched but said nothing. Was that what her mother had become? Rasa fodder?

'But the good news is,' Maya added brightly, 'Kelee has found the map of the tunnels.'

'Excellent!' The sparkle in Walnut's eyes reflected everyone's enthusiasm at the news.

'Unfortunately, however, we cannot make any escape plans until we find out where in the tunnels the prisoners are,' Maya continued.

'That's where I come in,' Twitchet meowed, jumping onto the table. 'I've been studying the map, I'm small and quick and I can see pretty well in the dark. I'm going to find them and tell them they must not feed a Rasa when it's fading.'

'Great idea.' A broad grin spread across Tynan's face. 'Things are looking up, after all.'

'We have already located a nearby tunnel and Twitchet will enter tonight,' Maya told them.

'Will you be able to help them escape?' Ariel asked hopefully, imagining the cat carrying a key in his mouth.

'I will try, but do not have expectations. We don't know what it will be like down there.'

Ariel sighed.

'Coming back to the forthcoming battle,' Tynan said with a thoughtful frown. 'The focus of the Emot's attack will be Ariel and, with Nick away, Walnut, you and I must be her primary defenders.'

'Why would I be the focus of their attack?' Ariel asked. 'There must be plenty of Warriors who are a bigger threat to Emot than me.'

Walnut sighed and glanced thoughtfully at Maya and Tynan.

'Perhaps it's time,' Tynan said.

'She must know sometime,' Maya added.

Ariel glanced from Walnut to Maya and back again. 'The Rasas have been targeting me from the moment one broke into my house. Why me?'

The old guide hesitated.

'I need to know … Now.'

Walnut nodded. 'There is a prophecy. We think it is about you, and it looks like Rasama thinks so too.'

'So, why haven't you told me already?'

'If a person knows a prophecy about themselves, they can behave differently to the prediction, thus voiding it. You would need to continue as if you had never heard it, or at least not rely on it to provide the desired outcome.'

'In other words, don't expect some magic to come from outside of yourself to fulfill the prophecy,' Maya explained.

Ariel fixed Walnut with a demanding stare. 'Tell me.'

14

Prophecy

'When the oily plague infects the land
And the nut has born no fruit,
When men feed demons without a care,
And few cut them at their root,
One will come to break the drought,
One bright to cut the dark,
One who wields the blade of Aarod,
One bearing the Copper Mark,
With four protectors they will come
To trap the demon king
And triumph over evil
Though no sound of blade shall ring.'

'The Blade of Aarod,' Ariel murmured—her magical blade, a dagger until she whispered an incantation to transform it into a sword. 'And the Copper Mark is supposed to be my hair.'

Walnut nodded.

'Are you the nut?'

'We think so, because none of my travellers have defeated Rasama. Yet.'

'Who are the protectors?'

'They would be Maya, Layla, Twitchet and myself.'

'What about Nick?'

'I'm not mentioned in it either, Ariel,' Tynan pointed out.

'Why couldn't Tynan and Nick be protectors?'

'The prophecy was originally written in the ancient language and the word used here for protector means a Noble One, which means someone who has defeated Rasama.'

'Twitchet has defeated Rasama?' Ariel exclaimed, looking at everyone in disbelief.

'Secret weapon,' Twitchet said.

'How can a cat defeat Rasama?'

'I wasn't a cat at the time.'

'Oh.'

'Hence the disguise,' Walnut said, 'and so long as Rasama doesn't know Twitchet is here, he will think we are one short.'

Tynan smiled. 'Now I understand.'

'I don't get it,' Ariel protested, 'how can you be sure who the protectors are?'

'The magic needed to stop Rasama from running away requires four Noble Ones, each with a different concentration of qualities of the Radiance,' Walnut explained. 'My Radiance has a red tinge, Maya's main colour is white, Layla's is green and Twitchet's is yellow.'

'I see.' But she didn't see at all.

'Well,' Tynan said abruptly, 'I had best be off and mobilise this army. Get a good night's sleep everyone. I expect we will be riding to Craggin Rocks tomorrow.' He nodded to Walnut and left the room.

Ariel gulped. All of a sudden, everything had changed. The ground seemed to fall away beneath her, leaving her hanging in unknown territory.

'I'll see you in the morning too, Ariel and Maya,' Walnut said. 'Here at seven for breakfast.'

'Travel well,' Maya said.

Walnut left to fly across the mountain and solicit help to defeat an army of demons that, apparently, were gathering for the express purpose of killing Ariel.

Great, she thought sarcastically. I wanted a more exciting life, now look what I've got, a whole army out to get me!

The courtyard gate creaked open and Yule walked through with Spud at her heels. She ushered the wombat back into his pen, then walked through the French doors and glanced from Ariel to Maya and back again. 'What's going on?'

After hearing the story, Yule went back to the office to *tidy up a few things* before dinner. Ariel invited Maya to eat with her and Yule, and although she declined, she didn't leave straight away.

'You are worried,' the old woman said.

Ariel nodded.

'You do not think you can kill Emot?'

Ariel shrugged. Maya waited. Ariel said nothing. Maya's gaze became so intense that it seemed to penetrate Ariel's skull and suddenly the words came tumbling out. 'It's Nick. When his face pops into my mind, I want him with me so much that it hurts. I'm not sure I can face Emot, let alone kill him, without Nick there. Sometimes I can cut through the whole thing and it isn't an issue, but other times, I'm just a mess. I hate it.'

'Try looking at it a different way,' Maya suggested. 'Instead of seeing him as a boyfriend, see him as a Radiant being who mirrors your own Radiance. Whatever Radiant qualities you see in him, look for them in yourself, and when you find them, claim them. Then every time you think of him, it will help clear your mind. If you do it well enough, you may find that your mind is elevated so far above your fears, that they will simply not be a problem any more. Try it.'

'Now?'

Maya nodded. 'Go on, take your time.'

Ariel closed her eyes and thought of Nick. She recalled meeting his eyes at the inn at Shifting Stones. Once again, she felt that pristine purity, that incredible power and that vast capacity for love that she'd seen in him that night. Once again, she saw the same in herself reflected in his eyes. She sat unmoving, feeling the all-pervasive power of the unlimited love that resided at the core of her being. She didn't need Nick around to be happy. She just had to develop the true courage of a Warrior, the courage to embrace this noble self—her birthright—every minute of the day and night.

She could do it in training sessions, but could she do it when she faced Emot?

✳✳✳

The next day after lunch, Ariel rode out at the head of the Warrior Army with Tynan. Walnut, Layla and a group of Warriors Tynan called the Green Company had already cleared Craggin Rocks of bands of Emots and now awaited them at a camp site.

Horden, a gruff Haba, rode beside her. Swirling tattoos covered his bare arms and chains hung off the fitted leather breast plate that sat over his T-shirt. All the Warriors, including Ariel, wore such garments, but only the Haba had decorated them with embossed patterns and studs. Ariel ran a hand over the smooth, body-hugging leather that protected her vital organs. Gauntlets gave her forearm protection, shin pads protected her calves, and caps above the armholes protected her shoulders.

An orderly column of Warriors, organised into companies, wound along the road behind them. Mounted Warriors rode at the head of each Company and the rest walked behind. The Red company came first, their red scarves fluttering in the wind, followed by the Yellow, Green and Blue Companies. At the rear of the army, draft horses pulled waggons laden with supplies.

Although the sun shone, a large area of cloud shrouded Diamond Peak, depriving Ariel of its inspiration. She wished Nick was beside her. He would want to be there.

'The Rasas will almost certainly remain in clan groups,' Tynan told her, 'so we have matched our companies to their targets. The White company consists of those who last defeated Bitah; Yellow are those who last defeated Amic; Red are those who have defeated Emot, and Green are those who have succeeded with Cogin. The Blues are the new recruits.

'While the companies engage the emanations, members of the telepathic circle will search for the Majors, who will no doubt hide. Layla will seek out Bitah, Yule will seek out Amic, Walnut and I will stay with you since Emot will probably not be able to resist making his way to you eventually. Maya will have the Light Brigade with her and be responsible for counteracting any black magic should the demons have any Magans with them.'

Ariel nodded, but said nothing, her gaze fixed on the sight ahead.

Huge rectangular blocks of sandstone thrust into the sky before them like an assortment of different sized apartment blocks and skyscrapers set in an otherwise deserted plain. The mammoth rocks filled Ariel with a mixture of awe and excitement. She couldn't wait to be amongst them, and could barely contain her excitement when they eventually entered the shadows beneath the sandstone blocks.

Wind and rain had softened their edges over the millennia; the dark flowing lines of minerals leached by the rain ran down them, like painted streams, and little grasses grew in their folds. Silence reigned beneath these monuments, as if the Warriors had wandered into a cathedral or the Great Hall. Here, the land itself called one to worship.

The army stopped to make camp in a large area near the centre of the rocks, and Horden, Tynan and Ariel joined the Green Company and the Noble Ones where they camped in a smaller space nearby. The members of the Green Company, mostly older Warriors, a few Haba, and one blue-cloaked Magan, already had their camp well set up, and they lounged around or stood in small groups in quiet conversation in a road-width area between two blocks. One stood around two stories high, the other probably three; before them and behind them blocks rose six stories or more.

Ariel dismounted but stayed close to the horses and sat with her back to the sandstone wall while Tynan spoke to Walnut, Layla and Maya, and Horden greeted various members of the group. She felt a little out of place in such a splendid company of Warriors with their regal bearing, unwavering presence and clear eyes that seemed to see everything in one glance.

They moved with the kind of grace that only comes from awareness. These Warriors had all defeated Cogin, and some had faced Rasama but, apart from the Noble Ones, none of them had succeeded in destroying him. Ariel sighed and wondered if she did manage to do what they hadn't, how long it would be before the Master Demon re-grew. Would there be others to cut him down again before he regained his strength?

Walnut walked over. Jali, the little green and orange King Parrot sat on his shoulder. 'Jali tells me that the Domos army should reach the plain in the morning; are you ready to face Emot?' The parrot cocked his head and looked at her with his bright eyes as if waiting for the answer.

She shook her head.

'Then I won't wait for you to try. We'll dispatch him as soon as we find him.' Jali waddled along Walnut's shoulder closer to Ariel, then leaned towards her and tilted his head as if unsure of what he heard.

'No, it's okay,' Ariel said. 'Let me try. I was just feeling a little overawed in this company.'

'Their Radiance is no different than yours,' Walnut replied, 'no better and no less either; they have just been training for longer in this life. But you have lifetimes of training behind you and are in fact every bit as capable as they are, if not more so.'

'How?'

'You have a rare determination and focus on your goal.'

Ariel shrugged. 'What if my focus isn't purely on my goal?'

Walnut chuckled. 'You told me yourself that Nick can help you get into the right mind state, so use him as your call to practice.'

'Have you been talking to Maya?'

Walnut grinned. 'This was never going to be a solo effort, Ariel. The Warriors are here to help you, and I think you do not want to fail them.'

She nodded.

'Then you know what to do.'

'I do.'

'Then do it, now, every moment, choose the sky over the clouds and join this fine company.'

Ariel nodded, and hoped she wouldn't let him down.

'I'll see you at dinner,' he said before walking back towards Tynan.

Ariel sighed, leaned the back of her head against the rock and closed her eyes. It would be dark soon. She should probably set up her bed-roll. A thin camp mattress awaited, but an image of a soft bed taunted her. She laughed it off, but a kind of wistful yearning lingered, and other things she wanted began to flit through her mind, silly things mostly and easy to let go, but the subtle sense of reaching for something remained as an undercurrent in her consciousness—almost as if Emots were creeping up on her.

They were.

Someone shouted a warning and waves of the red-eyed demons suddenly poured from clefts in the rocks on both sides of the camp. Layla and Walnut flew into the sky. Sceptre fire blasted from all directions and demons vaporised. Some shot frozen flames from their talons, but the barbs fell harmlessly on the ground in the presence of the Green Company. Many Emots fled back to the safety of the rocks, only to be blasted from above by Walnut and Layla.

Ariel scurried closer to the horses, keeping the rock at her back. The horses snorted and stamped but, well-trained as Warriors' mounts, they didn't bolt. She felt safe amongst their warm bodies surrounded by the smell of horse and leather, but her hand rested on the hilt of her dagger, just in case any demon came too close.

While everyone else blasted the demons with their sceptres, Maya simply stood still and chanted, and Ariel soon discovered that what she lacked in physical strength, she more than made up for in other skills. White light streamed from her chest and formed a pillar of white fire the size of a human. With another incantation, she sent it gliding towards a narrow passage where demons hid. 'Seek the dark ones,' she murmured. 'Give them light.' The demons' fiery barbs vaporised in Maya's ethereal pillar. One demon raced forward and slashed at it, but dissolved into nothing as soon as his talon touched the white flames.

A Magan far too elderly for Ariel to consider him much use in a battle, stood unmoving behind the horses, his back to the rock. He muttered to himself and waved a wand in a series of complex movements, then aimed it at the rock and drew it slowly to the side, as if pulling against something. Several Emots emerged from their hiding place behind the rock, struggling against the magic that drew them forth. Warriors set upon them and vaporised them all in a matter of seconds.

Ariel drew her dagger and turned it into a sword, but instead of running into battle like the others, she stayed amongst the horses, content to leave the attack to the professionals and protect herself should any get close. Unfortunately, one did.

She felt a presence behind her, and the unmistakable smell of Rasa washed over her. She swung around and gasped. An Emot so large that he could only be Emot himself stood before her, a gloating sneer on his oily face. Ariel glanced around but, busy with the onslaught of demons elsewhere, no one watched her and no one came to protect her. Her heart pounded like a drum played by a maniac, but the beast made no move to attack. He fixed his flaming eyes on hers and rooted her to the spot.

'At last,' he crooned, 'I meet the famous daughter of Aarod, spawn of my slave.'

'Slave?' Ariel croaked. Why wouldn't her feet move?

'She feeds us, and so tasty she is.' The fiery slit of his mouth curled up.

Horror brought bile to Ariel's throat. Wake up, she told herself. She'd expected Emot to use her mother as bait. She'd trained to handle it. With a deep breath, she expelled her fears.

'Willing, she is.' Emot lifted his talon leisurely and fired a shard of fire towards her.

Ariel shattered it with her sword, but he sent another before she had time to prepare, and it sliced into her heart, knocking the breath from her lungs. Images of her mother willingly feeding the foul creature flashed through Ariel's mind while Emot stood and grinned at her, waiting for a feed. She shook herself out of the vision and lunged at him. He flipped her blade aside with his talon and fired a volley of barbs. She shattered some of them with her sword, but others penetrated her defence and slipped through her skin like caresses. Her mind flitted from simple desires, like that for a warm bath, to something that pulled at her deepest desires.

She gritted her teeth and thrust again, but he parried the blow with infuriating ease and, with a smirk, shot an arrow of fire into her heart.

The sound of battle surrounded her, but Ariel found herself immersed in one of her fantasies. All she had ears for was Nick's voice, all she had eyes for was his face, his eyes, and all she could think about was his touch, his lips on hers and the blissful energy between them. He seemed to be there with her, but somehow just out of reach, a mere breath of wind between them. She reached towards him, craving the pleasure he promised, but the red-eyed Rasa Major ripped Nick from her grasp and reached his talon towards her neck. Ariel froze.

Suddenly, the demon dissolved with a sizzle. Ariel's eyes focused once more on her surroundings. Layla stood staring at her; the flaming sword in her hand burned the red blood of Emot from its blade.

Ariel blushed in embarrassment at her failure. 'I didn't think it would feel so real,' she whispered.

Layla sheathed her sword. 'Now you know,' she said curtly and walked away.

Once again silence reigned in the shadows of Craggin Rocks. No one spoke. They just carried on as if nothing had happened. Ariel wanted to scream that she was sorry, that she could do better, that she would do better next time, but she didn't, she just stood and stared stupidly into space.

Walnut brought her back to her senses when he landed lightly beside her. 'One's first meeting with a Major Rasa is called *getting the measure of his power.*'

Ariel sighed.

'Now sit,' he commanded.

Ariel obeyed without a word, and they sat cross-legged on the ground with their backs against a rock the size of a car.

His eyes fixed on her with a no nonsense gaze. 'How did he trap you?'

Ariel squirmed. Her failure with Emot had made it glaringly obvious just how much her fantasies had cost her.

'It was so real.'

'That is how it is with Emot. Now, what did he catch you with?'

'You know.'

'But you need to say it.'

She sighed and stared at the dirt ground beneath her fingernails. 'Nick.'

'Memories or fantasies.'

'Memories,' she lied.

Walnut nodded. 'Memories are just memories, precious and worth keeping, but we must remember that they are past and will never come again. To wish for them again will only prolong our grief at their passing.'

The old man's eyes moistened and, suddenly, Ariel realised that he spoke also of himself and Miramar.

'When the face of a loved one swims into our mind,' he continued quietly, 'we can say, *go away, it hurts to see you*, or *I want more of you, don't go* or you can pretend they aren't there, but those reactions don't help us. What we need to do is simply enjoy them, but let them pass on through. It is tempting to want to cling to those wonderful memories; Ariel, believe me, I know, but the holding on only causes us pain and it won't go away until you let go.'

'I'm so sorry, Walnut.' Ariel wrapped her arms around herself. 'At least Nick is still alive. I will see him again.'

'Perhaps,' Walnut replied, 'but perhaps not. One day he will die and if you can learn to let him go while he is still alive, it will be easier to let go when he is dead. He will die. You will die. But true love endures and one thing you can be sure of is that he does love you very much. I have seen it in his heart. He is good for you, but you must not let Emot turn your love into craving.'

Ariel nodded, determined not to fall into the same trap again.

'Sit quietly now,' Walnut instructed. 'Sit tall, like the mountain, relaxed and alert. Let your concerns fall away; breathe them out.'

A weight fell off Ariel's shoulders.

'Allow your mind to be spacious … look at what rises there.'

Ariel almost laughed. She knew what would rise. She was familiar with it now; the pain of separation, the angst of his absence, the desire to be with him, to touch him, to feel his touch on her and have him fill the hole in her heart. A fantasy formed in her mind and, instead of letting it pass, she reached out like an addict for her drug, craving its pleasure.

Walnut stared at her. She felt a change in the atmosphere and met his shocked eyes.

'I didn't realise,' he said bleakly. 'You hid this from me. This balm you've created. Do you realise how dangerous this is?'

Ariel gulped at his wrathful tone. 'I do now.'

'Do you want to prove Twitchet right?' he asked severely.

She shook her head. *Of course not.*

'Then don't buy into the fantasies. Now chant with me.' He began to chant the incantation for entering the Radiance.

Ariel joined in and the syllables soared around her and through her. They vibrated in every cell in her body and calmed her energy, but an alluring fantasy of Nick's return soon crept into her mind and she reached for it, turning her desire into craving.

'Look at it, Ariel; look directly,' Walnut commanded, his voice resonating with power. 'Look now.'

She obeyed.

Immediately, she looked, she saw the craving and it dissolved instantly. The released energy blasted through her with a power and purity that far surpassed any dubious pleasure she got from her fantasies. Her mind opened into a vast wholeness that in its endlessness, embraced Nick's essence as if there had never been, could never be, any separation. She knew this state and she knew how to get there, all she had to do was choose it above the other options.

'Do it,' Walnut commanded sternly. 'Every time. Never, ever let the fantasies take hold. You are not skilled enough to play with fire.'

15

Twitchet Underground

Twitchet scrambled through the small hole and sat blinking in the gloomy tunnel. His nose wrinkled at the smell of damp earth. *Add a rotten potato and it's an unpleasant mix in anyone's language, except for a Rasa of course. Come on furry disguise, let's execute this task and get out of here. No point staying in a Rasa den longer than necessary.*

As soon as his eyes had adjusted to the dark, he set off along the roughly-made tunnel. A couple of Rasas could walk side by side in the passageway but, by the feel of the rocks scattered on the floor, no one had walked this way for some time. Soon, his entrance hole had become a tiny pinpoint of light behind him.

The first intersection came sooner than expected, and Twitchet flashed onto the image of the map firmly entrenched in his mind. He aimed at the central chamber, well-positioned for general access and large enough to hold prisoners. The smoother floor on the new tunnel indicated more regular use, and without scattered rocks to impede his progress, he ran, skipping soundlessly along, heading deeper beneath the ground.

The route he and Maya had worked out took him along a convoluted series of passageways with various chambers off to the sides. Though his memory held the map well, his sense of

152

direction was unreliable in the dark and twisting tunnel. But when his tunnel intersected with a wide corridor lit by flaming torches, he figured he'd found a main thoroughfare, one he hoped would take him to Nadima.

'You're staying here,' a shrill voice echoed suddenly from up ahead.

Twitchet slowed and stayed close to the wall, his paws light and silent on the dirt floor.

'Why can't we share the glory too?' another Rasa whined. 'There's never been a battle like this before and I'm not allowed to go.'

'Stupid!' the other replied coldly.

Following the voices, the little cat peered into a huge cavern off the side of the tunnel. Two Amics, marked as such by their yellow eyes, stood only a few metres from him, silhouetted in the light of torches burning in niches in the walls.

'Some of us have to stay behind so the clan is strong enough to regenerate quickly if a protector gets our master. Go up there and you'll fade along with him.'

Another Amic, much larger than the first, moved smoothly towards them. 'Stop grumbling, Amic Dor,' he screeched. 'You may still get to join the battle. If our master fades, but regenerates quickly, he may wish to return and take some of us with him.'

'The battle will likely be over by then,' the smaller Amic grumbled.

'There will still be pickings,' the larger one hissed impatiently. 'Weakened Warriors to feed from.'

'And many targets who could strike our death blow.' The larger Amic suddenly raked the smaller one's face with his talons, and in the screeching that followed Twitchet streaked past the entrance to the cavern, undetected.

The voices echoed behind him.

'Coward,' the larger Rasa shrieked, 'you are weak. You must have grown too quickly and from poor fodder. Our master does well to leave you behind.'

'We are all newly grown,' Amic Dor sniffed. 'And I am overdue for feeding. Those going to the battle are feasting on the prisoners on my turn, and we are not allowed to go out to feed.'

'Because we must be here when regeneration is needed.'

'We will feed when the rest have finished,' the third Amic added.

The voices faded as Twitchet sped on through the dark, the map in his mind guiding his way. He wondered at the Amic's exchange—emanations with names and eloquence, feeding on a roster system! If a cat could sigh, he would have done so, and deeply.

A few minutes later, a hissing which built in intensity interrupted his thoughts. He crouched, ears flat, the fur on his back bristling. A low growl emanated from the back of his throat. He cut the sound immediately, and as he ran back the way he'd come, looking for somewhere to hide, he berated himself silently for not overriding his cat instincts sooner. He could not afford to draw attention to himself.

The snakish sound drew closer. Twitchet pressed himself into a niche in the wall just before a group of Amics glided through the tunnel towards him. The size and fierceness of the Amic at their head marked him as their Major, Amic himself. Flanked by torchbearers, his eyes blazed an intense yellow, and he hissed as he marched, as if humming a song. Twitchet flattened himself against the wall and froze, hoping they wouldn't look down.

Hundreds of emanations flowed past, leaving a sinking feeling in Twitchet's fur covered belly. If Amic could generate this many emanations in the time since his defeat by Ariel, then how many emanations did the undefeated Emot and Cogin have?

As soon as they'd passed from sight, Twitchet sprinted down the tunnel, his little heart pounding.

When he heard another group of Rasas coming his way, he scampered into a side tunnel, and took several turns before finding himself back on a main route. It was the sobbing that drew him the rest of the way, and the scene that presented itself when he poked his head into the central chamber brought an ache to his heart. He suspected that the only reason tears weren't running down his furry cheeks was that cats couldn't cry.

Three large cages full of hollow-eyed people backed onto the cavern walls. Some prisoners lay on the floor and sobbed; some wrapped their arms around their legs and rocked back and forth; some comforted others with soft words or an embrace. None had much flesh on them and all looked exhausted.

'Get rid of the dead-wood,' a voice commanded from a side room.

A group of Emots entered the cavern, unlocked the cells, dragged out prisoners who looked near-death and hauled them away down a tunnel. In one cell, the demons held a grey haired man in a tight grip while bodies were hauled away by their brethren. He couldn't move, but his chanting reached Twitchet's ears—a Warrior's incantation to sooth the prisoners and give them strength.

'We need more food,' a woman in another cell cried. 'We are no good to you dead.'

'Shut it, witch,' one of the Emots retorted.

They restrained her too while they walked through her cell lifting heads and kicking bodies to see who had energy left to sustain them. When she tried to protest, one of them clapped a clawed hand over her mouth. *Another Warrior.* But where was Nadima? The photo he'd memorised didn't match any of the faces in the cells, and he'd had a pretty good look when the beasts walked through. They locked the cells and carried the key to the room off the side. Twitchet couldn't see in but he suspected it would look like any guard room in any prison. Was this why they had become so sophisticated? All these memories, thoughts and feelings they fed on would provide a huge bank of behaviour to mimic. Twitchet felt his furry brow furrow. It was the obvious explanation, but he wasn't sure it was enough.

With the Rasas out of sight, Twitchet stepped into the cavern and sat on his haunches, wondering how to proceed. The man with the grey hair squatted beside a young girl in the cage nearest the cat, stroking her hair and speaking softly. He looked up and met Twitchet's eyes with a clear gaze. Twitchet dipped his head in acknowledgement, and the man returned the gesture, Warrior to Warrior. Twitchet scanned the room, then tilted his head to one side and waited. The man smiled and jerked his head towards a narrow passageway on the other side of the cavern. Twitchet dipped his head again, then scurried around the edge of the room and down the dark passageway.

A lamp glowed on the wall at the end, lighting a small cell. Twitchet heard no sound and no Rasas stood guard. He padded silently up to the bars and slipped through into the straw-covered cell. *Like animals. Wait. I'm an animal! There's nothing wrong with that. But even cats prefer carpet to straw.*

A bundle lay on a blanket with a shawl wrapped around thin shoulders. Fair hair fell across closed eyes and what would be a pretty face were it not for the grime. Nadima. Ariel's mother. He padded close and flicked his tail across her hand. She gasped and sat up, her eyes flicking nervously around the cell.

'Not a rat, a cat. Down here,' he said.

Nadima glanced down. Her eyes widened.

'I'm Twitchet. Walnut sent me.'

'What … what are you?'

Twitchet yawned. 'What do I look like?'

'A cat,' Nadima whispered, 'but you talk.'

'Tell me something I don't know.'

She narrowed her eyes at him. 'Where's Walnut?'

'Not here.' He sat on his haunches, wrapped his tail around him and fixed her with unblinking eyes.

She grimaced. 'Now you tell me something I don't know.'

'You did ask.'

'Fine. Can you get me out?'

'Not now. The place is swarming with Rasas, hundreds of them, from all of the clans.'

She sighed and the glimmer of hope in her eyes died. After a moment of silence, she barraged Twitchet with questions. He told her the good news—Ariel was alive and had defeated two Major demons already—and the bad news he watered down, seeing no point in adding to the woman's sorrow. She seemed to draw comfort by stroking his fur as they talked, and the cat in him purred with pleasure.

He didn't ask why the hordes weren't feeding on her, or how she maintained herself. She had to have struck some bargain to look so well under the circumstances. Before he left, he spoke to her from his most human place, bypassing the grumpy little cat he liked to play, to reassure her that all would be well.

'I am not a fool, Twitchet,' she said. 'I know the odds. You don't have to sugar coat the truth for me.'

He nodded, then gave her the message he would also deliver to everyone in the other cells. 'Remember this, at all costs; you must not feed a Rasa when it's fading.'

✳✳✳

The sun climbed in a partially clouded sky, and billows still shrouded the mountain peak despite a clear night—a cold shock after the warmth of Sheldra. At least it isn't raining, Ariel thought.

She stood with Walnut on a rise above Craggin Plain at the edge of the rocks and watched hundreds of unruly Domos, crude weapons clanking ominously, thunder onto the southern

157

side of the straw-coloured plain like a herd of wild animals. They wore animal skin skirts and little else apart from bone necklaces and ornaments in their woolly hair, and though they were too far away to see, Ariel knew their broad nostrils would be flaring and their eyes would be bulging with excitement beneath their heavy brows.

Ariel swallowed in a suddenly dry throat. She'd practised most of the night and again first thing this morning, but those weapons were real and the demons solid. How did she get herself into this? *Give me boring old school and exams any day!* Yet, despite her trepidation, something in her revelled in the day. She believed in the Warriors, in their quiet strength, their wisdom and compassionate humanity. In comparison to the Warriors' most noble qualities, the demons were nothing.

Warriors skirted around the edge of the rocks to their pre-assigned position and waited for the Domos to come closer.

Tynan rode up beside Ariel. 'How is the heir to the Blade of Aarod?'

'I'm fine, Tynan, but please, don't call me that.'

'Why? It is what you are,' he replied as he slid off his mount.

'She is more than that,' a thin quavering voice behind them said.

They turned to face the source of the words.

An ancient man with near sightless eyes stood behind them. He stared blankly at Ariel, then continued. 'She is also Ariel the Great, Champion of Noble Qualities, Lady of Light, Defeater of Demons and Liberator of human kind.'

Ariel stared at the old man in shock.

'Where is Nicholas the Great?' he asked.

'In my heart,' Ariel replied, wondering why she didn't say he was taking a group of travellers to the Observatory.

'That will do for now,' the man said, then he shuffled away, tapping the ground with a white cane.

'Who's that?' Ariel whispered.

'Morgan,' Tynan replied. 'One of Maya's Light Brigade, a powerful healer and skilled with white fire.'

'What did he mean with all that? Is he crazy?'

'Not at all.' Maya's voice emerged from a cluster of tiny spinning spheres of light that appeared in the air before them. 'Sometimes he speaks people's future names,' she continued as her form solidified. She fixed Ariel with a beatific smile.

Ariel snorted, she would never call herself any of those.

Others may, though. Ariel flinched at Walnut's words in her mind. He gave her a cheeky grin and raised an eyebrow. She remembered asking him his name when they first met; he'd said he had many names.

'You don't want to know,' he said, his eyes twinkling.

Tynan broke up their exchange. 'So, Ariel the Great, Defeater of Demons, are you ready to begin the battle?'

Ariel rolled her eyes. 'No. I want to watch television and eat chips and fizzy drink.'

The assembled company looked at her with horror, except for Walnut who laughed. His small frame shook with glee.

'I'm not joking,' she protested. Walnut laughed louder while the others looked even more startled and confused.

'Oh, all right then,' Ariel said sarcastically, 'I suppose we'd better get it over with.' She looked at their shocked faces, then chuckled along with Walnut. 'Sorry,' she grinned. 'I was joking, but ...well, I guess not entirely.'

'Come, Ariel,' Walnut said, taking her arm and leading her towards the horses that grazed peacefully behind them. 'It's time to set the plan in motion and ride to your future.'

Ariel mounted her horse, took a deep breath and brushed a fly from her nose. The sun shone fiercely bright and the day warmed rapidly. Much more heat and her leather breastplate would become a sauna. Not a comfortable thought. Ariel wanted the battle over with. Now. She wondered if it were possible to swim in the rushing river on the other side of the plain.

Tynan kneed his horse and trotted off. Ariel and Walnut followed. At the bottom of the hill, they galloped onto the plain. The Domos ran towards them, shouting in their harsh voices, and as soon as the Domos were close, Ariel, Walnut and Tynan turned and raced back the way they had come, leading the Domos to where the Blue, Green and Red companies waited. When the demons reached the edge of the rocks, the three Companies appeared, running or riding from their hiding places. The demons stopped. Some backed off only to be pushed forward with shouts and jeers by those behind them. After a moment of surprise, the Domos surged forward and the battle began.

The Green Company sprayed the Domos with sceptre fire, knocking out dozens at a time. Those who slipped between the blasts of white fire attacked the sword-bearing Warriors. Swords and axes clashed, sending the harsh sound of metal on metal resounding across the plain. The Domos' guttural curses sizzled as they dissolved harmlessly on the Warriors' curse shields.

Ariel, Tynan and Walnut galloped back into the cover of the rocks and up the path to the lookout where they had an unobstructed view of the dry grassy plain. They dismounted and watched the confrontation below. Ariel shook her head sadly, glad she wasn't down in the melee. She remembered the terror she'd felt when she faced an army of demons for the first time and felt for those who were new to battle.

A Warrior fell. Ariel held her breath and bit her lip until a Green Company horseman raced towards the fallen man and scooped him from the ground. He galloped away, taking the injured man to safety. Ariel breathed again, but this was only the beginning.

Rasas poured from a hole in the ground on the northern side of the plain. Tynan raised a pair of binoculars, then held a horn to his lips and blew one blast. 'White eyes,' he said as the White Company raced towards the demons of the Bitah clan. The Green Company swung their horses away from the Domos battle and galloped across the plain to join them. Together they cut the Bitahs off before they joined with the Domos.

'Yes,' Tynan exclaimed. 'We foiled that plan. And look, the next clan comes as we expected.' He pointed near the river where more Rasas flooded, like waves of oil, from another hole in the ground. After checking through the binoculars, he blew two blasts on his horn. 'Amics,' he explained as the Yellow Company moved out to meet the onslaught.

'Yellow eyes,' Ariel thought. How dare there be so many after I just demolished their boss!

As soon as the Yellow Company engaged the Amics, more Rasas swarmed from both holes. Ariel's heart pounded. Emots. She couldn't see their flaming red eyes from her vantage point, but she felt their magnetism. Their proud rippling figures looked almost beautiful. Ariel caught herself and wrenched her mind from such thoughts.

Tynan blew three blasts, and the Red Company turned away from the Domos and headed towards the Emots. As long as the Rasas remained in clan groups, Tynan's plan to keep the Warriors away from those they weren't ready to defeat worked, but Ariel watched with a heavy heart; their most generous estimate fell far short of the demons' actual numbers.

'Where's Maya?' Ariel asked.

16

The Battle of Craggin Plain

Walnut pointed to a block of sandstone the height of a two storied house about one hundred metres away. Maya sat on top with the twenty adepts of the Light Brigade. Powerful beams of Radiant Light poured from their chests and, guided by their hands, swept across the field like searchlights. The light, the responsive power of the Radiance, weakened any demon it touched and strengthened the Warriors. Where their light illuminated the battle, demons fell from the Warriors' swords with ease. Ariel followed a beam as it swept across the field to the southern side.

'Oh my God,' she whispered.

The Blue Company struggled against the remaining Domos. Axes came down on Warriors' necks and swords ran through their hearts.

'We have to go and help them,' Ariel said, turning to her horse.

'No,' Walnut and Tynan said together.

'But I can't bear to see these people dying for me,' she protested.

'They don't do it for you, Ariel,' Walnut said, 'they do it because they're Warriors. They've taken the pledge to defend the human race against the Serpentine demons. It's their fight too.'

Ariel buried her head in her hands and moaned.

'Damn,' Tynan muttered, 'we'd better get them out of there.' He raised his horn to his lips but Walnut stayed him with a hand on his arm.

'Look what comes.'

Ariel lifted her head.

A group of around one hundred Magans galloped up behind the Domos and, with expert horsemanship, turned quickly and rode along the back of the Domos army, blasting them with wand fire.

'Excellent,' Tynan said with relief.

With Warriors attacking them from both sides at once, many Domos scattered sideways, but the Magan horseman sped along the sides and picked the fleeing Domos off as they ran. Several Magans sat on their horses some distance from the battle and moved their wands in synchronisation. Domos began to stagger and slow as the magic took its toll. Ariel glanced at Tynan, pleased to see that much of the tension of the last few minutes had evaporated from his face.

'That was tight,' he murmured.

With the Domos battle under control, they scanned the rest of the field. As expected, they saw no sign of the Major Rasas. Their emanations poured from the holes and flooded the plain in flowing black figures. Ariel figured that they outnumbered the Warriors by around ten to one. Two long blasts on Tynan's horn split the Green Company sending a division each to assist the Whites, the Yellows and the Reds. But even though Warriors added their sceptre fire to the mix, demons forced them back towards the rocks.

'How can they have made so many?' Tynan muttered grimly.

'We have to find the Majors,' Ariel said urgently. 'We have to get it over with, before too many are hurt. Where are Yule and Layla?'

'Calm down, Ariel,' Walnut said. 'They'll find them eventually.'

Pillars of spitting, twirling fire flew from the Light Brigade and joined the battle. Demons vaporised with a touch, but still more came.

Ariel caught sight of Layla silhouetted against the sun. She flew along the edge of the battle, occasionally dipping into the fray to help out a Warrior, but even when Ariel borrowed the binoculars from Tynan, she couldn't see Yule who, without the power of flight, had to stay on the ground. She hoped it was a good sign. 'There's more Emots there than the others,' Ariel said. 'If we got rid of Emot, we could turn the battle.'

'Any idea where to find him?' Tynan quipped.

'I can draw him out. He'll come if I … make the right signals.'

Tynan grinned, despite the gravity of the battle. 'You're right; he won't be able to resist such a tasty morsel as you.'

Ariel grimaced. Was her struggle so obvious?

'Emot is like fire,' Walnut said. 'I don't want you starting something you can't stop.'

Ariel pressed her lips together. He'd made his lack of faith in her clear. 'At least I can fight the emanations,' she said determinedly. She mounted her horse and turned its head towards the downward trail.

'We can join the Yellow Company, I suppose,' Walnut said grudgingly.

'The Reds need my help more.'

Walnut grabbed her bridle. 'You wait for Tynan's orders like everyone else.'

'No one's going anywhere, just yet.' The chill in Tynan's voice made them swing around and stare into the sky where

Tynan trained his binoculars. Ariel gasped. A flock of Demon Wraiths sped towards them.

Layla appeared from the other side of the field and began blasting the nasty creatures. Walnut's bell rang above the sound of battle and he flew into the air. Tynan and Ariel could only watch helplessly as he hurtled across the sky to help the only other person in their army who could fly.

Walnut and Layla darted around the Wraiths, slamming them with lightning. Some fell in balls of flame, but many more remained to attack the flying Warriors. Tynan peered through the binoculars and sucked in a sharp breath.

'What?' Ariel asked. The Wraiths were too far away for her to see the details.

'Layla's arm is bleeding profusely, but she still fights.'

Walnut abruptly dropped height. Ariel gasped and clutched Tynan's arm.

'They have to get out of there,' he said. 'Damn, my telepathy went with Walnut.' He turned towards the Light Brigade, blew several short sharp blasts on his horn, then pointed to the battle in the sky and beckoned urgently to Walnut and Layla. 'Get out of there,' he growled.

Maya nodded and turned to the flying ones.

Walnut plummeted, seemingly out of control. Ariel screamed. But something flew beneath the falling Warrior and broke his fall. Ariel's eyes widened. Walnut sat firmly in the arms of a Haba seated on a flying horse.

'Sky Steeds,' Tynan exclaimed, clapping his hands.

Ariel raised her hand and shielded her eyes against the sun. More horses flew down from the north and surrounded the Wraiths. Sceptre fire blazed.

'Let me see.' Ariel reached for the binoculars. Tynan handed them over and she focused on the Sky Steeds. Their enormous wings beat the air, holding them steady while their riders, sitting on brightly coloured saddle cloths, hit the wraiths with a barrage of white fire, some from sceptres, and some from flaming swords. Demon Wraiths exploded or fell in charred pieces at the Habas' hands. While Walnut and Layla flew to safety, the Haba finished off the wraiths, then turned their attention to the rest of the battle. They swooped low, leaned over the side of their horses, sprayed the Rasa with white fire, then pulled up, circled overhead and swooped again.

Ariel tapped Tynan's arm and returned his binoculars. He peered through them while she scanned the battle with her naked eye. 'There's more,' she said, pointing to the bridge across the river. A column of Haba marched towards the battle. Their powerful and inspiring combat song drifted across the field. Once over the bridge, the Haba fanned out behind the Rasa forces. Only then did it look like the Warriors had a chance. Only then did the Rasa falter and the Warriors hold their ground, but still Rasas came to take the places of those that had vaporised. And still Warriors fell.

Walnut and Layla landed beside Ariel and Tynan. Blood ran down Layla's arm and her breath came short and fast.

'Go to the healers,' Tynan commanded. 'Walnut, are you all right?'

'Just a little shaken.'

A bell rang. Layla took off again.

'I want to go down,' Ariel said. 'I have to help.' She kicked her heels into her horse, but reined it in when Tynan spoke.

'Wait, who are these, running in from the south?'

Ariel stared where he pointed and smiled. 'Star Clan Domos! Good old Chief Torla. Look, Walnut, it's Day Star in front, doing his fleet footed thing.'

'I've never seen anything like it,' Tynan said, staring at the huge graceful Domos that strode across the countryside in great bounding steps. Around one hundred more of them jogged behind him in tight formation.

Walnut grinned. 'Our secret weapon.'

Tynan frowned. 'But they're going right past the Domos. That's no help.'

'They won't attack their own kind,' Walnut said, 'but I suspect they're going to finish off the Bitahs.'

Tynan raised his eyebrows.

Few Warriors even knew of the existence of this un-demonised clan of Domos, but Ariel and Nick had met them on their way to the Plateau of Bliss. Without Day Star's skill with the Water Spirits, they would never have made it across the river to their destination.

The Star Clan proved Walnut correct when they attacked the Bitahs. Tynan blew his horn and signalled the White Company to switch their attention to the remaining Domos. Ariel imagined how amazed the Warriors would be to see clean, well-attired Domos fighting beside them, no doubt grinning in delight at the prospect of a battle. The Star Clan tore into the Rasas with relish. Some picked them up in their big hands and broke them in two, laughing with glee.

'Time to go.' Ariel kicked her horse into action and cantered down the trail towards the battle. She didn't look back, but she waited at the bottom. Tynan and Walnut weren't far behind.

To Ariel's surprise, Tynan headed north.

'Yule's in trouble,' Walnut explained.

Ariel grimaced, then shook her head and galloped across the field to where the Red Company fought. Tynan would rescue Yule, and Walnut would follow her.

Pleased to be helping at last, Ariel threw herself into the fray with enthusiasm. She swiped some demon heads off from horseback, but when they began attacking the horse, she dismounted and slapped his flank, sending him away. Emots flooded around her but Walnut did a good job of keeping the hordes back while Ariel battled one at a time.

The Emots' presence fuelled an underlying sense of dissatisfaction, but she was determined not to let it undermine her. If she couldn't cope with these guys, Walnut would drag her off to help with lesser foes, and she needed the practice of battling Emot's emanations before she faced their boss.

A shout of joy went up from the other side of the field. Someone must have taken out one of the Majors. But where the Emots battled, apart from heartening the battle-weary Warriors, it made no difference.

'Bitah's gone,' Walnut shouted a moment later, his voice carrying easily over the sound of battle.

'Yule?' she shouted back, knowing that some kind of telepathic communication must have come his way.

'She's fine,' he replied.

If someone killed Emot, all his emanations would fade, just as the Bitahs had. Trouble was, the big bloke would be hiding to avoid that exact scenario. But Ariel knew how to draw him out. She bet he wasn't far away, and she fought on the edge of the battle. There, he might feel little enough danger from the other Warriors to try to taste her. But first, she would have to slip away from Walnut, or the big guy may not dare show his face.

She imagined Nick and yearned to feel his lips on hers and his arms holding her tight. The Emots around her flew into a frenzy of desire. They surged towards her. Walnut sprayed them with sceptre fire, but still they came. Ariel moved back, well behind Walnut and the other Warriors who were keeping the throngs away from her.

'What the hell are you doing?' Walnut shouted.

Ariel said nothing, she was too busy indulging in a very naughty fantasy of her and Nick. It worked. The largest Emot of all appeared from a crack in the rocks and glided towards her, flanked by two large emanations. She hadn't expected the bodyguards, but she couldn't suppress a grin as the Emot Major sped towards her. Tynan was right; he couldn't resist.

Walnut's sceptre fire rat-tatted like a machine gun as he fought to keep the emanations from her back, but she didn't stop the fantasy. She needed the big guy close enough to kill. Even if she couldn't kill Emot this time, at least he'd be out in the open where Walnut could.

'Pete, David,' Walnut shouted. 'Beside her.'

Walnut must have seen what she was doing, but he was giving her a chance. His trust buoyed her confidence. She could do this. She would be the one to take Emot out.

'Remember, Ariel,' Walnut yelled, 'your life is more important than beating him.'

When the Emot Major was a couple of metres away, Ariel brought her mind back to the present and faced him, sword ready, and mind calm and clear. Two Warriors flanked her now, and the bodyguards sized up their opponents but didn't move. Behind her, Walnut's sceptre fire slowed a little, but she trusted he'd keep the emanations off her back.

Emot's red-hot eyes bored into her with a powerful lust. 'Now, now, little one,' he crooned in a horribly seductive voice. 'That isn't very nice, luring me here to feed, then taking it away.' He chuckled. 'I see myself in you, darling. We're going to get on just fine.'

Ariel didn't flinch. She held his gaze, raised the blade of Aarod and fired a stream of white fire. He merely stepped smoothly to the side, his fiery mouth curling up at the corners as the flames sped past him. Muscles rippled beneath his oily, flowing skin, like a silk shirt so fine that it revealed the chest beneath.

He chuckled again. 'I shall enjoy this fight, for I think I shall feed well today.' He raised his talon and a barb of fire shot towards her.

'Wrong.' She ducked, closed the ground between them in a few swift steps and struck at the demon. He blocked with his talon and his bodyguards leapt forward. Pete and David stepped in and engaged them. Emot sprang forward, talon thrusting. Ariel parried, thrust, blocked and swiped in a deadly dance of sword and talon. Emot fought hard, fast and strong, and it took all Ariel's strength and concentration just to parry his deadly talon and hold her own against his onslaught. His second barb found its mark.

Ariel gasped as brilliant images flashed through her mind. First a soft bed, a glass of water, dead Warriors restored. Then her mother again, bound then freed and the question, always the question. What do you want? Ask and you shall have it. Ask me, Ariel. Ask me.

'Step back, Ariel,' Walnut called. She did, and a blast of sceptre fire singed the folds of Emot's skin.

'Curse you, old man!' Emot shouted and sent another barb towards Ariel. This time she cut it in half, then sent a ball of flame through her sword back to the demon. He grimaced as it grazed his arm, but he threw himself into the attack again, firing barbs and flashing his killing talon in rapid succession.

Emot seemed to fluctuate between trying to kill her and trying to feed on her. While his emanations kept everyone around her busy, he fed Ariel subtle glimpses of Nick. Quick at first, they built in number, length and emotional strength, creeping up on her amongst images of chocolate, beach holidays, soft beds and Emot's defeat.

The only breaks she got were when Walnut shot a lightning bolt at the feet of the demon, making him jump back and curse before continuing the attack. Once, she thought he was going to run away, but he must have been promised great rewards to take her out, because he stayed. Ariel made several light strikes, scratching him enough to make him wary, and he grazed her twice, almost softly, a strange feeling, alluring enough for her to have a faint desire to experience it again.

Gradually, he wove a spell around her, a barrage of little desires, nothing major, nothing she would call craving, until he hit her with Nick again and she faltered at the very real feeling of his lips on hers. Walnut blasted the feet of the demon and Ariel fell to the ground, pulling a barb from her arm and biting her lip to stop from crying out. Again, Walnut hit just in front of the demon.

'Time to take him out,' he said.

'No.' Ariel staggered to her feet. 'I can do this.'

17

Nick and Kestril

Eight hooves pummelled the earth. Manes and tails flew on galloping horses. Two riders, bent low to the saddle and moving as one with their beasts, sped out from Sheldra. One face like chiselled stone with deep green eyes probing ahead, alert for danger. The other, almost young enough to be his son, matched the elder in the intensity of their purpose. An unlikely alliance, Nick thought, but forged from their love for an old man, it would remain until they had removed the terrible danger that awaited him.

Kestril had said little when he found Nick and his group of travellers in the restaurant at the beach in the Lures, but in his sparse utterance Nick had heard much more than what the magician had spoken. Nick had frowned when he saw the black-bearded Magan in the doorway, his face in its usual impassive mask, his purple velvet cape and high black boots out of place in the modern beach suburb.

He strode directly to Nick's table, bowed briefly to the others and addressed Nick immediately in his gravely voice. 'Walnut and Ariel's lives are in grave danger, you must come now.'

The tone of his voice and the look in his eyes told Nick that *now* meant right now. Despite Nick's misgivings about the dour magician's ruse at Minion Hills, he wasn't going to risk not trusting him in this, or miss a good excuse to get back to Ariel.

'Sorry, everyone, I've got to go,' he announced, standing abruptly. He glanced around the table. John's eyebrows sat high on his forehead. Sarah's lips pursed in annoyance at the interruption and the others just stared with wide eyes. 'Lynlee will look after you,' he continued, not giving his sister a chance to refuse. 'In fact, she may even be willing to take you on to Observatory.' He turned his best pleading, puppy-dog eyes on her.

The blood drained from Lynlee's face. 'If Walnut is in danger then you must go,' she whispered, her golden curls bobbing around her fine-boned face. 'Of course I'll take them on for you.'

Nick hugged her, nodded a farewell to his stunned group of travellers, grabbed his pack and followed Kestril from the room. They hastened to the portal hidden in a back room of the beach-side Pavilion.

'Rasama has a plan to kill Walnut and Ariel with human slaves disguised as scholars,' Kestril told him as they strode along. 'There is a huge battle raging now on Craggin Plains. The slaves will strike while they are busy fighting.'

Nick increased his pace. In the heat of battle such a plan could work too easily. No demon could touch the old man, but humans could, and if Walnut wasn't there to protect her, Ariel would be easy pickings.

Walnut must not die.

Saddled horses waited for them outside the portal at Sheldra. They wasted no time mounting and urged their horses in haste. At Craggin Rocks, they rode into the Army's base camp on foaming horses and Kestril's request for fresh horses was acted on immediately and without question. As he changed horses,

Nick realised that though he'd never liked the man, Kestril's command of the situation impressed him, and he was grateful he had come to get him. Apparently, he not only knew that Nick would want to be by Ariel's side, but also honoured his relationship with her enough to facilitate it. The man was full of surprises.

Their new steeds champed at the bit and needed little urging to thunder out of the camp towards the battle. They sped along the track between the enormous Craggin Rocks, and soon the plain spread out before them, the battle raging in the distance.

Nick had never seen a battle like it before. Hundreds of Domos and Rasas covered the plain, the sheer size of the battle making the clash at the Observatory look like a child's party. He prayed they wouldn't be too late.

The cold wind rushed at Nick's ears, forced into his lungs and tossed his hair as he flew across the plain. The sound of thundering hooves and the jangling of bridle and bit rang in his ears. The smell of leather and linseed oil filled his nostrils. His body knew only the feel of the horse beneath him and the reins in his hands as he sought to outrun time and get to Walnut and Ariel before Rasama's plan came to fruition.

Following Kestril's lead, Nick halted his horse on a small rise on the edge of the battlefield and scanned the area. It appeared as if the Warriors had gotten the better of the feral Domos, but the Rasas numbers were too strong. Warriors were dying and Rasas gloating. The Warriors weren't losing, but they weren't winning either.

How would they ever find Ariel and Walnut?

'Seek her with your mind,' Kestril commanded.

For a moment, Nick wasn't sure what he meant, but the look in Kestril's eyes told him that he'd better work it out, and fast. He closed his eyes, opened his mind and extended his awareness across the field, seeking the energy that called to him, like a siren to sailors. Not a hopeful analogy, he thought, but possibly true. The battle's fierce energy washed over him, making it hard to pinpoint the buzz of Ariel's proximity. He'd never sought it before, and never been aware of it from such a distance. *Ariel, where are you?* A familiar energy emerged from the melee, weak, but enough to grab his attention. He pointed to the right and opened his eyes.

'There.' Kestril pointed to a spot amongst the Red Company where sceptre fire left plumes of smoke curling into the sky.

Nick nodded and, with a nudge from their heels, the horses cantered along the edge of the battle, dodging skirmishes and leaping fallen bodies. Nick drew his sword and cut down any demons that tried to stop them. Kestril blasted them into oblivion with his wand.

The Magan stopped abruptly. Nick drew his horse up beside him. 'Someone's moving in that scrub,' Kestril said, indicating an area of shrubs behind and not far from where, assisted by Walnut and two other Warriors, Ariel fought a large Rasa, no doubt Emot. Two people in hooded scholars' jackets darted from one bush to another, closing the distance between them and Walnut.

'I'll take them, you look after her,' Kestril said and heeled his horse into action.

Nick urged his horse on. Chunks of earth flew from its hooves, but Nick feared he wouldn't be fast enough. Walnut stood beside Ariel, blasting all the emanations that came close and, every now and then, shooting a thunderbolt in front of the big Rasa, enough to keep him off Ariel but allow her to finish him if she could. Under the circumstances, even Walnut would be hard-pressed to notice the assassins who now walked nonchalantly towards him.

Kestril galloped ahead of Nick, but there was no guarantee he would make it in time either. Nick rode hard, set his gaze on Ariel and sent her a blast of energy laden with warning.

Ariel gasped. No fiery barb had penetrated her skin, yet something slammed into her chest and spread through her limbs with a force and flavour that could only be Nick. How dare the demon steal something so precious and pure and use it against her. *Stuff you, demon.* She would not sully it with craving.

She gritted her teeth and struck out. The foul beast's eyes flared in surprise. He gripped at the laceration she'd made on his arm and backed away, eyes narrowing. If not him, then who? Where did the energy come from? Suddenly, inexplicably, Ariel knew Walnut was in danger. She glanced his way, and saw two brawny men with daggers glinting in their hands elbowing past demons towards him. Why weren't they knifing the demons?

'Walnut, behind you!' she shouted.

One of the men, his features half obscured by a hooded scholar jacket, raised a dagger ready to throw. At Ariel's voice, the old man spun in a blur of speed, his sceptre thundered out a lightning bolt and sent the man crashing to the ground. Walnut ducked the flying dagger but overbalanced and fell sideways. The other assassin lurched forward, dagger raised.

Ariel lunged towards him, but a spurt of blue fire hit him from behind and knocked him senseless. The dagger dropped harmlessly to the ground. Ariel gazed along the line of fire. Kestril sat, with his wand raised, on the back of an ebony horse steaming with exertion. His eyes met hers and his mouth opened in a warning she never heard.

A flare of raging fire sharpened to a red-hot point pierced her sword arm and twisted, tearing at the wound's raw edges and sending spasms of pain shooting through Ariel's exhausted body. A horrifically real image of Nick lying dismembered flooded her mind. A green-eyed Rasa stood smirking over him, wiping Nick's blood from his claws. Ariel screamed at the sight of Nick's staring dead eyes and craved his living presence beside her. Her arm hung limp and useless at her side and tears smarted in her eyes. She stared into the pitiless red eyes of Emot as he reared above her, holding a talon grown to the size of a sword ready to thrust through her heart.

'Got you,' he gloated.

Hoof beats thundered close, a bridle rattled and suddenly the smell of sweating horse surrounded Ariel as a large bay, nostrils flared, flanks foaming, reeled in and bowled Emot over, sprawling him on the ground. Ariel stared at the rider with a mixture of shock and relief. Nick reined in the horse, leaned out from the saddle and thrust his sword through Emot's heart before the demon could struggle to his feet.

'A fatal flaw in their nature,' Nick said as he turned his brilliant smile on Ariel. 'They like to revel in their victory before they've taken it.'

Ariel barely registered the Warriors cheering as the Emots dissolved around them. She staggered on legs suddenly turned to jelly. In a flash, Nick dismounted and caught her before she fell. He pulled the barb of fire from her arm, lowered her gently to the ground and placed his hand over the wound.

The world spun, Nick's face blurred and just before she passed out, she heard Kestril shout. 'Cogins!'

Nick's heart skipped a beat. Few had defeated Cogin and few were ready to now, least of all Nick. More cruel, vicious and sadistic than all the other Rasas, although jealousy was their favourite food, they fostered and feasted on every destructive tendency known to man.

'Damn,' Nick muttered, but he held his attention firmly on Ariel's wound. He laid his hands above the gash, breathed in and drew out the poison. It flowed from the wound like black blood. Once her blood ran clear again, he sent healing light to stop the pain, cleanse and repair the damage.

A horse whinnied. 'I'll find the Major,' he heard Kestril say. Walnut placed himself between Ariel and Nick and the wave of Cogins that swarmed towards them.

Thunderbolts flashed in fast succession and dozens of Cogin's emanations vaporised from Walnut's onslaught. Nick stayed with Ariel, happy to play a healer instead of a dead hero in this scene. He had no illusions about his present readiness to face a Cogin—zilch.

Another cheer went up, from further away this time.

'The Amics are gone,' someone yelled.

It made no difference to those facing the Cogins. Few of the Red Company were any more able to handle them than Nick, and more than Walnut could handle alone raced towards them across the plain.

A horn blew. Sky Steeds flew across the sky. The Cogin smell strengthened. Nick's heart raced. He hadn't defeated their Major, wasn't immune to their poison, and the last time he'd met an emanation at the Plateau, he'd failed. Ariel had saved him then, but in her present state, she couldn't even save herself. He suspected that he had little hope of protecting her, but if he didn't try, they would both be dead.

He was just about to ease Ariel from his lap and face the Cogins when Horden appeared, sceptre blasting. 'Stay with her, boy,' he shouted. 'The Green Company will deal with this lot.'

Ariel's eyes fluttered open. She glanced at her arm, then smiled up at him, and their eyes met in a shared acknowledgement of his healing. She sent him a thank you beyond words, then sat up, grabbed her sword from where it lay on the ground beside her and began to stand.

Nick grasped her arm and restrained her. 'Stay down. They're Cogins.'

'I don't care, we've got to help.' She shrugged him off and struggled to her feet. Nick scooped up his sword and leapt up after her.

'No!' Walnut shouted. 'Stay down. Leave them to me.'

Nick dropped to the ground and pulled her down after him. The most experienced Warriors surrounded them. Even Tynan had turned up to fight off the green-eyed monsters, but a Cogin squeezed through their defence and headed straight for Nick. Its eyes fixed on him with a look of malicious glee. Nick took a deep breath and stood to meet it. 'Stay down', he hissed when Ariel tried to follow him. He ignored her protests and, making sure that his mind was free of demon fodder, raised his sword.

'Master seeks you,' the beast slurred as it drew near. It whipped its talon up and fired a tiny green tornado. Nick darted out of its way, but another followed immediately. One scored a hit, and all Nick could see was Ariel standing in front of a cheering crowd with her dagger raised, about to kill Rasama. A searing jealousy rose, he blinked it away and swung his sword towards the grinning Cogin. Ariel's dagger got there first. The demon vaporised.

She turned to him with a grin. 'I owed you that.'

Nick just stared. She'd thrown her dagger and saved him from a Cogin emanation—again. But he should have been able to save himself! Jealousy spiked from him, drawing the eyes of every Cogin in the vicinity. Oblivious to the danger, Ariel reached down to scoop up her dagger. But while her attention was diverted, another Cogin broke through a gap in the Warriors' defences. This one didn't aim for Nick, his talon headed straight for Ariel's neck.

Nick couldn't move fast enough. His limbs felt heavy and seemed to move in slow motion as he sprang forward, sword in hand. 'Roll,' he shouted, hoping she'd get out of the way.

She looked up, eyes wide at the flowing figure lunging towards her, green fire lolling from its mouth. She rolled, but too late. The talon was just about to slice into her when the Cogin vaporised.

Warriors' cheers rang across the field.

Nick breathed again and fought to still his now shaky limbs. *Thank you, Kestril.*

Ariel looked around. 'Someone's taken Cogin out.'

'Thank goodness for that.' He sheathed his sword, grabbed her hand and helped her to her feet, then placed his fingers beneath her chin, tilted her face towards him and kissed her, good and hard. She responded with a fierce abandon that caught him by surprise.

'Well, it seems that you are both alive and well,' Walnut quipped.

Ariel broke the kiss and drew back. A pink tinge flushed her cheeks.

Nick suppressed a smile. He hadn't seen her quite so flustered before. 'I'm glad you're okay too,' he said to Walnut. 'I was worried there for a moment.'

'Yes indeed. Thank you for your timely arrival.'

'You have Kestril to thank for that.'

'Undoubtedly. I shall be with Tynan should you need me,' he added before walking away.

Nick turned his attention back to the girl before him.

'I've missed you,' she said.

'Missed you too,' he replied and kissed her again, softer and deeper this time. The barriers between them fell away, and they melted into a bliss so profound that they were more than immersed in it, they were it. When he could hardly breathe anymore, he released her lips and pulled her close, pressing her head into his shoulder. She sighed, her breath warm against his neck, and he rubbed circles on her back. It felt so right to have her in his arms.

Eventually, she pulled back. 'How come you're here? Did your travellers make it to the Observatory already?'

'No. Kestril came and got me from the Lures. Lynlee's taking them the rest of the way.'

'Looks like I owe the grumpy Magan.'

'Hey, brother!' someone called. Nick turned to the voice. A Haba Warrior strode towards him.

Nick grinned. 'Hey, Radric, good to see you.' He embraced his old friend, a quick, strong hug with the customary pat on the back.

'So this is the heir,' Radric said, bowing to Ariel. 'And a fitting princess for our little prince.'

Ariel's eyes widened, and she fought to suppress a grimace. Nick chuckled.

'You must camp with us tonight, brother,' Radric said. 'There'll be a party for sure.'

As an adopted member of the Haba clan Nick could hardly camp anywhere else. 'Is that okay with you?' he asked Ariel.

Ariel nodded. 'Sure.'

'Later then.' Radric nodded, dipped his head to Ariel, then strode off in the direction of the river.

18

Healing

Nick slipped his arm around Ariel's waist and turned to face the battlefield dotted with fallen Warriors. Scholars and ordinary students from the base camp were already lifting the injured onto stretchers and carrying them to an area close to the rocks.

'There's so many dead or wounded,' Ariel said. 'It's horrible.'

'I'm going to help heal,' Nick said, removing his arm from her waist.

'Then I'll be your nurse, Doctor.' Her eyes twinkled over a cheeky grin. She was flirting with him? That was new.

He took her hand and led her towards the makeshift hospital. 'Good, because I'm not letting you out of my sight again. You're not supposed to have battles without me, you know.'

'Sorry, we couldn't wait. I'm glad you turned up though.'

'Me too.'

'Do you have to go back?'

He shook his head. 'I'm not going to. Under the circumstances, it's perfectly reasonable to leave them to Lynlee. It's high time she got out of the Lures anyway.'

Ariel squeezed his hand and even skipped, apparently happy just to see him. Nick grinned. His absence hadn't been a bad thing after all.

An unconscious woman with extensive talon wounds lay at the edge of the rows of injured. Nick knelt beside her and held his hand over her heart. A faint pulse told him she still lived, but only just.

A pair of black demon kicker boots softened by a long pale skirt appeared beside him. Nick looked up. Maya stood above him, her eyes full of concern. 'I am afraid that this lady may be leaving us.'

Nick turned his attention back to the woman. 'Not just yet.' Healing power rose in his chest and shimmered into his palms. He held them above the deepest Rasa gash and the world stilled around him. He wasn't sure if it was reality or merely his perception of it, but the birds and animals became quiet, and the Warriors' voices hushed as the wound began to heal. When only a faint pink scar remained, the woman opened her eyes, smiled, then yawned and fell asleep.

Nick smiled, filled with a deep sense of satisfaction. All these years he'd fought his own power, never realising until Ariel came into his life that he could use it to heal.

'You have kept this skill from us, Nicholas,' Maya said. Nick looked up into her shining eyes. 'And what a great skill it is. The only other I know with such power is Morgan.'

He stood and accepted her praise with a nod. 'I only found out recently.' He glanced across to where Morgan sat on the ground beside a patient, his hands held above the wound just as Nick had done. The old man looked up. His sightless eyes roamed over Nick.

'When this is all over,' Maya said. 'You should return to Sheldra and study with him.'

'Good idea, but now, shall I find the worst ones?'

'Indeed, that is what Morgan does. The most seriously injured are over there with him.'

'Morgan called you Nicholas the Great,' Ariel said as they walked towards the ancient man.

'What?'

'He told me my future names too. Mind you, he didn't say which life I might get them in.'

'What were they?'

'I'm not going to tell you. It's too embarrassing.'

The old man's voice floated across the distance between them. 'Man of great power, Translator for the Ancients, Healer of the Sick, Protector of...,'

'I don't want to know,' Nick snapped, glaring at the old man.

'As you wish,' he said and returned his attention to his patient.

'Why don't you want to know?' Ariel asked.

'I don't want to have to live up to someone else's idea of what I should be.'

'But you're already all those things.'

'Just drop it, okay.' His voice came out more harshly than he intended.

She shrugged. 'I love you too, grump face.'

He sent a mock searing look her way, then grinned. 'Come on, let's make ourselves useful.'

'It looks like the assassins have regained consciousness,' Ariel said, pointing to where Walnut stood with Tynan, Kestril and two bound men in scholars' jackets.

Curiosity burned from her. 'You go, I have healing to do,' he said.

Ariel nodded. 'I'll join you soon.' She walked off and Nick turned to another patient.

Ariel recognised the bound men as Beak and Doram of the Menhirs. Doram was one of the men that had ambushed them outside of Minion Hills and Beak was the one who had killed Miramar. She wished Kestril had used full power on the black-hearted fellow. He should be dead.

'I see you escaped your kinsmen,' Walnut said to Beak, raising one eyebrow.

Beak spat.

'I should slit their throats and save my father the bother,' Kestril said in his usual growl.

'Or we could put them on trial at Sheldra,' Walnut said. 'They would be imprisoned and encouraged to redeem themselves.' He turned to Kestril. 'Any other options that don't involve their instant deaths at your hand?'

'If I return them to our clan, they would be tried for treason, and since Beak has rejected the Terrigal's punishment for Miramar's death, our clan would administer their own justice. The end result would be the same,' he replied.

'No!' Doram cried, his eyes wide and glassy with fear. 'I'd rather the rest of my life in a prison at Sheldra.'

'It is not your choice,' Kestril replied.

'And we have not committed treason,' said Beak. 'We did what we did for the benefit of our clan.'

'You were there, in the town square, when my father gave his latest orders to our people,' Kestril said calmly. 'He said, from this moment on, Menhirs, you will not lift arms against any Magan or our allies, the Warriors, without consulting me first. From now on our enemies are the demons, not human kind. You have gone against his orders. Therefore, you have committed treason and should be tried by the Menhirs for that crime, as well as for the attempted assassination of a Warrior, and in Beak's case, the murder of one.'

'If you take me back, cousin,' Beak replied, a smug expression on his face. 'I will charge you with treason also, for I

see that what I always suspected is true. You allied yourself with
the Warrior Clans and worked against the Menhirs and against
your father's wishes.'

'Kestril is not on trial here, Beak,' Walnut said. 'You are.'

'What will happen to them if they are tried by the
Menhirs?' Ariel asked.

'They will be executed by knife to the throat,' Kestril
replied without emotion.

'Hasn't there been enough killing already?'

'Look at him in Second Sight, Ariel,' Kestril said curtly.
'Look at the level of his infection. Can you find one gap where
the light shines through? I think not. I know my cousin and he is
determined once set on a course. If we do not deal with him
finally now, he will try again and again until he succeeds.'

'He could be imprisoned instead of executed.'

'It is not your place to speak for him,' Kestril growled.
'Only Walnut can mitigate his fate.'

Ariel grimaced, but said nothing more. She bet Nick
would happily see Kestril dispose of the man once and for all.

'If imprisoned, he could find a way to escape,' Kestril
continued. 'You and your protectors will never be safe from this
man.'

'He dreams of being master of the demons,' Walnut said,
his eyes looking into space. 'He sees himself with the Majors at
his side, doing his bidding, terrifying all people into submission.
He thinks that with them, he can have everything he wants.'

'Fool,' Kestril hissed, 'the demons are your masters, not
the other way around. Rasas submit only to one master, Rasama,
and humans who play with demon fire become charred beyond
recognition. The result of your path is that of a slave or a puppet;
either way it is Rasama's will that will be done.'

'Tynan, will you help Kestril take them home?' Walnut
asked.

'Of course. I am inclined to think that execution may be the kindest solution for this one anyway. That way he will not grow more Serpentine this lifetime.'

'Take one of the Light Brigade with you, Tynan, someone to prepare him before his execution,' Walnut said.

'You speak as if my sentence has already been decided,' Beak said, his eyes flicking nervously from face to face.

'Do you doubt the outcome of your trial, cousin?' Kestril asked in a voice more gentle than usual.

Beak didn't reply.

'What of me?' Doran whispered.

Everyone looked at Walnut, but it was Kestril who spoke. 'My father will decide your fate as well.'

Walnut nodded, and the poor Magan shivered with fear. Ariel hoped she'd never have to meet Kestril's father.

Tynan called to two Warriors who were talking nearby. 'Finch and Tyler, can you take these two back to Sheldra and put them in a cell for us, please?'

'Yes, sir,' they replied and bustled the two Magans away.

'I apologise for my clan, Walnut,' Kestril said. 'It pains me that, out of all the Mage Clans, it should be my kinsmen that have done these deeds.'

'Was it not also a kinsman that told you of the plan and thereby helped save mine and Ariel's lives? And was it not you, the son of Lord Menhir himself, who stopped the plan from its fruition?'

Kestril nodded grimly.

'Then consider your debt paid.' Walnut smiled and Kestril bowed his head in deference to the old man.

Ariel searched for Nick. She spied him, still working on those too injured to move, not far from where she'd last seen him.

Nick healed without pause. He had no idea how many he had tended to, or how much time had passed. He existed in a world of energy rather than matter, and only emerged from it when Ariel brought him sandwiches and insisted that he take a break to eat. They sat without speaking on the ground beneath a sun now high in the sky, and Nick continued his work as soon as he'd polished off the last of the sandwiches.

Eventually, Maya laid her hand on his arm and told him to stop.

'Why? There are still many wounded,' he replied.

'You are not used to this,' she replied, 'and not trained in the subtleties of healing. There is danger in doing too much at one time. The worst are healed and the others will soon be well again. You have done enough.'

'No. I'm fine.' He stood, but swayed on his feet.

Maya put her hands on her hips and pursed her lips. 'Feeling a little lightheaded, are you?'

The world shimmered around him. 'I was fine until you mentioned it.'

Ariel placed her hand on his arm and gave him a do-as-you're-told look. 'Just a few more, okay,' he protested.

'If a demon or an assassin came for Ariel now, could you protect her?' Maya asked.

Nick sighed. 'Okay, you have a point.'

Ariel and Nick found some horses and rode back to the base camp to pick up their gear, then headed towards the Haba camp by the river on the other side of the plain. As they rode, Ariel told Nick about the prophecy.

'So, no place for Tynan or me, huh?'

'You do have a place. With me, wherever I am. Anyway, the prophecy could be about four people. You, me, Tynan and Kestril.

'One will come to break the drought,
One bright to cut the dark,

One who wields the blade of Aarod,
One bearing the copper mark.'

'Nice try, Ariel, but I don't think that would be the general interpretation, and you'd have a bit of a struggle trying to match each of us with a line, especially when you have both the blade and the mark.'

'I'm not supposed to think about it anyway,' she said. 'Tell me about the Sky Steeds instead.' She glanced into the sky where several of the huge beasts flew without riders.

'They aren't domesticated, just permit the Haba to ride them when they need to. The Habas made a pledge to the Pathmaker to protect those on the Upper Reaches, so you can imagine how important the Sky Steeds are to them.'

'Need a lot of protecting up there, do we?' Ariel asked, looking up the mountain.

'Yeah,' Nick replied in a clipped tone. Things would get a lot harder before all this was over.

The cloud that had hidden the Peak all day now rose steadily, as if lifting its hat to celebrate the Warriors' success. They stopped to admire the sharp ridges highlighted in silver snow, shining boldly in contrast to the deep blue-shadowed gullies. Nick shivered. The Steps of Death were visible too, scarring the near kilometre-high cliff behind the stone walls and slate roof of the Hermitage. They'd left scar tissue on his soul too.

'We've got a long way to go,' Ariel said.

'Yeah.' He felt her trepidation, but he wasn't going to reassure her with platitudes. She knew the score.

'The Warriors won their battle today, but I lost mine,' she whispered.

'No one lost,' he replied. 'Your win has just been delayed.'

19

Camp at Rushing Waters

The Haba made camp among the scrubby trees on the Sheldra side of Rushing Waters River, and the afternoon was drawing to a close by the time Nick and Ariel arrived. They left their horses with a groom and searched for a campsite to share with their guide. 'This is a good spot for Walnut,' Ariel said, stopping between two roots of a large tree.

'And we can set up behind those rocks,' Nick said, pointing to a private nook. Ariel's heart beat a little faster.

'I went crazy without you,' she said as they dumped their packs.

'How crazy?' he asked with that familiar, and oh-so-missed, twinkle-eyed amusement.

'Loopy. I gave up even trying to talk to Dennis, and Yule only talked about old pieces of paper.'

He chuckled. 'What about me? Stuck with Robyn, Sarah and John!'

Ariel smiled, remembering the group she'd met at the Shifting Inn.

'They asked about you and were thrilled at your progress.' He stepped closer. 'I felt very proud of you.'

'Yeah, well, I would have died ten times over without you.'

He frowned and counted on his fingers. 'No, just five times, and you've saved me twice now, so we're nearly even.'

'Don't worry; you're still way ahead of me.'

He snorted as if it wasn't important, but his satisfaction at the comparison radiated from him like a warm fire. She draped her arms around his neck and kissed him.

'Mmm, I like this,' he mumbled through the kisses, 'but we should set up before dark.'

'Sure.' She pretended not to care, but she would rather have stayed kissing.

Walnut joined them at dusk, and after a rest and a wash in the river, Ariel and Nick cooked sausages. The comforting familiarity of the evening ritual made Ariel realise how much she'd missed camping with Nick and Walnut. She didn't care that her studies at Sheldra had been cut short. She just wanted to get moving up the path again.

She'd just finished her last sausage and cleaned up the remains of the salad when the deep bass of a big drum resounded across the camp.

Nick's eyes lit up. 'Great; they brought the drums.'

'Drums? What for?' Ariel asked.

'Duh? Playing.'

'Yeah, but . . .'

'You two go,' Walnut cut in. 'I'll clean up here.'

'Are you sure?' Nick asked.

'Quite sure. Go and enjoy yourselves.'

Nick grinned. 'Thanks, Walnut.'

He jumped up, beckoned to Ariel and set off towards the sound so fast that she had to run to catch up. They wove their way through the trees past colourfully embroidered tents until they found a solidly-built Haba man sitting at the edge of a clearing, slapping out a hypnotic rhythm on a djembe drum. His tattoo-covered flesh rippled with the beat. A large fire crackled nearby, and Habas gathered around, bubbling with excitement.

Other drummers arrived and sat cross-legged on the ground beside him. One by one they added their instruments to the beat. Drums of various pitches rang out in vibrant syncopation and, called by the sound, more Habas gathered, their faces glowing. Ariel couldn't help but share their enthusiasm.

Naked from the waist up, the firelight painted the drummers' chests with gold and revealed the extent of the fine tattoos that spiralled across their shoulders and down their arms and backs. One of the drummers gestured Nick over and pointed to a spare drum. Nick didn't even glance her way. He just strode over, ripped off his shirt, grabbed the drum and settled himself on the ground with the others. As if that were the cue, the pace and complexity of the music increased.

Excitement filled the crowd as the drums pounded out the Haba's joy in victory. The drummer's muscles rippled in the firelight, driving the power of the drums with strength and ease. Their faces glowed with pleasure and, completely immersed in the music, they played as one, the deep sounds of the big djembe skillfully accented with cross rhythms from smaller, tabla-style drums.

Ariel couldn't keep her eyes off Nick. An energetic and skilful drummer, the music emanated from every pore of his being. His finely muscled chest glistened in the flickering firelight, and he played the way he fought—totally present, his power completely under control, firmly directed and beautiful to watch. Ariel's breath hitched in her chest. She'd landed herself a gorgeous man. She wished she could share the news with Tamara, but her best friend remained a world away, outside the Hidden Realm, and oblivious of the demons that walked the ordinary world.

More musicians joined in, adding wind and percussion instruments, various sized wooden flutes, gongs, clap sticks, and a Haba version of a didgeridoo that produced a deep, resonating and somewhat haunting background to the other instruments.

As the tempo increased, a line of women entered the space. Their feet pounded the earth, their arms made curling pathways through the night air and their hips swayed in an energetic and alluring dance. They wore thick brocade belts around their hips and, following the lead of a lithe old woman, wove their dance in a tapestry of movement and colour.

Intoxicated by the music, Ariel's feet picked up the beat. The line of dancers passed in front of her, and the last in the line took Ariel's hand and swung her into the dance. The rhythm of the drums exploded inside her and the dance took over. Immersed in the shared experience, her feet pounded, torso pulsed and hips shimmied without conscious effort. The dancers, pure music in corporeal form, were as one with the drummers, synchronised to the hypnotic rhythm. The music swelled to a crescendo, then with one resounding beat, it stopped. An instant later, the crowd erupted into cheers.

Flushed and smiling, Ariel plonked herself breathlessly on the ground at the edge of the crowd. One of the musicians began to play a slow melody on a wooden flute, and the crowd settled again. A female Haba entered the space and began to sing in a clear, high-pitched voice, her hips swaying to the beat. The words of the ancient language wove its spell over the audience. The drummers began to play again, but Nick pulled on his shirt and joined Ariel. He sat beside her and slipped an arm around her shoulders.

'Where did you learn to play like that?' she asked.

'These guys,' he replied. 'I lived with them for a year. They adopted me into the clan.'

'That explains it.'

'And where did you learn to dance like that?'

She shrugged. 'Nowhere. I just can't not dance when the beat's so good. This music is amazing, and that woman's voice, I've never heard anything like it before.'

'It's a love song,' Nick whispered, his eyes twinkling.

Ariel stared at the starry-eyed singer. 'I thought so.'

'Actually, it sounds better if you don't understand the language,' Nick whispered, his breath warm against her neck. 'The words are really corny.'

Ariel giggled. Energised by the dance and seduced by the drums, she snuggled against Nick, enjoying the sensuality of their proximity. The intensity of their energetic connection didn't scare her anymore, instead it merely heightened her pleasure, and she stayed in his cosy embrace while a man joined the woman and the love song became a duo. Another more lively song followed, but when they called Nick back to the drums, he shook his head.

'Let's go,' he whispered.

She nodded, and he took her hand and led her through the crowd. The cool of the evening soon took the heat from her skin as they picked their way through the tents back to their camp, but Nick's hand remained in hers, and the warmth of his being spread through her body and pooled in her pelvis like liquid fire. As they drew near the river, the music faded into the background, overtaken by the sound of swiftly flowing water. They ambled along the bank, enjoying the clear starry night.

'Let's sit here for a while,' Ariel suggested before they arrived at their camp. 'I'm still too fired up to go to sleep yet.'

They sat and rested their backs against a large tree. Nick wrapped his arms around her and pulled her close. She curled into his chest and silently watched the river glistening in the moonlight, wishing that the feeling of safety would never end.

***

A green whirlwind tore down the tunnel towards Twitchet. He pressed himself flat against the ground as it flashed past in a blur, flinging dust and small stones in its wake. A spiraling column of flame followed, flickering sparks as it spun. It roared past, followed by a train of hot air. Twitchet's eyes widened. Curiosity killed the cat, he thought, but I have to see this.

He raced along the twisting tunnels after the flame. When it turned off the corridor, he peered around the corner into a large cavern with a high vaulted ceiling, many side pockets and magnificent stalactites dramatically lit by flickering torches. A group of Emots crowded around the flame in the centre of the cave, raised their arms above their heads, touched their talons together to form a canopy above the flame and chanted in a low hum. After only a few minutes, the emanations stepped back and lowered their arms. A full-sized, slightly wobbly outline of an Emot had replaced the flame—their leader, grown again. He glided weakly to a spot on a rock ledge, his emanations following close behind. Twitchet stayed, rooted to the spot, fascinated by this snip of Rasa life that probably no other Warrior had ever witnessed.

'Amic and Bitah will have to be born anew,' Emot said in a wavering voice, 'but Cogin lives still. We are greatly diminished but not defeated. I assure you that the spawn of Aarod will not be permitted to destroy us. I will feed on Emot Sai's witch and she will quickly make me strong, then I will return for her daughter and we shall all feed well. I have seen her weakness and she cannot fail to succumb to my traps.' The Emots gurgled with pleasure and their master stood and glided unsteadily towards the mouth of the cave.

The fur on Twitchet's back stood on end and he fled, navigating the tunnels at full speed, relying on his cat senses and hoping that his inner guidance system was leading him where he wanted to go. The tunnels narrowed, the air grew cooler and the rotten potato smell of Rasas faded. Even if it wasn't the right one, the blessed relief of an exit waited somewhere up ahead.

He sprang from the tunnel into the cool night air, ran behind a tree and waited until his little heart had stopped pounding. The sound of a rushing river filled his ears. The smell of barbequed sausage made his nose twitch and the light of campfires drew his eyes. Two Habas sat quietly on the ground nearby, apparently guarding the tunnel. Twitchet ambled along the riverbank towards the fires.

He found Ariel and Nick beneath a tree. She lay curled against his chest, wrapped in his arms. Even in the dim light of the moon reflected in the water, he could see the joy on their faces. His ears flicked and he padded silently towards them. 'It seems that my campaign against this outcome is a lost cause,' he meowed.

Ariel and Nick looked up in surprise. Nick grinned. 'Most absolutely and completely lost,' he said. He and Ariel's chuckles rang like a symphony of bells in the darkness.

'Did you find my mother?' Ariel asked, sitting up.

'I did, and she lives.'

Hope blossomed in Ariel's heart. She leaned forward. 'Tell me everything.'

'She appears to be handling her incarceration skillfully and is well in body and mind,' Twitchet told her.

'Can she escape?'

The little cat shook his head. 'It is as we thought. The tunnels are swarming with Rasas. The only way to be sure to get her and the other prisoners out unharmed is to remove all the demons at once by killing the Master Demon.'

Ariel sighed, and the little bubble of hope deflated, but she shrugged off the sense of impotence and impending doom and concentrated on her joy at having Nick by her side again. He wrapped an arm around her shoulders and drew her close.

Twitchet snorted and strode off, muttering about the unfortunate developments in Ariel and Nick's relationship. They chuckled at the departing figure, his tail held high, then Nick placed a finger under Ariel's chin, gently tilted her head towards him and kissed her. At last, she had him back. He deepened the kiss and her body tingled in places she'd never felt before. Overwhelming desires suddenly flooded through her as if a dam had burst. Everything she'd ever felt for him that she'd bottled up and hidden away was now free, swirling around her like snowflakes in a storm of emotion. She melted in his arms, her lips moving with his as if she couldn't bear even skin between them.

'That's different', he mumbled.

'I do have a soft and cuddly side,' she murmured before capturing his lips again.

'I like it. What happened to the ice queen?'

Ariel pulled back and stared across the river. 'She realised you were right; you already were a distraction.' She turned to face him. 'And I realised we could be dead tomorrow.'

He smiled and drew her back into his arms. His lips found hers again and suddenly, she couldn't get enough of him, his lips, his scent, his fingertips on her neck, his hands wreathed through her hair. Passion raced up her spine like wildfire, met Nick's desire and kindled it, like petrol thrown on flames. She pressed herself against him, willing to receive whatever he wanted to give.

He broke the embrace and sucked in a breath. 'Wow!'

Ariel blushed. Admitting her feelings for Nick after denying them for so long had set her hormones raging. She fanned her face. She wasn't used to this. 'I'm just glad you're back.'

He smiled and stroked her cheek. 'I'm glad too. And I'm relieved that we're finally together.'

Ariel slumped against the tree. 'Except for the mushy-brain syndrome.'

'The what?'

'Mushy brain. The you're-all-I-can-think-about see-saw ride.'

He chuckled. 'I'm flattered.'

'But I should be thinking about defeating demons, not about my next kiss.'

He shrugged. 'The demons will wait.'

Ariel nodded. 'I hope you're right.'

He grinned. 'I'm always right.'

'Pah!' She punched him playfully on the arm.

'Whoo, electricity!' Nick teased. He clutched his arm in mock pain and rolled on the ground.

Ariel giggled as she watched him. At least some of their relationship was normal.

He rolled back to her and cocked his head. 'What if I refused to kiss you?'

'Why would you do that?'

'To test for craving.'

She put her hands on her hips and pulled a face at him. 'I am not craving you.'

He grinned his cheekiest grin. 'Good. Then no more kisses. It's bed time.'

A wave of disappointment washed over her, and an image of her fantasy Nick bruising her lips with passion flicked into her mind. She should have let the image slip quietly away, but instead she wondered how she could get Nick into a tuxedo. He looked so good in it. She doubted the real Nick would be seen dead in a tie though.

'I felt that,' he said.

'What?'

'You went somewhere else.'

'Damn this energy thing,' she muttered. 'Why does it have to scream like an alarm when I lose it?'

'Or when I lose it. But whatever the reason, it's good for us, keeps us on our toes. We'll get there quicker together.'

Ariel smiled. 'When it's bad it's very, very bad, but when it's good, it's brilliant.'

He opened his arms. 'Come here, you.'

'What about the test?'

'It's over. You failed.' His eyes twinkled above a roguish grin.

'I did not. I just wandered into the future a little.'

'Chasing after what?'

'None of your business.'

He shrugged. 'Whatever it is, if you try to hold onto it, you're likely to find Emot sniffing about.'

She narrowed her eyes. 'Okay. I have a test for you.'

He raised an eyebrow. 'Are you going to try to make me jealous?'

She scooted close and sat before him. 'No; I'm going to give you a goodnight kiss and challenge you to find anything remotely like Emot food.'

'Deal.' His voice came out low and husky.

Ariel took a deep breath and, as she exhaled, let her thoughts drop like a stone into a pool. Love flowed from the peace and clarity that remained and spread throughout her being. She leaned forward, dropped her gaze to his full waiting lips and kissed him. Gently at first, then as he responded, the kiss deepened. She felt everything, every tingle, every thump of her heart, every spot that warmed, every urge to go deeper and further, and she noted every thought and every image and let them fade into the past. She needed nothing more than what the moment offered, and she immersed herself in the pleasure of it.

'Not a sign of it,' he murmured when the kiss ended. 'You passed.'

Ariel smiled. 'So did you.'

Nick wrapped an arm around her and drew her into an embrace. She snuggled in and rested her head on his shoulder. A moment later, he kissed the top of her head and declared it time for bed.

Back at camp, they found Walnut already snoring in his bedroll, and after a quick goodnight kiss from Nick, Ariel crawled into her sleeping bag. She lay awake listening to the drums until they faded into the night, leaving just the sound of crickets, frogs and the occasional owl.

It came just as she drifted off to sleep and shocked her awake with its vividness; her and Nick at her fantasy resort, warm water lapping on naked skin. No! No more fantasies, she told herself. Nick's here now. I have the real thing. But the real thing wasn't going to take her to that resort any time soon; never, actually, because it only existed in her imagination. He might engage in some of the same activities, however, minus the warm water.

Ariel giggled, then caught herself. She had a horrible sinking feeling that, despite already facing him twice, her battle with Emot had only just begun. The time for playing games was past. If she couldn't resist the lure of her fantasies, her quest would stall. She might even die. What would happen to her mother then?

20

Wildfire

Deep beneath the ground under Diamond Peak, Nadima gave her wet hair one last rub, hung a towel on the horizontal bars of her cage and smiled as she placed the shampoo neatly in the corner of the cell she had designated as her bathroom. Pleasing Emot Sai had its advantages.

A key clicked in the lock. She swung towards the sound and stared at the big Emot who opened the door. She hadn't expected him back today. He'd fed earlier and gone away satisfied. The demon's fluid form rippled like folds of fabric and his eyes flamed brilliant red against his black slimy skin.

'My master, Emot, comes,' he growled. 'You will feed him as he desires or I will punish you.' It was only then as he flicked it in warning, that Nadima saw the riding crop in his taloned hand.

'I will not resist him,' Nadima replied.

Emot Sai's mouth of flames curled into a smile. His master, Emot, the clan's Major, staggered along the corridor like a drunkard. Nadima's eyes widened at his state, little more than an outline, a surface of translucent black that shimmered in the air, a mere suggestion of form. She bit back a smile at his fate and waited without moving as he entered her cell and placed his talon on her neck.

'Feed me,' he demanded.

But Emot's talon raised nothing in Nadima. She had none of his favourite food to give him, not even a flicker of desire passing through that she could latch onto and turn into craving. She blinked in confusion and threw a look of pleading to Emot Sai. Without a sound, he threw a shard of flame that flew through the air and landed softly on the side of her head where it melted and formed an image in her mind. Her dead husband, Aarod, alive in the vision, stood before her. His arms wrapped around her and his lips pressed tenderly on hers. Then he stepped back, his eyes asking if she wanted more.

Of course, she did. Nadima would love to feel his kisses again—even from the fantasy Aarod Emot Sai had sent her—but whereas usually she would simply feel the desire and let it pass when it naturally faded, to feed the demon, she had to turn that simple desire into craving. She had to hold onto the desire and not let it go. She had to stir up memories and abandoned hopes while reminding herself that he wasn't here and she couldn't have him. More than anything she wanted her dead husband back, alive, and she told herself that repeatedly, ran it on a loop in her mind.

The illusory Aarod drew away even as he reached towards her with yearning in his eyes, and as Nadima's desire turned to craving, the warmth from the memories turned to angst in her heart, and love became pain. As a Warrior, she could have let it go at any time, but she gave herself over to it instead. She rolled around in her angst and churned it into a mire, like a pig in mud. Emot fed from Nadima's emotional sludge and gurgled with pleasure.

Emot Sai's smile grew smug as his master's form began to fill in from the sustenance Nadima provided. But, as Emot fed, Sai's smile slowly faded, and something bitter replaced his pride—jealousy. The image startled Nadima so much that she inadvertently cut the flow of craving.

'I have not finished,' Emot growled. 'Give me more.'

'That is all she can give in one day, Master,' Sai said.

'What do you mean?'

'I have never gotten more than that,' Sai lied. 'It seems that the stronger the Warrior, the less able they are to fall prey to their passions; they simply cannot do it. I assure you, Master, that she provides as much as she can and her rich flavour is very strengthening. Look how finely formed you are already.'

Emot looked down at his cloak-like form, solid now. He flexed his arms and a suggestion of muscles rippled beneath his shining skin. Nadima had indeed made him strong. 'Beat her then. I will have fear.'

'Food forced from a Warrior is bitter in comparison to those who know not how to fight,' Emot Sai said. 'There is plenty of easy Bitah food in the main cells, Master. The effort here is not worth it.'

Emot's eyes narrowed, but he nodded slowly. 'We will go where the fodder is easy then.'

They left the cell and the door clicked locked behind them, leaving Nadima with her amazement. Sai had protected her!

***

The cheerful voices of the Haba striking camp roused Ariel from her slumber. She opened her eyes to a brilliant blue sky and tree tops kissed with sunlight, promising a warm day. She looked through bleary eyes at Nick, still asleep in his sleeping bag nearby and burst out laughing.

A small ginger cat lay draped over his head, its head on his cheek and one languid paw curving around his jaw. One golden eye opened lazily and stared at her. 'It was the warmest place,' he purred.

Nick's eyes flew open. 'What's happening?'

'You have a live hat,' Ariel explained.

The hat leapt off and Nick sat up. Man and cat stared at each other, Twitchet doing his best to look endearingly innocent.

'I don't recall you asking permission to sleep on my head?' Nick's accusing tone didn't cloak the twinkle in his deep brown eyes.

'You were already asleep,' Twitchet replied. 'But what's the problem? You got a free head warmer.'

'You might've suffocated him,' Ariel pointed out.

'I wasn't on his nose. If I was, it wouldn't be red right now.'

Nick grimaced and slid his fingers through his gold flecked hair, ruffling it as if to shake something out. 'Just in case,' he muttered.

'I do not have fleas.'

'No, they're too smart to move in on you,' Ariel said with a grin.

'Lucky for them.' Twitchet stalked off, his tail straight up, the end twitching rhythmically as he walked.

Half an hour later, Ariel and Nick met Walnut, Twitchet, Radric and three other muscular Habas, who Walnut introduced as Dorn, Trone and Narbor, at the bridge over Rushing River on the eastern edge of Craggin plain. Walnut, in his battered straw hat, looked tiny besides the big Habas, but his powerful presence more than made up for his small stature.

The river, swollen with snow-melt, roared in their ears as they watched the proud and fearsome-looking Haba army cross in tight formation, three abreast, over the stone bridge. They turned left on the other side of the river and set off towards their town at the base of the escarpment, but Ariel and her escort planned to ride further east to the Hermitage which nestled at the base of the upper reaches of Diamond Peak.

When the last of the army had crossed over, Ariel and her escort mounted their horses—not the winged kind, unfortunately—and followed. Water thundered beneath them and splashed over the edge of the bridge, and the horses snorted and danced uneasily. Twitchet leapt onto Nick's lap and burrowed inside his jacket.

'What's the matter?' Ariel asked. 'Scared your hair-do will get ruined?'

Twitchet didn't bother to reply. Nick grinned and gave the little cat a friendly scratch behind the ear. 'Don't worry, Twitchet, you can blow dry it later.'

With gentle words of encouragement and reassuring pats for their mounts, the company passed over without incident. On the other side, they passed Haba riders strapping saddlebags on their Sky Steeds. Ariel marveled at the horses' thick bands of clearly defined muscle and enormous wings that beat the air with the sound of a windstorm as they galloped along the ground and lifted themselves into the air.

'Is there any chance they'd give me a ride sometime?' Ariel whispered to Nick.

He shrugged. 'You can only ask, but the Steed decides. It's up to them, not the Haba that rides them.'

'Have you had a go?'

He grinned. 'Yeah, and apart from facing Cogin, it was the single scariest thing I've ever done.'

'Why?'

'Though they go where the rider wants to go, the route they take might not be the one you'd expect, and they do like to play with their riders. If they make a rapid change of height or direction, it's easy to lose your seat.'

'What happened?'

'Well, I like fairground rides, you know,' he replied, 'but not hundreds of metres in the air. The horse thought he'd be funny and did a flip. I was strapped in well enough, but my lunch wasn't.'

'Oh.' Ariel pressed her lips together to stop a grin.

'It sounds funny now,' Nick mused, 'but it wasn't at the time.'

Ariel nodded, but she still wouldn't give up the chance to ride a flying horse if the opportunity ever came her way.

When the last of the Sky Steeds disappeared into the distance, a deep silence remained and the little company urged their horses into a trot, aiming to move quickly through the scrubby bush while they were fresh.

The air rapidly grew hotter and the horses' hooves crackled on the bone-dry leaves and twigs underfoot. The area above Rushing River hadn't seen rain for many months and the parched smell of dried leaves and straw-coloured grasses prickled Ariel's nose. The fiery sun soon turned the warm morning into a scorching day, and Ariel dragged her new wide-brimmed hat from the top of her pack and pulled it on. She was glad she'd worn her loose shirt, even though she sweated beneath the light-weight fabric, it protected her fair skin in a way sunscreen never could. Without it, she'd likely turn screaming red before midday.

They passed the desiccated corpses of animals that had died of starvation in the drought, and struggled on through the harsh unforgiving midday sun. Despite constant swigs from her water bottle, Ariel's mouth seemed continually dry. They stopped for lunch in a dried up stream—a bed of sand, flanked by pale-barked trees, wending its way into the distance—and after eating the bread, cheese and fruit the Habas had packed, they rested in the shade.

No one spoke in the oppressive heat. Ariel rested against a tree and hoped that the countless insects that inhabited the bark and soil would stay in their rightful places—away from her. She watched Nick who sat with his eyes closed against another tree, and decided that she did love him. She appreciated him, cared about him, and she'd do whatever she could to make him happy—including defeating Emot. And that meant loving him without being possessive and clingy.

Did that mean letting him go if he wanted to be elsewhere? She tried to imagine it, opened her heart and thought of his happiness instead of hers, and discovered that, yes, with an open heart, she could. What point would there be in holding onto to someone who didn't want to be with you?

Luckily, he did want to be with her, at least for now. He opened his eyes and winked at her, then smiled, laid his head back against the trunk and closed them again. Ariel smiled to herself, wondering if he'd sensed her feelings.

If so, what exactly had he felt? She closed her eyes, took a deep breath and felt what there was to feel—hot, and in more ways than one. Her hormones were at it again! She wasn't going to let Emot turn her desires into craving though. So she kept her mind focused on the present—anchored by the weight of her body on the ground—and let the fantasies of a cool swim pass on through her mind like a breeze. *Yay!* She could do this. Just feel it, enjoy it and let it go.

A horse whinnied. She opened her eyes. Dorn was giving the horses a carefully measured drink of water from their skin saddlebags. Ariel stopped short of draining her water bottle dry. She may need it later.

'Let's move on,' Walnut said. 'The day is still getting hotter and the longer we stay here, the thirstier we'll get.'

'Are you riding with me, Twitchet?' Nick asked after everyone had mounted.

The little cat lay in the heaviest shade, stretched out on his stomach as flat as a pancake, his limbs spread out almost at right angles to his limp body. He opened one eye. 'If you can lift me up.'

Nick slid off his horse, lifted the hot cat onto the front of his saddle and climbed up behind him. Twitchet positioned himself in the shade of Nick's partially open shirt and they set off once more.

The company walked their sweating horses in silence through long straw-coloured grasses, over sandy soil and under clumps of spindly trees. Sweat ran down Ariel's back. Nick unbuttoned the rest of his shirt, and the Haba stripped off their armour and rode bare-chested. Ariel couldn't help staring at the swirling tattoos that covered their glistening brown skin and accentuated the muscles on their chests and backs. If she ever got a tattoo, she'd get a Haba design for sure.

A breeze rose, but blew as hot as the day, and before long turned into a gale that flapped their clothing and grabbed at their hats until they stuffed them in their packs. The horses tossed their heads and whinnied as the wind whipped up grit from the barren earth and threw it into their eyes and noses. When the unmistakable smell of bushfire wafted over them, the horses bolted. Ariel clung to the pommel of the saddle, the reins slack in her hands as she struggled to stay on. Where was Kestril when you needed him? Last time her horse had bolted, the Magan had used magic to help her stay on, but now he and Tynan were taking Beak and Doram back to the home of the Menhirs. Uggh! She could just see the disgust in Kestril's eyes if she fell off. No, she wouldn't give him the satisfaction.

Gritting her teeth in determination, she risked taking her hands off the pommel for a moment to draw in the reins. Gradually, between quick grabs on the pommel, she eased the reins tighter, and smiled with satisfaction as she brought the horse under control. But still they galloped, for a thick pall of choking smoke billowed towards them, racing on the wind from above the path.

The smell of bush-fire struck fear into Ariel's heart. A demon they could face and beat, but wildfire … unless they could get to clear ground, a large body of water or a cave, they were lost. Even on a horse, could anyone outrun a fire in a wind as fierce as this? The intense heat sapped her energy, parched her throat and flayed her skin dry. Smoke stung her eyes and burned her lungs. Flames painted the sky red above the thick smoke, and a terrible roar filled her ears as the fire front came steadily closer. One glance at her companions showed that no one fared any better than her. They squinted ahead with grim expressions. Even Walnut looked uncharacteristically worried.

Waves of panic swept over her. No matter how much she let it go in her mind, the panic remained as a physical terror that gripped every cell in her body. Adrenaline pumped through her veins, screaming at her to move faster, to get away at all costs. Flying embers peppered the air, lighting spot fires where they fell to the ground. Flames exploded in front of them and the horses reared, whinnying in fright, their eyes rolling. Ariel jolted backwards and fell, hitting the ground with a bone-shaking thud. Her head bashed hard enough to make fireworks burst behind her eyes, and her horse fled, reins flapping.

More than one set of hooves thundered away. Who else had been thrown? The world spun around her. She tried to stand but staggered back, legs shaking, jellied by the shock. The burning smell blazed the back of her throat raw and her mouth tasted of ash. Slithers of black carbon, once twigs, floated around her like black snow, and the day turned to a furnace of red-tinged night.

The Haba tried in vain to control their rearing horses and Nick struggled to his feet a few metres away. Walnut had also lost his horse, but he stood quite still and stared into the flames. Ariel blinked through stinging tears, trying to clear her vision.

The pillars of flames that danced before them, only metres away, had searing blue eyes and teeth of hot white splinters. Fire Sprites. Their blazing legs kicked and jumped; their flickering torsos twisted and spun, and their arms of fire held flaming swords.

'Let them go,' Walnut shouted.

The Habas slipped from their mounts and drew their swords. The horses bolted. This was no ordinary fire, but could they quell it with swords? A Fire Sprite floated down in front of Ariel, radiating heat so fierce that she cowered back behind her hands. 'Your hair will burn,' it said in a voice that cracked like a whip, 'and your skin will melt.' Blue fire leapt from the pits of its eyes, spitting at her like snake tongues.

She scooted back and tried to stand again, but reeled from waves of dizziness. The Sprite's flaming sword flashed towards her. She rolled away just as Nick, brandishing his sword, leapt between her and the Sprite. Its arm fell to the ground, burnt into ash and fell apart, but the rest of it floated off the ground and stared down at them with a wary glint in its eyes. A new arm grew from its shoulder, blazing with light as if someone had thrown twigs on his fire.

'What has she ever done to you, Fire Sprite?' Nick shouted, glaring up at the sprite. Fury set his shoulders, blackened his voice and struck Ariel in the gut. His eyes blazed as bright as the flames around them.

'You humans are a blight on this world,' the Sprite crackled, its voice cutting across the roar of the fire like a thousand cracking whips, 'and fire purifies. It is our duty to raze your civilisation to the ground.' He slashed out with his sword of flames, but Nick met the blow, shattering the fire into sparks.

'If Rasama lives, things will get worse,' Nick shouted as he fought with the flaming spectre. 'He's whispered poison in your ears—lies!'

Ariel struggled to her feet and drew her blade. Her lungs burned. Her head felt thick and she could smell singed hair. She gasped for breath and heard the others coughing nearby, but could barely see them through the smoke as the fire-front drew steadily closer.

A bell tinkled from behind her, its pure tones bright against the crackling and roaring. Ariel glanced around. Walnut stood calmly, his left hand ringing the bell while his right hand waved his sceptre in a spiral that grew smaller and faster, then he drew his right arm back and flicked the sceptre towards the Fire Sprites. A mist burst from its tip and spread around the travellers. The Sprites catapulted backwards and the flames retreated, forced back by the mist. But not for long.

'Over here,' Walnut shouted. While the others raced over, he flicked his sceptre again and blasted a garbage bin-sized hole in the ground. Ariel's stomach twisted. They needed dynamite to make anything big enough to hold them all. Walnut pocketed his bell as they gathered around. 'Now drop your concepts, hold hands and close your eyes,' he said.

Ariel shook her head, but she reached for Nick and Walnut's hands all the same. 'We can't possibly fit in there,' she said.

'Only if you insist that is the case,' Walnut said, 'and we don't have time for that. Clear your mind, suspend all concepts and trust me.'

'Do as he says!' Nick hissed as he grabbed her hand. The electricity in his touch jolted her into submission and her eyes slammed shut.

'Do not open your eyes until I say or we will all die,' Walnut commanded in a voice so grim that disobedience was impossible. He chanted something low and quick, then Ariel felt a tug on her hand and followed Walnut as he led them, coughing and gasping, into a cool, earthy-smelling space. He chanted something else and the roaring of the fire faded away, leaving a weighty silence as the backdrop to their wracking coughs. 'Don't fall prey to concepts,' Walnut reminded them. 'Open your eyes, if you want to, but no speaking.'

Ariel opened her eyes and blinked in the pitch black. Walnut muttered something and his sceptre began to glow, illuminating the space. Curious faces stared wide-eyed at their refuge, a cave in the ground just big enough to hold them all. The

Habas stood quite still, their dark skin merging into the darkness and Walnut, his skin streaked with soot, stared before him as if into the space between worlds. Twitchet sat at Walnut's feet, licking ash off his marmalade coat. Nick looked the way she felt—hair filthy with ash, bloodshot eyes, black grime on his face with bright red flesh shining through in patches. Nevertheless he managed a smile and kept a firm grip on her hand.

Ariel anchored her mind to the tip of Walnut's glowing sceptre. Whenever a hint of a question arose, she kept her mind firmly on that sceptre and let the thought pass without hindrance. They died before fully formed. Better a dead thought than a dead person.

The air in the hole grew thick with the smell of sweat, ash, and burnt flesh and hair, but it wasn't long before Walnut spoke again. 'Now we leave. Same as before. Hands. Eyes. Minds clear.'

The company held hands again and they closed their eyes. Walnut muttered an incantation and they heard dirt falling away from the entrance. A gust of fresh air wafted in. Although tainted with smoke, it was a welcome relief.

Walnut tugged gently on Ariel's hand and led the party outside. 'You may open your eyes now,' he said when they'd stopped moving. They dropped their hands and opened their eyes.

The fire had passed. Ariel scanned the surrealistic landscape blackened by the inferno. Only the seared rocks and charred skeletons of the occasional tree remained, and a few fading embers smoldered or flickered with tenacious flames. The last billows of smoke faded near the river.

Everyone turned to stare in amazement at the relatively small hole that Walnut had blasted out of the earth.

'Impossible,' Dorn muttered.

'I didn't feel like I was shrinking,' Ariel said.

'You weren't,' Walnut told her with a grin.

'Then you made the hole bigger.'

The old man chuckled. 'The hole did not grow bigger and you did not grow smaller, nor did both things happen, and nor did neither of them happen.'

Ariel blinked; her mind stopped.

Nick grinned. 'I knew you'd say that.'

The Haba grinned as if they'd heard it all before and, like Ariel, didn't understand it in the least but knew that understanding wasn't the point. A conceptual mind could never understand something that was beyond concepts, and if they'd thought about what they were doing, they never could have entered that impossible refuge. Yet they had and, although they breathed raggedly through raw lungs and looked through stinging smoke-battered eyes, they were alive to prove that they had been in that hole and had come out again.

'I thought we were dead there for a moment,' she whispered to Nick.

'So did I,' he replied, 'but a close call with death makes life all the sweeter.' He brushed a straggle of hair from her sticky face and kissed her forehead. He smelt of sweat and dirt and smoke, and she didn't care.

What she did care about was her pack, gone with the horse, and everything she needed with it, including the irreplaceable old guidebook with its handwritten annotations—maybe burnt to ashes now—along with the photo of her mother that she'd tucked inside it before she left home. She literally had nothing apart from the clothes on her back. No clean clothes, no sleeping bag, no hairbrush, no face cream, not even a toothbrush. A kind of grief swept over her, a lonely sinking feeling.

'Is anyone burnt?' Walnut asked.

'My paws,' Twitchet replied. 'And my tail is singed.'

Sure enough, the fur on the tip of the little cat's tail was black and shrivelled.

'I think my back is,' Dorn said, his voice tight with pain.

'Let me look at it,' Nick said quietly. The injured Haba turned and

Nick sucked in a breath at the sight of the large blisters and patch of skin seared white on the Haba's back. He held his hands above the burns and closed his eyes. No one spoke as Nick's power embraced them all in silent concentration. After several moments, he dropped his hands, opened his eyes and smiled at the results. The wound had become healthy pink skin. Ariel shook her head in amazement. What a gift he had.

Twitchet butted his furry head against Nick's leg. He glanced down. The cat held one paw up and cocked his head as if to say, *me next?* 'Sure, little fella. Ariel, can you hold him for me please?'

Ariel lifted the cat without even a smidgen of banter passing between them, and after Nick had healed Twitchet's paws, the company set off on foot.

'I hope the horses are safe,' Radric said.

The others nodded their agreement, but the fire had been fierce and its speed enormous. The animals would have had to make it to the river before the fire. The travellers walked fast, keen to get out of the heat of the relentless sun. The smell of barbequed animals and shifting grey ash tickled their noses, and blowflies buzzed around them. Heat radiated from the smoldering earth, and with their water bottles gone with the horses, Nick figured that everyone's throat was as painfully parched as his. Thankfully, the wind dropped, and as the day wore on and they climbed towards the Hermitage, the air cooled, bringing blessed relief to the raw skin on his cheeks.

'Was there magic in that wind, Walnut?' he asked.

'The way it came and went so quickly makes it extremely likely,' Walnut replied.

Nick nodded and Walnut answered his next question before he even formed the words.

'Any Magan not in the Minion Hills at the time could have missed the binding and, unfortunately, those not near their homelands are likely to be the most dangerous.'

21

The Hermitage

Ariel and her escort—a ragged-looking band after the trauma of the fire—trudged across the plain towards the Hermitage. The pristine snow-capped summit of Diamond Peak drew Ariel's gaze. It called to her, urging her onwards and upwards and, despite her growing exhaustion, a joyful enthusiasm at the prospect of the next stage of her journey bubbled up in her.

The last of the smoke haze wafted away as they drew close to the Hermitage, and Ariel saw the building clearly at last. Perched on a rocky outcrop, it rose as if from the stone beneath it—rough uncut stone like the oldest of the Magan dwellings. Double-storied and similar in size to Tynan's house at the Observatory, this stark, imposing building with small windows had an austere air about it, like a castle without battlements.

They arrived bone-achingly weary at the front door at dusk. The blessedly cool mountain air and prospect of a shower lifted Ariel's spirits, and as the ancient wooden door of the Hermitage creaked open, excitement rose at the prospect of exploring this ancient building.

An old man with bright blue eyes stepped out. His wispy white hair stuck up at odd angles, and he scanned the company with a mixture of surprise and relief. 'Thank Aya you're all right,' he exclaimed in a voice almost as creaky as the door. 'We saw the fire and . . .' His eyes rested on Ariel and his face cracked into a wide grin showing several missing teeth. 'Ah, little Ariel.' He stepped forward and clasped her hand eagerly in his. 'Welcome home. How I have longed to see you here again.'

Ariel's eyes widened. 'Home?'

'This is where you were born,' Walnut hastened to explain.

The old man frowned, a little affronted. 'Doesn't she know?'

Ariel shook her head. Nick gawked at her as if she'd grown horns or something. Apparently, he hadn't known either. She looked up at the high walls above her. This was home? When?

'You lived here before your father died,' Walnut explained. 'This is Geordie, the Hermitage's caretaker. Now, can we come in, Geordie, or are we going to have to spend the night on the doorstep?'

'Oh my goodness, no,' he replied. 'Please do come in. The fire is already lit in the kitchen and Deirdre has aired your rooms.' He took Ariel by the arm and led her inside, calling for the housekeeper.

'I think we've become invisible,' Twitchet meowed behind her. 'Old Copper-locks has stolen the show.'

'Copper-locks!' Nick chuckled. 'That's a good one. Let's go round to the side door.'

Ariel didn't hear the Haba's reply as they walked away. She stood in a wide, cool entrance hall, stark in its contrast to the ornate luxury of Tynan's house, the cosy warmth of Miramar's house and the simple grandeur of the buildings at Sheldra. This was rough-walled, floored in plain stone and completely unadorned.

A plump red-faced woman appeared through one of the doors off the entranceway. She beamed with pleasure through a halo of frizzy grey hair. 'Ariel, my darling child,' she announced.

'My goodness, look how you've grown. But, oh, what a mess you are.'

Ariel smiled weakly. Who was this person?

'I suppose you don't remember your old Aunty Deidre now, do you?' she continued.

'Aunty?' Ariel squeaked. No one had told her she had an Aunty.

'This is Deidre, the housekeeper, Geordie's wife,' Walnut explained. 'She isn't really your Aunty, but she liked you to call her that when you were small.'

'Oh.' Ariel gulped. 'Hi.'

'Would you like a cup of tea?' Deidre asked.

Ariel shrugged; she didn't care about tea. All she wanted was a shower and some clean clothes. But she was thirsty—very thirsty.

'Water,' she croaked, swallowing in her too dry throat. Would she ever get rid of the taste of fire?

'Of course, dears, do come this way.'

She led them down a corridor past a dining room and a sitting room, then into a huge, old-fashioned, kitchen. A white-wood table, smooth from countless scrubbings, sat in the centre. Cast iron pots and pans hung from hooks on one wall, and bunches of herbs dried above a large wood-fired stove. Ariel followed Walnut's lead and sank into a chair at the table, grateful to rest her legs at last.

Deidre drew two large glasses of water from a tap above an over-sized sink, handed them one each, then filled a jug with more water and placed it on the table. Then she leaned against the sink and watched Ariel the way mothers of little children do when their offspring do something clever.

'Where are your things?' she asked when Walnut had drained his glass.

'The horses ran off in the fire,' he replied. 'All our gear was on them, except what you see.'

'Oh my goodness. Thank Aya you weren't burnt to death.'

Walnut nodded but offered no further explanation. 'Ariel will want some clean clothes. Can you find something for her?'

'Of course. Nadima didn't take everything when she left. There will be something in her room for Ariel.'

'I'll show her up,' Walnut said. 'Put the kettle on and I'll join you in a while, and I hope you've plenty in the larder; those boys will be hungry.'

'Oh, yes. What happened to your Haba friends?' Deidre glanced behind them as if she thought they should be hiding there.

A door on the other side of the room opened and Nick walked in followed by the four Habas. 'Hi, Deidre,' he said. 'We washed the worst of the soot off outside—didn't want to muss up your lovely kitchen.'

'And just as well that is too,' she replied, folding her arms across her chest in mock sternness.

Walnut caught Ariel's eye and jerked his head towards the door they'd entered by. She followed him out of the kitchen, grateful for the silence after Geordie and Deidre's overwhelming welcome. Nick's voice, as he introduced the Habas, faded behind the thick stone walls.

Walnut led her further along the corridor past another door. 'The library,' he said.

Ariel nodded and trailed him up a set of stairs. A strange feeling settled over her. What was this dingy place to her? Its austere walls seemed to seep into her and nudge at long-forgotten memories she never knew she had.

Walnut stopped outside a door in the middle of the upper floor. No polished finishes or brass knobs here, just sturdy wood, unadorned but planed smooth, even the knob. 'The Maloney family rooms,' he declared, gesturing to the door.

Ariel fitted her hand around the smooth knob, turned it and pushed the door open. The foundations of her life cracked at the sight of the cosy living room—something she never knew existed, but now remembered, as if from another life. Even in the rapidly fading light, the saffron coloured walls, thick maroon curtains and rich tapestries made a striking décor, but more powerful were the memories awakened by that room. Ariel's eyes moistened and something tugged at the centre of her chest. She'd been three years old when her father died, too young to remember him, but in this room, she recalled his loving presence, the sound of his laughter and the feel of his strong warm arms around her.

Walnut slipped an arm around her shoulders, and gave her a squeeze. 'This is where your father grew up and where he lived with Nadima and then with you,' he told her. 'The Hermitage is the seat of the heirs to the Blade of Aarod, Ariel. Your family heritage is as much a part of this place as the mortar between the stones.'

Ariel sniffed. Why hadn't Nadima told her about this? Fine antique furniture filled the room—a comfortable looking sofa and matching chairs, a shiny-topped table with curved legs, an elegant sideboard displaying fine china and a glass-fronted cabinet containing silverware. A pot bellied stove nestled against the far wall with a blackened kettle on the hearth, and a small coffee table with a tiled surface sat against the wall beside it. On the top, a pottery teapot rested as if set down only a moment before. Ariel imagined her mother squatting on the floor making tea. Tears rose in her eyes, but she wiped them away. How different her life would have been had they never left.

'That's your room, over there,' Walnut said, pointing to a door in the wall on the right-hand side.

She stared at it. This one and the other internal door on the left-hand wall gleamed, their red wood and brass knobs polished to a shine. I'm glad I don't have to polish them, she thought.

Walnut followed her to the door. 'Apart from Deidre keeping it dust-free, I believe it's unchanged from the day I helped Nadima pack a few things and take you to the portal.'

Ariel took a deep breath, opened the door and peered inside, but no painful memories presented themselves, just a little girl's room so delightful that it made Ariel smile. Bright, modern tapestries warmed the stone walls and, on the bed, a fluffy feather blanket, wrapped in a flower-patterned lemon cover, promised a warm night. Books and toys filled the shelves and a thick brown rug that invited toe-snuggling lay on the floor by the bed.

'You can move back in if you like or we can give you another room if you'd prefer,' Walnut said.

'No, I'll stay here.' The residue of her family's long presence within these walls filled her with a deep sense of comfort and belonging. It wasn't the sort of place she would have picked for a home if given a choice, but in some strange way, she felt she belonged here in a way that she had never belonged in the suburb where she had lived most of her life.

Back in the living room, Walnut lit an oil lamp and started the fire—which someone had kindly left set. 'It heats the hot water tank for the bathroom across the hall,' he explained. 'You'll have warm water soon and it'll be hot in half an hour. Your parents' room is that one.' He indicated the door on the other side of the living room. 'You should find something there to change into.'

Ariel nodded and looked vaguely around. Was this a dream?

Walnut watched her closely. 'It's your place as much as your mother's, you know.'

She nodded again, but said nothing.

'Do you want me to stay for a while?'

'No, I'm fine. Just worn out.'

'Good. I'll put Nick in the room next to yours, but he'll have to share your bathroom if that's okay.'

'That's fine. Where will you be?'

'Other end of the hall, and our Haba friends will have the downstairs suite.' He showed her how to work the flues on the fire and light the oil lamps then left her alone.

As soon as he'd gone, Ariel explored the bathroom across the hall. A huge bathtub with clawed feet welcomed her from its spot in the middle of the green-tiled room. Perfect! A cheerful rainbow-covered shower curtain hung above it, and even the shower head was huge—the size of a saucer. Shiny white tiles topped with an elegant decorative strip of gold filigree rose three quarters of the way up the wall. Fresh towels hung on a rack on the wall beside the tub, and a face-washer sat, neatly folded, on the side of the hand basin. It felt as if she'd walked into an expensive antique hotel.

A mirror hung above the sink, but Ariel had no desire to see if she looked as bad as she felt. She splashed her face with cold water, rubbed the face-washer over it and dried off on one of the towels. The bathroom felt lived in now.

A cabinet hung on the wall next to the basin, and inside Ariel discovered an old pot of face cream—which smelt just fine—some perfumed oils, extra soap, headache tablets, a tube of toothpaste and a toothbrush still in its packet. She felt a lot less adrift with these simple objects at hand, as if their possession anchored her to the safety of normality. In the cupboard below the sink, she found, amongst various other things, an unopened packet of feminine products. She smiled, pleased she wouldn't have to broach the subject with Deidre.

After adding more fuel to the fire in the living room, Ariel approached the door to her parents' bedroom with some trepidation. Would she find any trace of her father in there? A reminder of who she had lost before she had a chance to know him. She opened the door, stepped inside and let out a low whistle. An impressive king-sized wooden bed with a canopy and drapery took up most of the room. Bedside tables, a dressing table with an oval mirror, two large chests of drawers and two wardrobes completed the red wood set. The room felt ritzy and elegant but also comfortable and cheerful.

It had the same granite walls as the rest of the building on its outer and corridor wall, and the same high, narrow windows. Like Ariel's room, the side walls were plastered smooth, but painted a soft mushroom colour instead of the sunny yellow in her room. To Ariel's relief or disappointment, or maybe a bit of both—she wasn't sure which—no obvious reminders of the previous occupants remained. The room was neat and tidy and, no doubt thanks to Deidre, not a spot of dust lay on the well-polished surfaces.

Ariel glanced from one chest of drawers to the other. Were her father's things still in one of them? If so, she didn't want to see them. Presuming that the set next to the dressing table belonged to her mother, she slid open the top drawer and peeked inside. Socks and underwear—not much of it, just a few things left behind. She drew out a pair of knickers, they looked about the right size, but the bra was a lost cause. She would wash her own and go without until it dried. In the drawers below, she found a few faded T-shirts, a pair of track pants and a couple of sloppy sweaters. She drew out the steely blue sweater. The water should be hot enough by now.

A strange kind of relief washed over Ariel as she left her parents' room with fresh clothes in hand, as if she'd been ferreting amongst the possessions of the dead without permission and had narrowly escaped detection. She shivered and hoped the water was truly hot.

After a warm shower, a change of clothes and a quick rest on the sofa, Ariel closed down the flue on the pot belly stove, picked up the oil lamp and headed towards the kitchen. The light of the lamp flickered her shadow into strange shapes on the stone walls, and she shivered in the deepening chill. The large drafty corridors felt eerie and lonely in the dark, and she hurried to find a haven from the apprehension that stirred in her gut.

By the time Ariel joined the others in the large, thankfully warm and well-lit kitchen, Twitchet had already installed himself by the stove.

'Look out, here comes Thomas,' Nick said just after Ariel walked in.

'Who's Thomas?'

Nick tilted his head towards the large black cat with white paws that strode into the room. His proud bearing and air of disdain clearly communicated his status as king cat of the castle. He stopped a metre from Twitchet and growled a warning.

'Now, Thomas,' Deidre warned him, 'be nice to our guest.'

'Hello,' Twitchet meowed, not moving from his place by the fire.

Thomas bared his teeth and hissed.

'Now don't be like that,' Twitchet said, standing up. 'I'm willing to share.'

Thomas hissed again, leapt forward and took a swipe at Twitchet, then turned his back and stalked out of the room.

Twitchet merely blinked. 'That went well,' he declared before resuming his spot.

Everyone laughed.

'Poor Thomas,' Geordie said.

'I'm afraid Twitchet isn't well endowed with social skills,' Walnut said apologetically.

'I'd better feed him in the hall,' Geordie added. 'He won't like that.'

'Tough,' Twitchet meowed.

'Now, don't be a naughty kitty,' Deidre said condescendingly, though the smile in her eyes showed she had already developed a soft spot for the little cat.

Twitchet buried his face in his paws—a picture of embarrassment. Deidre nonchalantly continued with preparation for dinner.

After a generous roast dinner followed by apple pie, and a profusion of compliments to the cook, Walnut, Ariel, Nick, Deidre, Geordie and the four Habas retired to the lamp-lit sitting room where they gathered around a roaring fire. A red-patterned rug warmed the granite floor, and a huge tapestry of a Warrior battling a blue-eyed Rasa hung on the wall opposite the large windows and French doors. Ariel peeked through one of the small panes but saw no further than the terrace. Darkness blocked the view.

'The tapestry shows the Pathmaker killing Rasama,' Deidre said as she pulled the thick red curtains across. 'It's supposed to inspire us all, but I'm happy just to help others get there, at least in this lifetime.'

Brown leather sofas and easy chairs filled the room, along with the requisite coffee tables, some bookshelves and a couple of square tables. The Habas settled at one of them and Dorn pulled out a pack of cards. The others sat around the fire, and Geordie found some Haba beer in the cellar. The big men accepted it gratefully but, to Radric's obvious amusement, Nick politely refused. Ariel's eyes soon grew heavy and she excused herself and took herself and her lamp up the stairs to her room.

Back in the Maloney family sitting room, Ariel stoked up the stove again and waited for it to roar before turning down the flue for the night. The oil lamp cast a warm glow around the room and Ariel stretched out on the lounge, enjoying the homely feeling. All she needed now was a mother to join her.

22

Nick draws a line

A soft knock sounded at the door. 'It's Nick.'

'Come in.'

He did, along with her favourite smile, though it didn't disguise the tiredness around his eyes. 'Make a dome tonight and remember I'm right next door. Walnut says that behind the blue tapestry in your room is a door onto the corridor and my door is right next to it.'

'Okay.' She climbed off the couch and walked over to him. 'Does your room have a fire?'

'Not one that's going, why?'

'You could sleep in here if you want.'

'It's okay. I'll be cosy enough once I'm under the blankets, and I can always ask Twitchet to sleep on my head.'

'It looked to me like he wasn't going to leave the sitting room fire.'

'I know,' Nick replied, 'but I can live in hope.'

Ariel chuckled at his dead-pan expression. It cracked into an affectionate smile and his eyes locked on hers.

'Goodnight.' He tilted his head and leaned forward. Her whole being tingled with anticipation. Their lips met and a powerful current surged between them. The walls of Ariel's being dissolved into him as if she'd fallen into a pool of bliss. Fire raced through her veins and she pressed herself against him.

Never again would she fight his desire. The flood gates that had kept her passion locked away were open now; her fervour released and flowed without hindrance. Now that she'd accepted their mutual attraction, she saw no reason to put a limit on how far they might go. She could be dead tomorrow. Letting go of her inhibitions made her feel free in a way she had never felt before.

She slid his shirt out of his trousers and ran her hands over the muscles on his back. Her fingers trailed across a scar on his shoulder then down, fingertips tingling against his smooth skin. She brought her hands to his chest, stroked the soft hair there and delighted when his stomach muscles grew taut beneath her fingers. They slid lower and traced the skin around the top of his trousers.

'Whoo, hold on there,' Nick extracted himself from her, exhaling forcefully, his eyes wide.

'What's wrong?' Her mind was clear, her awareness centred. She felt no neediness, no desperate craving, just a nice relaxed … readiness.

'Nothing's wrong.' He stroked her cheek. 'We just shouldn't get too physical, that's all.'

'What?' Ariel stepped back. 'Are you serious? First, you refuse to leave me alone, then you ignore me completely, then you go back to seducing me at every opportunity, and now when I can't resist you anymore, you don't want me. And you accused me of running hot and cold!'

'I told you I didn't want anything more than kissing and cuddling.' He raised an eyebrow in challenge. 'Isn't that enough for you? … Or do you want me to make love to you?' He teased her with twinkling eyes and a curled lip.

Ariel opened her mouth but nothing came out. He'd been so direct. She blushed, looked at the floor and shrugged. 'Sometime.'

'Now?' His voice melted like sweet chocolate. He took a step closer, placed his finger under her chin and gently lifted her head, fixing his penetrating eyes on hers, igniting the charge between them.

She squirmed and drew her eyes away. He'd called her bluff. *Damn him.* He knew her too well. 'Not *right* now,' she mumbled, 'but we should just let it happen naturally … one day.'

'I agree,' he replied, 'but not until after I've defeated Cogin. That's why, until then, we have to stop before it's too hard not to.' He grimaced at the double meaning and shrugged apologetically.

Heat rose to Ariel's face, but she ignored it. 'What's Cogin got to do with it?'

He shook his head. 'Remember the sledgehammer my feral beast likes to throw at you occasionally.'

Ariel twisted her mouth in frustration. He referred to the painful and unpredictable surges of energy that flew her way when his jealousy got out of control, or when she threw up a psychic wall to keep him out. 'But everything's been wonderful since the Plateau,' she protested. 'Not even a little zap, just … delicious.' She stroked his cheek.

He put his hand on hers and shook his head sadly. 'I won't risk hurting you, and I can't be sure that I won't until Cogin is dead from my sword. Can you imagine how painful it would be if our energy got all twisted up while we're that close?'

'You wouldn't be jealous, and I wouldn't close off. Not then, not if …' *Not if we're making love* she wanted to say, but couldn't bring herself to speak the words.

'You can't guarantee that. One passion can easily ignite another, and we don't know what games Cogin is capable of playing, or where or when he might send his minions to attack.'

'I'm prepared to risk it.'

'Well, I'm not. I'd never forgive myself if I hurt you, and I can't afford to lose control and let Cogin in.'

'You're scared.'

He snorted and his face grew hard. 'Yeah. Too right I am. And you wanna know why? You wanna know just how screwed up I am?'

Ariel bit her lip, not sure she wanted to hear this.

'Today, when we arrived here and Walnut mentioned that this is where you were born, do you know what I thought?'

Ariel shook her head, too stunned by his vehemence to say anything.

'I thought about how you had everything going for you, the Blade of Aarod, the prophecy, daughter of the Maloney family and now a high birth.'

'What high birth and what's the big deal about my family?'

'You don't know?' He seemed genuinely surprised at her ignorance.

She shook her head.

'The Maloneys are the oldest family on the mountain, the closest thing we have to aristocrats. You're practically a princess, and I'm a baker's son. Add to that, the fact that very few are born this high in the mountain, and those that are have climbed at least this far in previous lives, and that puts you way ahead of me. *That* is what I thought when I found out where you had been born. How pathetic is that?'

'Oh, Nick. This isn't a competition.'

'I know, but we're talking about layers of conditioning here, my whole childhood of never being good enough, always falling in the shadow of my brother and always struggling to beat him, wanting more than anything to, just once in my life, come out on top, and be the one my parents are proud of. I know how stupid that mindset is; I peel it away like a layer off an onion; I think I'm over it, and I am for a while, until I discover that it's still there, smaller, but still there. I keep stripping away the layers, but my psyche is one hell of an onion, and I never know when some stupid little thing will set it off and make me ten years old again and insanely jealous.' He stared at her, checking that he'd made himself clear.

She sank onto a chair. 'I get it.'

'Do you? Really? Did I ever tell you how I killed my brother?'

'Stop it! I know how he died. Stop punishing yourself for something you didn't do.' *And stop punishing me!* She met his gaze, opened her heart and absorbed his pain and fury. His eyes remained steely for a moment, then softened. He slumped into the chair beside her and buried his head in his hands, deflated like an empty balloon.

'Sorry,' he mumbled. 'I just want you to understand.'

'I do.' She rubbed his back, the way her mother had rubbed hers whenever she'd been upset. But how could she, an only child and the apple of her mother's eye, how could she possibly understand what his childhood had been like? Was no father better than a bad one as Nick had always claimed? Was that another thing for him to hold against her? That she hadn't had a father around?

Ariel stood and kissed the top of his head. 'I think we should go to bed. It's been a long day.'

One goodnight kiss and ten minutes later, Ariel lay alone in her single bed wishing she was in a king-sized one with Nick. Their interaction before bed showed her how far the fantasies she'd comforted herself with in his absence had taken her from reality. The Nick she'd dreamed about hadn't drawn a line he refused to cross. He'd been thrilled with her new willingness, not scared of his own energy or that some demon would use their intimate moments to attack. That night it took a lot of discipline for Ariel to clear her mind and not welcome a fantasy with open arms.

***

Next morning, Ariel awoke to find the fire out and the air chilly. She dressed quickly and raced downstairs, grateful for the fluffy slippers she'd found in her mother's room. Tendrils of cold grey light seeped into the corridors and leached some of the cheerfulness from the kitchen, but Deidre soon had the wood stove roaring, the kettle boiling and bacon sizzling in a pan. Ariel helped lay the table in the kitchen and make the toast, and when the Habas poked their head in asking about breakfast, Deidre told them to stay out of her way and come when they heard the gong.

Nick didn't appear until five minutes after the gong. Everyone else was squeezed around the table in the kitchen, eating bacon and eggs with tea and toast.

'You're lucky I kept some bacon for you,' Deidre said, hands on hips.

'Good morning, sleeping beauty,' Radric mocked.

'Glad you could make it,' Dorn said.

'Yeah, we wouldn't have wanted to have to eat your breakfast for you,' Narbor added sarcastically.

Ariel had never had breakfast with seven men before, and she felt out of place amongst their cheerful camaraderie, but Nick handled their ribbing with practised ease, and after they'd shuffled around to give him space, their bantering soon faded in favour of eating.

'I suggest you two take a portal to Sheldra today,' Walnut said. 'You can replace your things and Ariel can shop for whatever she needs.'

'Great!' At last Ariel was going to use one of the mysterious transport portals. But there was one problem. She

231

leaned close to Walnut, who sat next to her, and whispered. 'I've used up all my money.' She hadn't needed much so far. Many people didn't charge Walnut or his travellers for anything. Even so, what she had managed to grab on her way out the door of her old home had gone.

'That's no problem,' he assured her, his kindly eyes holding hers. 'The Maloney family safe is here, and since you're one of the only two Maloneys left, I think that Geordie might open it for you and let you help yourself. There's plenty there.'

Nick nearly choked on his bacon.

Walnut turned a piercing gaze on his protege. 'True nobility is earned, not given,' he said sternly.

Nick pressed his lips together, and Ariel wondered what he'd thought to evoke such a statement from Walnut. Something about paupers and princesses, she suspected.

'Make sure you get everything she'll need for the upper reaches,' Walnut continued.

Nick nodded. 'Do you want me to get anything for you, Deidre?'

'No, deary, Geordie will do that,' she replied, pouring herself yet another cup of tea. 'You and Ariel go off and have fun.'

'Do any of the shops have Magan clothes?' Ariel asked Nick.

'There is one. Why, do you want a disguise?'

She pulled a duh-face and punched him on the arm. 'No; I want one of those cool belts.'

'Ouch.' He rubbed the spot where she'd hit him. 'I'm not buying you any more weights.'

'I can't believe I'm going shopping with a man.'

'What's wrong with that?' he countered with feigned innocence. 'It can't be worse than it is for a man shopping with a woman.'

'You think? Men try to rush you and grumble all the time, and when you ask them if anything looks good, they always say, yes, even if it's the most hideous thing you've ever seen.'

'Oh, you've had a lot of experience shopping with men, have you?' He smirked.

'Tamara brought her boyfriend Mitch once. It was a nightmare. They ended up arguing like an old married couple.'

Nick chuckled. 'I promise not to do that, but only if you don't take hours trying to decide everything.'

'Actually, I make decisions very quickly.'

He raised his eyebrows. 'We'll see.'

Ariel narrowed her eyes at the challenge in Nick's eyes. He just grinned. 'How about we get a little collar and a bell for Twitchet too?' she asked.

'No way, Copper-locks,' Twitchet growled from his spot by the fire.

'What?' Ariel spun around, not sure she'd heard correctly.

Nick stifled a laugh. Twitchet tucked his paws underneath him and closed his eyes.

'Did you just call me Copper-locks?' Ariel asked in a scandalized tone.

'I think that's lovely,' Deidre said as she stood and began clearing the table. 'Copper-locks and the four Haba. We could make a tale about your journey here.'

'And while you're at it, you should probably make a new tail for Twitchet, just in case he mysteriously loses his,' Ariel retorted.

The rest of the company snickered.

'Idle threats,' Twitchet said, but he tucked his tail in close to his body nevertheless.

Deidre bent down to stroke him. 'Aw, she wouldn't do anything to your lovely little tail.'

'Excuse me.' Twitchet stood. 'I think I feel a fur ball coming up.'

'Oh!' Deidre jumped back, and Twitchet shot out the door, leaving everyone chuckling.

'Would you excuse me, Deidre?' Walnut asked when they'd recovered. 'I'd like to spend a little time outside before we train this morning.'

'Of course,' Deidre replied.

Walnut stood and pushed back his chair. 'Let's meet in the training room in half an hour.'

Everyone nodded.

'Why don't you go out too, dear?' Deidre said to Ariel. 'I'll clear up here and it is lovely out.'

'I'll help clean up,' Nick said.

'No, let the Haba do it,' Radric said. 'You go and enjoy the view. We see it everyday.'

'Thanks, Radric,' Nick replied.

Nick led Ariel through the sitting room, cold and still without the crackling fire of the night before, and onto the terrace where the early morning sun began its job of warming the day. Her eyes lit up at the vista spread below them. She hadn't looked over the landscape since the Observatory, and today not a single cloud obscured the sight.

There had been no view from beneath the huge trees of the well-named Morbid Forest. At the Plateau of Bliss they had only looked east over the ocean, and they had seen nothing of the rest of the realm when crossing the treacherous Magan lands of Minion Hills. The lower slopes of the realm were not visible from Sheldra nor were the plains to its north, but the Hermitage sat high enough for an unobstructed view in all directions.

The ocean sparkled in the east, its great waves crashing onto the rocks far below, and the sky merged with the pale blue sea at the distant horizon. The vastness of the view eased the tension hiding in Ariel's chest and made breathing easier than it had been for days.

To the south lay her past, the off-mountain city she grew up in. Its skyscrapers stood proudly far below, like golden spires in the morning sun. Its suburbs flowed like patterned cloth over the lows hills and around the glistening harbour, and beyond stretched pale green and gold fields. Most people down there had no idea that this Hidden Realm existed. Nor did they see the demons that roamed among them, sapping their energy and turning their pleasures to pain. They had no idea that they hosted an alien parasite—the Serpentine—or that it was in danger of taking control of the human race.

Here, at her family home, the meaning of her place in the line of Aarod became clear. This was not some random label, it was something encoded in her DNA, an impetus to climb to the diamond at the very top of the Hidden Realm and defeat the demon that would otherwise prevent her from standing on that peak and taking command over the view. Even here, so far below the peak, it held Ariel transfixed.

The rising sun kissed the landscape with gold, sparkled off the turrets, domes and spires of the Plateau of Bliss, glistened on the surface of Lake Sheldra, and made mighty shadows at Craggin Rocks. Although it did little to warm them at that early hour, it promised another hot day to come.

'We've come a long way,' Nick said.

Ariel nodded. Although the Minion Hills obscured the Observatory, their vantage point sat just high enough to see the other markers of her journey on the lower slopes—the tops of the transparent domes of the Lures, the monumental rock face at Stone Cliff and the village of Shifting Stones.

But what of the future? She turned around and looked up. Her heart skipped a beat. The upper reaches of Diamond Peak rose majestically before her, topped by the shimmering gown of snow at the summit. She had come a long way across the foothills, but her mountain climbing hadn't even begun, and she knew now, only too well, the kind of demons that waited on those steep slopes to kill or enslave her. As always, the prospect of her journey excited and terrified her in equal measures. She did have two demons down though—only three to go—and had covered three quarters of the travelling distance. It was just unfortunate that the last portion would make the lower slopes look like a children's game. With a sigh, she turned back to the known.

'I don't like the look of that cloud.' Nick pointed to a grey blanket encroaching almost imperceptibly from the west. 'I'd say this warm weather won't last long.'

'Let's go for a run,' Ariel suggested. 'Just for fun.'

'What? For fun? Are you joking?'

'No. I like running.'

He snorted. 'You're welcome to it.' He left, shaking his head as if she'd said something crazy, and left her to her disappointment.

She'd imagined them running together, along a beach, but clearly that really was just a fantasy.

23

Another Feral Magan

A volley of wand and sceptre fire suddenly exploded through the still morning air. Ariel jumped. A shot of adrenalin pumped through her veins and, without a word, she and Nick raced towards the sound, drawing their weapons and setting magic shields as they ran. At the north-eastern corner of the building, they stopped and peered around.

On the ragged slope behind the Hermitage, Walnut crouched at the back of a ledge, dodging wand fire and blasting lightning into the rocks above. Nick glanced at Ariel. She nodded, agreeing to the plan she'd read in his eyes. They split up. Ariel scrambled to the east of the assassin, ducking between rocks and trees, and Nick climbed stealthily around to the west.

Ariel held her breath as she came within range of the attacker. A dark-haired Magan's head appeared above the rocks. He fired his wand at Walnut, then ducked under cover before the old guide's answering fire could catch him. When the attacker appeared again, she blasted a beam of brilliant white fire from the end of her sword—ten out of ten for awesomeness—and hit him in the side. He flinched, spun in her direction and returned fire.

She threw herself to the ground. A rock sizzled behind her, and the smell of wand fire—like burnt magnesium—filled the air. A blast sounded from the other side of Walnut. Nick, probably. Beams of sceptre fire crackled overhead and shattered rocks around the assassin. Movement below her caught her eye. The Haba guards had arrived and added their sceptres to the scuffle. Suddenly outnumbered, the green-cloaked Magan slunk off into the rocks above the Hermitage with Nick and the Haba in zealous pursuit. Ariel scrambled from her hiding place to join them, but Walnut called out.

'Stay, Ariel. Help me down.'

Warned by the muted pain in his voice, she hurried towards him. After slipping on the loose dirt between the rocks, she stumbled onto the ledge beside the old man. He leaned against the rock, breathing shallowly, his eyes closed. Ariel gasped at the fist-sized hole burnt through his shirt on his shoulder. She raced to his side, lifted the burned cloth and peered in, sucking in a sharp breath when she saw the depth of the wound. 'Ouch.'

'It is sad times indeed when an old man can't sit innocently in the fresh air without someone trying to kill him,' Walnut muttered.

Ariel stood and shouted up the mountain. 'Nick! Come back. Walnut needs you!' But the crackle of wand fire drowned her voice.

'Don't fuss,' Walnut said, clambering to his feet. 'I'll live.'

She helped him up and, keeping her eyes and hands away from the burn, supported his small frame as he walked across the ledge. She tried sending a mental message to Nick, hoping that their energetic connection might become telepathic, but she got no response. They made their way unsteadily down the steps carved in the rock and across the open area towards the Hermitage.

Geordie met them as he raced out the back door, sword in hand. 'Oh my goodness,' he declared, then ran back inside calling for Deidre.

Ariel planned to take Walnut to the kitchen where it was warm and light, but, even though he leaned heavily on her, he insisted on going to his rooms upstairs.

'I'll be all right,' he assured her, though his voice lacked its usual vibrancy. 'I just need to lie still.' Ariel's heart twisted. The old man suddenly seemed terribly frail, and although he showed little pain, the burn must be excruciating.

Walnut's rooms had a similar layout to Ariel's and, warmed by thick carpets, curtains and tapestries, had the same cosy feel. The sun hadn't penetrated the cold stone corridors, but embers still glowed in Walnut's little stove in his living room, and the thick walls retained the warmth. As they passed through the living room into his bedroom, Ariel sensed that, unlike his sparsely furnished room at Sheldra, this place was his home.

She eased him onto his bed, and Deidre arrived with an ice-filled cloth. She placed it straight on the wound, told Ariel she'd be back in a jiff with the right herbs, then bustled off again making tut-tutting sounds. Walnut lay unmoving on his bed, his eyes closed. 'Leave me. I'm fine,' he whispered, but he didn't sound fine at all.

Ariel waited for a couple of minutes, then when he didn't move or speak again, she went into his sitting room, stoked up the fire and looked around. A small table and three chairs claimed one corner of the room. A large desk next to a set of shelves laden with books occupied another corner. The requisite sofa sat at an angle to the fire, and a small shrine to the great guides nestled against the wall to the left of his bedroom door. A photo of Maya, his own guide, took the central position.

A lump rose in Ariel's throat when she saw the framed photograph on the desk. Taken at the back of the Hermitage in the snow, the photo showed Ariel's mother holding baby Ariel in her arms with her smiling husband beside her, his arm firmly around Nadima's waist. Kestril stood stiffly at Aarod's side and Walnut grinned happily beside Nadima.

Pieces of Ariel's life shifted and fell into place. No wonder Walnut had seemed so familiar the first time she'd seen him. No wonder he felt like a grandfather to her. Tears pricked the corners of her eyes. Why hadn't Nadima told her? She felt so much rich history in this place, stories Nadima had never told her, and memories that should have been hers, but her mother had allowed her to forget.

Footsteps ran up the stairs. 'Ariel, where are you?' Nick's voice echoed along the stone corridor.

'Here!' She stuck her head out the door.

He strode swiftly along the corridor towards her, his face taut with concern. 'What's wrong? Are you all right?'

'I'm fine but Walnut's not,' she replied, and led him straight into Walnut's bedroom where the old guide lay unmoving on the bed.

Nick knelt beside the bed, lifted Deidre's icepack and handed it to Ariel, then held his hands over the wound. His eyes turned dark and moist, his breathing deepened and slowed, but the wound remained unchanged. He frowned. Ariel chewed her lip, willing the healing to be successful. 'Okay, you can stop that now, Walnut,' Nick murmured a moment later. 'In this, I'm quicker than you.'

'And more skilled, without a doubt,' the old man whispered.

Both men breathed more deeply then, and the wound gradually healed. Nick dropped his hands. Walnut opened his eyes and grinned. Ariel breathed freely again.

'Out of the way, quickly,' Deidre shouted, bustling into the room. 'Come on, let me near him.'

Ariel and Nick stepped aside. Walnut sat up, and Ariel suppressed a giggle at his cheeky little boy grin.

Deidre frowned and glanced from smiling face to smiling face. 'What?' She lifted the burnt edge of Walnut's shirt and peered in, then turned on Ariel. 'Are you playing tricks on old Deidre?'

'No. Nick healed him.'

Deidre peered at Nick. 'No!'

'Yes,' Nick replied, nodding his head.

Geordie arrived just as Twitchet bounded onto the bed and they both peered at Walnut's shoulder.

'Good job, lover boy,' Twitchet said. 'They told me it was bad.'

'It was,' Geordie confirmed. 'I saw it.'

'Well, I never,' Deidre said. 'You could have told me not to bother with all this.' She indicated her basket of poultices.

'Sorry, Deidre,' Ariel replied. 'I didn't know if Nick would come back in time.'

'Did you catch the fellow?' Walnut asked.

Nick shook his head. 'A Doharven according to the colour of his cloak. The others were still looking when I came back. I had a feeling I was needed.' He looked at Ariel. 'Was that you?'

She grinned and nodded.

'Good work.' His eyes twinkled, and she felt his excitement at the prospect of developing telepathic communication.

'I'm lost,' Twitchet meowed from where he'd settled on Walnut's lap.

'Tough,' Ariel replied dismissively.

Twitchet growled.

'Why aren't you kind to the sweet little kitty?' Deidre asked Ariel in a scolding tone.

'It's just play, Deidre, banter, for fun. I don't really mean it and neither does he. Actually, I'm very fond of him.'

'I don't believe it,' Twitchet replied, but his expression looked a lot like a smile.

Walnut stroked him and Twitchet began to purr.

'Radric came back,' Geordie told them. 'He said Trone and Narbor will stay on lookout. I'll go and tell them you are all right.'

'Thank you,' Walnut replied as Geordie left, then he looked brightly at the others and swung his legs over the edge of the bed. 'Time to train,' he said gaily.

'Oh, no,' Deidre protested, 'you have to rest first.'

Walnut stood and walked from the room, chuckling. Ariel and Nick followed.

'He is impossible,' Deidre grumbled as she collected her basket.

'What was Walnut doing when you told him to stop?' Ariel asked Nick as they walked down the stairs.

'He'd put himself in a sort of coma,' Nick explained, 'a way to focus on healing. Given enough time, he probably could have healed himself, but it slowed me down.'

'Wow.'

'Yeah. Noble ones have all sorts of useful powers.'

***

In the library, several high, narrow windows spilled crisp light across the floor to ceiling bookshelves. Two reading lamps sat on a large table—the only electric lights in the building other than one standard lamp in the sitting room next door and a general light in the kitchen. With only oil lamps to light the rest of the building, there'd be no reading in bed at the Hermitage, Ariel thought as she followed Nick through the ancient, well-stocked library to the training room.

The pungent smell of incense wafted over them as they stepped through the door into a moderately-sized room. It had the same kind of windows as the library, with the addition of coloured glass in the uppermost panes which cast warm red and gold light into an otherwise chilly room. Directly ahead, against the stone wall, sat a shrine to the guides of the past—a multitude of small statues and framed images on a cloth-covered cabinet. Paintings on cloth hangings, depicting the Radiant Bodies of the Noble Ones, hung on the walls. Ariel wondered, if she defeated Rasama and stood on the summit of Diamond Peak like they had, would someone paint her like this, decked in silks and jewels and emitting rays of light?

Nick sat on a cushion and waited quietly while Ariel wandered around the room, feasting on the rich imagery, and letting the atmosphere inspire her mind into a deep clear stillness. Walnut arrived just as she discovered a photo of Maya on the shrine.

'That one is Greystar,' he said, pointing to the photograph of a tall thin man with a long white beard.

'He looks like a wizard,' Ariel said.

Walnut chuckled. 'Indeed he does.' He then named the rest of the guides whose images sat on the shrine. 'Your training now,' he continued, as he settled on the floor and gestured for Ariel to do the same, 'will gradually move towards experiencing yourself in your Radiant Body and learning to direct the power of your Radiance in ways that are highly effective on the Radiant Layer of reality and, if one is skilled enough, can also be used to affect the material plane.'

Magic?

Walnut cleared his throat. 'Affecting the Radiant Layer of reality is more than adequate for defeating demons,' he said sternly.

Ariel blushed. Walnut had already warned her not to focus on trying to manipulate the physical world until she had defeated Rasama. Don't get stuck in the Magan's byway, he had told her—meaning not to make gaining magical power more important than defeating the demons. Evidently, once she had killed Rasama, magical ability would come naturally.

Deidre, Radric and Dorn walked in and took a seat on the floor. Geordie sat on a chair behind them.

'Where's Twitchet?' Nick asked.

'He's going to try to make up with Thomas,' Geordie replied dryly, but his eyes smiled.

Nick raised his eyebrows in amusement. 'I'd say that's a lost cause.'

'Let us begin,' Walnut said.

In the stillness of that ancient room, every thought that arose in Ariel's mind slipped away as easily as it had come. After a few minutes of silence, Walnut began chanting the Pathmaker's incantation. Ariel joined the chant and, following Walnut's instructions, imagined the Pathmaker's body of golden Light alive in the space before her.

Rainbow light streamed from him and filled every pore of her being. Her Serpentine shrivelled in the brilliance and her body lightened, as if shrugging off its physical form. Her mind soared and flew into the luminous figure, merged, one with him, then dissolved into a pinpoint of light. As the light itself vanished into space, Ariel's mind expanded into the endless crystal clarity of her Radiant Nature.

For many minutes, the company stayed without moving, enjoying their mental freedom, feeling their joint power and directing it where they wished or, like Ariel, focusing on strengthening their ability to maintain that mind state regardless of what might arise.

Twitchet slunk into the room and sat between Nick and Deidre just as Walnut closed the session.

'Oh, Twitchet, dear,' Deidre said, peering at a fresh scratch on the little cat's nose.

'Don't fuss, it's nothing,' Twitchet replied.

'What happened?' Nick asked, a twinkle of amusement in his eyes.

Twitchet said nothing.

'I told him Thomas might be offended if he tried to help him catch that rat,' Geordie said with a grin.

'I'll never understand the feline mind,' Twitchet grumbled.

'What about your own?' Deidre asked.

Twitchet ignored her and sidled up to Nick. 'Can I borrow your finger for a moment?'

Nick obligingly placed his finger on the cat's nose, healing it instantly. 'There, all done,' he declared.

Everyone left to get on with their day then, except for Ariel. Walnut gave her some extra anti-Emot training. 'All of your training has been to bring your mind home to its natural stillness and clarity, and to rest there, without chasing after the thoughts, feelings and perceptions that draw you away from your true self. All Emot really does is make it harder to do that. He lures you with the promise of pleasure, praise, gain and even fame, and an untrained mind reaches for these hollow dreams instead of being satisfied with reality.

'You know how vivid he can make these promises, and do not think that your tendency to crave the pleasure Nick brings you has disappeared just because he has returned. You must remain vigilant. Enjoy your pleasure, but don't try to hold onto it or chase after it.' He fixed her with a piercing gaze, the kind that penetrated the depths of her mind. She met it without a single thought. 'What is your weapon?' he asked. A test.

'Recognise the hooks and dissolve them by seeing them for what they are, just an illusion, a hollow promise.'

'Exactly, shine the light of your awareness onto the darkness and it dissolves instantly.'

'Then send the energy of the unobscured light down my blade and ram it into the beast's gut.'

Walnut chuckled. 'Ten out of ten.'

Ariel scanned the room. With her mind open after the morning practice, everything seemed slightly dreamlike anyway,

even the granite walls, their solidity a kind of frozen luminosity.
'I've been doing okay,' she said.

24

Shopping

Nick led Ariel out the door at the end of the downstairs corridor and down a short, covered walkway to a garage-sized building. Inside, a transparent, pyramid-shaped Portal the size of a large lift swirled with rainbow light. Ariel marvelled at the beauty of the perfect geometric form and the power of the mind that made it.

'So how do we drive it?' she asked, stopping outside the door.

'Think of where you want to go and visualise it clearly,' Nick replied, 'but only think of one place or you could find yourself flickering.'

'Flickering?' She didn't like the sound of that.

'Yeah, if you don't give the portal clear directions, it gets confused about where to take you and you can end up with your molecules sort of flickering in and out of different places.'

'Ew, how do you get out of that?'

'Think clearly, but I've never heard of it actually happening, after all, you only have to hold your focus for a couple of seconds, so it isn't really that hard.'

'The thought of flickering should be enough to keep your mind in the right place.'

'Yeah. Are you ready?'

Ariel nodded, slid the glass door open and stepped into the swirling rainbows. Nick followed and closed the door behind him, his eyes shining in the magical light. He took her hand and gave her a reassuring smile.

'Think of Sheldra, close your eyes and off we go.'

Ariel visualised the Great Hall at the University of Sheldra, and a low hum filled the portal. The light felt like a warm wind dancing around her. Her skin tingled uncomfortably; her body grew light and she sensed herself tumbling through space. A roar like a raging windstorm filled her ears. She lost all sensation for a moment, then it returned with a gut load of nausea.

'We're here,' Nick said.

She opened her eyes, staggered sideways and fell into Nick's arms, clutching her stomach.

'It's lucky I came with you,' he said, helping her to stand.

'You didn't say it'd make me feel sick,' she complained.

'It doesn't make me sick,' he replied, opening the door. 'Take a seat.' He gestured to a bench outside the portal. 'Now I know why they have them.'

Ariel staggered from the portal, slumped onto the wooden bench and breathed deeply until her head cleared. The Sheldra portal sat under a roof supported by granite columns in a leafy park just outside the University grounds. Around them buzzed the township of Sheldra, and the people going about their busy lives as usual made Ariel feel as if she inhabited a slightly different reality, as if she existed one step back and to the side of everyone else. When her legs felt stable enough to walk on, she declared it time to go, and they ambled hand in hand out of the park and down the main street of Sheldra. The bright sunny day, the pretty façades of the old buildings and the sheer ordinariness of their shopping trip soon brought Ariel back to reality. Just girlfriend and boyfriend, like any teenage couple, she thought happily. Except that Nick wasn't a teenager.

He took her to a well-stocked camping shop first and Ariel was delighted to find a much improved later model of her sleeping tube, the lightweight one-person tent she'd had on her pack. Apparently, whoever owned the shop bought their goods from off-mountain. 'Maybe it was a good thing we lost the packs,' she mused as they paid.

She didn't think that when she bought a new copy of *The Guide to the Mountain Path*, though. The latest version didn't have the beautiful gold embossed title like the one Maya had given her, or the handwritten notes in the side margins. It didn't have the same strong paper or the sweet smell, and it lacked the presence of other fingers turning its pages, or curious eyes feasting on its secrets.

Ariel was, however, thrilled with the leather Magan belt. Wide enough to be a mini skirt and covered in pockets of various useful sizes, she'd wanted one ever since she'd first seen one in the village of Carvell deep in the Minion Hills. She couldn't resist a fine woollen tunic, soft shirt and skinny-leg jeans to go under it, either. Had she brought too many Magan style clothes? No. With her copper-coloured hair, no one would ever mistake her for a Magan.

Nick never once complained, and she gave him little reason to since she was quick to decide what she wanted, and whenever she asked his opinion, he gave an honest appraisal.

'The green definitely suits you better,' he said when she showed him two different sweaters, 'and you look great in the Magan pants. No, that's not right, you look great in everything. What I meant to say was that the Magan pants look good on you. Too good actually.' He grinned mischievously and brushed his fingers gently over her cheek. His eyes fixed on hers, the energetic communication unmistakably predatory, but where she'd rejected it before, she revelled in it now. She also recognised the love that flowed with it and realised how much she loved his constant attention, even when she hadn't admitted it and had been fending him off. She wouldn't take him for granted again.

'Will you still pounce on me when I'm old and grey?' she asked, only half joking.

'Definitely,' he replied, dead serious. 'I take Walnut and Miramar as my model.'

She smiled and felt the soft spot in the centre of her chest weep for what Walnut had lost when Miramar died. They had been like young lovers, living each moment together as if it were their last. Just as well, Ariel thought, for Miramar's death at the hands of a Mage Clan Magan was a sudden tragedy. A death that had been meant for her!

'Where have you gone?' Nick asked, watching the far away look in her eyes.

'Minion Hills, Miramar's house,' she replied.

Nick sighed. 'Me too.' He took her hand, lifted it to his lips and kissed her knuckles. 'I never want to miss a moment with you.'

She grinned, grabbed his hand, pulled him into the change room and closed the door.

His eyes widened. 'What are you doing?'

'Having fun.' She kissed him expectantly. He kissed her back, but briefly, then disentangled himself from her arms like some kind of prim schoolmaster.

Who was this person? This wasn't how it was supposed to happen. Her preferred version of reality flashed into her mind: a tangle of arms, lips and skin against glorious skin, plus the excitement of a forbidden place. That was the real Nick, surely. Did the one before her have some kind of thou-shalt-not-kiss-in-public phobia? She'd seen no indication of it before.

He put his hand on the door knob, preparing to leave, but she slipped between him and the door and wrapped her arms around his neck. 'Scaredy cat,' she teased.

He jerked away.

'Oh, for God's sake! It's just a cuddle.'

He shook his head. 'No, it's a lot more dangerous than that. It's clammy, sticky Emot food and, frankly, it makes me feel a little claustrophobic.'

Ariel recoiled as if he'd slapped her face. A mixture of guilt and rejection coiled in her gut.

He pushed past her and left the room. Ariel fought back tears.

She bought the sweater while he waited outside and joined him with some trepidation.

'Let's have lunch,' he said, thankfully with no sign of the distaste he'd shown in the shop. 'There's a lovely little cafe in the park.'

Ariel nodded and followed him silently, across a verdant lawn and past bright flowerbeds and a children's playground, to a cafe overlooking a small lake. They sat on the terrace in the shade of a leafy tree, ordered open sandwiches and salad and watched the swans on the lake as they ate. The energy flowed clean and clear between them. He even reached across the table and held her hand as if to reassure her that he loved her.

Something tightened in her chest, and suddenly, she feared losing him so much that she wanted to rope him to her side and never let him loose.

He dropped her hand abruptly. 'There it is again.'

She rolled her eyes. 'I just like being with you, that's all.'

Nick's lips curled in a bemused smile. 'I like being with you too; but if I'm scared that the pleasure won't last and I cling to it like a drowning man to a lifebuoy, or crave it like an alcoholic desperate for a drink, then it's Emot food.'

Ariel frowned. 'I wouldn't have been clingy if you hadn't pushed me away.'

'I wouldn't have pushed you away if you hadn't been clingy.'

'What's wrong with wanting a cuddle?'

'Nothing, if that's all it is, but it wasn't, you were expecting me to be what you want me to be, but maybe that isn't who I am.'

Ariel's jaw dropped. 'You can't know that!'

He snorted. 'It's me. I can feel it, remember? You're holding on so tight it's suffocating.'

Ariel gulped. 'I really did just want a cuddle.'

Another raised eyebrow. 'Trust me. I'm not going to run away.'

He could be killed though, and there was a green-eyed demon keen to make that happen. Ariel placed her hand on the centre of her chest, breathed away the tightness and drew her mind back to the present where Nick sat alive and well before her. How could she appreciate the present if her mind was worrying about a future that may never happen?

He pulled a delicate white flower from the bunch in a vase on the table, curled his fingers around it and held his hand in front of him, in a loose fist, fingers towards the ground. 'We fear letting go because we think this will happen.' He released his fingers and the flower fluttered to the ground. 'But actually, it's like this.' He picked up the flower and curled his fingers around it again, but this time he turned his hand so that his palm faced upwards. Slowly, he unfurled his fingers, revealing the fragile bell-shaped flower, nestled safely in the palm of his hand.

'But we're so scared we'll lose things that this is what we do.' He closed his fingers over the flower once more and squeezed until the skin on his knuckles stretched taut with tension. When he unfurled his fingers, the flower, battered beyond repair, its petals bruised and broken, lay like a corpse in his hand, and there were marks where his fingernails had dug into his palms.

'All we let go of is the pain.' He took her hand and stroked her fingers. 'No moment will ever come again like this one and knowing that makes everything so much more vibrant and precious. If I try to make each moment permanent, or try to make it into something else, I lose that.'

'Yeah; I know.' So what if he isn't into kissing in a change room, who cares?

Nick nodded. 'And how does this feel now, this precious moment?' He ran his finger across her throat.

She smiled and closed her eyes. 'Precious; very precious.'

After lunch, they wandered over to the University to pick up some things from Nick's room, but they crept away without seeing Yule, Maya or Layla. They didn't want to have to explain anything just then, and Layla and Maya would join them at the Hermitage as soon as they had finished teaching the course that the battle of Craggin Plain had terminated so abruptly for Ariel.

The Portal ride back to the Hermitage went more smoothly than Ariel's first attempt. The roaring sound, and the whirling and falling sensations were just as intense, but she arrived feeling just dizzy, instead of both sick and dizzy. Light cloud cover had begun to descend over the peak, and the temperature was slowly dropping, but the view down the mountain remained unobscured. For now.

'Ah, the youngsters are back,' Geordie said when Nick and Ariel wandered into the kitchen after stowing their packages in their rooms. 'Come with me; I have something for you.'

Ariel glanced at Nick, but he just shrugged his shoulders and gave her an I-know-nothing kind of look.

Geordie led them to the stables, stopped just outside the door and told them to stand still and close their eyes. They did. His footsteps faded into the stables and, a moment later, hooves clattered towards them on the cobblestones, bridles jangled and horses snorted, eager to run. Ariel smelt the unmistakable smell of horse and leather, and felt warm horsey breath on her hand.

'You can open them now,' Geordie said.

She opened her eyes, smiled at the pretty bay mare in front of her and stroked her velvety nose. 'She's lovely.'

'And so's this one,' Nick added, patting the black gelding nuzzling his stomach in search of a treat.

'Walnut said you might enjoy some riding,' Geordie said. 'So these are yours while you're here. Yours is Mandy, Ariel, and, Nick, yours is called Grey. Don't ask me why. That's the name he came with, but they're both Magan horses.'

Ariel smiled. 'Thank you, Geordie; I'd love to have a ride.'

'Off you go then.'

Ariel glanced at Nick. He nodded. 'Now's as good a time as any.'

They mounted their horses and Geordie adjusted their stirrups. 'By the way, has there been any sign of the Magan?' Nick asked.

The old man shook his head. 'The Haba think he's disappeared down a Rasa hole. They can't find one, but it's probably just well hidden. You'll be safe on the open land.'

'So long as no one lights another fire,' Ariel said dourly.

'Won't do any harm now,' Geordie replied. 'There's nothing left to burn.' He patted Grey's rump. 'Off you go now.'

Five minutes later, Nick raced Ariel across the plain, hair and manes flying behind them. Blackened earth flicked from the thundering hooves and Ariel's heart soared with the excitement of riding for pure pleasure.

***

After their ride, Ariel and Nick returned, invigorated, to the Hermitage and discovered Kestril and Tynan sitting at the table in the kitchen. Tynan had a pot of tea in front of him and sipped from a fine china cup and Kestril gripped a large cup steaming with the aroma of strong coffee. The contrast between the two men couldn't have been greater, one with fair hair and beard, the other with hair and beard as black as night.

Tynan stood to greet them, smiling broadly. His eyes crinkled behind his spectacles. 'Ah, Nick, my boy, and Ariel, good to see you. Walnut tells us you had another close escape on the way here.'

'Luckily, he was with us,' Nick replied as he shook Tynan's long fingered hand. The tall scientist wore two large silver rings and one of his characteristic flowing shirts, this one mauve. His sword hung on a sturdy leather belt at his side.

Ariel felt Kestril's intense green eyes on her and turned to face him. He returned her stare coolly, his rugged face impassive. What was it with him? The olive-skinned man wore his usual Magan gear—leather pants and jerkin over a soft white shirt and the purple velvet cape of a Menhir. Though a Magan, he also carried the sceptre of a Warrior in a pouch on his belt, right next to his wand and sharp gilded knife. This combination of Mage Clan magician and advanced Warrior made him a rare and dangerous man, one that Ariel still couldn't fathom.

25

The Past Unveiled

After a quick afternoon tea, Ariel joined Walnut for another practice session. When they had finished, he took a fist-sized embroidered bag from the cupboard under the shrine and handed it to her.

'What is it?'

His eyes twinkled above a characteristically cheeky grin. 'Open it and find out.'

'She can be so slow sometimes,' Twitchet meowed from where he sat on the sofa.

'Go chase rats,' Ariel replied.

'Can't. I promised Thomas I'd leave it to him. But I might see if I can sniff out where that Magan went.'

'Good idea,' Walnut said.

Twitchet ambled from the room while Ariel pulled a double-sided, hand-painted drum from the bag. 'What's this for?' she asked, running her fingers over the letters embroidered on the cloth handle.

'Magan script,' Walnut said, 'made long before the clans split, when Magans still actively supported those who sought the peak.'

'I mean, what's the drum for?'

'Calling demons.'

'Great,' Ariel said sarcastically. 'Do I get to choose which ones and how many?'

'That depends.'

'On?'

'What you're thinking at the time.'

'Oh.'

'You hold it like this.' He took the drum and showed her how to position her fingers between the two halves of the drum and grasp the handle in her hand. 'Then you flick your wrist, like this.' As he rotated his forearm rapidly backwards and forwards, two beads on strings flew against the sides of the drum and made a quick, sharp rhythm. He handed her back the drum. 'When you're ready, I want you to call up Emot.'

Suddenly, Ariel felt as if she was sliding down a long slippery slope pushed from behind by some unstoppable force. She had nothing to hold onto, nothing to stop her downward movement, and at the bottom of the slide waited a huge mouth with glistening sharp teeth.

'Think about him as you roll the drum,' Walnut continued, 'and stop as soon as he or an emanation appears.'

'I suppose if I keep going I get the whole army, do I?' Ariel asked, only half joking.

'I think your arm would fall off long before that happened,' Walnut assured her with a twinkle in his eye. 'Of course, it's up to you, but I would like you to give it a go in the next day or so. Let me know when you're ready.'

Ariel nodded, but she couldn't stop that sinking feeling. Emot terrified her in a way the other Major Rasas didn't. They scared her too, of course, but there was something deeply seductive about Emot, something she didn't dare admit to Walnut. Even so, she figured she might as well give it a try. She'd have plenty of back up if anything went wrong. 'How about tomorrow after training?'

'Perfect,' Walnut said. 'And before you go to sleep tonight, review everything you learnt with Layla and Maya. Now, go, Tynan will be waiting.'

She met the sword master behind the Hermitage, keen to get moving, for the sun that had greeted their arrival at the Hermitage had disappeared beneath an icy cloud. The thick cloud cover showed no sign of lifting and a chill had settled over the mountain.

✳✳✳

After dinner, the Warriors assembled in the sitting room to enjoy the fire and company. Two of the four Haba guards stayed outside on watch while the other two played cards with Tynan, Geordie, Deidre and Nick. Walnut read in one of the comfy chairs and Ariel curled up in the other with a notebook, trying to remember the main points from her studies with Layla and Maya. She stared at the few sentences she'd written on the page. They were just words, black ink on white paper, a sound spoken or thought; she might remember them and understand them, but did she know them enough to live them? She doubted it, but consoled herself that at least she was working on it.

The door opened and closed. Ariel shivered involuntarily, and not from the cool of the night that slipped in with the late arrival. She knew without looking that it was Kestril. He had said nothing during dinner, but she'd felt his cool gaze on her. Since Walnut had said that the Magan would accompany them on the next leg of her journey, she figured it high time they sorted out whatever his problem was. She took a deep breath and sat beside him on the sofa.

'Why do you hate me?'

He turned his gaze from the fire to her, his green eyes piercing in their intensity, his face impassive as usual. 'I don't hate you.'

'You look at me like you do.'

One side of his lip curled up and he snorted. 'I don't mean to,' he said before turning back to the fire.

'If it's not hatred, then what is it?' Kestril didn't reply or move; was he even considering her question? 'How can I trust you if I don't know how you feel about me?' she continued.

He snorted disdainfully, but looked at her again. 'I am used to people mistrusting me. Why should I care whether you do?'

'I don't know, I guess I thought you might prefer me to trust you.'

'I don't require anything from you.' Once again, he returned his attention to the fire.

Ariel sighed. *This is like trying to squeeze oil from a rock.* 'Why do you look at me so coldly sometimes?'

Kestril's jaw tightened, but he kept his eyes firmly on the fire.

'Tell me.' She glared at him—a dose of his own medicine.

He sighed, no doubt realising that she wasn't about to give up. 'You remind me too much of your father and mother.'

Ariel blinked in surprise. 'Didn't you like them?'

'Huh!' He turned abruptly, eyes flashing onto hers. 'Your father was my best friend … Your hair … when I see it, I see him. You're a constant reminder of what I couldn't prevent.'

'Oh.' That wasn't the kind of answer she expected at all. 'I'm sorry.'

Kestril snorted gloomily. 'So am I, Ariel. So am I.'

'What about my mother? Was she your friend too?'

'I think she hated me, and she certainly never trusted me.'

Ariel frowned. 'I see.'

'You see nothing.'

Ariel swallowed. The conversation was more difficult than she had feared. 'Then help me to see,' she pleaded. 'Why didn't Nadima like you?'

'I don't know.' His tone hinted at poorly concealed pain. 'Perhaps she resented how close I was to Aarod. We were like brothers.'

Ariel nodded and they both stared into the fire. 'How did he die?' she whispered a moment later.

Kestril closed his eyes, his normally impassive expression broken with pain. He took a deep breath. 'He fell.'

Ariel's chest tightened at how difficult this was for him. 'From where?'

'We were on the scree slope above Madyi. Someone, Rasama I expect, for Cogin was dead at Aarod's hand, set a huge rock rolling down the slope. It came quickly and we leapt to the side, but Aarod slipped on the gravel and fell.' Kestril's eyes glazed over, as if gazing back in time, and his jaw clenched as he fought, unsuccessfully, to stop the rage and grief from showing on his face. 'I called out but couldn't do anything to help him. The scree was unstable, the rock almost upon us. I saw that Aarod had landed on a ledge, saw him wave, trying to reassure me that he was all right. The rock crashed past me, close enough that I felt the wind of its passing. It landed on your father and crushed him to death.'

Neither Kestril nor Ariel moved or spoke for some time. He brought his expression under control, but she could feel his pain—his pain, her pain, Nadima's pain. She felt his regret and frustration at his inability to save her father.

'I couldn't even reach him,' he murmured, his eyes moist. 'I set the light above him and I rolled enough shingle down to cover the visible parts of his body, and that was the best I could do for the one man I would happily have given my life for.'

Ariel's heart cracked open. She wanted to embrace him, to help heal the pain, but he remained Kestril, remote and untouchable. He'd gone far away, back on that cursed slope again, and Ariel found herself reliving the memory with him.

The demon's laughter rang in his ears. Tears pricked at the corner of his eyes and a sick feeling twisted his gut. His heart had shattered, crushed along with Aarod. Anger and grief throbbed through his being and, though he wanted to rail around in it like a madman, like the well trained Warrior that he was, he simply watched it pass. At least he hadn't fed the demon, he thought grimly. He hadn't the heart to go on alone and he hadn't been back since. So much had been lost that day, and Aarod's death had rendered the prophecy a lie.

He had wondered how he could tell Nadima, so immersed as she was in her little girl. No, he couldn't face her. He couldn't be the bearer of such terrible news. But the thought of Aarod's daughter had made him turn back and look around. The blade of Aarod glinted in the sunlight from where it lay just off the track, still where it had fallen from Aarod's hand as he fell. Kestril picked up the dagger and stood once again on that fateful spot, looking down over a man-sized rock and a pile of stones where Aarod's body lay.

Your daughter still lives, Aarod, and she too has the mark. I will make sure that she gets this blade and when the time comes, I will help her fulfill the prophecy. I swear on your body, my good friend, that I will protect your daughter with my life.'

He could not tell Ariel this with words. His voice would surely break if he tried to speak of the unspeakable.

Ariel blinked as the flickering fire at the Hermitage came back into focus. Kestril still stared into the flames. Had he known she'd seen his memory? Had he called her in? If not, how did she get there? She didn't have the heart to ask, so she never did find out. 'Thanks for telling me,' Ariel said quietly after a moment. 'Perhaps one day you could tell me about your good times together. Nadima never said anything about my father and I'd like to know what sort of a man he was.'

'He was the best kind.' Kestril's features softened. 'Kind, reliable, funny, brave, strong, both mentally and physically. We were so close, Ariel, so close to the top of the mountain. We were still young enough to think ourselves invincible and perhaps we should have waited for Walnut that day, but even he couldn't have saved Aarod from that rock.'

Ariel put her hand on Kestril's arm and smiled at him. 'I can see that he had a good friend in you, Kestril. If my father trusted you, then I do too.'

'Huh!' Kestril snorted. 'I could be lying. I could have killed him myself. No one would know for sure.'

'No. I would know,' Ariel corrected him and looked directly into his eyes. *I saw it.*

Kestril raised one eyebrow. 'Is that so? Then I was right to be careful around you.'

Ariel grinned and Kestril actually smiled. The icy barrier between them had begun to melt. 'I'm glad we talked. Thanks. I'm off to bed now.' She stood and headed towards the door. 'Goodnight.'

'Wait, I'm coming too.' Nick stood as she passed the card table.

'Aw, come on, one more hand,' Radric complained.

Nick slapped his friend on the back and grinned. 'Tomorrow. Okay?'

'We should go too,' Dorn said.

Radric nodded. 'Tomorrow and I'll beat the pants off you.'

Nick chuckled and opened the door for Ariel. They walked down the chilly stone corridor past oil lamps set on tables against the wall. At the bottom of the stairs, several sat on a table and Ariel lit one to carry with them.

'Don't you need one?' she asked.

He shook his head. 'Mine's in my room, that's why I wanted to come up with you. I don't fancy navigating my way upstairs in the dark.'

Ariel agreed. Both the Observatory and Sheldra had had gas lamps set in the wall, a big improvement in convenience over these low-tech hand-held lights. The dimness of the light here took a bit of getting used to.

'I hear you're going to call Emot,' he said as they walked along the upstairs corridor.

'Walnut's idea, not mine.'

'Are you ready?'

She shrugged.

They stopped outside the Maloney family rooms. 'As your tutor, I suggest a test is in order,' he said. She didn't have to ask to know exactly what kind of test he referred to. He leaned towards her, eyes twinkling roguishly and planted a delicious kiss on her lips. 'Mmm, not bad,' he mumbled, then kissed her some more, passionately this time.

Ariel almost purred like a kitten with cream at the pleasure flowing through her body, but the memory of his disgust at her clinging made her cautious, and she watched her mind carefully, so carefully, in fact, that no fantasy lured her, even when his kisses became neck nibbles and he pulled her close against him.

'Excellent. You passed with flying colours,' he said, and reached around her to open the door.

She lit the lamp on her table—refilled by Geordie every day—then Nick bade her goodnight and took the lamp they had carried to his room one door down.

Ariel sighed as the door closed behind him. She didn't want to have to be so cautious with him. Their physical relationship should be free and natural, not hobbled by this fear of creating Emot food. She had imagined them being closer now that she'd stopped trying to keep him away, but it seemed that the more she wanted him, the more he withdrew. She wanted the old Nick back.

She shouldn't expect more, she told herself as she sat on her bed, it would only lead to disappointment, but the seed of discontent would not be so easily dismissed; it sat in her heart like a smoldering lump of coal. She thought of Kestril's revelation instead, and that led her to wonder if she would ever see her mother again.

In the past, such thoughts would have left her feeling helpless, but Maya had shown her how to help. Ariel sat tall and whispered the incantation for connecting with her Radiance. The power of it swelled in her chest, then burst forth in the form of Radiant Light. She imagined her mother and sent the light to strengthen her and weaken any Serpentine in or around her, be it in parasite or demon form. Even if it didn't help Nadima much, Ariel thought, it sure made her feel better. At least she'd done something.

***

Emot Sai, his face twisted with fury, burst into the cell with two other Rasas. He pulled Nadima roughly from her chair—another perk from pleasing him—and kicked it out of the way. Nadima cringed and her heart beat faster. He hadn't treated her like that for a long time.

'What tricks are you up to, witch?' he screamed. One of his henchmen grabbed her from behind and held so tightly that his claws dug into her arms. 'Why have I not grown when you feed me as I demand?'

'Perhaps I am too weak to sustain you, Master,' she replied, using the deferential tone that pleased him.

His face twitched and the fire in his eyes flickered up his face. 'Your flavour is good, but I do not grow stronger. Whatever magic you have used against me will stop now. No one tricks Emot Sai and gets away with it!'

Nadima recoiled in fear. She'd never seen him so angry. 'Sorry, Emot Sai, I don't know what's wrong.'

'You lie! But now, my pretty one, it's time to give up your tricks. Stop your cruel magic or I will use this little instrument on you. It will cause me no pain, but for you, it will not be pleasant.'

He raised his arm. A knife gleamed in his hand, and his sly smile became triumphant.

Nadima's heart leapt into a sprint. He knew her weakest spot, physical pain. He'd always got his way by inflicting it on her, but he paid a price. When he'd pushed his talon into her flesh, making her scream with agony, she'd sent Radiant Power to the wound and made his talon burn so fiercely that he couldn't stand it. Though she mostly succumbed to his will before he gave up, he'd not resorted to inflicting pain since she'd begun feeding him on demand. Now he could cut her without risking a burning talon. She was at his mercy, and mercy was not something demons were known for.

'You don't need to do that, Sai,' she said. 'I'll let you grow, I promise. Give it a day or two and you'll see.'

'We'll be watching you carefully now, night and day. Any tricks and you can be sure I'll demand the spicy flavour of pain again and again until you beg for mercy.' He laughed cruelly and placed his talon on her neck. Obediently, she fed him with fear that he would carry out his threat. 'Good,' he said after a few moments, 'but your fear has a nasty metallic tang. Give me my favourite flavour.'

Once again, Nadima obeyed and gave herself over to craving the unbearably sensuous touch of his talon resting on her neck. She still limited feeding the big Rasa too much of this particular flavour, and so far, he'd been happy with what she provided. Luckily, Emot Sai didn't want to work too hard for his meal, and he wanted the best possible flavour. For her health and sanity, she needed to hook into that desire now, but she waited until he was satisfied before she spoke again. 'Will you allow me to cleanse myself still, so that I can remain strong enough to feed you?'

'You will still have water provided,' he growled.

'I refer to my inner self. You've seen others fade away after feeding Rasas for too long. That will happen to me unless you allow me one magic. It is harmless to you and will not stop you growing, but it will prevent me from becoming weaker and will keep my flavour pure.'

His eyes narrowed, so that instead of flames, brilliant embers burned behind the slits.

Nadima wondered if he was reaching into the Rasa's shared memory bank to find a picture borrowed from some human brain that would show him what to do. He would find nothing though. No Warrior had been in this situation before. How would he decide what would he do? He hesitated, unsure, so she provided him with an answer. 'Let me show you. You'll see how harmless it is.'

'Go on, but we will be watching closely.'

Nadima set a white light above her head and chanted the incantation that caused it to drip like nectar. The light washed through her body and flushed out the Serpentine that, stimulated by feeding him, had grown around her Radiant Light body. She hoped he couldn't see the slimy black parasite—invisible to all without the Second Sight and part of the network that created the demons. If he couldn't see it, the magic would look harmless; if he could, then he had to decide if diminishing part of the entity he belonged to was an acceptable trade for his own satisfaction.

'Very well,' he growled several moments after she'd dissolved the light.

Nadima reined in a smile and bowed her head to him in deference, knowing it would please him, but in reply, he merely nodded to the henchman holding her. He threw her roughly on the ground, and the Rasas glided from the cell, slamming the door shut behind them.

Nadima crawled to her mattress, lay still and thought of Walnut. His Radiant Form appeared before her in her mind, streamed multicoloured light into every cell in her body, then shrunk into a pinprick of light and dissolved into the centre of her chest. She slept then, free of fear and pain, and awakened with her courage and determination renewed.

After that, a Rasa watched her every hour of the day, especially closely when Emot Sai came to feed. She fed him a smorgasbord of different flavours, offering everything except her craving for his touch, and she fed him quickly, trying to satisfy him before he remembered his favourite flavour. She only provided craving when he insisted on it, and she continued to fade out the flow instead of letting it wear itself out in its own time. She had to risk his wrath at her subterfuge should he find out, for every moment she immersed herself in the painful yearning his touch evoked in her, its lure strengthened and her resistance weakened. The risk of addiction, of complete subjugation to his will, was too high if she didn't retain some control.

After Emot Sai had finished feeding each day, they let her do, what they called, the cleansing magic, but at night they wouldn't allow her to sit up—her guard fired flaming shards at her through the bars if she tried. She didn't risk using her Radiant Light to dissolve the Rasas anymore, unless the guard fell asleep while she was awake—an unfortunately rare occurrence.

One morning, Emot Sai visited early, even before the lamps had been lit in the tunnel. He dragged her roughly from her bed and jerked her to her feet.

'No more inferior flavours,' he hissed.

She faced him impassively, resigned to her fate, knowing the demand he would make of her.

'You will feed me always on your craving for my touch.' His words, their power strengthened by his deathly tone, ripped her last support from beneath her.

'Please, Sai, please,' she begged. 'I feed you enough, I don't undermine you anymore, allow me this last shred of dignity.'

His lips curled into a cruel smile, and he stroked her neck where it gave her the most pleasure. 'Resist, and I will show you the consequences.'

She did, and from along the corridor someone screamed. Nadima's stomach twisted. 'Please. Not that.'

'Willingly crave my touch every time I feed,' Emot Sai whispered seductively. 'Or I will make you watch what we do to them.'

With tears in her eyes, Nadima resisted no more. Her subjugation was complete.

26

Calling Emot

Ariel woke when the pale light crept over the windowsill and the bird's morning call reached its peak. She groaned and buried her head under the pillow. Her life was a roller coaster of demons, training, and a love that was so much more complicated than she could have imagined.

'Grrr.' She rolled onto her back and lifted the pillow off her face. A little girl's room surrounded her, but whoever that three-year-old had been was long gone, only a trace of her in the toys left behind. And where was the nearly eighteen-year-old that, only a few weeks ago, had been preparing for school exams and complaining about her life being boring? Ariel barely recognised herself in what she had so rapidly become—A Defeater of Demons well on her way to becoming a Lady of Light, maybe even a Liberator of Human Kind. Trouble was, before she could become that, she would have to be a Champion of Noble Qualities and that meant defeating Emot, amongst others.

She felt like crying. Was it because she didn't know who she was anymore, or because she had to face a demon she wasn't ready for? She didn't have to, but why not get it over with? I just need a good training session, she told herself, then I'll be ready.

Morning training relaxed Ariel and cleared her mind so that everything that arose in it eased gently away like waves falling back into the ocean. All she had to do was maintain that. As extra support, she awakened the powerful force of her heartfelt desire to help free humankind from the Serpentine and used it to propel silver light from the centre of her chest into the universe. This light of love—poison to Serpentine and demons—spread out in all directions and weakened every form of the parasitic Serpentine that it touched. She smiled with satisfaction as she imagined the light eating away at Emot like acid.

When she had completed her preparations, Ariel led Nick and Walnut to the open area at the back of the Hermitage for her meeting with Emot. Pale grey clouds hung low above them, and Ariel shivered in air that threatened snow.

'We'll hide in case he doesn't come because we're here, but we'll deal with any emanations he brings. Just yell if you want us to get him,' Nick told her.

Ariel nodded. 'I will, don't worry.'

'Good luck,' he smiled and kissed her gently.

'Stay clear,' Walnut told her, his piercing gaze locking on hers.

She nodded and met his gaze, confident in the clarity of her mind. He smiled and nodded his approval, then he and Nick moved off to station themselves nearby. Ariel blew on her hands and rubbed them together before taking the drum from the bag slung across her shoulder and holding it ready.

She checked that her mind was stable—so far so good—then she took a deep breath, exhaled slowly and faced the place where the Magan assassin had disappeared. With a flick of her wrist the drum began its call. 'Come to me, Emot, if you dare. To feed or kill without a care,' she chanted.

Nothing stirred in the lumps of granite fallen from the escarpment that rose up behind the Hermitage. Would he come? Ariel shifted her weight restlessly. She wanted to get it over with and get back indoors to the fire. The breeze grew stronger, and even colder, and still the demon didn't appear. She was considering abandoning the battle when the unmistakable smell of Rasa wafted towards her. She turned into the breeze and gulped, ceasing her chant as the black fluid form of Emot glided between the rocks towards her. He stopped several metres away, a safe distance. His flaming eyes fixed on hers and flushed her with warmth. Was that normal? Shouldn't she be terrified?

'What do you offer me, little one?' he said in a deep smooth voice.

'A chance to feed or kill,' she replied in the traditional way.

'Or be killed,' he replied. 'I am not stupid, and though your offer is tempting indeed, I will not come closer unless your protectors reveal themselves.'

Ariel just stared at him.

'Then I shall not play with you today,' he replied. 'Nor will I come should you call again. I will choose the time and the place.'

He turned away but Ariel called after him. 'No, don't go. Walnut, Nick, come out.'

Emot turned back, his lips curling slightly. Walnut and Nick stepped out of their hiding places. Nick watched the demon with narrowed eyes. 'Send them away,' Emot demanded.

Ariel shook her head, her heart raced and her limbs trembled at the thought of being alone with him.

'Mmm,' the demon mused. 'The old man then, get rid of him and I will call assistance to match your pretty boyfriend.'

Ariel looked at Walnut in desperation. She wasn't prepared for this bargaining. Walnut beckoned to Nick and they joined her.

'It's up to you,' Walnut said quietly.

'Can't you just make yourself invisible and still be here?' Ariel asked.

He shook his head. 'Invisibility spells do not work on demons. They are attuned to our energy more than our visible form, so we can't fool them that way, but Nick is quite capable of protecting you by himself and I will watch from upstairs. How strong do you feel?'

Ariel shrugged and glanced at the Rasa waiting for her. She didn't know if she could defeat him yet, but she didn't want him to go away without having a chance to try. 'I'll be all right so long as Nick can protect me.'

'I don't have a problem with Emots.'

'All right. Keep clear.' Walnut walked towards the Hermitage.

Emot's slit of a mouth curled into a twisted smile. 'I look forward to this.' He pulled his arms back, stretching his chest. A suggestion of muscles flexed beneath his slimy skin. 'Step aside, boy.' He glided closer, skin rippling. Ariel and Nick drew their swords. 'Further apart,' he insisted.

Nick glanced at Ariel. 'It's okay,' she assured him. He moved several metres away, then inched closer until Emot shot him with a glare.

'Enough!' The demon's feeding talon grew long, and he and Ariel faced each other without moving while three emanations glided towards them. 'They will keep lover boy busy,' he said. Liquid fire dripped from his mouth.

Ariel ran at him.

'Yes, come to me, little one,' he crooned seductively, then stepped aside. Her sword thrust into nothing.

The emanations attacked Nick. He blocked their blows and landed a few of his own, his sword cracking a rhythm against their steel-hard talons.

Slithers of fire burst from Emot's talon and raced towards Ariel. She swung her blade, flashing in the cold light, and hacked the brittle flames into pieces. They fell, fading onto the ground, but one found its mark. Ariel's sword froze in a chest block, her eyes wide with shock. Nick's arms were around her, his lips on hers, one hand sliding down her stomach. Heat flushed her cheeks and her limbs trembled. How could a demon make it so real?

Nick's voice came from far away, as if through a watery barrier, but it couldn't be him; his lips were fixed on hers with an abandon she'd never felt in him before, and her mind leapt into an imagined future that she couldn't let go of because Emot made it so shockingly real and delightfully intoxicating.

'Ariel?' Nick called, still fending off the emanations.

'You're … here,' she gasped.

What was the sleazy bastard doing to her? 'It's Emot,' Nick reminded her. 'In your mind.' He struck one of the emanations a deadly blow. It sizzled into nothing.

Emot's cold laughter rang out as he fired another flame. 'Now I take you away and she craves for more.'

Nick risked a glance. Ariel's eyes had glazed over. Did she even see the demon any more?

'So weak, so predictable,' Emot gloated and laid his talon on her neck.

Yep, she'd gone into Emot's la la land. 'Ariel!' Nick yelled. 'Wake up!' The beast stood casually, feasting, occasionally shooting fire to stir her craving.

Nick growled in frustration. He wasn't supposed to dispatch the demon for her unless she asked, but it was time to override that injunction. He lunged at one of the remaining Emots and dispatched him with a thrust through his neck. The last emanation moved between Nick and Ariel, fighting to allow his master to feed.

Emot could have killed her by now, but he was playing with her. The thought sickened Nick, but the demon's weakness also gave him time. He would not let the sleaze-bag kill his girl. His determination aroused more power and speed. He whirled around his foe and vaporised him with a blow to the head. Then, before Emot realised his defence was gone, Nick sprang forward and plunged his sword straight through the demon's side. Emot screeched in anger, spitting fire. Ariel screamed.

'I'll be back for more,' Emot hissed as he faded into a faint red shadow then vanished like a gust of wind.

Nick sheathed his sword and turned to Ariel just in time to see her horrified face before she fled around the side of the building. He raced after her, turning the corner in time to see her ride from the stables and urge her horse into a gallop. He hurried to find his own horse.

Geordie stood outside the stables, staring after Ariel with a bemused expression. 'My goodness, you're both keen this morning,' he said as Nick ran up. 'Luckily, I've got them saddled already.' He pointed to Grey standing calmly nearby, his reins twisted round a tethering hook.

'Thanks.' Nick untied the reins and swung himself into the saddle.

'Looks like you'd better catch that little filly,' Geordie said, still watching her.

'I intend to,' Nick said. *She might run faster than me, but I'm faster on a horse.* He turned the horse's head towards the open plain, gave him a good kick in the flanks and urged him after Ariel's fleeing horse.

The finely bred Magan mount took up the challenge. Nick leaned into the gallop, riding like a jockey, his body moving in perfect synchronisation with the horse as they sped relentlessly towards Ariel. Grey's mane flew in Nick's face. His neck warmed Nick's cheek. His smell filled Nick's nose, and the sound of hooves denting the earth, bridle jangling and horse panting filled his ears. He'd felt the edge of desperation in Ariel as she fled. He couldn't let her out of his sight.

Gradually, they gained on the fleeing mare. 'Wait!' he called as he drew close. Ariel's thick auburn hair streamed out behind her, and tears streamed down her face. 'Ariel. Stop! Please.'

'Go away!'

He rode up beside her and tried to grab the reins from her hands, but she turned the horse away. Nick raced ahead and cut her off. Mandy stopped, panting heavily, and before Ariel could urge her on again, Nick grabbed the horse's bridle and held her firm.

'Let her go!'

'Ride's over, Ariel,' he said.

She growled in frustration, slid from her horse, stomped several metres away and slumped to the ground.

Nick dismounted. 'Stay here,' he said to the horses and gave them each a reassuring pat before walking over to her. She batted stones from side to side in the dirt in front of her. 'What is so terrible?' he asked.

'You saw,' she muttered.

'I saw Emot being Emot, and I saw a Warrior in training, learning how to defeat him.'

'What you saw was a Warrior failing!'

Nick shrugged. 'So what? It happens to all of us.' He knelt beside her.

'Don't touch me!' She jumped up and stepped away. 'I'm disgusting.'

'No,' Nick said softly. He stood and took a cautious step towards her. Even the cornered-wild-animal look in her eyes didn't mar her beauty. 'You're just upset, and that's fine.' He opened his arms, inviting her in. 'Come on.'

She shook her head, picked up some stones and half-heartedly threw them at him. He ducked each one and began to chuckle. The wild animal had transformed into a petulant child. 'So, you're laughing at me now, are you?' she said. 'Is that supposed to make me feel better?'

'I'm not laughing at you; I'm laughing at him.' Nick pointed behind her at the furious tear-streaked gimp with wild green hair and muddy coloured skin. It pelted her with stones and hissed through pointed teeth.

Ariel swung around. 'Dammit,' she growled, but instead of following the protocol for getting rid of Gimps, she grabbed a handful of stones and lobbed them back at him. The little demon took up the challenge with glee, and they hurled missiles and insults at each other while Nick shook his head in disbelief.

'All right,' Ariel said after a moment or two. 'Come here.' She beckoned to the Gimp. He crept closer, his head cocked, eyes suspicious. His bulging eyes followed her hand as she reached towards him. When she patted his head, he ducked away, blinking furiously. 'Aw, you're quite cute really, aren't you?' Ariel said warmly. The Gimp faded into nothing.

Nick took a few steps closer.

'It's all right,' she said, turning to him. 'I'm safe again.'

'Thank goodness.' He took her in his arms and squeezed her tight.

'Sorry,' she mumbled.

'Nothing to be sorry about,' he said. She snorted, but he didn't confront her with it. Walnut would do the debriefing later, and the temperature had dropped alarmingly. 'You're freezing. Let's get back before it snows.'

Ariel looked up. 'Clouds,' she said wearily, 'just clouds in the sky.'

Nick nodded. He knew the analogy. 'And you aren't the clouds. You're the sky, the big blue sky that's always there behind them.' She sighed, and Nick kept his arm around her as they walked back to the horses. He knew how she felt—not a bit like the sky. She felt dirty and grey. The gritty energy of it rolled off her in waves.

After their break and with their sweat chilling in the cold wind, the horses didn't need any urging. They took off at a gallop towards the warm stable. The first flakes of snow fell as they entered the compound, and they cantered right up to the stable, dismounted immediately and led the horses inside.

Kestril stood with Geordie by the empty stalls. They stopped talking and looked up as Ariel and Nick came in, concern evident on both faces.

'Take her inside,' Kestril said. 'I'll fix the horses.'

Nick glanced at Ariel. She stared into space with glazed eyes. 'Thanks, Kestril. Maybe a warm bath, hey?'

'I hope that's all she needs,' Kestril said quietly.

'I'm fine,' Ariel said as Nick put his arm around her and led her to the door. 'I'm just cold. A bath is a great idea.'

Nick certainly hoped it would do the trick and bring her back to herself.

At the bottom of the stairs, Ariel stopped. 'I need to be alone for a bit,' she said. 'I'll join you in the kitchen when I've regained use of my limbs.' She blew on her hands and Nick kissed her icy fingers.

'I'll wait outside your rooms,' he said.

'No way. It's freezing in the corridor and I want a couple of hours alone. Go where it's warm. I'll be okay.'

'Are you sure?'

'I'm just going to run a bath and soak in it until I can feel my toes again. I really don't need a bodyguard for that. Give me a break, Nick, please.'

Nick wondered how long it would take Emot to reform. He'd have to have either a human slave or a lot of emanations nearby to regrow before Ariel had finished her bath. And surely he wouldn't dare walk into a place full of Warriors who would lop his head off on sight. 'All right, milady. Whatever your heart desires.'

'Whatever?'

'Ah … well, let's say, whatever this rather flawed knight can manage.'

'Hmph. See you later then, Flawed Knight.' She raced up the stairs, leaving Nick unsuccessfully trying to read the tone of her voice.

27

Seduction

Ariel's footsteps shattered the silence in the upstairs corridor, and the inclement weather choked the light from the few narrow windows so that little penetrated the gloom. She shivered, but not just from the cold. She'd seriously overestimated her ability to defeat Emot, and his attack had left a residue in her body, a subtle tingling of anticipation. If she let it go and looked at it directly, it would dissolve, but she didn't. She enjoyed its promise of pleasure. Like a guilty secret, she hated it, yet held it to her breast like some kind of charm.

Emot had caught her with her fantasies, like a worm on a hook, and she'd gobbled it up like a starving fish. The bath would ease the tension in her body and help wash the craving away.

Just before she got to her rooms, Nick called out from behind her.

'Wait, and don't turn around. I've got a present for you.'

Ariel stopped. Her skin prickled as Nick drew closer. His powerful energy preceded him, hot and flickering. He smelt different, as if he had aftershave on. She tried to turn, but he placed his warm hands on her head and held it firm.

'Stand still. Close your eyes, and don't look around,' he said in a deeply seductive voice. Its unfamiliar cadence rang a warning, but his lips caressed her neck and the flicker of doubt faded from her mind.

The walls of the corridor dissolved around her. The grey snow-laden sky faded away, and Ariel stood in front of Nick on a private terrace beside a natural steaming pool. Soft lights placed subtly amongst the rocks and trees illuminated the area, protecting them from the surrounding darkness. Some part of her rejected the scene as impossible, but a greater part embraced it, eager for it to be real.

'Tonight's the night,' Nick whispered. His arms wrapped around her waist. His lips brushed her neck. 'I hope you like the setting.'

'It's lovely,' she said, taking in the plush surroundings.

In one smooth motion, he dropped her robe off her shoulders and turned her towards him, pulling her close. She trembled as his bare chest touched her bikini clad body. 'Shall we swim before or after?' he asked.

'After.' She sighed.

But in the stone corridor at the Hermitage, a demon stood behind Ariel, sending flickers of fiery images into her mind. A warning pushed its way into her awareness. Why was Nick so willing all of a sudden, and weren't they in the Hermitage? The resort faded as the feeling of the Rasa's slimy body behind her dawned in her consciousness. She recognised the taint of demon beneath the aftershave and realised that it was not Nick's lips on her neck, but Emot's talon.

He must have had plenty of emanations nearby to bring him back so quickly. But when *she* killed him, since she hadn't done it before, the blast of her Radiant Power would shock the demon so much that it would flow through to his emanations and vaporise them as well. Then Rasama would have to grow a new Emot from his own body, a much longer process.

Ariel fought back her disgust and slid her hand towards her dagger, but the talon disappeared from her neck. She spun around in time to see Emot gliding noiselessly down the corridor. She should run after him and kill him, but her legs felt like jelly and her confidence was shattered. She stumbled into her room and threw herself on the bed. Why did she let him get to her? Hadn't she already failed spectacularly enough for one day?

Ariel hated herself for her weakness and did everything her training had taught her not to do. She welcomed her guilt and self-hate with open arms. She relived her shame over and over, reminding herself how stupid she was and how much was at stake. She deserved to suffer! But in that suffering, she understood how Nick had suffered in the same way that day on Shifting Stones when he'd growled at her and his energy had hit her like a battering ram. Knowing that he still battled the residue of his past, her heart went out to him, and thinking of him drew her from her self-obsession.

She heaved herself from her bed, wrapped herself in her new Magan-style alpaca shawl and stared through the narrow window panes. Perhaps the sight of the pure white snow fluttering to the ground would help her feel clean again, but all she felt was a thirst for more of the romantic, sensuous Nick in the fantasy. That Nick didn't hold back in case he got too turned on to stop, or his desire roused some feral energy he couldn't control. That Nick didn't turn his back on her, or twist his face in disgust, and he was even more handsome. There was no harm in a little fantasy, she thought, so long as she didn't get trapped in it. And she wouldn't. She could watch it like a television show, just sit back and let it flow on through.

'Will you stand for me again, little one?' The voice, a sloppy impersonation of Nick, but still seductive, came from behind her.

Emot! Again.

She shouldn't even consider it, but … *I'll pretend; get him close then stab him.* And she would have another little taste of the fantasy Nick first—Emot made him so deliciously real—but she would be careful. She would not be caught.

The demon moved close behind her. 'Don't turn,' he crooned and placed an oily hand on her neck. Images flickered into her mind.

The light of dawn pierced between the curtains, she smelt the faint sulphur smell of the hot pools, heard the breeze whispering in the palm trees, felt the sheets on her naked body and tasted Nick's lips on hers … The barrage of sensations overwhelmed her and knocked her from her centre of awareness. Her perception of it as just a fantasy faded quickly amid a tangle of limbs, twisted sheets and oil-slicked bodies. A sleazy voice broke the magic. 'We'd better leave you hungry for next time.'

Not Nick!

Ariel opened her eyes and swung around, her hand fumbled for her dagger, but it was too late. Emot glided, smoothly, silently out the door and her legs felt like rubber again. She groaned and slumped onto the bed, wrapped her arms around herself and rolled from side to side, trying to quell the roaring in her head and the flames in her body.

This couldn't be happening. It was all too much—way too much. Exhaustion swamped her, and she buried her head beneath her pillow and gave herself to the glorious forgetfulness of sleep.

She slipped in and out of sleep and tasted a smorgasbord of delicious dream flavours as the demon infiltrated her dreams. In the unawareness of slumber he teased her mercilessly until he'd turned her desires into craving. Nick may have popped his head in to check on her and found her sleeping, but maybe that was a dream too.

Someone, or something, did open the door quietly and glide to the bed where she lay. It had to be Nick that removed the pillow from her head, settled himself smoothly behind her and set her blood on fire, but she couldn't be sure. Her dreams seemed to be turning into reality, and reality felt more like a dream.

'Have no fear of me, little one. I'll not hurt you,' the Nick impersonator purred. 'The flavour of your craving is ecstasy for me.' Ariel, limp against his chest, moaned at the alluring touch on her neck. 'Feed me willingly and I'll protect you,' he promised.

She never heard the warning that whispered from the depth of her consciousness, for the warm arms of her fantasy lover and the feel of silken sheets on naked skin demanded all her attention. The demon's touch became Nick's lips, and a strange, brittle kind of pleasure coursed through her veins. It wrapped her in a mindless blankness that shrouded her problems but also her awareness. The demon fed her fantasies so real that she mistook them for reality, and she fed him her craving for more.

It seemed as if she had found the obliteration of all pain and the fulfilment of all desires, but when the touch withdrew, the brittle quality of the pleasure sharpened like edges of glass in her skin, and the only thing that would return it to pleasure was more of the demon's touch. 'Don't stop', she murmured.

'Later, my darling,' he crooned. His weight lifted off the bed. 'I shall return.' She felt his presence glide out the door. It clicked shut behind him.

His absence was agony. Not a breath of fantasy remained and the stark reality of life had never felt so bereft of pleasure—a lack that could be easily fixed by the simple touch of a demon. She felt like a half-dead fish dangling on a fisherman's line, unable to open her mouth for fear of losing the flavour that sweetened the hook, and she could think of nothing other than the return of smoothness to her shattered senses. She lay, as if drugged, completely fixated on the demon's return. She didn't crave the demon, but she did crave the pleasure his feeding brought her. Before the hour was up, Emot lay once again behind her on the bed, and, this time, she welcomed his presence.

'You've made me very strong, little one. I enjoy that, and you enjoy it too, don't you?'

Ariel didn't reply—something in her vaguely remembered that she was supposed to defeat demons, not make them stronger.

'Say you enjoy it,' he hissed.

'I do,' she mumbled obediently, and put her head on the side to facilitate his feeding. He sipped from the fire inside her, drawing it out though his talon, like liquid through a straw.

The echoes of footsteps from further down the corridor reached her room, and the demon froze, listening. 'I must go.'

'No,' she croaked.

'Hush, little one, and fear not,' he crooned in his oily voice. 'I shall return, for I am as addicted to your deliciously sweet flavour as you are to me.' He slipped off the bed and glided away.

Someone knocked on the door to the Maloney rooms.

'Ariel, it's Nick. You've been ages. Can I come in?'

She didn't answer. Her lover never knocked.

'Ariel?' He sounded worried now. 'Are you there? Are you all right?'

Still she didn't answer.

Nick opened the door into Ariel's sitting room and his heart skipped a beat. The room was empty but the putrid smell of a Rasa lingered. He strode into Ariel's bedroom and found her lying on the bed, eyes glazed, staring at the ceiling. 'What happened?'

She didn't reply. He ran to the bed, grasped her by the shoulders, and lifted her, but she flopped like a rag doll and avoided his gaze. A weight settled in the centre of his chest, a horrible kind of knowing. 'He's been here, hasn't he?' No answer. He shook her. 'Ariel! Look at me. Answer me!'

She frowned. 'Who?'

'Emot, the Rasa, the demon. Remember?'

She squinted up at him. 'You're not my lover.'

'It's me. It's Nick. I'm here.' His voice took on a pleading tone.

'No, your hair isn't golden.' Her words ran together.

Some twisted energy form flew from her and punched a hole in his chest. He grimaced and let her go. She flopped back onto the bed with an ugly smile. 'Oh, Ariel, what has he done to you?' No reply. Again.

Was she drunk, or drugged? He leaned over and looked into her eyes, but what he saw there was not Ariel. No energy danced between them. He switched to Second Sight and confirmed what he'd feared. Thick red-tipped ropes of Serpentine almost completely obscured her radiance. Had she fed Emot willingly?

'Touche,' she slurred. Her eyes burned like molten steel.

Nick recoiled from the truth in her eyes and switched back to normal view to shut out the evidence of her crime. He had to get the demon that did this, and he had the distinct feeling that he wasn't far away. The smell hadn't gone. He bet the Rasa was hiding in the living room, primping himself up for another attack.

'I'll see you soon,' he said loud enough for any lurking demon to hear, then he opened and closed the door that lead directly from Ariel's room into the corridor. He drew his sword without a sound, crept into position behind the door to the sitting room and waited.

Ariel suddenly staggered to her feet and ran towards him, snarling, her hands held out, fingers like claws. He fixed his gaze on her glaring eyes and blasted her with raw power, hopefully enough to sear the demon out of her. She recoiled as if hit, staggered for a moment, then passed out. He caught her before she hit the floor and carried her to the bed.

'Sorry, Ariel, wherever you are,' he murmured as he lowered her carefully onto the tangled sheets. He returned to his post behind the door and cursed himself for leaving her alone.

Five minutes later, Emot, huge and solid, glided into the room just as Ariel returned to consciousness. She sat up with a smile and opened her arms in welcome, but Nick stepped from behind the door and beheaded the demon in one smooth stroke. Ariel fainted. The demon faded into a faint red flame and flew out the door.

The demon had been so strong that Nick suspected it wouldn't be long before his emanations returned him to full form and he'd be back for Ariel. Since he had already killed this Major Rasa once, now, no matter how many times he lopped off the beast's head, the demon's emanations would not dissolve along with their master. That only happened the first time a Warrior killed the head of one of the clans, and it was the reason why Walnut could not effectively kill Rasama for them. Nick cast one last agonised look at the prone Ariel, then sprinted down the corridor to find Walnut.

He found him and Twitchet in the kitchen, and when Nick told them about Ariel's condition, a flash of horror passed across the old man's face. 'Maya and Layla have just arrived; Twitchet, find them and tell them to join us, and quickly.'

The cat raced off, and Nick followed Walnut back up the stairs. He strode into Ariel's room and stood beside Walnut. She sat on the bed and stared at the old man with a blank gaze. Tears stained her face. 'Ariel, my dear, what has become of you?' Walnut asked.

She buried her head in her hands. 'I fed Emot,' she croaked.

He smiled and sat beside her. 'At least you know what you've done.' He wrapped his arm around her and drew her close. 'Just relax; we'll sort you out in a jiffy.' The old man began to breathe deeply and Nick switched to Second Sight.

As he had expected, every time Walnut took a breath, he inhaled some of the red-tinged black slime that obscured Ariel's Light and drew it into the centre of his chest where it dissolved harmlessly in the Light of his Radiance. When he breathed out, healing white light flowed from his heart centre, wrapped around Ariel and weakened her Serpentine. It ate into the slime like acid on metal.

Tiny spheres of light appeared in the room and formed into Maya's ample body. As always, her long white hair flowed liberally over the pale floaty fabric of a full-length dress. Bright eyes beamed from her wrinkled face and quickly took in the situation. Without a word, she sat on the other side of Ariel and began the same process, drawing out the Serpentine and directing white light into the quivering frame in Walnut's arms.

Nick just stood and stared, his mind numb with horror.

'We must get her to the training room,' Maya said after a few minutes. 'It will help to be there.'

Ariel looked up. 'I want him,' she whispered, her eyes red—and not just from crying.

Walnut exchanged a concerned glance with Maya.

'If she wants him, she must have fed him several times,' Maya whispered. 'This is very bad.'

Walnut stroked the damp hair from Ariel's forehead. 'It's all through her.'

Layla, in a quirky green tunic that matched the vibrant colour of her short spiky hair, burst into the room and Twitchet bolted in before the tapestry swung across the doorway. 'Is it too late?' Layla asked, her face etched with concern as she took in Ariel's diminished state.

'It may have become a habit already, but she does know what she has done. Let us hope that knowing is strong enough to counter the craving.' Twitchet jumped onto the bed and stared at Ariel. 'Don't say anything,' Walnut warned him, then he turned to Nick. 'Let's get her to the training room.'

Nick lifted Ariel gently in his arms, his heart sinking at Walnut's words. Once the Serpentine had solidified, it could take months to remove it.

'Don't worry, Nick, she's strong,' Walnut reassured him.

As he carried her downstairs, Nick sent every bit of healing energy he could find into Ariel's limp form. The slightly desperate edge to it probably tainted the energy and rendered it less effective, but he'd get himself together as soon as he'd settled her.

Just outside the training room, she looked up at him and a whisper of a smile flickered on her face. 'Nick,' she murmured. 'I feel terrible.'

Relief swept over him as he recognised Ariel in her eyes again. 'It's okay, you just got sick. We're going to make you better. Okay?'

She nodded, smiled weakly, then sighed and, closing her eyes, rested her head against his chest.

'Here, put her here,' Walnut said, pulling a chair into the centre of the room. Nick set her gently on the chair, but she flopped to one side and nearly fell off. 'Try to sit up, Ariel. It will make the healing easier,' Walnut said.

Her body suddenly became rigid. Her eyes flew open and her gaze flicked around the room. 'Where is he? What have you done to him?' She turned on Nick with a look of pure hatred born of thwarted craving.

A bolt of clammy energy whacked him in the chest. He gasped and struggled to cope with the suffocating air that suddenly surrounded him. Every fibre of his being recoiled from the manic look in her eyes. What had Emot lured her with? The green-eyed monster stirred inside him, but Nick dissolved it with an inner smile. No way would he be jealous of a demon.

Ariel—the remorseful one again—buried her head in her hands.

Walnut and Layla brought four chairs and arranged them, one in each cardinal direction, around the patient. Maya and Twitchet joined them, and they sat, one on each chair. With each in-breath, they drew Serpentine out of Ariel, and with each out breath, they filled her with the cool white light of their Radiance.

Unsure where he should be, Nick stood behind Ariel, his hands on her shoulders, holding her firm against the back of the chair. When she seemed to be able to sit by herself without flopping, Walnut gestured for him to go behind Maya's chair. But it felt wrong. He never disobeyed his guide, but his legs resisted walking from that circle, away from Ariel, and he had to force himself to do as the old man wished.

The spot in the centre of his chest throbbed, blasted open by the shock of Ariel's condition—painful, yes, but it also gave him direct access to the responsive quality of his Radiance. He stood obediently behind Maya, tuned into that Radiance and directed its healing power with all the love he could muster.

'Ariel,' Maya asked, 'can you hear me?'

'Mmm.'

'You are sick, you have a disease in you that we must get rid of, but we need your help, you have to want to be well and to get rid of Emot's taint. Do you want that?'

'Mmm.' Ariel nodded vaguely.

Maya shook her head sadly at the half-hearted response. Walnut drew his chair in front of Ariel and sat, fixing his gaze on her. Nick switched to Second Sight. The old man radiated pure rainbow light, clear, warm and peaceful. 'Ariel, do you know who I am?' he asked.

She looked up and smiled, and the joy in it lifted Nick's heart. 'Walnut.'

'Do you remember why you're climbing the mountain?'

Ariel's hands flew to the centre of her chest, and she drew herself up, strong for the first time since Nick had discovered her. 'Like a mountain.' Hope resonated in her voice. The tension faded from her face and clarity returned to her gaze. Walnut's smile of relief mirrored Nick's.

'Mum. I have to rescue her and all the others from the … the … demons.' Her voice weakened at the last words and tears came to her eyes. 'I've done something terrible,' she confessed.

28

Addiction

Shivers wracked Ariel's body. Nick took off his jacket, strode into the centre of the circle and wrapped it around her, then he stayed, standing behind her chair. It didn't matter where anyone else thought he should be; he knew he had to be there, right behind her.

'Do you regret it?' Walnut asked.

'Regret! I wish I was dead.' The tears dried up in the face of her self-hatred. She grabbed her hair at the roots and tugged violently. Nick laid his hands on hers, and sent calming energy flowing through his palms. Her fingers relaxed and released her hair.

Walnut glanced thoughtfully at Nick before turning his attention back to Ariel. 'Can you make a vow not to feed Emot ever again, a vow you will keep at the cost of your life?'

'I'd rather be dead than do it again, but I don't know if I can stop myself,' she replied. 'I enjoyed it! How horrible is that? I did the complete opposite of what I wanted to do. It'd be better if I was dead, at least I wouldn't make him stronger. Ugh.'

Nick forced his curling fingers to relax. Her battle with Emot mirrored his with Cogin and he wished, more than anything, that she could be free of that suffering.

'We need you alive, Ariel,' Walnut continued. 'If you were dead, the demons would win, and the window of opportunity your life has brought will be closed forever.'

'But I can't be sure I'd resist.'

'I'll help.' Nick felt his unwavering commitment wrap around her.

'If you make the vow, you will be able to heal,' Walnut continued. 'But if you don't commit yourself to not feeding Emot again, the healing may fail. Your will must be set strong. We can prevent what grew in you this afternoon from solidifying, and we can diminish it to some extent, but you must complete the healing yourself and train solidly until you are ready to face the demon again. Will you do this?'

Ariel closed her eyes, but said nothing. Walnut returned to the healing circle with his chair and, apart from their breathing as the four Noble Ones worked on drawing out the newly grown Serpentine, no sound broke the stillness in the room. Despite their efforts, little Serpentine came out. Ariel still held to her demon. Nick remained where he was, his hands on Ariel's shoulders and, seeking to help, opened the energetic channel between them. He nearly jerked his hands away to cut off the intensity of her pain. Emot had aroused an intoxicating and incapacitating thirst in her, one she craved as pleasure, but was, in truth, the pain of dissatisfaction and the promise of fulfilment that would never be realised.

She reached up and rested her hands on his. 'I vow on pain of death that I will not feed Emot again.'

Even with her declaration, and despite Walnut, Maya, Layla and Twitchet's efforts, Ariel's Serpentine was setting. Walnut gestured Nick out of the circle again, but he didn't move. There had to be a place for him. He was as much a part of this team as the others.

'Let him stay,' Twitchet growled.

Nick acknowledged the unexpected support with a brief smile.

Walnut glanced at the cat and some unspoken communication passed between them. 'Do what you need to do,' he said after a moment.

Given permission, Nick followed his intuition. He collected a chair, placed it in front of Ariel, then sat and held her gaze gently in his. Though he saw little of the Ariel he loved, he knew she was in there somewhere. He felt his love, pure and all-encompassing, gathered it together and sent it to her on his gaze. As blazing white light, it flowed, like an electric current along a wire, and melted the protective shell she'd built around her Serpentine. The demon spawn softened and began to flow more easily from her. The atmosphere in the room lightened, along with Nick's heart, and the Noble Ones continued the now quickening healing process. Gradually, Ariel returned to herself. Nick saw it in her eyes and her growing smile, and he felt the bliss of their love replace the mockery of it in Emot's hollow promises.

A quarter of an hour later, Walnut stood. 'That is sufficient emergency treatment. Much of the new growth is diminished and I think we've stopped any more solidification. Ariel should be able to remove the remaining coils with the healing practice.'

Nick leaned forward and hugged Ariel. She squeezed him back.

'Nick, you are to remain with her at all times,' Walnut continued. 'I'll ask Geordie to put another bed in her room for overnight. Ariel, you are not to allow one single thought to escape your gaze, and you will do the healing practice every moment you aren't asleep, eating or taking a walk. You will remain in silence to assist you in distinguishing reality from your thoughts and desires. Are there any questions?'

Everyone shook their heads, except Twitchet who simply washed his paws. 'It'll be no use if she invites him back,' he said through a mouthful of paw.

Ariel glared at him. 'I won't.'

Twitchet cocked his head to one side, stared at her for a moment, then turned his back and stalked from the room. Maya, Twitchet and Layla headed for the door.

'Layla, wait,' Walnut said. 'Will you stay with Ariel while I talk to Nick, please?'

'Sure.'

Walnut drew Nick outside the room. 'When he comes back, get him immediately. I don't want her to see him at all if it can be avoided.'

Nick nodded.

***

Nick suspected that the Noble Ones had much to talk about, but they barely spoke at lunch, presumably to help Ariel in her silence. She ate little, and when Nick had finished, she mimed going to bed, so he accompanied her upstairs.

He watched her from a chair across the room as she slept, curled on her side, as beautiful as a porcelain doll. With only the even sound of her breathing to accompany him on his vigil, he soon dozed, half-awake, half-asleep. But even through his half-slumber, he sensed when a demonic presence grew in the room. His eyes jerked open and his nostrils flared at the unmistakable smell of Rasa.

A dark shape with eyes like burning coals stood over Ariel's bed. Tongues of flame licked from its slitted mouth and a long talon rested on her exposed neck. 'There's no need to protect her from me, Nick,' Emot growled, not looking at him. 'I would never harm her.'

Nick's hand slid to the hilt of his sword and he prepared to spring.

'And there's no point either, because she wants me back, even now she willingly feeds me in her sleep.'

It was only then that Nick noticed the blissful look on both their faces, and how Ariel held her neck exposed for the demon. He should have dispatched it immediately, but the sight both horrified and fascinated him. How could she bear the smell, or did she not smell it anymore?

'Her flavour is the most exquisite I have ever tasted,' the demon gloated. 'Rasama wants her dead, but I want to feed from her. Allow me this and I will protect her from him. We can protect her together and share her flavour.' Ecstasy dripped from every word.

Nick leapt to his feet, sword swinging, and sliced through the demon's neck in one swift motion. 'Never!'

'She wants me. I'll be back,' the demon purred as he faded away.

Ariel pulled the blankets closer around her and snuggled further down into the bed, but she couldn't settle. Something burned into her back. Her eyes flashed open and she swung her head around. Nick sat in a chair watching her, the power of his gaze like an electric current between them.

'Do you remember any dreams?' No emotion showed on his face and his voice, though soft, gave little indication of his feelings.

She shook her head, then something better forgotten surfaced. She pushed it down and turned away from him. The blankets no longer kept her warm and the shiver that wracked her body echoed deep in her soul. Nick touched her shoulder and tears of shame and regret flowed down her cheeks. His hands stroked her hair. His lips kissed her forehead. And her heart wrenched, knowing he felt her pain.

'Ariel,' he whispered, 'what can I do?'

At first, she didn't reply, too lost in her misery to respond, but even misery eases if you don't keep thinking about its cause, and once freed from the grip of her desolation, she wiped the back of her hand across her eyes and sat up, pulling the blankets around her. She looked Nick in the eye, opening the channel between them, and knew he'd understood her before she spoke. 'Hold me.'

He gathered her into his arms and pulled her close. She felt him soften, surrendering to her as she did to him. Their minds and hearts merged and opened. Their awareness sharpened, and in the embrace of this deepest love, all was forgiven, healed and renewed. Neither wanted to break the connection, it was too perfect, too complete. But eventually, Nick lowered her onto the bed and lay behind her. With his body shielding her back, he slipped the blanket over them both, and there they remained, his arms wrapped protectively around her.

When Walnut came to call them for dinner, he found them like that, sound asleep.

Ariel heard Walnut's voice, but didn't know if she was awake or asleep. She dwelt in an aimless shifting state, sometimes in light, sometimes in dark, sometimes in pleasure, but mostly in pain. Someone pressed up against her back, their body fitted close to hers, arms warm around her. She moaned and tilted her head, opening her neck with a sigh, but no hot talon ignited her craving.

Nick awoke as soon as she moved. He saw her neck expectantly exposed and sniffed, but smelt no demon. *Thank goodness.* Sleeping through an attack would be intolerable. He stroked her neck and sent healing energy to soothe her restlessness and guide her back into sleep.

Walnut stood at the window and turned when he spoke. 'She may well take refuge in sleep for a while.' Dusk had crept into the room. Its grey light aged the old guide, highlighted the tension in his usually serene face. The weariness in his eyes reminded Nick of Walnut's mortality, something he didn't want to face, especially not now.

Nick unwound himself from Ariel's sleeping form and joined Walnut at the window. 'He came to her while she slept,' he whispered, watching her face, so peaceful now. 'She called him in a dream and fed him from there.' The centre of his chest ached as he recalled the demon trying to make its bargain.

Walnut frowned. 'Then she has become habituated to his feeding.'

'She's addicted?'

'It appears so,' he replied gravely.

Nick shook his head. 'How could it happen so fast?'

'The battle on Craggin Plain must have weakened her more than I realised. The barbs he fired into her probably stayed viable and seeded her dreams. He'd only have to visit her a few times in a short period on top of that to tighten his noose.'

Nick exhaled forcefully. 'I should never have left her alone.'

'It's not your fault. This kind of highly focused targetting is not normal. None of us even considered the possibility.'

'What do we do?'

Walnut sighed. 'Make sure he doesn't feed from her again.'

Nick glanced at the old man. 'But if she wants it?' Worry gnawed at his gut, an unfamiliar and disturbing feeling.

'She doesn't really want it. She just can't stop. It's a habit now, a habit we have to help her break.' He turned back to the view. Clouds of freezing white gathered outside, threatening snow.

Ariel shifted restlessly in her sleep, drawing Nick's gaze. The air before her began to shimmer and she tilted her head, sighing through parted lips. Her eyes opened as the shadowy form of Emot appeared before her bed. His taloned hand reached towards her exposed neck.

Nick's hand flew to his sword, but the power of command in Walnut's voice stayed his hand. 'You have no place here, demon.' His low tone had a strange echo to it and Emot dissolved even before the old man had fully turned to face him.

'No,' Ariel screamed as Emot disappeared.

She began to shake. Nick didn't hesitate. He took her in his arms and held her until the shaking subsided. Though her energy felt sharp, hot and painful to him, he didn't shy away. He opened the soft spot in the centre of his chest and willingly accepted her pain. The burning of her craving dissolved in the cool calm of his Radiance, and he sent healing energy back to her, willing it to soothe her and help her to let go.

Walnut placed a chair by her bedside and sat, watching them, his expression unreadable. When Ariel had calmed, he looked directly into her eyes. 'Ariel,' he said firmly, 'you have become habituated to feeding the demon. You are calling on him without knowing what you are doing. We will not allow you to feed him again, but if you are to ever live anywhere other than the addicts' ward in the hospital at Sheldra, or roam as a starving ghost, then you must break the habit.'

Ariel flinched as if Walnut had slapped her in the face. Nick swallowed, his throat suddenly dry. He hadn't realised it was that bad.

'I thought you'd healed me. I wanted to be healed,' Ariel whispered, tears springing to her eyes. Nick took her hand and sent her as much reassurance as he could muster. Had it helped? He couldn't tell. She wouldn't meet his searching gaze.

'We removed the newly grown Serpentine, but you are not only allowing Emot to feed, you appear to be encouraging it,' Walnut said.

Ariel flinched, and stared at the ground, her expression twisted into one of disgust—for herself. 'I've broken my vow. I want to die.'

'That is not necessary,' the old man replied, 'but renewing your vow and continuing the training is. We can support you, but only you can remove the habit. It will take willpower, but I'm sure you can do it.'

Ariel's lips pressed together, but she nodded her assent. 'What do I do now?'

Walnut sighed. 'We will not let the demon get anywhere near you. Your body will have to adjust to the lack of his feeding. This may be painful, but you will have Nick. I will not deprive you of him again.'

Ariel looked at the man she had finally accepted as her partner and her eyes filled with tears. 'I failed. I'm sorry,' she murmured before looking away.

Nick smiled his encouragement. 'We haven't failed. The battle's still to be fought.'

'Nick's right,' Walnut said, his eyes crinkling at the corners, 'this is just a set back, an illness you need to recover from, that's all. Just remember why you're on this mountain. Never forget that. You have to get better for everyone's sake.'

She turned moist eyes on the old man. 'This could happen to Mum, couldn't it?'

Walnut nodded slowly, his expression grave. 'It is a great danger for one trapped as she is.'

Ariel shook her head. 'Poor Mum. I hope she's tougher than I am.'

Nick's hand strayed to the middle of his chest. The ache of Ariel's desire to free her mother from suffering sat there as if it belonged to him.

'Use that compassion to help free yourself,' Walnut suggested.

Hope flared in Ariel's eyes, like a beacon in the darkness.

'Draw her suffering into yourself and it will dissolve your Serpentine,' he continued. 'Maya would have taught you that.'

Ariel nodded. 'She did, but I forgot about it.'

'Well, now is the time to remember. It is part of your prescription for wellness. Alternate the healing practice with this one, and you help your mother and yourself at the same time.'

A smile lit Ariel's face.

Walnut stood. 'I'll bring you some dinner.'

'We can come down,' Nick said.

Walnut shook his head. 'I think it best you stay here tonight. And, yes, I know Deidre can bring it, but I don't want her to see Ariel like this. It would only upset her.'

Nick followed Walnut into the corridor, but held the tapestry back so they could still see her through the open door. 'Have you seen this sort of thing before?' he asked.

Walnut nodded.

'What happened to them?'

Walnut frowned, considering the question, but said nothing until Nick narrowed his eyes, placed his hands on his hips and leveled his strongest stare at the old man. 'I need to know.'

'Of course you do. But please, don't get depressed. Ariel is stronger than the others I've seen and getting through this will only make her stronger.'

Nick raised his eyebrows expectantly, signaling to him to get on with it.

Walnut sighed, his expression uncharacteristically grim. 'The first one I knew was never cured. He tried to keep Emot with him all the time and got violent when anyone tried to kill the demon. He went to live in the back blocks of Minion Hills. Last seen, he had turned into a starving ghost. The second one was apparently cured but had a relapse and lived most of the remaining years of her life in the addicts' ward under a twenty-four hour demon watch. Another died in Emot's arms after feeding him all her life. Though most were cured, I never knew any that were able to go on to defeat Emot afterwards.'

Nick's heart sank at the news. 'We have to get her through this. She has to defeat that bastard.' He almost scared himself with his vehemence.

'And she will, Nick. She will,' Walnut assured him.

'What makes you so sure?'

'The others didn't have anyone like you.' He raised his eyebrows and pursed his lips, challenging Nick to deny it.

Nick shook his head. What difference did that make? The prophecy didn't even mention him.

29

𝓑reaking the 𝓗abit

Ariel sat on her bed, back straight, staring into the space in front of her. Her hours of training kicked in; her confusion dropped like a stone thrown into a deep pool and her mind settled. Nick sat on a chair beside her, lamp light painting his features with gold.

'Do you think of him?' he had asked when she'd finished picking over the food Walnut had brought. At first she had wanted none of it, but he'd resorted to feeding her with a spoon until she promised to eat something herself.

The question had shocked her. 'No. Not him,' she had replied. 'It's you I think of. He just happens to be the one who's there.'

'Me?'

'Of course, you're what I want, not him.'

He had frowned then, not reassured, and after raking his hand through his already wildly tousled hair, had declared it time for healing. And so they sat.

From the centre of her chest, Ariel drew a ball of brilliant silvery white light, rolled it up her spine, flung it out the top of her head and left it floating a foot above her. Healing syllables

302

flowed on her breath in a rhythmical chant and liquid light began to drip from the gleaming star.

The healing nectar washed, like a raging flood, through every cell of her body and flushed out the Serpentine. Keen for freedom from the demon's taint, she urged the nectar on, chanting stronger and faster. The Serpentine flowed, like old pus and viscous soot-laden blood, from every orifice and pore of her skin and slid, like cold oil, down her body onto the stone floor where it vaporised.

A leaden weight lifted from Ariel's being and her body became as clear as crystal. The nectar kept flowing and filled her like a glass of luminous milk, lifting her energy and strengthening her resolve. The star of white light descended down her spine and she transformed into pure Radiant Light. Shimmering rays of multicoloured light burst from her chest and spread healing power in all directions. She became a vast, brilliant light that touched all beings throughout the universe with rays of love so pure that Serpentine dissolved on contact.

After a time, she folded the outer world into herself then dissolved into a point of light. The light fell into itself and melted into nothing. Ariel had turned inside out, all reference points gone, nothing left with which to define herself. She remained there, her mind resting comfortably in space, nowhere.

An image of her mother trapped in the darkness of a demon's nest appeared in her mind. She felt her mother's anguish as if it was her own and, borne on her breath as Maya had taught her, she used that compassion to heal both their pain. Breathing in, darkness dissolved into Light; breathing out, Light eased the darkness. Serpentine stood no chance in the brilliance at the core of Ariel's being.

This was the pattern of her healing.

Exhaustion eventually claimed Ariel, and after a shower, she sank onto the bed and promptly fell asleep.

Thick stone walls dripping with water surrounded her. The place smelt of cold stone, Rasa and fear. Weak light filtered through a tiny barred window too high to look out of, and hissing snakes of shiny black Serpentine covered the floor. Screams stuck in Ariel's throat. The snakes writhed up and around her legs, their long red tongues flickering like fire.

She tried to shake them off and run, but she couldn't move, crippled by an overwhelming sense of helplessness. She screamed, but it came out as a strangled gasp. The Serpentine snakes licked at her with putrid tongues and climbed up around her chest. They wriggled down her arms and pinned her hands behind her back, then slithered over her face, sending her into a blind, gasping panic. Tears of horror streamed down her face, but still her screams wouldn't sound. The snakes covered every inch of her body, smothering her. She couldn't breathe.

Death looked her in the eye and she awoke in a sweat of terror, arms flailing against an imaginary foe.

Nick raced to her side. 'What is it? What's wrong?'

She threw herself into his arms. 'He's killing me,' she croaked.

He stroked her hair. 'No. We're not going to let him.' His voice rang with determination.

✳✳✳

Twice that night Nick woke to find Emot in the room, and twice he killed the demon before he tasted his prey. He still managed to wake before Ariel, and he didn't want to disturb her, so they arrived late in the kitchen for breakfast. Only Deidre remained in the room and her frosty manner told them she wasn't too pleased with their tardiness.

'Walnut wants you in the sitting room,' she told Nick when they'd finished breakfast. 'Ariel, you're to stay here.'

Ariel glanced from Deidre to Nick with a frown.

304

'It's okay. I won't be long,' Nick said.

'Oh heavens,' Deidre said. 'Surely, you can do without him for a while.'

'Of course I can,' she replied. 'See you soon.'

Nick strode into the sitting room. Maya, Layla and Twitchet had gathered in front of the fire with Walnut. A war council?

'So that is how it is,' Walnut was saying.

'And when do you think she will be ready to face Emot again?' Maya asked.

Nick perched on the arm of the sofa as Walnut replied. 'I don't know, and it would be counterproductive to pressure her. If she fails again, it could set the journey back indefinitely.'

'The demons are becoming stronger by the day,' Layla said.

'I know, but I won't consider moving on until she has defeated Emot.'

The others nodded in agreement.

'The healing is going well,' Maya pointed out. 'Surely, it is just a matter of time before she is strong enough.'

'Not necessarily,' Twitchet said. 'The healing practice will get her back to where she was, but to defeat Emot, she has to be stronger than she was before.'

'Don't forget that other cases like this indicate that there is a great possibility that she may never be strong enough to succeed against Emot,' Layla said.

Nick shook his head. 'No. She has to be well enough. We have to make sure of it.' Four pairs of eyes fixed on him, as if only then noticing that he had joined them.

'Nick is right,' Walnut agreed. 'It is time to add other things to her prescription.'

'Tomorrow we are resuming the trainings we began at Sheldra anyway.' Maya's voice sounded thin and her form flickered a little.

'Yes, of course, she needs all that,' Walnut agreed, 'but more importantly, she needs to look at the specific fantasy that he caught her with, so that next time she doesn't fail to apply the training to it. I think she is ready to face that now. Nick, do you agree?'

Nick shrugged, surprised and flattered that Walnut had asked his opinion. 'I guess so.'

'So we find her weak spot and make sure it isn't weak anymore.'

'We all know what her weak spot is now, don't we?' Twitchet put in. 'Or should I say, *who* her weak spot is.'

Nick frowned. 'I thought you'd given up harassing us over our relationship.'

'I have,' Twitchet replied. 'I'm just stating the obvious.'

'Now don't you two get going,' Layla scolded. 'What is, is. Let's move on to working with it.'

'Let me do it,' Nick said. 'I know her better than anyone. I can get her off whatever fantasy he fed her.'

'What? Make the cause of the illness, the healer?' Twitchet sneered.

'That's not a new idea, Twitchet,' Layla said. 'It's how vaccinations work.'

'But it is dangerous,' Maya put in. 'Too much and you get the disease. It could make her worse.'

The company fell silent, each pondering the situation.

'Mind you,' Twitchet meowed, 'I have noticed that the flip side of this weakness Ariel has,' he fixed his yellow eyes unblinkingly on Nick, 'is that this energetic connection she has with him is also one of her strengths. You saw its power when we gave her the emergency treatment. Coupled with his healing capacity, I think we should risk it.'

They all stared at Twitchet, surprised by his unexpected support for the idea. 'You know I favour fast dramatic methods,' he explained, 'and they are not without danger, but I think it is what is needed in this case. If we are too cautious and too gentle with her, we may wait a very long time.'

'You think I shouldn't be gentle?' Nick asked.

'Confessing to you might be quite confronting for her,' Twitchet replied. 'You'll probably have to push her a bit. That's all. But you're the healer. Do it your way.'

'Seriously? Now you're letting me do it my way. We could have avoided this whole disaster if you'd supported me back in the Morbid Forest.'

'I didn't trust you then.'

'And you do now?'

'Frankly, you're the best shot we have.'

Nick shook his head with a mixture of amazement and annoyance.

'That's decided then,' Walnut said. 'Nick will be Ariel's vaccination against Emot.'

Nick collected Ariel from the kitchen and took her to the training room where he bade her sit and let her mind settle. He sat beside her and fine-tuned his awareness, preparing himself as he would for facing a demon. Then he adjusted his chair until he sat directly in front of her.

'What images did Emot show you, Ariel?' he asked.

His eyes penetrated her to the core, stripping her naked. She tore her gaze from his. 'I … why do you want to know?'

'So we can make sure he doesn't catch you with it again.'

'Again. Oh God. I have to face him again.' She trembled at the thought, conveniently forgotten until now.

Nick nodded. 'If you want to fulfil the prophecy.'

'I do, but I don't know if I can defeat him anymore.'

'Look at me, Ariel.'

She did, and he pinned her with his gaze, fixed her in place like a helpless butterfly on a board.

'You will defeat him. I know it. The strength is there in you. I feel it. I always have.'

She dropped her gaze and shook her head. He didn't know that. He couldn't know the hold Emot had on her, even now. But Nick didn't let her go; he lifted her chin, forcing her to look at him.

'I don't care what you think, right now; I'm going to make sure that you can defeat him.' His voice rang with a surety that almost convinced her—almost. 'We have to look at what he hooked you with and make sure that next time you recognise it for what it really is.'

She turned away, unable to bear the penetrating intensity of his gaze. 'I know what it is. It's a demon's fantasy, that's all. It just seemed very real at the time.'

'What was it?'

She shook her head.

'Look at me, Ariel. Stay open. This is a healing. You must tell me.'

She shook her head again.

He grasped her chin and swung her head back to face him. 'Tell me.' His voice was gentle, but his eyes blazed with intensity and his energy urged her to tell the painful truth.

She closed her eyes tight against the tears that threatened her composure. 'What does the content matter?'

'It matters because he hooked you with it, because something in the content was enticing enough for you to forget it was just a fantasy. Maybe enticing enough that you didn't even want to remember.'

She opened her eyes and shot him a look of defiance. 'Shouldn't I be talking to Walnut about this?'

'Don't avoid the issue.'

'I'm not, it's just . . .' He was right; she was avoiding it. 'It's too personal with you.' She looked away again.

'That's why you have to tell me.' His voice had a hard edge now.

'That doesn't make sense.'

'Yes it does, because it could come between us. Do you want that?' He grabbed her chin and forced her to look at him again.

'Of course not.'

'Then tell me.' His voice rose.

'Let me go.' She slapped his hand away and stared at the ground. Should she leave? No. He was trying to help her and Walnut would only send her back.

'It's only hurting because you're holding on,' he whispered, his voice so tender that she wanted to cry.

She nodded, recognising the truth. Yes, she had to open to him, to the painful, embarrassing reality. Even without their eyes connecting, she could feel his questioning. It felt as if he dug around in her mind, looking under the carpets for the dirt she had hidden away. 'Stop looking at me like that,' she growled, uncomfortable under his scrutiny.

But the mental gaze intensified and he prised her mind open. 'Stop fighting and let me in,' he said. She relaxed a little and felt him seeking the place she had barricaded against him. 'I have a sense of something now,' he told her, 'but it's best you give me the details. I might imagine them worse than they are.'

She sighed. 'It's embarrassing.'

'I know, but I'm not going to judge you. He threw it at you.'

Silence. Ariel battled two desires, one to confess, and the other to hide. One brought her closer to Nick, the other created a gulf between them.

'Trust me.'

'We were lovers, and it was nice,' she confessed after a moment.

Nick stifled a chuckle.

'That doesn't help!' She picked up a cushion and thumped him with it. Quick as a flash, he grabbed it off her and thumped her back. She grabbed another one and fought back, hitting and ducking. They ended up rolling around on the floor, laughing until they could fight no more for lack of breath.

'Sorry,' he said sheepishly.

'I forgive you.' She smiled and curled up against him, cherishing the feel of his body against hers, the energy flowing easily between them, just how it should be, always. A vision of them more intimately connected slipped into her mind, something she never imagined in such detail until Emot fed her the image and the feelings that went with it.

Nick froze for a moment, then gently disengaged himself from her with a sigh. 'There it is.' He stood, walked to the window and stared silently into the snow.

Ariel pressed her lips together. Heat flushed her face, embarrassed that she was still vulnerable to Emot. As if called, he appeared before her and reached his talon towards her neck, oblivious of Nick's presence. 'Nick!' she screamed.

'So hungry for you, little one,' he managed to purr before Nick grabbed his sword and beheaded him.

'This is getting to be a habit,' Nick muttered as he sheathed his sword.

Ariel buried her face in a cushion and bit back tears.

Nick sat beside her and stroked her back. 'We just have to stick with it.'

'He won't come straight back, will he?'

Nick shrugged. 'He does seem to have a lot of back up and the louder you call, the sooner he'll be back. How did you call him? What were you thinking?'

'I won't do it again,' she stated flatly.

'Tell me. The details.'

She bit her lip and looked stubbornly at the floor.

'Ariel,' he growled.

She sighed. 'Images, feelings, it was just a quick glimpse.'

'About?' He fixed her with a stare that told her he wouldn't give up.

She relented. 'You! Okay! You and me. Together.'

He merely nodded, unsurprised. 'What hooked you?'

She stared at him. 'Fine, if you're going to insist, I'll tell you. You're not dangerous, you don't hold back, or turn away when I … you know. I don't have to be careful all the time. There's nothing between us … Nothing … and it feels nice.' She shrugged.

'And it's not real. It's not me. It's a dream me,' Nick said. 'If you want me to match your fantasy, then you'll be disappointed.'

'But one day it could be like that,' she protested.

'Then you're living in the future and missing the present. I'm here, Ariel, this is me. Here. Now. I'm not perfect. I can't fulfill your dreams, but if you want me, then you have to let go of the fantasy and accept me as I am.'

Ariel grimaced. Sometimes the truth sucked.

'So, it's hard to give up your perfect Nick, is it? Even though he's an illusion?'

She narrowed her eyes at him but he just grinned.

'You know why you can't resist Emot?'

Ariel shot him a frosty glare.

'You're so keen to jump into his fantasies that you don't even realise he's there. It's no wonder you haven't defeated him.' She sent mental daggers his way, but they melted in the love he blasted at her. 'Tell me what you have to do?' he asked. 'You know, and I know you know.' He waited while she took a deep breath then forcefully blew the air out through her mouth.

'I have to let go of the fantasy and be satisfied with reality, here, now, in the present.'

Nick nodded. 'Wouldn't it get boring after a while anyway?'

'What do you mean?'

'Is it the same every time?'

'Not exactly. There are different ones and versions of them.'

'Even so, it's your mind he's made the fantasy from. That means there won't be anything unexpected or new. Reality has to be much more fun because you never know what's going to happen next.' He leapt to his feet, scooped her up in his arms, raced outside and dumped her in a patch of snow. Ariel screamed.

'You creep,' she shouted, brushing off the snow as she stood up.

Splat! A snowball hit her in the chest. She looked up. Nick grinned, a challenge. 'I'm a very good shot. It's lucky I'm not aiming at your head.' He fired another one, hitting her on the shoulder as she stooped down to roll her own snowball.

Ariel scooped up some snow, rolled it into a ball and hurled it back at him. He ducked out of the way, but his ball scored another hit on her. She made snowballs and threw them back as fast as she could, but Nick was faster. Her shots often flew wide of their mark, whereas his hit her nearly every time. *Damn him!* Her hands froze and her nose dripped, but he stood between her and the Hermitage, and he wouldn't let her past without a fight.

'Are you going to drop the fantasy idol and accept the real creep?' he shouted, 'or shall I aim for your head and bash your stupidity out of you?'

'That's not fair,' she yelled back.

'Reality isn't fair, but it's alive and unknown and challenging. So what's it to be?' He stopped, hand up, a snowball aimed at her head.

'You wouldn't,' she growled and hit him square in the chest with a ball of mush.

He didn't move, just grinned mischievously. 'Wouldn't I?'

Ariel stared at him, wondering.

'Well,' he demanded. 'What's it to be?'

She walked towards him, took the melting snowball from his hand and smashed it on his head. He grabbed her wrist, wrestled her to the ground, and sat on top of her, a triumphant gleam in his eyes.

'Would you ever have come up with this one?' he asked.

'Why would I want to?' she replied, rolling her eyes.

He kissed her luxuriously on the lips, then drew back, grinning. 'Because snow is so deliciously cold.'

She chuckled. 'Okay, point taken, Sir Nick.'

'You haven't answered my question?'

'Okay. I'll take the horribly cold, wet creep that I'm madly in love with.'

He chuckled and got off her.

'Well done,' Twitchet meowed. They turned to find him sitting high and dry on the terrace wall. 'Brutal but effective.'

'Thanks for the vote of confidence, Twitchet,' Nick said sarcastically, 'but it wasn't planned.'

'And neither should it have been,' he replied.

Ariel got up and brushed herself down. Melted snow soaked her clothes. 'I'll have to change now,' she complained.

'I hope it was exciting enough to lure you away from Emot's little stories,' Nick said.

'Quite possibly, but I don't know. It has to compete with a luxury resort in summer.'

'Oh, you want heat, do you?' He picked her up again, raced her upstairs with her giggling all the way and dumped her in front of the fire in her sitting room. 'You'd better take your clothes off,' he said and burst out laughing.

She looked at him, wide-eyed, her mouth open in shock.

'Twitchet would mention dinner at this point,' Nick said.

Ariel shut her mouth, met his gaze with a challenge and began stripping off.

Nick sighed. 'Unfortunately, I'm only human, and a flawed one at that, so I'd better leave. You have five minutes to change, and when I come back I'll be very boring for the rest of the day.' Then he was gone.

Ariel couldn't stop grinning as she stepped out of her sopping clothes. She felt lighter than she had since Nick had left for Shifting Stones and somehow the whole battle she'd had with Emot since then seemed unreal. 'I'm going to kick this habit,' she muttered. She wrapped herself in her mother's old dressing gown, sat on the sofa and remembered each of the alluring fantasies. They flicked through her mind like a slide show, and she shattered each one with a glance. In the light of reality, they looked stupid, impossible or simply embarrassing.

When Nick returned, Ariel was sitting cross-legged on the floor, stroking her neck absently. 'The sky is definitely better than the clouds,' she told him.

Nick knelt beside her, removed her hand from her neck and kissed her there. 'Only I should touch you on that spot,' he whispered. 'Promise me you'll not let anyone else have access to your beautiful neck.'

Ariel laughed. 'I promise, Mr. Vampire.'

30

The Demon Returns

Although something had shifted after Ariel's snow fight with Nick, Emot's lures still crept into her mind. She felt him nearby, calling to her, and suspected that only Lalya, who guarded her sometimes, and Nick's vigilance kept him away. As the day drew on, her desire to feel his touch grew stronger, but when she caught a glimpse of him lurking in the corridor after morning tea, Nick stepped between them and the demon ran away. Emot returned as she walked onto the terrace after a session with Layla, and the only reason Ariel didn't run to him and offer herself to his intoxicating touch was Layla's presence just inside the French doors behind her.

The demon fixed his eyes, burning with lust, on her, and it was all she could do to keep her feet rooted to the spot. 'I can't,' she managed to whisper, but he either didn't hear or was desperate enough for her not to care. He scanned the area, then drew closer, apparently thinking her alone. She should have run away, but her longing for his touch kept her there. She hoped Layla had been distracted and they truly were alone, but just as Emot's talon touched her neck, Layla appeared behind him and lopped off his head.

315

Ariel felt as if her lifeline had been broken and she'd been cast adrift in a wild ocean. Shudders wracked her body. Layla sheathed her sword, came up beside her and gave her a hug. She wriggled from her grasp and spun around. 'Stop doing that,' she yelled.

'What? Killing the demon or giving you a hug? You need both.'

'I'll decide what I need and what I don't.'

'You need the demon, do you? That will free your mother, will it?'

'Damn you. Damn him. Damn everything.' Ariel stomped inside and threw herself on the sofa in the sitting room.

'What's in your mind?' Layla asked, following her in.

'And stop asking me that. Why does everyone ask me that?'

'You know why.'

She did too. Every time she drifted into a daydream, whoever accompanied her said those words, forcing her to choose reality over the fantasy. She should know better than to complain, but when jitters took her over, all she wanted was to get rid of them.

Nick walked into the sitting room and glanced from Ariel's miserable face to Layla's concerned one. 'What's the matter?'

'The usual,' Layla replied. She sat on one of the comfy chairs and stared at Ariel.

Nick nodded, walked behind the sofa and began stroking her hair. 'Do you want me, or a fantasy of me?' he asked. Again. A ploy of his to keep her focused. She batted his hand away, but he just chuckled, then lifted her hair from her neck and ran a row of kisses down her bare skin, kisses to match anything Emot offered. She sighed and reached up and ran her hand through his hair.

He tumbled over the back of the couch, sat beside her and turned his lips loose on hers. 'Which Nick?' he asked through kisses.

'This one,' she replied, and, right then, she did. It was when he stopped that the other Nick appeared in her mind, offering more, much more. Did she really want that, anyway?

'And now?' He sat back and watched her closely.

'You'll do,' she replied and let the fantasy Nick fade away.

'Interesting methods you have, Doctor Nick,' Layla quipped.

'The cure has to fit the illness.'

Layla stood. 'It's time for your group healing session.'

Nick stood and offered Ariel his hand.

She took it and, hand in hand, they followed Layla to the training room. She liked the healing sessions. They helped stop the shuddering and they left her feeling clean and positive, whereas Emot's touch left her feeling dirty and full of self-loathing. Only when he came close did the latter eclipse the former.

After the healing sessions, though diminished, the Serpentine came back, like her hair returning to waves after straightening. If she could have stayed in her Radiant Mind, she could have stayed free of the Serpentine, but she couldn't.

'You just need more stability in your mind,' Walnut told her, 'so it always remains tuned to what is, not what you'd like things to be.'

***

Late that afternoon, Nick suggested a walk.

'I don't know, Nick. I'm kind of tired. I'd like to go to bed … to rest.'

He smiled. 'Sure, but let's just get a breath of fresh air first.'

317

Ariel hesitated. She felt Emot nearby. She should go, get away from him. 'Okay.'

The cold air promised more snow, so they grabbed their coats and scarves from the hall stand and headed to the door at the end of the corridor. Nick opened the door for her, but Ariel stopped and shook her head. Emot yearned for her, his desire palpable somewhere behind her. She hesitated.

'Go on,' Nick urged, 'before we freeze the place out.'

Ariel's head felt thick and her heart pounded. She swayed between two extremes, what she should do and what she yearned to feel, just one more time.

'Where is he?' Nick asked in a low voice.

She shrugged.

'Tell me and I'll slit the bastard's throat. Then we can go outside without a demon breathing down our necks.'

'No!' She turned to him, horrified. She couldn't bear the shudders again.

Nick slammed the door shut and turned on her. 'Listen!' His sharp tone sliced through her fumbled senses, his stalwart patience replaced with wrath. 'If you can't find the will to give up this obscene fetish for yourself, then do it for me, because I can't stand to see you crumble, and if it's not enough to do it for me, then do it for everyone else.'

She stared at him in shock. The force of his sudden anger buffeted her like a hot raging wind. 'Why are you shouting at me?' she whispered.

'Because I care, and I'll do more than shout if I have to,' he replied. 'Next time you make any noise or, so help me, any movement that remotely looks like you're inviting that demon for dinner, I'll give you a solid blast of . . .' His angry gaze thundered into her eyes so powerfully that she flinched as if he'd slapped her.

'Of what?' Her voice wavered. The concern beneath the pain in his eyes tugged at her heart and blasted the demon from her mind.

'Try me and you'll find out.' His eyes challenged her, but his lips curled slightly upwards. He opened the door again and, suitably chastised, Ariel stepped outside into the pale grey light.

Flakes of snow flurried around them in swirls of white and their breath came out in puffs of white. They walked through the garden without a word, watching the landscape transform before them as the snow began to settle.

'You're going to have to work really hard to break this,' Nick said after a while. 'It's disgusting what that bastard's done to you.'

Ariel's heart dropped at the cold disparaging tone in his voice. 'You don't love me anymore, do you?' she asked, not looking at him.

He snorted. 'I love you no matter what, but I hate what you're doing.'

The last bit of the sentence came across with a touch of venom. Ariel pursed her lips. The snow increased all of a sudden, falling from the sky in blankets. 'Let's go. I'm getting cold,' she said brusquely and turned back towards the building that rose impressively grey and austere behind them.

✳✳✳

That evening Ariel joined the others in the sitting room after dinner. The lamp light washed her friends with a soft golden glow. The murmur of their talk rose and fell over the crackling fire, and the smell of coffee permeated the air. A cosy, comfortable scene that nurtured her fragile sense of self.

She listened to Tynan's stories, laughed at Nick and Walnut's jokes, and noticed that Maya did little apart from stare into the fire. Ariel felt a growing frailty about her, but even in her silence, the ancient one's presence was a great comfort. Only Kestril didn't join them.

Tynan stood in front of the fire, twiddling his thumbs behind his back. 'Everyone is very pleased with your progress and from what Walnut tells me,' he declared, 'Nick's skill as a healer and demon beheader may become quite legendary.'

'I don't think Ariel would want this turned into one of your stories, Tynan,' Nick said.

'Whoever kills Rasama must put up with the story of her journey becoming well known. It's inspiration for everyone else.'

Ariel narrowed her eyes at the tall scientist. 'Then wait until I've killed him.'

'Of course, Miss.' He bowed deeply, a look of amusement on his face.

Ariel eased back into the old sofa and absent-mindedly began caressing her neck.

Nick rose from his place on the other side of the fire, walked over and sat on the arm of the sofa beside her. 'He's left his mark on you, hasn't he?' he said dryly.

'What?' Ariel turned with a frown, but in reply, Nick merely stroked her neck.

'Oh that,' she murmured, blushing slightly.

'Yes, that.'

'It's just a scar. Walnut says it will fade in time.' She kept her voice light.

'It's not the scar I'm concerned about.'

'I'm going to kill him, Nick. I promise you, nothing of him will remain.'

'Good.' He smiled, then bent over and kissed her gently, right on the spot where Emot had fed.

Ariel closed her eyes and luxuriated in the moment. Her mind roamed ahead, seeking more pleasure, imagining where it might lead if they went to her room now. *What's in your mind,*

Ariel? The day's mantra, programmed into her skull by repetition, jolted her back to the present.

'That's better,' Nick mumbled.

Ariel flushed. He could feel her craving so, of course, he could feel when it dissolved. Vigilance. *You must be always vigilant,* Walnut had said; *tether your mind to the post of present reality, as it is.* She turned her attention to the room, the sounds, the feeling, and the temperature— warm with the fire roaring.

Nick slid onto the sofa beside her and slipped his arm around her shoulders. The energy flowed cool and clean between them. How could she ever have mistaken the thirst that Emot aroused in her for the smooth deep nectar of her connection with Nick?

Twitchet jumped onto the arm that Nick had vacated. 'I suppose you've come to gloat, have you?' Ariel asked.

'What sort of a cat do you think I am?' he replied. 'Petty? No. Gloating is for Rasas. It is unfortunate that what I feared came to pass, but that is not the purpose of my sitting here.'

'Then what is?'

'I had hoped to commend you on your progress, but it seems that you still have a lot of work to do in your social skills.'

Ariel opened her mouth to fire something back at him, but before she could think of anything, Nick stood and picked the little cat up by the scruff of his neck. Twitchet hung limply in his hand, a look of reluctant resignation in his eyes as Nick carried him to the door and threw him outside.

'That's a major defect of this form,' Twitchet muttered, as the door closed behind him.

✳✳✳

Something woke Nick early in the morning. Not a sound, not a smell, not a sight, but a feeling like a ripple in his energy field. The dim grey light of dawn was just seeping through the narrow windows, and Nick peered through bleary eyes at the room around him. Ariel moaned in her bed. Nick leapt from his, grabbed his sword from the dressing table, then froze, horrified at the sight before him.

Emot sat on the bed next to Ariel, one arm snaking around her. Her head lay against his shoulder, and he rested a talon on her exposed neck. Gentle smiles wreathed their faces— but not for long. Nick made no effort to handle his jealous rage, he let it burst from him and smash into them.

They both jerked as if slapped and their heads snapped towards him, eyes wide with surprise. Nick caught the demon's gaze in his and held it firm. As Emot faded from the strength of Nick's focus, he cried out. 'Cogin will make short work of you!'

'Pah!' Nick spat and turned his fury on Ariel.

She fell back, her hand on her chest. Yep, she'd got it.

He stepped towards her, glaring. 'You said you wouldn't do it again!'

'I won't. Not again. I promise.'

'Promises aren't enough. They won't save you from the addicts' wing at Sheldra and they won't save you from me.' He blasted her again. Let her feel what her demon games did to him.

'Please,' she gasped. 'I can't bear it when you're like this.'

'And I can't bear to see you feeding him,' he shouted. 'You had everything going for you and now you're just throwing it all away, and on what? Your own selfish desires. What about your mother? What about the Serpentine infesting the world? What about me and Walnut and the others who love you?'

Ariel burst into tears.

'Get real, Ariel. Everything is at stake here! Everything!'

'Not you and me?' she whispered in a strangled voice.

'Why not, if you're so willing to trade me for a demon.'

'It's you I want, not him!'

'It doesn't look like that to me!'

Walnut burst into the room. 'Get out of here, Nick.' The tone of his voice allowed no disobedience.

Nick stared at him, jaw clenched.

'This is not helping,' Walnut continued. 'I'm surprised Cogin hasn't come to get you. Now get out of here and take that Gimp with you.'

Nick swung around. A bright green gimp scowled at him from under the window. It followed him as he stormed from the room, cursing under his breath.

Ariel stared miserably at Walnut, waiting for his fury, but he simply pulled up a chair and sat opposite the bed.

'Nick has said enough,' he said. 'Now, sit and look at me.'

Ariel gulped, knowing what he wanted. How could she look into his eyes now without dying of shame? But she knew he would insist, so she gathered her courage, sat straight and looked at him. No judgement showed in his gaze, just a love that held her without conditions. In the power of his gaze, her shame dissolved along with the last vestiges of craving—gone, as if the demon had never existed.

'The ultimate healer is the Radiance,' he said. 'Remain in that long enough or consistently enough and your craving will dissolve before it's even formed.'

He began to chant, and Ariel felt the room fill with a presence that was one and many at the same time. She switched to Second Sight and gasped. Luminous beings made entirely of tiny spinning spots of rainbow light hovered around her. Multicoloured light radiated from them in a glorious display of awareness, and they emitted a quiet, low hum. Walnut had called on the great guides of the past.

'Open your heart, Ariel.' Walnut's voice resonated with the power of all the guides. 'Open to those who made the path and walked it before you, to those who passed on what they learnt from their guides so that you too can walk the path with that knowledge intact. Open to them with deepest respect and gratitude and you will open to the deepest level of your Radiance.' He chanted again and she joined in. The incantation opened a channel to the Great Guides around her, and in the light of their all-encompassing, endless love that made no judgements and asked nothing in return, she opened, layer by layer, further than she'd thought possible.

She could do this. She would not be a victim to someone else's whims, not even those of her darkest desires.

Nick returned, his shame at his outburst palpable in the rarefied atmosphere of the room. He didn't speak and they didn't move. He just sat on the chair opposite the bed and joined their meditation. Ariel felt the burden of his guilt lift and his mind merge with theirs in a peace so profound that even the cause of his guilt dissolved as if it had never existed. Nevertheless, he apologised as soon as Walnut had closed the session.

'No harm done,' the old guide said.

'If Cogin had been here, I would have been feeding him, too,' Nick said dourly.

'Cogin was here,' Layla said, poking her head around the door. Her spiky hair waved above a cheeky grin and twinkling eyes. 'I caught him on the way in. You must have called pretty strongly, Nick. I heard the shouting and figured it wasn't a good time for you to battle him, so I beheaded him for you.'

'Oh,' Nick replied. 'Thanks.'

'No problem. I love chopping their heads off.' She giggled and left.

'Trust the sky in you, Ariel. Do not listen to the clouds,' Walnut said as he followed Layla from the room. 'And no more words about this.'

31

Conquest

Nadima awoke to the clang of her cell door opening and a stronger Rasa smell than usual. Heavy eyelids and a body still quivering with exhaustion proved she couldn't have slept long.

'Bring some light. Let her see me,' commanded a voice deeper than Emot Sai's and far more deadly—the major of the Emot clan himself! 'Get her up and hold her firm.'

While some minion scurried away to bring another flaming torch, Emot Sai grabbed her, dragged her from the floor and held her tight as he'd had lesser Emots secure her for him. She lifted her head and schooled her face into an impassive mask, hopefully before he saw her shock at his form, so much larger and more solid than on his last visit. Light from the flaming torch on the wall outside the cell flickered ominously on his oily black skin.

'Do you know who I am, witch?' Emot hissed.

She nodded.

'Say it!' His upper lip twisted into a malevolent grin.

'Emot,' she whispered.

'Very good. And now that you know who faces you, do you tremble with fearful expectation?'

Though only partially true, Nadima nodded.

The demon slid smoothly across the stone floor until he stood before her. His fiery red eyes raked her body.

'Turn her around,' he commanded.

Emot Sai obliged.

'You have done well to subjugate this one, Emot Sai.'

'She will not resist, Master,' Emot Sai said proudly.

'She is a fitting meal for Emot, just like her spawn.' Emot ran his talon along the line of Nadima's jaw and up behind her ear.

Despite herself, Nadima trembled at his touch and flinched at the mention of Ariel. Emot didn't miss it, and Emot Sai gurgled his pleasure as he pressed against Nadima's back.

'Yes, she feeds me, your beloved Ariel, feeds me willingly. That's why I'm so strong, see the fine density of my form,' Emot gloated.

'If she feeds you then why are you here?'

'A small set back, of no consequence and not your daughter's doing. She waits for me. In fact, she does nothing but wait for her lover's return.'

'You lie!'

He merely laughed, picked something off his chest and held it up for her to see. Nadima bit her lip, struggling to maintain her calm. Several auburn hairs hung from his fingers.

'She comes as close to me as Emot Sai does to you now,' Emot continued, stepping back. 'And I drink the flame of her craving while she craves the pleasure I offer, just as you do with Emot Sai as he feeds on you now.'

Her jailor's talon touched Nadima's neck and she stifled a sigh. The familiar rhythm of his deep purr rumbled against her back.

'My turn,' Emot droned.

Emot Sai grunted, a hint of displeasure in his tone. Did he not want to share? Emot stepped closer and Nadima trembled in trepidation. Even without his talon on her neck, she found Emot Sai's presence behind her uncomfortably comforting.

'My pleasure for you is even greater than his,' Emot crooned as he stroked her neck where he would feed, preparing her for his touch.

Nadima gasped; waves of tantalising expectation rushed through her body. How could Ariel, so young and untrained, possibly resist such allure? The thought provided a convenient emotion to feed the Rasa—hopelessness. To keep it flowing, she reminded herself of the terrible consequences for the world should Ariel truly be addicted. Warriors trained for years to avoid this kind of mental torture. At least she knew how to get herself out of it.

'Let loose your craving, my love,' Emot purred when she eased out of the hopelessness. Emot Sai shifted uneasily behind her and his hands squeezed harder around her arms. 'Feel the exquisite pleasure of unrequited desire,' Emot continued, stroking her neck again. Nadima swooned with pleasure.

She didn't dare resist. If Emot Sai told his master how he'd gotten his way, she'd be placing a potent weapon into the hands of the enemy. The only real way out of this mess was to kill Emot, and quickly. But how? She knew a way, but was her command of the Light strong enough? He would kill her if she failed, but perhaps it was better to die trying than to endure being a demon's slave.

She turned to the demon and smiled her most alluring smile. 'Come lie with me,' she said, taking his taloned hand.

'Watch out Master, the witch has tricks,' Emot Sai spat.

Shut up, Sai.

'Don't tell me what to do!' Emot screeched at his underling and sent a slap of fire to punish him. 'Stand by the door and feed on the leftovers. She's mine now.'

Emot Sai whined and his face twisted in misery as Emot lay beside Nadima on her bed. He slithered close to her, the strength of his smell raising bile. But she faced her revulsion and it dissolved under her scrutiny. She had to remain in control.

He began caressing her with greasy hands, but she held them still. 'There's no need for you to do anything,' she whispered, 'I will feed you of my own free will. Let me caress you, just place your talon on my neck and enjoy.'

'Oh my, you are even better than your daughter, even more willing,' Emot wallowed in his triumph. As she'd hoped, she'd caught his interest with something different, and hopefully it would hold him long enough.

It had caught her jailer's attention as well. Emot Sai watched from the door with a bitter expression. She had never lain with him. For a moment, his eyes flamed green. *He is jealous!* Nadima had no time to consider the ramifications; she had to begin.

She ran her hands across his chest. 'Feel my craving for your feeding,' she whispered, and though one part of her mind yearned for the pleasure his talon would provide, she focused on an image of Walnut in his Radiant Form. Give me the power, she prayed silently, open my heart so the Radiance flows unchecked. Instantly, she felt his presence, as if he was there beside her.

The demon sipped on her craving, but she fooled him, feeding him only her craving for the success of her plan and ignoring the pleasure of his touch completely. She could never have fooled Emot Sai that way. He knew the flavour of every one of her emotions.

'More,' Emot swooned.

'Look into my eyes,' she whispered. 'Feed on the gaze of desire.'

He obeyed, amazing Nadima with his willingness. Her offer had completely disarmed him. Drawing on her deepest experience of her Radiant Power, and bolstered by her sense of Walnut's presence, unbeknownst to the demon, each time she breathed in, she drew some of his black slimy form into the centre of her chest where it dissolved in the brilliance of her Radiance. Each time she breathed out, brilliant white light poured out and consumed some of his flesh. The demon's form flickered and lost its solidity. Nadima drew on more power than she knew she had, but was it enough? It had to be quick, very quick.

Emot's eyelids grew heavy and his gaze dropped.

'Master,' Emot Sai whispered.

Nadima glanced at him. The struggle in his expression tugged at her heart, but he too was weakening, fading with his master who was locked in the embrace of Nadima's fearless love.

'It's a trick,' Sai managed to get out in a feeble voice.

Walnut! Nadima called silently. Lend me the power of the guides of the past.

Light blazed from her chest and sucked Serpentine from the demon. Layer by layer, it vaporised in the brilliance.

'What treachery is this?' Emot pulled away from her and tried to scramble to his feet, but the Light held him firm and ate into his form like acid. 'Let me go, bitch!' Though full of passion, his voice thinned as he faded into a mere wisp of red light, then into nothing. Nadima smiled. Emot would never hunt her again.

A cheer rose from prisoners down the hall. Nadima turned her gaze on Emot Sai. He was fading fast and the lesser emanations had already dissolved. Sai fell to his knees before her. 'Please,' he begged. 'Feed me. Quickly, my love, before it's too late. I will serve you, protect you, and bow down to you, only save me. I want to live.'

A mere shadow of Emot Sai groveled before her.

'I have been good to you,' he whispered, the fire gone from his eyes. 'Would you repay me with death?'

Nadima shook her head. 'Ah, Sai, do you really think I could trust you? If I feed you now, you will be the new Emot and you will do what Emot must do.'

'No, I swear. I will not hunt others,' he vowed in a barely audible voice, a last desperate attempt to stay alive. 'My existence and Emot's power will be in your hands. I surrender to you, Nadima. I am your slave.' His eyes closed, too weak to speak, too weak to move, his form, barely there, now reached only to her knees.

Adrenaline suddenly pumped through Nadima's veins, driven by the possibility of an alternative vision. 'You foul idiot, stinking creature of evil. You disgust me,' she spat, recalling her most bitter memories of the demon's work. 'I hate you and all your kind for what you do to people, the pain you cause, the terror you instill.' She crawled to what was left of Emot Sai, took his talon, almost transparent now, and placed it on her neck.

A slither of fire flared in the depths of the demon's eyes. 'My love, my love,' he crooned as he fed on the thick soup of her anger. 'I am yours forever.'

Tears formed in Nadima's eyes at the pleasure of his touch, and she fed him on a rich cocktail of emotion, all garnished with fear for the future. What was she doing? Was she addicted after all?

Emot Sai's form grew and began to solidify, but when his head, still not fully corporeal, reached Nadima's chin, she ceased her immersion in the flow of emotion, cutting off his sustenance.

'More,' he begged.

'No, Sai,' she said softly, removing his talon from her neck. 'I cannot let you be as strong as you were before. You will have to live in a diminished state or not live at all.'

'But I am Emot now. I must have the strength to take succession and a form to match my status.' He clambered to his feet, flexed his muscles and drew himself up, his eyes flaring with excitement.

Nadima stood, easily a head above him and stared down the disdain in his eyes. 'You are in no position to ask for anything. I will test your allegiance and, if you prove trustworthy, I can afford to let you be stronger, but if you fail me, I will demolish you with one glance. The deal is simple, do as I say, or die.'

Sai's shoulders slumped, the fire faded from his eyes and, after a moment, he replied in a subdued tone. 'I will do as you wish.'

'Good,' Nadima nodded. 'Now, the rules.'

Sai groaned and Nadima chuckled. 'Remember the alternative, my Rasa friend.' She patted his head and his eyes burned with shame and fury. 'This was your idea, Sai. I would have let you fade had you not begged me to save you. In return you must bind yourself to me, be the slave you promised. Swear that you will protect me above yourself, follow my command without question, and that you will not feed without my permission or create emanations.'

He glared at her. 'Perhaps I would rather die,' he muttered bitterly.

'The choice is yours,' Nadima said without emotion.

Sai said nothing for a moment, then rallied. 'In return, you will feed me yourself,' he said with as much dignity as he could muster. 'Give me that much, my love. For me there is no greater pleasure than my talon on your neck, sipping your sweet nectar. For this alone I will do as you command.'

Nadima considered the deal. Did she dare continue feeding him herself? Did she dare not to? With a sigh, she decided. She needed him to help free the prisoners before Cogins swarmed the place, and what better way to ensure his servitude than by feeding his addiction. She could get rid of Emot Sai later.

'It's a deal, Sai. Serve me well and you will have your pleasure.'

The Emot smiled and bowed, but his next sentence disturbed Nadima more than she wanted to admit. 'Then you will have your pleasure too, Mistress.'

'You are the slave, Sai. Don't forget that.'

'Of course, Mistress.' With a smirk, he reached his talon towards her.

She slapped it away. 'First, we free the prisoners.'

'No,' Sai protested. 'Now the Emots are gone, the Cogins will take over. I cannot go against the Cogin.'

'Then look into my eyes, Emot Sai, and say goodbye forever.'

He stared at the ground, shaking his head in misery, but after a moment, he shuffled a hand amongst the folds of his skin and drew out a large key. 'You do it,' he said. 'I will stay here where the Cogin won't see me.'

'No. You will come with me and protect me as you vowed. If we meet Cogins, you will tell them that you are Emot now and that I am your slave. In their presence I will give you the status you crave. Only you and I will know which of us is truly the slave.'

Emot Sai's thin lips twisted into a lopsided smile. 'As you wish, Mistress.'

Nadima peered into the main cavern. Only one lantern burned, tainting the air with its oily fumes, and the few Domos in attendance slept on their straw beds. Not one Rasa in sight. Luckily, Emot had chosen the evening for his visit.

Clutching the key in her hand, Nadima stepped into the cavern; but, at the same time, two burley Rasas appeared out of a tunnel. Green eyes flickered like a windstorm on their viscous faces and green saliva dripped from the slit of their mouth. Nadima swallowed and stepped back, hiding the key behind her back. She had forgotten there were two Cogins stationed close to the cages.

'Well, well, what have we here, Cogin Ra?' one of the Cogin growled, his face twisting into a sadistic smile.

'I'd say Emot's finished and now it's our turn to play.' The second Cogin chuckled and rubbed his hands together with glee.

'Emot is not finished,' Sai said in a deep voice, stepping out of the shadows behind Nadima, 'and for as long as I survive, it is not your turn. This Warrior is my slave.'

'Then where are your emanations, Emot, and why are you so slim?' the Cogin sneered.

'I had a setback elsewhere,' Sai replied. 'But I will soon be restored. My slave has planned a special feast for me and my emanations are gathering in our own quarters. They will all share the spoils of my conquest. Unfortunately for you, we will only be serving Emot food.'

'Why are you here then when your quarters are that way?' Cogin Ra asked suspiciously.

'The prisoners are coming with us,' Sai replied. 'They are the feast.'

'This is foolish, Emot. With only you to guard them, they could escape. Why not bring your clan here?'

'It is a plan too subtle for Cogins,' Sai replied disdainfully. 'Prisoners rarely provide Emots' favourite flavour. This way, we make them think they are going to escape and then we feed on their lust for freedom.' The lie fell flawlessly from his lips.

'Impressive,' the other Cogin said.

'What if they do escape?' Cogin Ra demanded. 'You will have the fury of Cogin and Rasama on you.'

'My emanations can easily herd them back again. Besides, they will never find their way out of our labyrinth.'

'That is true, Cogin Ra,' the second Cogin agreed.

'I cannot let you take the prisoners from here without a guard,' Cogin Ra said.

'I wonder if you can stop me,' Sai said. 'I am a Major after all and you are merely an emanation.'

The two Cogins looked uneasily at each other.

'When this feast is over, I will make a plan for you too,' Nadima said in her sweetest voice. 'I will find a way to get the prisoners to give you Cogin food.'

The Cogin looked somewhat mollified but unconvinced.

'What else do you think is going on here?' Sai asked them. 'Do you think I am trying to free the prisoners? Ridiculous. What would I gain from that? Go back to your chamber. I will call if I need a Cogin.'

The two Cogins looked at each other, then Cogin Ra shrugged. 'It is no business of ours, anyway,' he said. 'We get little satisfaction from this lot and if the prisoners escape, it will be on your head, not ours.'

'They will not escape through my plan,' Sai said and pushed past the Cogin.

Nadima smiled to herself. No, they will escape through my plan.

The Cogin begrudgingly made way and retired to their chamber. Nadima breathed a sigh of relief. Her story had passed its first test. She placed her hand on Sai's arm. 'You did well. I'm impressed.'

'I stick to my bargain. You stick to yours.'

The sleeping Domos had awoken during the conversation and they stood awaiting the new Emot's orders. Nadima shot him a reminder glance.

'Go,' he said to the Domos. 'Go home; you are not needed here anymore.'

The Domos grinned. 'Thank you, Master,' they said with a bow, then turned and raced down one of the tunnels.

Nadima smiled at Sai. He smiled back, pleased with himself. Lust glittered in his eyes. She turned away and walked to the largest cell. 'Bob,' she whispered through the bars. 'Where are you? We're getting out of here.'

Several prisoners lifted their heads and stared at her through bloodshot eyes. Many lay crowded on straw beds, but few slept.

'Nadima?' A tall grey-haired man stood up in the middle of the cell. 'How wonderful to see you. Did you say we're getting out?' He frowned at Emot Sai as he stepped over the prisoners and came towards her.

'Yes,' she whispered, 'but we must be quiet.'

A murmur ran through the cells and people began getting to their feet, their faces glowing with hope.

'You have an Emot with you. *The* Emot, I suspect,' Bob pointed out, an unspoken question in his eyes.

'It's complicated, Bob, and we don't have time for answers now,' she replied. 'All you need to know is that he's under my control, and he's promised to guide us out of here.'

Bob raised his eyebrows and turned his gaze on Sai. The demon nodded sullenly. 'But what is a demon's promise worth?'

'If it wasn't for his promises, there would have been a lot of torture in these cells,' Nadima replied.

'If we are escaping, then what is that demon doing here?' a woman asked.

'He's going to show us the way out.' A whisper of surprise and disbelief spread through the cells.

'Why wouldn't he lead us into a trap?' the woman asked.

'I heard him tell the Cogin that she was his slave,' a man nearby said. 'That sounds more likely to me. All the Emots disappeared except him, so she must have fed him before he dissolved. Only a slave would do that.'

'Whether you trust me or not is up to you,' Nadima replied. 'I'll not defend myself, but I'll lead any of you out who want to come with me. You can stay if you want.'

'Why do you bother with them?' Sai growled. 'Let us go alone.'

Nadima shook her head. 'Give them time.'

'I do not care about them, but the longer we wait, the more likely it is that Cogin will get suspicious. Do you think those emanations will not tell their master?'

'I'll risk it,' a woman said. 'Where can she lead us that would be worse than staying here?'

Many nodded, but some still looked skeptical.

'You will have to be silent all the way,' Nadima said, 'and you must do as you are told or we could all be discovered. Also, you must not attack the demon. Without him we will get hopelessly lost.' Hope and despair, tentative trust and blatant suspicion played on the prisoners' faces. What did you expect? she asked herself. 'How many Warriors do we have?'

Several people in each cell raised their hands.

Nadima nodded. 'I am going to let the Warriors out now, so we can work out a plan. The rest of you need to stay in the cells until we're ready to move out. The two Cogins are suspicious. If they come back, it's best that things look as normal as possible.'

A murmur went through the prisoners. It sounded to Nadima like a mixture of agreement and suspicion.

'Let the Warriors out, Sai. It will help them trust you,' she whispered, handing him the keys, 'and others will be less inclined to want to rush out.'

'You ask me too much already,' he grumbled.

'Sai, please. I have risked everything to save you.'

'Don't forget, I do the same to please you.'

'I will keep my word.'

He glared at her, but took the keys and glided to the first door where, with a pained look on his face, he let out Bob and several others, then closed the door and did the same with the other two cells. Nadima kept her eyes on the exit the two Cogins had taken.

'Bob,' she whispered as he joined her. 'Will you trust me? I can't take them all out without help, and if someone does something wrong we will all be … well, killed probably.'

'I trust you, Nadima, but not him.' He nodded towards Sai who was gliding back towards them. 'And do you? Really?'

'In this, yes, because I have what he wants. Isn't that right, Sai?'

'Yes, mistress,' he replied, his eyes glittering. With amusement?

'Sai?' Bob asked.

'It was his name before . . .' Nadima shrugged.

'Ah, before. I understand.' Bob nodded.

'It's the only way we'll get out.'

'I suspect you are right, that's why you have my support.'

'Believe me, Bob, I know what I'm doing.'

'I hope so. For your sake.'

32

Escape

'Can you speak to the Warriors?' Nadima asked Bob. 'We need their support; they know you and we must hurry.'

He nodded and Nadima beckoned the other Warriors over. They joined her and Bob, but kept their distance from Emot Sai.

'Nadima is an old friend and the wife of the last holder of the Blade of Aarod,' Bob told them. 'I trust her and ask that you do so too, so that we can get these people out of here. Do we have your support?'

'I don't like it,' a Warrior woman said. 'But any escape attempt will have its risks, and there is no point staying here. It's true we'd be unlikely to find our way out on our own, so if she has some hold over this Emot, then I agree that she should have our support.'

The others nodded. Nadima smiled. Sai flicked his talons together, and all eyes turned to him. Nadima shook her head and he dropped his hands to his sides.

'Thank you,' Nadima said. 'I need you to station yourself along the line of people and help the untrained to be silent and courageous. Do you agree to help this way?'

They nodded.

'Good. Bob will be my second in command and will take messages along the line.'

'And the Rasa?' a man asked. 'What about him?'

'He will do as I tell him, but when another demon appears, we will act as if I am the slave and he is the master.'

'I wonder which way it really is,' one of the Warriors murmured.

'Tell him,' Nadima commanded Sai.

'Must I say it?' he hissed. 'It is bad enough that it's true.'

'Say it, *Emot*.'

'Unfortunately, she is my mistress,' the new Emot growled. His words appeared to satisfy the Warriors.

A young Warrior with *Dean* scrawled across his T-shirt stepped forward. 'Where is my sword, *demon*?'

'You treat me with disdain and expect me to give you a weapon,' Sai replied. 'I don't think so.'

'Where is it, Sai?' Nadima asked.

'This wasn't in the bargain,' he growled.

'What if we meet Cogin? What will he do to you? With a sword we could save you from him.'

'What makes you think you could defeat him? And why would I give a weapon to one who would kill me at the first opportunity?'

'If you are really his mistress,' Dean interjected, 'then he should do what you tell him to. Why don't you punish him?'

Sai growled, his killing talon extended, and he lifted his hand, ready to strike.

'No.' Nadima placed a restraining hand on the demon's arm, then turned to the boy. 'Go away, young man. We don't have time for this.'

Dean curled his top lip in distaste and stood his ground until Bob commanded him away with a jerk of his head.

'I did not agree to be the butt of a baby Warrior's scorn,' Emot Sai growled.

'Are you hungry?' Nadima whispered.

Sai's eyes flared and his face softened.

'Show me where the weapons are.'

His face twitched with humiliation at the power she had over him, but he nodded and led the way towards a narrow corridor off the main cavern.

Bob moved to follow.

'It's okay, Bob,' Nadima said. 'I need you to let the prisoners out, divide them into groups, one for each warrior, then wait. I'll be back soon.'

As soon as they were out of sight of the Warriors, Emot Sai stopped and turned to Nadima. 'Do not tease me, my love.' She saw the frustration in his eyes.

'I do not tease you. Give me the weapons and you can feed.'

He smiled, a strange twisted thing, and led her along the tunnel to an alcove where several swords and a sceptre lay. She took the weapons, wondering which Warrior the sceptre belonged to, then stood and presented her neck to the demon. He purred contentedly until she cut the flow.

'I need more,' he whined.

'Not now.' She wiped her hand across the place where he'd fed and handed him two swords to carry.

He looked at them in surprise. 'You trust me?'

'Should I not?'

He shook his head.

'Good, get us out of here.'

When they returned to the others, if any of the Warriors noticed that Sai had grown a little, they never mentioned it.

'Dean will not be taking charge of a group,' Bob told her. 'I have released Melanie who, though not a Warrior, will do a good job.'

'Dean will be in my group,' an older woman standing beside Bob said, 'where perhaps he will learn how not to taint the name of Warrior with arrogance and anger.'

'Thank you,' Nadima replied.

'I will take Dean's weapon,' Bob said. 'Who owns these others?'

'The sceptre is mine,' the older woman said. Nadima could see by her gracious bearing that she spoke the truth. 'I will take the rear of the line.'

'Good idea,' Bob said.

'What's your name?' Nadima asked the woman as Bob gave out the rest of the weapons and allocated the owners their place in the line.

'Natalie,' she replied.

'You are the most advanced Warrior here,' Nadima said. 'Do you wish to lead or give some direction?'

'No, I think you are doing just fine, my dear. Sometimes radical, unorthodox means are necessary, but I do pray that you have the strength to dispatch your demon as soon as we are free.'

'I'm counting on it,' Nadima said and Sai hissed quietly from his place close behind her. She shot him a reassuring taste of craving, then told the Warriors the story they would use as explanation should they meet other demons. 'You will need to keep your weapons hidden, or we will not look like prisoners. Use them only on my command.' The warriors nodded. 'Now, lead us quickly, Sai,' Nadima said, smiling at him. 'We have lost enough time already.'

His eyes flared—with pleasure or irritation, she couldn't tell—but he led the prisoners, roughly eight to ten in six groups, up a tunnel lit at irregular intervals with burning torches set on the walls. Many had gone out, presumably from lack of oil, and some sputtered and died as they passed. The prisoners stumbled along in darkness, until Bob and two of the other Warriors took the next torches from the wall and carried them. After that, they moved swiftly along a long gradually rising segment, until Emot Sai slowed as they came to an intersection.

'Wait here,' he told Bob.

Nadima followed the demon a short way along the right hand fork until satisfied that no one came their way, then they led the prisoners on. A hundred metres further along, they stopped again. Rasa voices echoed down the tunnel towards them. The prisoners, eyes glinting fearfully in the flickering torchlight, pressed back against the tunnel walls.

'Rasama must be very powerful to grow our master so quickly and strongly,' a Rasa said in an arrogant voice.

'And Master has done well to make so many Amics in such a short time and provide a source of fodder within the nest. We can look forward to a long life I think, brother,' another added.

Several of them laughed together.

'Babies,' the new Emot muttered. 'They know nothing.'

The Amics turned the corner and stopped, their eyes flickering over the line of trembling prisoners.

'Emot?' the leader asked.

'Of course,' the new Emot replied. 'And the fodder on demand is my doing, not Amic's.'

'Hmph. Our master told us it was in cells in the central chamber.'

'It was, but we are taking them to the Emot nest for a special feast for my people. You may feed here. The prisoners will not be back in the central cells until morning.'

The Amics grunted their agreement and came towards the prisoners with their feeding talons extended.

'Not this one,' Sai growled as the leader placed his talon on Nadima. 'She is mine alone.'

The Amic shrugged and Bob stepped forward to take Nadima's place. His hand rested on the short sword hidden beneath his shirt and he glanced questioningly at Nadima. She shook her head, almost imperceptibly, and Bob quietly submitted to the Amic's need.

Nadima and Bob had placed the strongest non-trained prisoners in the first group and had told them to give themselves to their fear if they asked them to feed any Rasas. Now, they fed the Amics without hesitation.

'Have you enslaved them all, Emot?' the leader of the Amics asked when he was satiated. 'They are very willing.'

'Emots have ways that other Rasa clans can't even dream of,' he replied. 'Now return to your nest.'

The Amics nodded and turned back obediently. As soon as they were out of hearing, the prisoners followed.

'The inferior Rasa clans are easily satisfied and have no imagination,' the new Emot whispered.

The escapees negotiated several intersections and T-junctions without meeting any more demons, then Emot led them into an enormous cavern. 'They can hide here for a while,' he told Nadima. 'I want to show you my palace and we should check the Cogin trails before moving on.'

'Your palace?'

He nodded and led her to the back of the cavern. 'This is the Emots' nest.' He puffed up his chest. 'I am lord of this place now and one day it will be full of my emanations. They will honour and obey me and bring me the best slaves.'

Nadima raised her eyebrows, but said nothing. A timely reminder, she thought, realising that he would do whatever he could to make his dream a reality.

'And this is Emot's palace,' he said as he led her into a smaller cavern connected to the large one.

Nadima's jaw dropped. Throughout the cavern, huge stalactites and stalagmites joined to make columns and arches; lanterns in niches in the wall illuminated them in subtle and pleasing ways.

'It is the best of all the caverns. Rasama gave it to us because it suits our disposition. Emots enjoy beautiful things.' The way he looked at her made Nadima squirm. 'Look at this.'

He showed her a natural air vent in the back corner and as she looked up at the tiny speck of daylight many metres above, he stepped close.

'I will feed now. ' He placed his talon on her neck.

Nadima bashed it away. 'Not until I say!' She tried to move past him, but he pressed her back against the wall.

A muscle next to his mouth twitched and his eyes narrowed. His voice came out as a hiss. 'Here, we will do as I say, for this is my place and I am lord here.' His talon flashed towards her and penetrated just beneath her collarbone.

Nadima gasped, but caught the rising fear and anger and dissolved it before he could feed.

He pushed the talon in deeper and twisted it in the wound. 'Bitah food will do.'

Nadima gritted her teeth against the pain. 'You don't need to do that,' she said. 'I'll not feed you that way. Take it out.' She put a finger under his chin and lifted it until her gaze fixed on his eyes.

His arm went limp, the talon withdrew and he began to shrink. 'No,' he cried, unable to wrench his eyes away even though her gaze diminished him. 'Cruel Nadima. What of our bargain?'

'The bargain was that I am your mistress. You are not my master and this is why.'

'You will never get out without me.'

She released him. 'That is why you are still alive.' She pushed past the weakened Rasa. 'Come, I will feed you when we are free.'

'No Cogin will ever believe I am Emot in this state.'

She stopped and turned back. 'Then let them watch me feed you willingly.'

His eyes flared, no doubt excited by the idea of showing off his domination of her, but the accompanying smile faded quickly. 'Please, Nadima,' he begged, 'just a little. Back to how I was. I cannot go out like this. I am too weak.'

She sighed. 'Give me a baby wombat any day,' she muttered. 'Okay, Sai, just a little, but not your favourite, and in future don't forget who is mistress and who is slave.'

'It is hard for me here in my palace,' he grumbled.

After the feeding, they returned to the main Emot cavern, checked the tunnels ahead and took the prisoners to the next intersection. There, they waited in silence for a few minutes, listening. Just as they began to move again, Rasa voices echoed down the tunnel. Bob hid his torch behind him and beckoned the prisoners back against the side of the tunnel.

A group of Cogin glided along the tunnel, luckily too engrossed in boasting of their conquests to notice the prisoners frozen against the wall of a side tunnel.

'We are nearer to the Cogin's nest now,' Emot Sai whispered. 'We must be careful.'

With a start, Nadima realised that they were now going away from the Emots' nest. Their story would no longer hold. She mentioned it to Bob and with a determined look on his face, he patted the sword at his side. She prayed they wouldn't have to use it. Probably only Natalie had the ability to succeed against the deadly Cogin.

The prisoners crossed the intersection one group at a time, while Emot and Nadima remained at the junction. The last group had just gone across and Nadima and Emot stepped into the main tunnel after them when another band of Cogin rounded the corner and strode silently towards them.

Nadima's heart skipped a beat and she motioned a warning to the prisoners still in sight along the tunnel. They bobbed to the ground and Dean pulled the nearest torch from the wall and stamped it out. A moment later, three large Cogins stopped in front of Emot and Nadima. Her palms sweated and a wave of fear arose, but she dissolved it with a glance.

'Are you Emot?' the leader asked.

'Of course,' the new Emot replied, puffing himself up.

'You are very small for a major,' the Cogin said. The three of them laughed.

The new Emot's face twitched. 'A small set back,' he growled. 'Nevertheless, I am a major and you are mere emanations. You will speak to me as you should or not at all.'

'Apologies, my lord,' the leader replied. 'And who is this?'

'My slave.'

'Then why does she not feed you?'

'She is a Warrior. Her flavour is very rich. I take it in small doses.'

The leader of the band narrowed his eyes at Nadima. 'We are going to check on the prisoners. Cogin sensed that Emot was dead.'

'I am the new Emot. She fed me to keep me alive.'

'How do I get a slave like that?' one of the other Cogins asked.

'By serving your master well,' Sai hissed, glaring at him.

'But why are you going away from your nest?' the leader asked. 'Do you not need to recover and create emanations?'

'I do, but she craves fresh air and I feed on her craving,' Sai replied, impressing Nadima with his ability to improvise. Perhaps they could get out of this without a battle that, even if they won, would alert every Rasa in the tunnels.

'I say this is suspicious,' the Cogin leader said. 'Our Master warned us to be careful. You must come and explain yourself to him.'

'Watch her feed me willingly and you will see the truth of my story,' Sai countered.

'That I'd like to see,' the second Cogin said.

'Very well,' said the first.

'Come, slave,' Sai growled. 'Feed me your best.' His eyes glittered and his mouth twisted into a smile.

Nadima obeyed. She knew he would enjoy proving his subjugation of her, so she didn't provide his favourite flavour.

'More, slave. More,' he hissed when she ceased the flow.

Nadima glared a warning at him but gave him another taste. The new Emot's talon lingered on her neck even after she had stopped the flow.

'Are you satisfied?' he asked the Cogin when he finally withdrew.

'If she feeds me too, I will believe you,' the leader said.

'She is my slave. I do not share her. A Cogin should understand that.'

'One taste and my suspicions will be allayed.'

'What do I care about your suspicions? I am Emot Major.'

'Not yet, I think,' the Cogin replied. 'You are still too weak.'

'I will remember your insolence when I have my full succession.'

'You may taste Rasama's wrath before then.'

'I will willingly feed him, Master, if that is your desire,' Nadima said. They couldn't afford a battle such as this.

'I have no time for this,' the new Emot said. 'I have a clan to create. Feed him and let us be on our way.'

'Perhaps I can feed on your jealousy, Emot,' the Cogin chuckled.

'You have two seconds!'

Five seconds later, the new Emot brushed the smiling Cogin's talon off Nadima's neck. 'She is good,' the Cogin gloated.

'Your master does not understand the ways of Emots,' Emot said and gestured the Cogin down the tunnel. 'When you see him again, tell him if he wants my secrets he must teach his emanations more respect.'

The leader of the Cogin band nodded grimly and walked down the tunnel towards the cells. Nadima breathed a sigh of relief and they took off in the other direction.

'Good feed,' Sai murmured.

Nadima ignored him. He was stronger than she wanted him to be, but he had done well and, blinded by his addiction for her, seemed almost as keen as she to get out of the tunnels.

They hurried to the head of the line of prisoners, aware that as soon as the group of Cogins found the cells empty, they would come back this way for sure. Before they got to where Bob waited, a Rasa voice rang out.

'Prisoners!'

Someone screamed and the sound of steel on talon rang along the tunnel.

'At arms, Warriors,' she shouted and ran the rest of the way to the head of the line, gathering the armed Warriors as she went.

Bob struggled against a Cogin, while several more fed from the first group of terrified prisoners. One already lay dead on the ground. The other Warriors ran up and joined in the fray, attacking the Cogins with vigour but, clearly, none of them had the skill or training to defeat them. Only Bob and she had defeated Emot and she had no weapon against them, except … Where was Sai? She looked desperately around but he'd disappeared.

'Damn,' Nadima muttered. Could the prisoners rush past the Cogin and take their chances in the rest of the tunnels?

One of the Warriors cried out and fell to the ground; blood poured from his chest. Bob backed off, unable to make a strike.

'Stop,' Nadima cried, running out before the Cogins. 'Stop. We will feed you.'

They stopped and stared at her through narrowed eyes.

'We are Emot's slaves. We will feed you.'

'Slaves?' one Cogin said. 'Then why do these ones have weapons?'

'Because they are Warriors,' Natalie replied, stepping out from the crowd, her sceptre raised; 'and Warriors are not demons' slaves.' With one volley of sceptre fire, she completely wiped out the group of Cogin.

'Oh Natalie,' Nadima cried throwing herself around the older woman's neck. 'Thank Aya you're here.'

'I'm only sorry these old legs couldn't get to the front more quickly,' she said, looking at the two young men that lay dead on the ground. 'Take the rest on,' she told Nadima. 'I will set the light above them and follow you.'

Nadima nodded and beckoned the prisoners on. 'You take them, Bob,' she whispered.

'Don't wait for him, Nadima,' Bob replied. 'He's probably run off. The air's fresher here. We can't be far now. Let's just follow our noses.'

'Go. I'll catch you up.'

Bob shook his head, but walked on without her.

Nadima stayed against the wall and when the last prisoner had passed, she spied her Emot wandering up the tunnel behind them.

'It is done,' Natalie said as, with the help of sceptre magic, she finished covering the dead men's bodies. She followed Nadima's gaze. 'Do we still need him?'

'We are not out yet and he needs me,' Nadima replied.

'That is a strange thing for a Warrior to say.'

'Do you judge me?'

'No, but I wonder.'

'In time, you will see.'

'Be careful.'

Nadima nodded and when the elderly Warrior had followed the others, the new Emot glided up to her.

'I refuse to fight against my own kind,' he said.

'I did not ask you to.'

'Then let us go.'

Nadima nodded. 'I'm glad you came back,' she said as they set off up the tunnel.

'I cannot stay away from you, Nadima.'

They moved quickly to the head of the escapees, arriving just as a band of Bitahs appeared in the tunnel in front of them.

'It is Bitah himself,' the old Sai whispered. 'You must feed me, quickly. Another Major will never believe I am Emot in this state.'

Nadima frowned. Could she risk it? Not if there was another way. 'Bob,' she whispered. 'Bring the Warriors, we must use our gaze.'

Bob slipped back along the line as the Bitah and his gang drew close.

'Emot?' Bitah asked as the two groups met. 'What are you doing with these prisoners? Is this treason?'

The new Emot drew himself up but before he could speak, Nadima took his talon and placed it on her neck.

'We are slaves. We feed Emot willingly with his favourite food.' She roused the strangely painful pleasure of yearning to feed him and he grew visibly, then she quickly stopped the flow.

'All slaves, Emot? These few have the look of Warriors about them.' He indicated the Warriors that came up behind Nadima. 'No Rasa, not even Emot, could achieve such as this.'

'I do not lie,' Sai said. 'You have just met the most powerful Emot ever known.'

'Look at our faces,' Nadima said, sidling close to her Emot, 'you will see our craving for our master's touch in our eyes.'

Emot flinched, but the Bitahs curiosity overcame their caution and they looked into the prisoners' eyes. Immediately, the Warriors who had already defeated Bitah locked their gazes on those before them, and the demons began to dissolve.

'No!' Emot Sai screamed. 'Stop this at once!'

The Warriors ignored him. The Bitahs faded into a wisp of white and disappeared down the tunnel. A joyful murmur rose from the escapees.

'I will not lead you anymore,' Emot growled at Nadima.

'You must,' she whispered in reply. 'We are bound together, you and I.' He looked at her with such painful yearning that her heart twisted in sadness for him. 'Feed me now, or our bargain is broken.'

Nadima stared at him but he avoided her eyes.

'I can assure you that I will slice quite a few of these weaklings into pieces before any of you kill me.'

He was right. Few of the Warriors with them had the ability to defeat even a weakened Emot. Nadima sighed, motioned to Bob to turn away and when the prisoners had all looked away, she extended her neck and stood still while Emot fed. Once again, she cut the flow before he could grow too strong, but he said nothing and led them on.

33

Freedom

The fire in the sitting room crackled cheerfully and Deidre's knitting needles clicked in an easy rhythm. Walnut sat, reading, in one of the battered easy chairs. Geordie dozed on the floor by the fire with Twitchet on a cushion at his feet. Maya had already gone to bed. Layla had flown to her home somewhere on the upper reaches, and Ariel curled up against Nick's chest on the sofa.

'We really should go to bed,' he murmured.

'Mmm.' She made no move to go.

He chuckled and stroked her shoulder.

Someone shouted from outside. Two voices. Geordie's eyes flew open and everyone looked up, listening. 'I'll see what's going on,' Geordie said, pulling himself to his feet.

'What's that strange noise?' Deidre asked. 'It's getting closer.'

A bubbling sound came from outside. Or was it more like humming? Ariel wondered. No; not humming. 'It sounds like voices,' she said, sitting up, 'lots of them.'

Walnut stood and placed his book on the coffee table. 'I'll go and see. Nick, stay here with Ariel.' He strode out the door.

Twitchet scampered after him.

Deidre pushed her knitting into a soft bag and walked from the room, leaving Ariel and Nick staring after her.

'Why did Walnut tell us to stay?' Ariel asked.

'Invalids shouldn't get excited,' he replied with a grin.

Ariel rolled her eyes.

✸✸✸

A ragged procession with Nadima at its head scrambled from a hole in the ground with shouts of joy as their lungs filled with fresh air and their eyes beheld the twinkling golden lights of the Hermitage not far away. They scrambled through the boulders towards it, stumbling in a darkness broken only by the light of the Rasa lanterns they had wrenched from the walls.

'People to the west!' someone shouted from the Hermitage.

A torch swung over them and settled on Nadima. Even when she shaded her eyes, she couldn't see the person behind it.

'They're friends,' a voice shouted, and the figure with the torch walked to meet them. 'Nadima! Blessed Aya, am I pleased to see you.' The voice had an English accent. Tynan? He lowered the torch as he drew close and Nadima smiled when she saw that the man behind it was indeed Tynan. 'I feared we'd never see you again.'

'It's good to be out.'

'I don't doubt it.' He turned to the demon hovering close to her side. 'But what is that Rasa doing there?'

Nadima turned to Bob. 'Take them on, Bob, please.'

'Don't be hard on her,' Bob said as he beckoned to the others, 'we only got out because of him.' He nodded to Nadima, then led the procession of ex-prisoners towards the Hermitage.

'In that case,' Tynan said as the ragged band of ex-prisoners walked past them, 'the question is, why is this Emot at your side?' He glared at the demon.

'*The* Emot,' the demon hissed.

'Emot himself!' Horror and disbelief laced Tynan's voice. 'Nadima, what have you done?'

Nadima took a deep breath and drew herself up. She would not be ashamed. She had harmed no one. She had defeated Emot and freed the prisoners. 'I defeated Emot. This one was an emanation, my jailer. He promised his allegiance in return for his life. With him under my control, I saw a way to escape.'

'So you fed him as he faded!' Tynan turned a fierce gaze on her.

'How else could I have kept him alive?'

'But you created the new Emot!'

'Created and control,' Nadima corrected. 'Don't worry, my friend. I am not this one's slave. He is mine.'

The new Emot flinched at the word. His lip twitched, and it did not go unnoticed. Tynan eyed the demon with suspicion.

'Rasama would have a new Emot quickly enough anyway,' Nadima continued, 'and that one would do what Emots have always done. This one, however, will not create emanations because I forbid it. I doubt he has the strength on what I feed him anyway.'

'You feed him still! Are you mad?'

'I would not foist that task on another.'

'Are you sure of your motivation?'

Nadima glared at Tynan. How dare he question her? Emot Sai pressed closer to her. She shrugged him away. 'So long as there is an Emot, Rasama will have no need to create another, so we can continue without the threat of an Emot army. Besides, we would not have escaped without Sai.'

'Sai?'

'My name was Emot Sai, before I became Emot. ' He drew himself up to his full height, diminished as it was, and puffed out his chest.

'You call him by a familiar name too! Nadima, this is too much, too dangerous!'

Nadima sighed. 'We spent a long time together, Tynan. He was as kind to me as he could be under the circumstances, and Emot Sai as a name is a bit of a mouthful.'

'I don't like it,' Tynan said through clenched teeth. 'You can't trust a Rasa, even if he is indebted to you.'

'How do you know that? Have you ever tested it?' she retorted.

Tynan pursed his lips.

'Look at him, Tynan, look hard. He cares for me in his way. Don't you think that might change him?'

'I think that is a very dangerous belief, Nadima. Demons are not capable of caring. If they could manage it, it would kill them.'

Perhaps it will kill him, Nadima thought, glancing at her demon.

'And how might such a belief change you?' he asked. 'What if you become too fond of him?'

'I am no fool!'

'And I'll be watching … for your sake. Rasas can take on disguises, so why not a simple mask of compliance?' He turned to the new Emot. 'One step in the wrong direction and I'll kill you myself, regardless of what she wants. Understand, demon?'

Emot's eyes blazed with indignation. 'I will not give you the satisfaction.'

'My goodness, what have we here?' Walnut's voice preceded the slight figure emerging from the darkness. He held his sceptre high so that its soft white light illuminated their faces, creating a circle of light in the darkness. 'My, my, this is a new development,' he exclaimed as he took in the faces before him. 'Dearest Nadima, it's so wonderful to have you back.' He gave her a big hug, then stepped back, regarded her closely for a moment, then turned his attention to the Rasa at her side. 'They are all talking about the escape, saying how they would never have gotten out without you. So on their behalf, Emot, I thank you.'

Tynan rolled his eyes in disgust. 'You're thanking a Rasa! What is happening to the world?'

'Your subjugation is a welcome development,' Walnut continued.

'I have a deal with Nadima, that is all. I keep my part as long as she keeps hers.'

Tynan stared at the demon. Emot met the Warrior's eyes without flinching. Even as he began to fade, he did not try to wrench his gaze away.

'Stop it!' Nadima shouted and pushed Tynan away, breaking the eye contact. 'I'll dispose of him when I'm ready!'

Emot smiled. Nadima wanted to kick him for that little ruse.

'Are you sure you're not the slave?' Tynan asked. 'Look at her, Walnut, defending a Rasa. What good can become of that?' He turned abruptly and walked away.

'Thanks for the welcome home, Tynan,' Nadima said sarcastically. 'It's good to see you again after all these years.'

Tynan stopped and sighed, then turned back. 'I'm sorry, Nadima. Of course I'm pleased to see you, and to see you well. Your … slave … just took me by surprise, that's all. I'll see you soon.'

Nadima sighed as she watched him stride away.

'Tynan,' Walnut called after him, 'have Ariel wait for us upstairs and, if anyone asks, tell them we are disposing of the demon.'

Tynan nodded and Sai growled.

'Relax, demon,' Walnut said. 'Nadima will decide what to do with you, not me.'

'Ariel is here?' Nadima's heart leapt.

'Indeed and she is on her way to Rasama as predicted.'

'Thank Aya. How is she?'

'She is doing well. You will see her soon, but first we must attend to this demon who hangs at your side like a pet.'

Nadima glanced at Emot then back to the old man. 'Do you think I'm a fool too?'

'No, my dear. I think you are very brave. For a weaker Warrior, it would be suicide, and even for you it is a dangerous course, but since you have defeated Emot, you should be strong enough to remain in control.' Walnut observed the new Emot impassively. The demon stood very still.

'He looks hungry,' Walnut observed. 'No doubt food is your part of the bargain.'

'Indeed,' Emot replied smoothly, his eyes flickering brightly, 'she gives me my favourite. She craves my touch.'

'Sai!' Nadima scolded. 'Keep your mouth shut!'

'Yes, Mistress.' He bowed with mock respect.

'I see,' Walnut said, one eyebrow lifting.

'He has agreed not to hunt or create emanations so long as I feed him, and I can turn the craving on and off at will,' Nadima explained. 'He's very compliant when he's fed his favourite.'

'He has done what you wanted, Nadima. Why keep him?'

'Surely you can see how a weak, enslaved Emot can help the situation.' Emot's grimace showed his distaste at Nadima's choice of words.

'Perhaps, but is that your only motivation?'

Nadima stared at the stone walls of the home she had shared with her beloved husband and where she had birthed her daughter. 'Okay,' she blurted out, 'so I'm fond of him, and feeding him what he wants is easy for me, and yes, it does give me pleasure. But I have defeated Emot. I am not in any danger.'

'Except that, as you should know, Nadima, regardless of whether or not you have defeated Emot, the more you feed him, the more of a habit it becomes. And pleasurable habits in particular can be very hard to break.'

'Yes, I do know that, and if it becomes a problem then I will stop.'

'Once it's a problem, it will be hard to stop.'

'What do you want me to do then? Let him starve?' Emot sidled closer to her and she patted his head.

'No; it will be kinder to dissolve him quickly.'

Emot hissed and Nadima shook her head.

'It's not fair to kill him so long as he keeps to his side of the bargain.'

'But he is Emot, perhaps not strong enough to take full succession, but Emot nevertheless. You will not be able to suppress his instincts for long.'

'I'll keep a close eye on him.'

'Perhaps we can find someone else to help you with the task of feeding him. We can wean him off you slowly.'

'You mean wean me off him, don't you?'

'Only if it applies.'

'I will accept your daughter as a fitting substitute,' Emot said with a sly grin.

'No!' Walnut and Nadima exclaimed together.

Emot chuckled, his eyes glinting wickedly.

'You stay away from her,' Nadima growled.

'Of course, Mistress, as long as you keep our bargain.'

'You see what I mean?' Walnut said.

'And you see what I mean. He will do as he's told so long as I feed him.'

'Perhaps, but don't fool yourself. He is still dangerous. We will have to put him in a cell.'

'A cell!' Emot shouted. 'I did not agree to this bargain to be locked away from all sustenance.'

'It's either that or death, I'm afraid,' Walnut said.

The demon curled his lip in distaste. Nadima caught the hatred burning in his eyes before he turned and fled, gliding swiftly into the darkness. Walnut's hand blurred as he reached for his sceptre. The flash of white light brought Emot to his knees before he had gone more than a few metres.

Nadima ran to his side, followed more sedately by Walnut. 'I could have killed you,' he said, looking down at the weakened demon. 'You remain only because she wishes it. Now, go where she commands or I will finish the job.'

***

'Tell me, Nick,' Ariel asked, getting to her feet. 'How do enough people to make a noise like that suddenly appear up here?'

'I was wondering that myself.' He leaned back on the couch and stretched.

'Tunnels. It's the only answer.' She grinned then turned and walked out the door with Nick close behind.

Tynan strode down the corridor towards them. 'Hold it there, you two. Nick, take her upstairs. Walnut's orders.'

'Why?' Ariel asked. 'What's going on?'

'There's a bunch of people escaped from the demon's nest. A lot of them are pretty traumatised. Walnut doesn't want you to see them yet.'

'Mum,' Ariel gasped. 'Is she?'

'She's with them, she's fine, but she's not here yet. I'm sure Walnut will bring her to you as soon as she arrives.'

Deidre bustled along the corridor towards them. 'Come on, all of you, don't just stand there. We need everyone to help. They need blankets, beds made up. Oh, there's so much to do.' She pushed past them.

'I'm coming,' Tynan said. 'Nick, Ariel, upstairs, now.'

'We need them too,' Deidre called back.

Ariel glared at Tynan. 'Why can't we help?'

'Walnut wants you to wait upstairs for him. Come now, it's late, you should be getting ready for bed anyway.'

'It's Mum, isn't it? Something's wrong.'

'She's fine.'

'Then what!' Ariel nearly shouted.

Tynan sighed and glanced helplessly at Nick. 'For now just go upstairs and wait for Walnut … please.'

'Come on, Ariel.' Nick took her arm. 'There'll be a good reason for this.'

Ariel grimaced but allowed Nick to lead her upstairs.

***

'Come, Sai,' Nadima said, helping the demon to his feet. 'We'll find a place where you'll be safe.'

'I will not be locked away,' he growled, not moving.

'You cannot stay beside me here,' Nadima said. 'The Warriors would kill you, and if you refuse my instructions, I will not feed you.'

'There are others who will,' he replied, sullen as a little child.

'Come on, let's get him out of the way,' Walnut said.

Nadima took a deep breath, smiled seductively at the demon and sent him a taste of craving. 'Come.'

The new Emot's top lip began to twitch. His eyes blazed with desire and, after a moment, he followed her meekly.

Walnut led them to the side of the Hermitage and down a set of steps to the basement beneath. The darkness in the cells was so thick that it sucked up much of the sceptre light, and the dank smell collected at the back of Nadima's throat and ate into her bones. Under threat from Walnut that he would kill him, and with a promise from Nadima that she would feed him, Emot Sai entered the cell and they locked him in.

'She will find me no matter where you put me,' he said. 'I will sing to her and she will come. She will restore me to my full glory. She cannot resist me.'

'She is too well-protected,' Walnut told him. 'You will never feed from her.'

The steely expression on Walnut's face sent a tremor down Nadima's spine. 'Who is he talking about?'

'I will explain later.'

'She fed the old Emot and she will continue to feed the new one,' Emot gloated. 'The bars will not hold me when the little one calls.'

'She will not call. She is past that,' Walnut replied.

'Walnut? Where is Ariel?'

'Don't worry, Nadima. She is here. She is safe and she'll want to see you as soon as possible, but she must not know that Emot is down here. No one must know he is here. They must all think you have killed him. Trust me, you must say nothing of this.'

'She will know I am here soon enough anyway.' Emot's eyes blazed in the darkness.

Nadima stared at him in horror. 'Oh, no! I've brought a Major Rasa right to Ariel.'

'True, but she has to defeat Emot regardless of which incarnation it is. Perhaps with this one it will be easier for her.'

The demon growled, low and menacing.

Nadima glanced at him. If the prophecy were true, Emot Sai would die at the hands of her daughter. Why was that idea so repulsive to her?

Walnut touched her arm. 'Come.'

'You go, Walnut. I'll come soon. I have a bargain to keep.' He was already too strong for her liking, but he deserved his reward.

Walnut sighed. 'You have only the time it takes me to organise someone to keep watch over him, and that won't be long.'

Nadima nodded. 'It won't take long. I'll see you soon.'

When Walnut left, Nadima leaned against the bars and offered her neck. 'So hungry for you,' Sai murmured as he swept towards her, fire dripping from his mouth.

***

Walnut arrived at the Maloney family rooms to find Ariel pacing the floor of her bedroom and Nick perched on the edge of the bed with an exasperated look on his face. The old guide stepped into the room and quietly closed the door behind him.

'What's going on?' Ariel demanded, rushing up to him. 'What is it? Why can't I go down?'

'Steady on,' he replied, his palms up in front of him. 'I didn't want you to be upset, that's all.'

'Upset! You think not telling me what's going on won't upset me.'

'Sit down.'

'No.'

'There's a cute little gimp behind you,' Nick said.

Ariel glanced at the bedraggled creature then slumped onto the bed.

'Your mother managed to get a Rasa to lead the prisoners out,' Walnut explained.

'Wow.' *Her mother did that!* 'So she's a hero. Why did I have to wait for you to tell me?'

'People have attitudes, prejudices. I didn't want you to hear the story coloured by other people's ignorance.'

Ariel frowned and shook her head. How did she get a Rasa to lead her out? 'So she did a deal with a Rasa. Under the circumstances, I don't see what's wrong with that.' But what sort of deal would you have to make? And what kind of relationship would you have to have with it for it to stick to the bargain?

'It was an Emot,' Walnut said.

'Oh. Is … is she addicted?'

'No. She killed Emot.'

Ariel gasped. 'She killed him.' *How could she?* Ariel caught the rising anger quickly, but the fact that it rose at all scared her. She should be pleased.

A shadow passed over Walnut's face.

'That's great,' Nick said. 'It means we'll get a break from him for a while.'

Walnut didn't move.

'Walnut?'

'Rasama is strong. We must remain vigilant. The new Emot is not far away.'

Ariel frowned at the flood of conflicting emotions raging inside her.

'Your mother will be here soon,' Walnut said. 'I've told Maya to send her up.'

34

Reunion

When Nadima walked into the warm glow of the Maloney family rooms with Maya, silent tears flooded back with the memories. Life in the demon's nest had been so unreal, so unlike anything she had known before that she hadn't felt as if she'd returned to the mountain. Now, she faced the inescapable reality of what being on the mountain meant. Memories she'd pushed away for fifteen years stared her in the face. They were all here, all except Aarod.

'I must be more fragile than I thought,' she whispered, wiping away her tears.

Maya smiled kindly and patted her back.

Every object had its story, and pain touched every joyful memory, but the pain made the joy stand out in sharp relief. If the price of her happy life with Aarod was pain at its loss, then she would bear that pain willingly.

The door between the Maloney sitting room and Ariel's bedroom opened quietly and Walnut peeked his head into the room. 'I thought I heard someone. Come, Ariel. Your mother is here.'

Ariel had always thought that she would race to embrace her mother if she ever saw her again, but when she stepped through the door, all she could do was stare. Nadima looked older, graver. Grimy clothes hung off her thin frame, and her fair hair, streaked with more grey than Ariel remembered, hung lankly around a sallow face. None of that disturbed her, but Nadima's eyes did. Not the dark rings around them, but the look inside them. A haunted, pained look, a touch of shame, and something Ariel had never seen in anyone before, a sense of something illicit. What had Nadima done to give her such a look?

'Ariel,' her mother whispered, almost a rasp.

'Mum.' The word felt too cool but she couldn't say it any other way. She wanted to ask her mother why she hadn't told her about the mountain, but something stopped her. It would be like opening a Pandora's Box; a million questions would come tumbling out, accusations, defences. Her mother wasn't up to that. Yet.

Nadima stepped forward, tears in her eyes, holding out her arms. Ariel stepped into them obediently and melted in the warmth of her mother's love.

'Are you all right, Mum?'

'I'm fine, darling, just fine.' Nadima stroked her daughter's hair and held her close. Tears wet Ariel's shoulder. She pulled away. The colour drained from Nadima's face. 'What is it?'

'You … you need a shower,' Ariel stammered. She didn't mean to say it, but something had hit a raw spot. Something creepy and illogical. Not a demon in disguise, like the Amic that had tried to kill her, something else.

'It's true, I do smell,' Nadima's weak attempt at a smile didn't cover the hurt in her eyes.

'Come, Nadima, let's get you comfortable.' Maya took Nadima's arm and bustled her out the door.

Ariel bit her lip. 'That went well,' she said sarcastically.

Nick touched her arm and raised an eyebrow, a question in his eyes.

'She … she smelt like Emot,' Ariel blathered. 'And her neck. The scars. They're so thick … It's creepy. And if she killed Emot, then how was there one left to lead her out?'

Walnut returned her stare with a calm, steady gaze. 'After she killed Emot, she did a deal with an emanation. She kept him alive in return for her freedom.'

Ariel shook her head in disbelief. What a deal. Nadima must have been very sure of him, close even. How close? Something fierce and yearning shot through her heart. She breathed out slowly and let it pass. 'So he's Emot now. Where is he?'

Nick flicked a worried glance at Walnut.

'We have dealt with him,' the old man said in a tired voice.

Ariel shuddered involuntarily and Nick slipped his arm around her. 'I'm fine,' she muttered.

'Your mother was in a very tricky situation,' Walnut continued. 'She got to know a Rasa probably better than anyone ever has and she used that to her advantage. All that matters is that she is safe and well and she has defeated Emot. Now you must do the same.'

Ariel felt like her mother had spent a night with her boyfriend then murdered him, and the fact that she could even feel like that made her feel sick to her core. There were other feelings too, things too vague and fleeting to capture, and they left her with a gnawing unease.

'Let's go and help Deidre,' Walnut suggested.

Downstairs, Deidre had organised washing, feeding and sleeping quarters for the sudden intake of people. She had opened up the large drawing room and herded the escapees there before assigning as many as she could to bedrooms.

Geordie had fired up the boilers and by the time Ariel and Nick arrived to help, people had lined up for showers. Tynan,

Kestril and Geordie set up camp beds and handed out blankets and clothing.

'Just in time,' Deidre said when Ariel and Nick entered the kitchen—central command. 'You can start washing clothes. They're dumping them in piles outside the bathrooms.'

'We're washing clothes at this time of night!' Ariel couldn't believe her ears.

'They can hardly get back into filthy things after a shower, now can they?' Deidre retorted. 'And we might as well get them washed and hung out so they'll be dry by morning.'

'Oh, yeah.' Deidre always managed to make Ariel feel like a child.

'The basket is in the laundry,' she said as she turned and walked away.

Nick grinned. 'Come on, washer-maid, let's get to work.'

Ariel groaned when she saw the big stone tubs and hand operated wringer. 'Oh, for electricity and white goods.'

Nick turned on the taps and ran a mix of cold and steaming hot water. 'We only need to get the smell out,' he reassured her.

Kestril came to turn the rollers and push the clothes through, and Deidre and Tynan pegged the flattened clothes onto lines strung around the boiler room. By the time they had finished, the skin on Ariel's hands looked like prunes.

'You should have worn gloves,' Deidre said when she caught Ariel studying her hands. 'They're in the cupboard over there.'

'Now you tell me!'

Nick yawned. 'Let's get to bed.'

They made their way along the corridor past the drawing room scattered with makeshift beds and people tossing and turning as they tried to sleep. Even though people filled every bedroom, most of the doors to the upstairs rooms remained open. Ariel figured that, after their imprisonment, they wouldn't ever want to be shut in again. Maya stepped out of the door to the Maloney family sitting room as Ariel walked up.

'Your mother is in bed. Don't disturb her now,' she said. 'You can speak to her in the morning.'

Ariel felt quite content to leave her mother alone. 'Did you tell her about me and Emot?'

'Yes,' Maya replied, her ancient eyes piercing. 'I wasn't going to until the morning, but after you acted so strange, I had to.'

'Yeah. Sorry about that. What did she say?'
'Nothing.'
'Nothing at all?'
'Not one thing.'

***

When Ariel woke the next morning she found Nick's bed empty, and when he didn't turn up after ten minutes had passed, she realised that in the fiasco of her reunion with her mother, she'd forgotten to introduce him.

A few minutes after she'd dressed, he knocked quietly on the door under the tapestry.

'I think it's better I'm formally introduced to my girlfriend's mother, before she finds me sleeping in her bedroom,' Nick explained when Ariel opened the door.

She frowned. 'I'm sure you were in that bed when I went to sleep last night.'

'I was. I just got out as soon as I woke in case she came in. At least I'm dressed now.'

'It's feels weird having Mum back. I mean, sneaking about like this. You and I aren't an issue for anyone else—apart from Twitchet and even he's got over it.'

'We don't know if it's an issue for her or not. I'm just being cautious; don't want to get off on the wrong foot.'

'I guess.' She scraped the curtains back, letting in a flood of grey, and peered at the sky. Flashes of blue appeared between the billows of grey and white.

'You're pleased she's back though, right?' Nick asked.

'Of course, I'm pleased.' She turned away from the window. 'It's just strange to have her here, and she's … she's different.'

'She's been stuck in a demon's nest. That's got to do something to you.'

'I know, and I feel terrible about last night. It was just a shock seeing her so different and realising that she … knew Emot like I do.'

She caught the grimace on Nick's face before he turned and headed for the door into the corridor. 'Let's get breakfast.'

Ariel sighed. 'Just a minute.' She walked into the living room and picked up the hoody she'd left there the night before. The door to her mother's bedroom opened. Ariel looked up, startled by Nadima's sudden appearance and the maelstrom of emotions it set off.

Nadima smiled. 'I hope you feel better this morning.' She stepped forward, her arms outstretched.

Ariel snorted. 'Why didn't you tell me about all this, about the mountain, the Serpentine, the demons, the prophecy, my place at Sheldra?'

'Oh, so that's what it's about.' Nadima lowered her arms and took a deep breath.

'You should have told me. You could have saved me all that stress over exams I didn't need to pass and shown me that that wasn't all there was, that my future could be something else.' A furious red gimp snuck up behind her and began chewing on her ankles. She kicked it off.

'Even if you had believed me, what would you have done, while you waited for the sight to come? Twiddle your thumbs at school. And what if the sight hadn't come? You would have needed those exams then.'

'I was born on the mountain, Mother, or did you forget that? I didn't have to wait for my sight to come; I just had to not forget it. But you let me forget!' The gimp dug his teeth in. Ariel slapped it away. It stepped back and raised its little fists, preparing for a fight.

'It was better you forgot, for a while.'

'No, the forgetting was for you. I could have known so much more. I could have been a Warrior before that demon kidnapped you. I could have saved you from all that.' The Gimp punched her on the calf.

'When you were young, just after we left the mountain, I tried to train you, but you refused, and you didn't want to hear anything about Warriors and mountains. It made you miss your daddy. In the end, I gave up, and waited for a time when you were more mature, when I could explain things. I couldn't afford to turn you off the task that you had been born to do. What if you refused to come up the mountain? I had to wait until you were ready, in case you rejected the whole idea so strongly that it closed your sight forever.'

Silence.

'You were kidnapped and I almost died because I didn't know,' Ariel muttered. The Gimp kicked her in the shins.

'I made a misjudgment … I've never claimed to be perfect.'

Ariel glared at her mother, then spun away from her and stormed out of the room, slamming the door behind her. The Gimp ran after her. She stopped and faced it. 'Fine, I'm a jerk. Just like you.' She smiled at the little demon. It blinked twice, then vaporised.

Ariel found Nick already in the kitchen, stirring a huge pot of porridge on the wood stove.

'Make yourself useful,' Deidre said, handing her two bowls. 'Feed yourself, then you can feed everyone else without keeling over from low blood sugar.' She shooed Nick aside and dragged the pot to the cooler side of the stove. Ariel dolloped some porridge into the bowls and set them on the table. They'd just sat and begun to eat when her mother entered.

Ariel stood. 'Sorry, Mum. I didn't mean to be horrible. I'm really glad you're safe.' She opened her arms. Nadima walked over, and in their embrace, the weeks of separation faded away, pushed aside by the unbreakable bond of a love well-forged over many years.

'Me too,' Nadima said.

'I should jolly well hope so,' Deidre muttered.

Ariel broke the embrace first. 'Can I introduce you to someone?'

'Of course.'

Ariel smiled and gestured to Nick. He stood, a slightly nervous cast to his smile. 'Mum, this is Nick. Nick, this is my mother, Nadima.'

Nick stepped forward and offered his hand. 'Pleased to meet you.'

Nadima stared at his hand for a moment before taking it.

'We're together,' Ariel said.

'You.' Nadima raised her eyebrows. 'You have a boyfriend?'

'She does indeed,' Walnut said from his place at the end of the table.

Nadima grinned, then frowned.

I bet she thinks he's a bit old for me, Ariel thought as she and Nick returned to their breakfast.

'They are very good together,' Walnut said.

'He takes really good care of me,' Ariel said as she and Nick returned to their breakfast.

Nadima shook her head. 'So much has changed in so little time … The prisoners. I must see them.'

'They're all fine. Deidre has them organised, and the mountain folk have left already. Eat some porridge,' Walnut said.

'I hate porridge. But it's better than Domos gruel and that's pretty much all I've had for a while.'

'Sounds horrible.' Ariel scraped the last mouthful of porridge from her bowl. 'But this is the best porridge I've ever had.'

'Have sugar and cream,' Walnut suggested.

But Nadima froze, the blood drained from her face and she stared across the room at the grim-faced man who stood in the doorway. Kestril. Ariel tried to read her mother's expression, a mixture of loathing and fear and something strange Ariel couldn't put her finger on.

He strode across the room, stood before Nadima and looked directly into her eyes. 'I'm sorry.'

Ariel blinked. What was he sorry for? That she was free? His words made no sense.

'So am I,' Nadima replied, glaring back. Her eyes grew moist, but the magician never flinched, he merely nodded, clicked his heels together, turned swiftly and strode from the room.

Nadima wiped her eyes.

'Mum?' Ariel asked, pushing back her chair, 'are you okay?'

Nadima said nothing, and in a flash, Walnut stood before her. 'You defeat Emot with the power of love and compassion, yet you cannot forgive Kestril?'

Nadima gulped. 'I will,' she stammered. 'I just need time.'

'And just how much more do you need?' He fixed her with a penetrating stare. Ariel knew how it felt to be under such scrutiny, but Nadima didn't appear uncomfortable. She returned his gaze without emotion, then helped herself to porridge.

'What was that all about?' Ariel whispered when Walnut sat down again.

'Some pain takes a long time to heal.'

✳✳✳

Maya, Nadima, Walnut and Layla spent the day caring for the prisoners who hadn't already returned to their homes, mostly those from off the mountain, those who had had no idea that such a place existed before they stepped from the tunnel outside the Hermitage. The Warriors helped them to come to terms with their experience, explained the ways of the mountain and laid out the expanded options for their future. Twitchet gave furry little animal therapy by putting on his most charming manners and allowing himself to be stroked and pampered by everyone. The others refilled the woodshed, helped in the kitchen and washed the linen.

Ariel took a break from the kitchen and surreptitiously watched Nadima speaking to a group of women. Was that really her mother? How could it be?

Her mother didn't belong here. She belonged at home, in the house by the stream where Ariel had always known her; a pretty, warm-hearted woman who often sat with an injured animal on her lap, or a pencil and sketch-pad in her hand. Her mother wasn't this woman with a sword at her side, this Warrior and demon slayer, this person the traumatised ex-prisoners looked up to as a heroine. Ariel didn't know this person.

This Nadima, her mother had kept from her, just as she had kept the existence of the mountain a secret. Ariel turned away before her mother could see her looking.

Nadima's healing came from caring for the others and, wanting to prove she could do without him, she didn't go near Emot Sai. Besides that, she wanted to spend some time with her

373

daughter. She saw Ariel across the room and left the group of women to join her.

'Have you forgiven me yet?' she asked to Ariel's back.

Ariel sighed and turned around. 'I guess.'

Nadima smiled a smile that was exactly the Nadima she remembered. 'I'd like to hear about your adventures. They tell me you have defeated Bitah and Amic. That's quite an achievement in such a short time.'

'But I'm not doing so well now, am I?' Ariel muttered, surprising herself with the depth of her feeling. Where did that come from?

Nadima raised her eyebrows. 'You have no need to be ashamed.'

'No?' Ariel looked up. 'That's easy for you to say. You were a prisoner. You had to do what you did.'

'You think that made it easy?' Nadima's voice rose slightly. 'You don't have to feed a demon. You don't have one that you can't run away from. You're free. You don't have to indulge in your shame.'

Ariel felt small under the steady gaze of Nadima's steel blue eyes. She knew she should have dropped the whole thing then, but she had a bizarre, stupid urge to prove how despicable she was. 'Exactly, and what you did showed you were strong. What I've done just shows how weak I am.'

Nadima shook her head. 'I didn't feel strong. I felt weak and ashamed, and I often fed my Emot on it. But I also learned to cut through it, and I saw how shame weakened me, just like it weakens you. If you must indulge, at least indulge in your strengths.'

Ariel rolled her eyes at Nadima's parental tone. 'But you didn't get addicted. I did.'

'I almost did.' For a moment, Nadima's eyes took on a faraway look.

'But you didn't, you defeated him, but I … I don't know if I can.' Ariel bit her lip and looked at the ground. How come she was confessing all this to her mother?

'Are you going to make that thought into reality by believing in it?' Nadima asked.

Ariel sighed. That sounded like her mother. 'But you fed Emot, you must know what it's like. That hollow ache that's always there, him calling to you, and you know that if you call back, he'll come to you. I won't call anymore, but when he comes, even if I can resist feeding him, I don't know if I could kill him. I'm not even sure that I want that ache to go away.'

Nadima said nothing. She didn't have to. Now, in the depth of the silence, they both knew what this was all about. Something they had both experienced, something that others would never fully understand; the terrible lure of an Emot. Ariel could taste it on her tongue.

'How did you do it?' Ariel asked.

Nadima paused for a moment. 'I thought of Walnut and Maya and their unfailing faith in me, and I thought of Aarod, of how courageous he was. I thought of you, of how much I loved you and wanted to see you again, to hold you in my arms, and I thought of how I wanted to be free. When I remembered what real freedom felt like, I realised that all I was killing was pain.'

Silence.

Ariel snorted. 'Funny how hard it is to do it, though.'

'Yes. But you have to kill him, because that ache is poison,' Nadima whispered, 'and if you don't cut it out, it'll spread right through you, and eventually it'll kill you. You've seen the wasted prisoners. It's only a matter of time.'

The spot in the centre of Ariel's chest murmured in empathy as she remembered the dull lethargy and vacant eyes of the prisoners that were worst affected by feeding the demons.

'And it would kill everyone you love to have to watch you do it,' Nadima added.

35

Defeat

The musty smell of the stone walls reminded Nadima of her incarceration in the demon's nest, and her heart fluttered in empathy as Emot Sai looked at her with disgust from where he huddled in the corner. His eyes had lost their flame, only embers remained.

'Take a break, Dorn,' Nadima said to the Haba guard.

'Are you sure?'

'Yes, go on, get some fresh air.'

'Well, I sure could do with some of that.' He grinned and handed Nadima the keys. She smiled and realised that she barely noticed the smell of demon anymore.

'I'll come and get you when I'm done,' she said.

'Okay, don't feed him too much; he's good like that, too weak to complain anymore.'

Nadima nodded and Dorn left.

'Don't look at me like that.' Nadima opened the cell door.

'You betrayed me,' he croaked. 'I kept my part of the bargain, but you didn't. You agreed to feed me. I didn't expect you to give me full power, but this!'

She flinched, uncomfortable at how deeply his words cut. She didn't bother to remind him that it was no less than what he did to her.

'There is no dignity in this,' he continued. 'Such a state is not fitting for Emot, not even for an emanation. Better I had died quickly with my master than this painful, ignoble death.'

'I'm sorry. I had to stop for a while. I had to prove I could. I didn't realise you would weaken so quickly.'

'Pah! I care not for your excuses, only that you keep to your part of the bargain as I have kept to mine. I was to be by your side, your protector, not a sniveling captive. Allow me some dignity, Nadima; allow me some stature worthy of your Emot Sai.'

'This can't go on, Sai. It's not good for either of us.' Tears pricked her eyes as she opened the cell door and stepped aside.

He struggled to stand but staggered and fell back, gasping for air. 'You release me?' he asked. 'You are going to unleash me on the world?'

'Either way, there will be an Emot to hunt people.'

'What are you saying?'

'When Rasama realises you are too weak to assume full succession, I suspect he will simply make a new Emot.'

The demon's eyes flared. 'Then I would be redundant!'

'It could be worse than that.'

'Nothing is worse than that. I would prefer death.'

'And I expect that's just what Rasama would arrange for you.'

The muscles in Sai's face twitched with anger. 'Then you must make me strong enough to assume the succession.'

'I can't do that.'

'You mean you won't.'

'I will make you strong enough to leave here, then you can find others to feed you.'

'But the one I want is here.'

'No, you can't have her. You must leave this place. If you try to hunt her, I shall kill you myself.'

'If you kept me fed to full power, I wouldn't have to hunt anyone else. I would be strong enough to take the succession and Rasama would not find me weak.'

'But I will not allow you to make emanations, so Rasama will still realise that something is wrong.'

'Then let me create emanations. I will keep them under control.'

'That's impossible. One way or another, Rasama will make sure that there is an Emot worthy of the name. Without you, I wouldn't have escaped, so I am giving you the chance to be that Emot, but you must leave here.'

'Then come with me,' he said, his tone softening. 'If I have you, I will not need to hunt your daughter.'

Nadima shook her head. 'That's impossible.'

'Why do you think I helped you? Why do you think I stuck to the bargain?'

Nadima shook her head and stepped back, cautioned by the anger in his voice.

He looked up at her with baleful eyes. 'Because I crave your flavour above everything. I, Emot, who creates addictions in my prey, I am addicted to you, my prey! And look what has become of me. I am not worthy of my name.'

Nadima bit her lip. She had never seen him vulnerable before and it tugged at her heart, but she knew what she had to do. 'If you stay with me, you will die. I can't protect you anymore. Nick is not the only one who is keen to kill you.'

'Ah, Nick.' Sai reached into Emot's memories, not yet fully his own. 'The boyfriend. A nuisance.'

'Go, Sai, I release you.'

'Then feed me for I cannot walk from here like this.'

'Yes, I will feed you one last time.' She knelt beside him, placed his talon on her neck, leant against the wall and closed her eyes. Then she aroused a craving for the strange pleasure of his touch and gave herself over to it.

'Ah, my sweet, sweet Nadima, enjoy it my love, enjoy,' the demon crooned.

Nadima sighed. This would be the last time she would ever have the touch of an Emot on her throat, so why not enjoy it. She fell into a swoon, and when she tried to stop feeding him, he caressed her neck and it seemed to her that Aarod ran his fingers over her skin, that his hands stroked her hair, and his lips kissed her shoulder.

It was Emot, well satiated, that stopped the feeding. Nadima came back to the present with a jolt. Her eyes jerked open as the big Emot stood and drew himself up to his full height. His eyes blazed. Brilliant red fire dripped from their sockets. His leech-like skin shone on his now solid form, and his arm muscles flexed with power. He was magnificent and he knew it.

Nadima gasped and ran for the door, but the demon got there before her, slipped through and slammed the door in her shocked face.

What had she done?

'No, Sai,' she pleaded. 'This is not the way. If they see you like this, they will kill you immediately.'

'Huh!' he spat. 'I am not Sai any more, and you will not call me that. I am truly Emot now. With the strength you gave me, I have taken the full succession. I have Emot's memories and my task is clear. I will take one meal from your lovely daughter, then I will kill her.'

'No, Sai, please!'

'Emot, you will call me Emot,' he growled.

Nadima ignored his outburst. 'Her protectors will kill you and you have no emanations, you will not regrow. Hunt elsewhere, for your sake!'

'You do not fool me,' he sneered. 'You care nothing for me, and your daughter will die regardless. My predecessor was foolish, he wanted her flavour more than her death, but I have learned the folly of that and I will do what he could not. I will be worthy of the Emot succession. I will dispatch the threat to Rasama and he will reward me well.'

Nadima shook her head. She could not believe how stupid she had been to let her guard down at the last moment. *Never trust a demon!*

'Oh, and in case you really do care, do not fear for my safety for I will create some emanations before I visit Ariel. You gave me enough strength even for that.' He laughed coldly. 'Farewell, Nadima, I will miss your sweet flavour, but I would rather live without you than starve in your shadow.'

As Emot glided up the stairs with a satisfied smirk on his face, Nadima rattled the bars and shouted. 'Dorn! Help! The demon's escaped!'

❋❋❋

Ariel lifted her down jacket from the hook by the side door and slipped it on, while Nick donned his own jacket. She zipped up the zipper, then searched her pockets. 'Wait a minute, I forgot my gloves. I'll grab them, won't be long.'

She dashed back up the stairs two at a time. Nick began to follow her. 'It's okay, you don't have to come,' she called back.

A shaft of sunlight angled through the window in Ariel's room, illuminating the dust motes that flew up as she sifted through a pile of clothing thrown on top of the chair. She had just located her gloves when she smelt the unmistakable smell, felt the unmistakable presence and heard the unmistakable voice behind her.

'Stand for me, little one.' His voice crackled slightly.

Ariel froze, unable to move, tasting that familiar mixture of fear and yearning. The demon glided up behind her, his hot body pleasantly warm in the cold room.

'They've been cruel to keep us apart,' he said. Ariel shuddered. He pressed against her back, purring with pleasure, then brushed her collar aside and stroked her bare neck. Her shuddering ceased, but tears pricked her eyes.

'I've missed your delicious craving.' The heat of his voice fanned the back of her neck. 'Say you've missed me, little one, I know you have.' The tip of his talon traced gently along her neck, but when she didn't reply, he hissed. 'Say it.'

'I missed you,' she whispered in a quivering voice. But this wasn't really her Emot. It was another one with the same memories.

'You mustn't let them keep us apart,' the demon purred.

The comforting predictability, the promise of pleasure lured her as always, but this time she knew she had a choice. Freedom or enslavement? Could she prise herself loose from his grip? The fantasy Nick appeared in her mind, ready to play out the stories once more, but she remembered the delightful grinning face of the real Nick throwing her into the snow. She wouldn't be able to bear the agony on his face if she failed.

Turn, turn, she told herself, and the moment she turned her mind to look into itself, she pierced her yearning with awareness. It shattered, releasing the vibrant, blissful clarity of her mind. Freedom! She had only one thing left to do. Her hand slid to her dagger.

The demon released his lips from her with a scream. His body crumpled on the floor. His talons grasped at her, vainly trying to retain a grip on existence. 'Treachery,' he wailed, steam rising from his eyes.

Ariel turned to him, the dagger in her hand dripping with his red, hot blood.

He clutched at the deep hole the blade had left in his chest. 'Do not do this,' he pleaded. 'Feed me once more and I will give you much pleasure.'

Ariel watched him fade before her. 'All you ever do, Emot, is take. I will not be feeding you again.'

'Nadima! My love!' Emot wailed as the light went out in his eyes. His voice faded into silence and he disappeared.

Ariel frowned at his final words. He'd two-timed her with her mother! That was more than weird. It was disgusting. She shook her head. Thank goodness it was over.

Nick's worried voice preceded him along the corridor. 'Ariel! What's taking so long?'

Nick burst into the room, his heart racing as he took in her frozen form, her eyes staring at an empty space on the floor and, worse, the smell, unmistakably that of a Rasa demon.

She lifted her head and looked at him with a lazy smile. 'You're too late. He's gone.'

Nick's heart plummeted. 'Not Emot. Say you didn't,' he pleaded.

'Oh, but I did.' The smile turned triumphant, her face so bright that it chilled him to his core. How could she? 'I stood still for him, Nick. I let him stand behind me and, sorry, but I let him stroke my neck.'

Her left hand stroked her neck and, for a moment, Nick wanted to vomit. Why did she have to torment him by telling him the details?

'But I didn't feed him.' She grinned. 'I stabbed him. The dagger was perfect. The sword would have been too large.' She lifted her right arm out from the side of her body, and Nick began to breathe again. She held the blade of Aarod. Red liquid dissolved into nothing as it dripped off the blade. A shaft of sunlight crept over her back and her hair erupted into a halo of fiery gold. Power blazed from her eyes and the powerful serenity on her face held him transfixed.

Nick thought she looked like some sort of avenging angel, but he reined in his desire to take her in his arms. If she could torment him by making him think she'd fed Emot again, then he wasn't going to gush over her victory. At least not yet. 'You risked his talon on your neck?' he scolded her.

Ariel sheathed the blade and tossed her hair over her shoulders. The sparkle of triumph lit her eyes.

'You were either incredibly brave or incredibly stupid. Probably both,' he chuckled. 'But I don't care. I'm just glad it's over.' He pulled her to him, pressed his lips against hers and tasted the sweet flow of pure love, free of craving. 'Congratulations,' he murmured between kisses.

Nick called Tynan, Maya, Nadima, Twitchet, Kestril and Walnut to the sitting room.

'What's this all about?' Tynan asked as they settled on various chairs.

'A story, Tynan,' Nick began, and as he told the story of Emot's defeat, every set of eyes turned to Ariel. All except one. Nadima stared out the window into the falling snow instead of at the triumphant face of her daughter. Nick thought she looked more grieved than pleased.

Nadima did not ask if it was right or wrong to grieve over the death of a demon, she simply felt what she felt. Emot Sai was gone, never to return. Yes, he was just a demon but, even if it was self-serving, he had helped her.

Walnut sat beside Nadima on the couch and slid his arm around her shoulders. 'Amazing things, Rasas,' he said quietly.

'Are you sure they aren't sentient?' Nadima thought of Emot Sai's complex array of emotions and the way he pleaded for his life.

'In a way they are, I suppose,' he replied. 'After all, they connect to the mind of the one they're targeting and mimic their hopes and fears, their thought patterns and their emotions. Even so, they do not exist without us, they are merely an illusion, an expression of our own emotions. Any sentience they have is purely an extension of our own.'

Nadima sighed. 'What are weeds, after all? Just unwanted plants with excellent survival strategies.'

'But even weeds can have beautiful flowers,' Walnut said, 'and a plant in sunlight has bigger and brighter flowers than it does in the shade. Emot Sai reflected some of your sunlight, Nadima, and it was that in him that you grew fond of.'

'I suppose so, but if Rasas are a reflection of ourselves, then he showed me a strange twisted part of me and I'm relieved to be rid of it.'

Walnut smiled and gave her a hug.

'So, now that's all over, you can move on at last,' Tynan said to Ariel, excitement sparkling in his eyes. 'Phase three can begin. We can make plans this evening.'

'Wait,' Walnut interjected. 'Ariel may need a bit more time.'

Tynan rubbed his chin thoughtfully. 'I suppose she must have some Cogin preparation before she leaves.'

'She also has a decision to make.'

'What's to be decided? Ariel's not going to back out now, are you?' He turned to her.

'Tynan, please,' Walnut said. 'She must decide for herself whether or not she wishes to seek out the Master Demon.'

Ariel frowned. 'You mean I have a choice?'

'There is always a choice,' Walnut replied.

Ariel shook her head. 'Not for me. How could I turn my back on the prophecy?'

'A prophecy is only a prophecy if it comes true, and it will not come to fruition unless your commitment to defeating Rasama is unfailing.'

Ariel looked around the gathering of expectant faces and back to Walnut. 'Do you really think I could bear their disappointment?'

'You cannot do this just because others expect you to, or because you think you should. That is not sufficient motivation to overcome the trials that lie ahead of you.'

Something leaden dropped into the pit of Ariel's stomach at the mention of trials. Hadn't she had enough of them? 'Then what is sufficient reason?'

'You will know it when you find it. It is something that makes you sure to the marrow of your bones, so that when you are facing death, you will not flinch and provide Rasama with the fuel he needs to survive.'

'She shouldn't have to make such a decision now,' Nadima said, touching Walnut's sleeve. 'She needs time to recover and train more. You forget that she's barely more than a child.'

'I am not a child,' Ariel retorted. 'Haven't you noticed what I've been doing while you've been away?'

Nadima's eyes widened. 'I'm sorry. I didn't mean you were a child. Just, well, you're so young. Aarod had seen much more life before he went to the upper reaches and . . .' Nadima bit her lip.

'And he never came back,' Ariel finished. 'And you don't want me to go in case I don't come back either.'

'No. I . . .' Nadima sighed. 'Yes.'

'The same reason you didn't want me on the mountain in the first place.'

Nadima shrugged.

Ariel turned to Walnut. 'The job's only half done. I'm not giving up.'

'And I will guide you no further until you find a reason to continue that will give you the unfailing courage you need to defeat Rasama.'

'Can't you just tell me what it is?'

'I can, but then you could fool yourself and think you have that motivation when you don't. It is better you find it for yourself.'

'How long do I have?'

'As long as you need.'

Ariel grimaced. 'I don't have time for riddles. Rasama gets stronger by the minute. The longer I leave it, the harder it'll be.'

'Perhaps, but there is no point continuing without a valid reason.'

'Rasama won't rest until I'm dead, so I can't rest until I've killed him.'

Walnut just smiled.

Wrong answer.

Maya and Layla left the room. Twitchet curled up on his cushion by the fire. Nadima stared out the window. Nick and Tynan talked, and Walnut sat silently, his expression, once again, one of perfect serenity.

Why did she want to carry on? Or did she? Really?

Wouldn't she rather just take Nick and go off-mountain somewhere, somewhere safe, far away from demons. Ariel snorted at the thought. It didn't matter where she went; even if she couldn't see them, she'd know the demons were there. Every night, all she had to do was watch the news on television and she'd see Rasama's control over humankind growing. How could she live with herself, knowing that she had given up a chance to stop that?

She thought of how wrecked the prisoners had been after feeding the demons and how messed up her addiction to Emot had made her. All over the world, people lived in the same situation, only they didn't know why. Most of the human race was an unknowing host to the parasite. She was one of the few who knew how to stop it.

Ariel faced her guide. 'If I turn my back on this, I turn my back on every being in the universe. I can't do that. I have to go on. For everyone. Is that good enough?'

He nodded. 'Such a sentiment is exactly what is needed to help free you from the limitations of your ordinary self. And only when that limitation has been cast aside can you defeat the Master Demon.'

Ariel nodded. She had tasted that boundlessness. She could do this. 'What about Nick?'

Walnut grinned. 'He has known that answer for some time. His riddle is of a different kind.' He turned to Tynan. 'You may make your plans now, sword master.'

The story continues in

Eternal Destiny

Ariel and Nick face their deepest fears and their greatest challenge as they search for the Master Demon who holds the key to the future of mankind. Slay him and the world goes free; fail, and it falls irrevocably into violence and chaos.

Guided by a wisdom master of a mystical tradition that uses mind power as the basis of powerful magic, the assault party travels from the ancient granite walls of the Hermitage, up the Steps of Death, and through a labyrinth of shifting gorges to the Palace of Skulls. Even if Nick wins his struggle with the scars of his past and defeats the green-eyed head of the Cogin clan, they still must cross the scree slope, where the bones of Ariel's father lie, to get to the ice caves beneath the summit where the Master Demon awaits.

The journey is extraordinary, the enemies are deadly and the ending is mind-blowing.

✳✳✳

If you liked this book, don't forget to tell your friends about it and leave a review online. I'd love to hear what you think. Find out more about my books and visit my blog at http://tahlianewland.com. You can also follow 'TahliaNewland' on Twitter; like 'Tahlia Newland, author,' on Facebook, and be my fan on Goodreads.

'An entertaining and uplifting read.' Linda Gillard, best selling author of A House of Silence.

'An extremely original mix of real life difficult situations and magical elements sprung from the imaginations of main characters Carly and Dylan, as they envision ways to overcome everyday challenges, problems and obstacles.' Krisi Keley, author.

'This is a story about understanding, kindness and compassion, uniquely told with surreal fantasy elements, and is both entertaining and thought-provoking.' Kevin Berry, editor.

A Matter of Perception

Take a journey into a world where the hidden becomes manifest, and the lines between fantasy and reality blur. This collection of imaginative and entertaining stories about ghosts, sirens, demons, magical glasses and ordinary people will warm your heart and make you smile, shiver, and maybe even wonder about the nature of reality itself. The theme of individual perception as a result of our assumptions, beliefs and emotional experience bind these otherwise diverse stories into a unified whole.

This ebook collection of magical realism and urban fantasy stories is available at all ebook stores worldwide.

And the rest of The Diamond Peak Series

Lethal Inheritance #1
Stalking Shadows #2
Eternal Destiny #4

Acknowledgements

Thank you to the wonderful people who helped me transform this book from a jumble of words into a book ready for publication. I thank my husband, Chris for his ongoing support and excellent structural editing, and my daughter Kimberley Rose for her role as a beta reader and teen consultant.

A special thanks to Krisi Keley for her particularly insightful and valuable conceptual editing, and also for her careful line and copy-editing. I also thank Satyo Sulliven for her helpful comments and suggestions.. Thank you also to the people who take the time to read my book and write reviews. I greatly appreciate your support.

To my cover models, Jocab Brookfield and Kimberley Newland, thanks for your patience and willingness. Thanks also to my mother and stepfather for their ongoing generosity and support.

Last, but not least, I thank Sogyal Rinpoche for his inspiration and blessing.

About the Author

Tahlia Newland, author of the multi-award-winning Diamond Peak Series, writes heart-warming and inspiring magical realism and contemporary fantasy. She is also an editor, a reviewer, an occasional high school teacher, and a mask-maker who loves creating digital art and sitting on her veranda staring at the rain forest.

Before writing full time, she had over 20 years' experience in scripting and performing in Visual Theatre and Theatre in Education. She has had extensive training in meditation and Buddhist philosophy and lives in Australia with a husband, a teenage daughter, and a cheeky Burmese cat called George.

Glossary

Amic

Head of the Amic Rasa demon clan. Preferred food-arrogance and prejudice. His emanations are Amics.

Bitah

Head of the Bitah Rasa demon clan. Preferred food-fear, anger and hatred. His emanations are Bitahs.

Cogin

Head of the Cogin Rasa demon clan. Preferred food-jealousy. His emanations are Cogins.

Diamond Peak

Name of the mountain in the Hidden Realm and home to Rasama, Master of the Rasa Demons. Stepping on the diamond at the peak shatters your Serpentine and gives immunity to re-infection.

Domos

A demonised being, so full of Serpentine and under its wiles that they are considered demons. They live in family groups near villages and towns and amuse themselves by stirring up trouble with the townsfolk.

Emot

Head of the Emot Rasa demon clan. Preferred food-greed, craving and attachment. His emanations are Emots.

Gimp

A minor demon. They appear when people feel mild negativity, like irritation or suspicion. They are a nuisance, but generally not harmful unless one follows you continuously or grows large. They usually fade away if you laugh at or ignore them, vaporise if you look them clearly in the eye and grow larger and stronger if you get angry with them.

Hidden Realms

Realms that exist on the Radiant Layer of reality. Only those who have developed Second Sight can see or enter them. They exist alongside but unperceived from our ordinary reality.

Layers of reality

The Manifest or Ordinary layer—ordinary reality as we know it.

The Essential Layer—the formless, open, creative space from which everything emerges. It cannot be seen, but can be experienced through the mind.

The Radiant Layer—a layer of reality where phenomena arisen from the Essential layer exist as a wealth of rainbow-like forms. If the right conditions are present, these ethereal forms can solidify further and manifest at the grosser Manifest or Ordinary Layer of reality. Those with subtle vision can manipulate these forms with mind power, ie magic.

Light Body

A person's energetic body, made of Radiant Light.

Major Rasas

One of four of the Master Demon's bodyguards and head of one of the Rasa clans-Bitah, Amic, Emot and Cogin. They each have their own territory on the mountain and are connected energetically with Rasama. When he dies, they also die.

Noble One

A Warrior who has stepped on the diamond at the top of Diamond Peak. They are free of, and immune to, Serpentine infection. Unlike those who are infected, they are not connected to the Serpentine system.

Protective Dome

An invisible dome a Warrior creates with Radiant Light. A semi-permeable membrane that lets in air covers a lattice framework. The dome keeps out anything not invited in.

Radiant Light

The five coloured light-white, yellow, red, green and blue-that is the essence of every person's being. It can be obscured, but not destroyed, and can be seen by those who have Second Sight. Warriors learn how to access and direct it in order to kill demons. It can also be understood as Radiant Power manifesting as light.

Radiant Power

The power inherent in Radiant Light. It can be accessed through the mind and directed to kill demons, destroy Serpentine and manipulate phenomena at the Radiant Layer of reality. Warriors learn how to access it through incantation, the transformation of thoughts and emotions, or by seeing it directly.

Rasa

Rasa demons feed on negative emotions and smell like rotting potatoes. They are made from Serpentine and linked energetically to it and to the Major Rasa of their clan. When their clan Major dies, any Rasa in that clan unfortunate enough to be above ground at the time also dies.

Rasama

The Master Demon, head of the Rasa demons. He lives in caves just beneath the top of Diamond peak and rarely moves from there. His energetic connection with the Serpentine allows him to bring infected people under his control and thus create violence and chaos, which provides a ready food source for the Serpentine and his demons.

He can be killed with Radiant Power, and if the Warrior is not a Noble One and therefore still infected with Serpentine, the blast that kills Rasama travels via the Warrior's Serpentine through the Serpentine's energetic network, wiping it out as it goes. Thus, all the Rasa demons die and all Serpentine dissolves except for a small root that remains in those infected.

Rasama can re-grow from the Serpentine in a badly infected person. He then creates new Majors and they create new Rasas. To prevent his power over the human race becoming absolute, he must be killed regularly and the longer between his deaths, the more powerful he becomes.

Second Sight

A way of seeing the Radiant Layer of reality.

Serpentine

A snake-like energy parasite, invisible except to those with Second Sight. It lives on an energetic plane where it wraps itself around a person's Light Body. Black and slimy, it feeds on the host's negative emotions and encourages negativity in those it infects. It can be poisoned with positive emotions and destroyed with Radiant Light.

Smog / spores

In Second Sight, smog can be seen around the heads of those infected by Serpentine. This is made of Serpentine Spores that spread to others and take root in the fertile ground of negativity. Radiant Light destroys the spores.